The Donor

The Donor

CHRISTIAAN BARNARD

MICHAEL JOSEPH
LONDON

MICHAEL JOSEPH LTD

Published by the Penguin Group
27 Wrights Lane, London w8 5 tz
Viking Penguin Inc., 375 Hudson Street, New York, New York 10014, USA
Penguin Books Australia Ltd, Ringwood, Victoria, Australia
Penguin Books Canada Ltd, 10 Alcorn Avenue, Toronto, Ontario, Canada m4v 3b2
Penguin Books (NZ) Ltd, 182–190 Wairau Road, Auckland 10, New Zealand

Penguin Books Ltd, Registered Offices: Harmondsworth, Middlesex, England

First published 1996
1 3 5 7 9 10 8 6 4 2

Set in 11.75/13.5pt Monotype Garamond
Typeset by Datix International Limited, Bungay, Suffolk
Printed in England by Clays Ltd, St Ives plc

ISBN 0 7181 41520

ACKNOWLEDGEMENTS

I wish to convey my sincere thanks and appreciation to the various departments of the Medical School of the University of Cape Town who helped with information and references. In this respect I would like to mention the Department of Cardiology, Cardiac Surgery, Human Genetics, Neurology, Biochemistry, Neurophysiology, and the staff of the Medical Library.

I also wish to express my gratitude to Professor Jannie de Villiers, Dr Tobie de Villiers, Professor Peter Jacobs, Professor Eugene Dowdle, Professor Annette du Toit, Professor E. van Rensburg, Dr David Cooper and Hamilton Naki.

To my dear friend Bob Molloy without whose encouragement and assistance this book would never have been completed, I say thank you very much.

Finally, to my wife Karin who with great commitment and patience typed the manuscript and inserted the amendments, I dedicate this book.

AUTHOR'S NOTE

To the layman, genetic engineering has long been a Pandora's box which, once opened, will curse mankind for ever with the horrors of genetically altered life forms. Pandora, of course, had blessings as well as curses in her box. Critics of the work have paid little attention to this aspect and most often have represented genetic engineering as negative, leading only to disease and destruction.

In fact, such is the universal concern regarding the consequences of the outcome of genetic manipulation, most countries have laid down ethical guidelines within which they expect their scientists to conduct research. Most of these are really safety rules, which any competent researcher would observe without question.

What, then, is the track record of genetic engineering, ushered in almost two decades ago with Crick and Watson's discovery of the DNA genetic code? Surprisingly, and in view of the alarm generated by that early work, it has all been positive. Today we have a range of genetically altered bacteria: oil-eating microbes that clean up spillage, long-life tomatoes, tailor-made laboratory mice for cancer research and even goats which can be designed to supply drugs in their milk. Other fears have centred on human gene manipulation, the search for the genetically perfect body and the possibility of identifying for abortion purposes embryos with genetic defects.

The search for knowledge and truth should never be curtailed but the ways in which the findings are used certainly call for control. Like the veneer of civilization which overlies human savagery, the ethical barriers between the pure scientist and misapplied research findings remain thin.

This story is one of good intentions gone wrong, and some of the myriad ways in which we can mislead ourselves.

CHAPTER I

R odney Barnes had never seen a real hangman's rope before, much less fixed around a human neck. The body hung, suspended below the open trap door of the prison gallows, turning slightly.

Brutally efficient, thought Barnes, and wished himself somewhere else. He was waiting with three other men – the doctor, the superintendent of the prison and the hangman – and he and Dr Rood, the district surgeon, watched as two warders brought the prisoner into the execution chamber. A barren room: four concrete walls, painted a light green colour, with a ceiling also of concrete from which five strong iron hooks were suspended six feet apart. A single light, recessed in the middle of the ceiling, cast a shadow on the wall of a rope with a hangman's noose.

The monotony of the plain concrete floor was interrupted by a wooden trap door, which ran virtually the whole width of the room; below each hook some macabre mind had helpfully painted two footprints on the wood indicating the ideal position. The trap door was skirted by an iron railing to prevent anyone walking on it. There was only one opening in this barrier through which the condemned could be guided by the two warders from the outside of the railing onto one set of footprints. Only the condemned man was privileged to walk onto the trap door. One more item remained: a lever, resembling the brake handle of an early motor car, on the left side of the trap door.

Whatever his previous criminal history the condemned prisoner, a muscular young white man with arms trussed behind his back, was a pathetic sight. Stumbling on jellied legs, half carried

I

to the railed-off trap door, he sobbed and mumbled appeals to the warders. Once on the trap door, his legs gave way. A warder on either side leaned over the rails to hold him upright while the hangman slipped a hood over his head, placed the rope around his neck and checked that the noose was snugly in position behind the right ear. Why the right ear? Barnes wondered. What the hell difference would it make if it was placed anywhere else? He supposed it was all part of the black art of taking a human life according to prison regulations. What was the judicial formula? 'You will be taken from here to the place of your execution and there hanged by the neck until you are dead.' Wasn't that what the judge was supposed to say when pronouncing sentence? The execution party moved like clockwork. Do they practise this kind of thing? Barnes mused.

There was no fumbling, no missed movement. No one got in anyone's way. Barely seconds after the prisoner appeared he was prepared for death, the trap dropped from under his feet and he fell into the void.

The crack of breaking bone was distinct, like the snap of a twig. Barnes felt the nausea rise. Dr Rood had told him that the drop had been calculated according to body weight and length, ensuring a clean break without major trauma to the neck – the judicial procedure called for death by hanging, not decapitation. A mistake in the length of the drop could easily take off a man's head. In this place of justice it was important that the law be followed to the letter.

At that moment the prison doctor touched Barnes's arm and pointed to the steps leading down to the retrieval room. He followed like an automaton, glad of the need to move.

It was a mistake. He realized that as soon as he saw the dangling body. Could he stomach regularly being part of this? He knew that beneath the hood the cadaver's eyes were popping out of the sockets under the skull pressure caused by the rope. The same pressure had forced the tongue from the open mouth and the legs cycled feebly in a nervous reflex.

Barnes's medical training told him that the man was clinically dead, brain-stem snapped at the base of the neck, yet the body continued to twitch and jerk. The sphincter muscles had relaxed at the moment of death, voiding the bowels and raising a strong smell of faeces in the small chamber.

'Dr Barnes?'

He jerked – he hadn't heard a word the prison doctor had said. The paunchy little man in the white coat, stethoscope in hand, was smiling. 'Sorry, Dr Rood, you were saying . . .'

The doctor's smile broadened. He found Barnes's squeamishness funny.

God knows there was little enough to smile about, Barnes thought, but I suppose the man has to find humour where he can. Rood had earlier told him he had attended almost a thousand executions and still found it a draining experience.

'The heart is still beating. It can take up to fifteen minutes before we have complete cessation. Until then I'm afraid you won't be able to touch the body,' said Rood, exerting his official ownership of the corpse.

Barnes suppressed his irritation. The prison service used an outdated definition of clinical death, based on the absence of heart-beat. It meant some delay before he could remove the cadaver's heart. A lengthy interview with the Minister of Justice had failed to change the department's ruling.

'You'll need a change in the law for that,' the Minister – overweight, chainsmoking and stressed – had said. They were standing at the window of his office overlooking the urban landscape of Pretoria. A beautiful city, laid out in attractive tree-lined grids and squares as a worthy administrative capital of the country, it was now a riot of colour at the height of the jacaranda season. The dazzling blue and green of the trees flamed on every street, traffic bustled and people smiled. The Pretorians loved their city and often boasted they would live in no other. Clearly the mood of the metropolis had not penetrated up here to the Minister's office high on the hill where the administration buildings dominated the skyline.

His face sombre, the Minister stared out of the window. Of

early settler farming stock – his family had buried some seven generations in this land – he had a farmer's natural courtesy that seemed ill-suited to the demands of being the country's supreme arbiter of justice. It wasn't an ideal post to hold at a time when the country's political future was in doubt, when law and order was under threat from faction fighting – and the Minister's own hold on office was tenuous. What would a man have done in a previous life to be condemned to this job? Barnes pondered, remembering an Asian doctor in his student days who had believed in the doctrine of reincarnation.

'Dr Barnes, even if you were able to take a human heart as soon after death as you wanted, how could you get it alive to Cape Town for transplant? At best, with jet transport, it takes two hours.'

Barnes felt better. This was safe ground. He had lectured his students endlessly on this very point, fund-raised at countless dinners and been interviewed at length in print and on talk shows.

The Minister lit another cigarette and frowned again at the city below. 'I was always under the impression that the human heart dies when it stops beating, with the body.'

Barnes caught himself as he was about to launch into his 'the heart is just a pump' routine. Instead, he soberly sketched the history and background of heart transplants. It wouldn't help his case if the Minister suspected he was being lectured. Using a heart attack as an example, he pointed out that the most important thing was to maintain the flow of blood to the brain. Even when the heart was completely still it could be made to perform by massage or regular squeezing, which forced the blood to flow. This could be done by pressure on the chest or, in a surgical situation, by squeezing the heart directly. Electro-shock would restart the heart unless the heart muscle was too severely damaged. At normal temperatures the brain could survive for three or four minutes without blood-flow. It was possible to increase this survival time by lowering the body temperature. The latest definition of death depended on clinical findings which indicated that the brain had died. The patient could be clinically dead while the heart continued to beat.

Barnes warmed to his topic. 'Let's take the situation where the heart stops beating after death. This happens in judicial hanging. At the end of the drop the body's fall is suddenly arrested by the rope around the neck. The muscle in the neck is not strong enough to take the strain and a fracture or dislocation of the upper two bones of the spinal column occurs. This ruptures the brain-stem and the brain is literally disconnected from the rest of the body.'

A severely dressed middle-aged woman entered the office, carrying a tray of coffee. The Minister turned to thank her in his courteous way and looked at Barnes. 'Coffee, doctor?' The woman poured and left, not without a curious glance at the famous face of the surgeon.

Barnes took a cup and watched the Minister light a third cigarette. Judging from his body bulk and heavy smoking habit he could become a classic heart-attack victim. Not for the first time he wondered why so much of modern medicine had to do with politics. Why was he, a cardio-thoracic surgeon at the forefront of research into heart transplantation, standing here in the office of the Minister of Justice when he could be much more useful in an operating theatre?

Like all leaders in any field, Barnes had come up against the inevitable barrier to progress – the political reluctance to move into unknown territory. Man dreaded the unknown and politicians were quick to sense when people – and for people read voters – felt things were moving too fast. The heart-transplant barrier had been broken years before. With the rejection problem well under control, such operations were now almost routine. But the shortage of donor organs had remained a constant problem, and nowhere more so than in the field of heart transplants.

The layman still saw the heart as the seat of life, some the soul. For most people it held a special significance, as the focus of love and emotion. Relatives of terminally ill and brain-dead patients were reluctant to donate this most mystical of organs.

But to Rodney Barnes the heart was just a pump: the better its condition, the greater the chance of a successful transplant. Many times he had watched patients die, choking out their lives while waiting for a donor. Worse, he had watched surgeons transplant hearts in less than optimum condition, only to see the patient's suffering prolonged. Most hearts came from brain-dead accident victims, and were already stressed from trauma. Often the transplant was further delayed by a maze of red tape and form-filling, set up by medical authorities anxious to avoid malpractice claims by anguished relatives. Little wonder that transplant surgeons worked with inferior donor material, which reduced the chances of a successful outcome. What was needed was a supply of donor hearts in good condition, on time and to order.

An impossible dream – until Barnes read an angry editorial against capital punishment. He'd never had strong feelings one way or the other, except perhaps a vague recall of childhood biblical instruction. The Bible, he remembered, demanded an eye for an eye, which he supposed meant a life for a life. What had made him sit bolt upright and drop the rest of the newspaper on the floor were the figures for executions.

The Department of Justice was hanging up to three convicted murderers a week. Most were healthy young men in their prime, no doubt with equally healthy organs. Here was the supply: in good condition, on time and to order. Within days he had charmed his way through rising tiers of secretaries, penetrated the bureaucracy and had made an appointment with the Minister. His name, known far beyond the world of medicine, opened the doors.

The meeting proved a pleasant surprise. Ben Voos was that best of all combinations, farmer turned politician become statesman. Even the opposition agreed he had brought humanity to the job, dealing as it did with the lives of thousands in an era of political and civil turmoil. 'The relatives can claim it,' he answered, when Barnes asked what happened to the bodies of those executed. 'There is even a little chapel next to the gallows where, if they so wish, a service can be held for the departed loved one.'

He listened in silence to Barnes's proposal that the department give him permission to take suitable hearts as donor material.

'But what could you do with the dead heart of a murderer?' Voos clearly had trouble seeing Barnes's view.

Here it was again, the layman's idea of the stilled heart as a dead organ. Thank God it isn't so, thought Barnes. If that had been the case, open-heart surgery would never have got off the ground. It had long been the practice in surgery to stop the heart, sometimes for hours, while performing delicate work on it. Before the technique had been perfected, exposure and accurate stitching of the tensely beating heart had been almost impossible.

He had to ensure that the Minister saw the clinical point of view. 'I'm told there is a doctor present at every hanging to declare the prisoner dead only after the heart stops beating.'

'Not only for that reason,' the Minister spoke quickly. 'Also to see that the execution is carried out humanely.'

Jesus, thought Barnes. How can taking a man's life by hanging be done humanely? He let the thought go. 'You realize that this is quite unnecessary. The prisoner is dead at the moment his fall is halted by the noose, isn't he?'

'Yes, but the heart is still beating.'

Barnes had to stop himself sighing in exasperation. The Afrikaners in power believed emphatically that their actions were guided by God so he decided to exploit this weakness in the armour of the Minister. 'I recently read an article by Dr C. Pallace, from the Royal Postgraduate Medical School at Hammersmith Hospital, in which he stated that the concept of brain-death is not new. In many older cultures the human death was understood as the departure of the conscious soul from the body or the loss of the breath of life. The words which stand for soul are the same in many languages as for breath: *nephesh* in Hebrew, *urach* in Aramaic, *phenuma* in Greek, *spiritus* in Latin, *havas* or *nephs* in Arabic and the ghost in the old English sense. In Genesis 2:7 the association between breath and life is clearly stated, "And the Lord fashioned man of dust of earth and instilled in his nostrils the breath of life and the man became a living creature." Nowhere in the early religious writings do you read about the heart-beat and the pulse as determinants of life or death.'

'But the heart will eventually stop?' The Minister was not giving up.

'Yes, sir. If we do nothing the heart stops after a few minutes only because, with the death of the brain-stem, the breathing reflex stops. The heart slowly loses its supply of oxygen and eventually dies. If I were to connect the person to a ventilator the heart would continue to beat.'

'For ever?' The Minister was thinking aloud, brow wrinkled.

'No, no,' said Barnes, anxious to clarify the point. 'That is one of the problems still unsolved. We can breathe for them, feed them, correct the metabolic disturbance, do everything possible in our state of knowledge but within a few hours or days the circulation begins to fail and the heart deteriorates. That said, research is constantly ongoing and we are adding to our knowledge all the time.'

'It seems to me there is a lot you doctors do not know about death?' The Minister made it seem like a question.

'Yes and no.' Barnes was quick to respond. 'It's mainly a matter of semantics. In the medical and legal professions there is a general agreement on the notion that loss of brain function is death.'

'If I understand you correctly, doctor, then death as we laymen know it is more a process than an event?' The Minister looked more alert and had stopped smoking for the first time in the conversation.

'I spoke to the district surgeon who said he had to wait until the heart stopped beating before the body can be lowered from the noose.' Barnes had thought about this many times: it would cost him precious minutes in his race to save the heart from deterioration.

'Yes, that is the law,' the Minister interjected.

Barnes had reached the crux of his argument. 'You probably realize there is no legal reason why the body could not be lowered while the heart is still beating. You remember – a beating heart in a dead human being?'

There was silence. The Minister turned back to the window where the afternoon shadows were lengthening. The silence stretched. 'Maybe we can review these regulations,' he said at last.

'It would be better if I get to the heart before it stops beating. The biggest problem is to stop the blood from clotting and clogging the smaller vessels supplying the heart muscle. If this is allowed to happen the heart cannot be started again. It must be done as soon as possible after the circulation stops.'

'How will you overcome the problem?'

'As soon as the body is lowered to the floor I will inject an anti-coagulant into a vein in the arm.'

'An anti-coagulant?'

'Yes, heparin – a drug that prevents the blood from clotting.'

Putting both hands on his own chest and pushing down on his breastbone, Barnes explained, 'By squeezing the heart be-tween the breastbone and the spine I can start the circulation again – allowing the heparin to mix with the blood of the whole body.'

'Ah, your "heart massage" process?'

Barnes saw he was winning. 'You did say there was a small operating theatre near the execution chamber?' he asked.

'Yes – fairly well equipped I'm told. It was used when the law allowed the removal of skin, bone and other parts.'

'I can supply all the instruments I need in a sterilized con-tainer. All I want is a table and a good light,' Barnes said, hardly able to believe the direction this was taking.

'That is already available.' The Minister still looked uncertain. 'But I suggest you go and see for yourself.'

So he had permission to attend a hanging! Like most people, Barnes had no morbid desire to view a violent judicial death but his professional curiosity was aroused. His heart-rate climbed at the thought.

The Minister coughed. Barnes realized he had been staring into space. 'Sorry. I've just been thinking that once the body has been heparinized I have to get to the heart as soon as possible to minimize damage.'

'Damage?'

'The damage that will result from the heart being warm without a flow of blood to the muscle.'

'So you are not going to restart the heart?'

'No. That would complicate the procedure. If I set out all my instruments in the operating room before the hanging, and am scrubbed up, gowned and ready, the body can then be placed on the table as soon as it is heparinized. It will take only a few seconds to cover it with sterile drapes and I can start to remove the heart without delay.'

The Minister was intrigued by the idea of having sterile conditions for a dead man. 'The same conditions as for an operation?'

'Yes. The removal of the heart must be done with the same precautions against infection as for any other operation on a live patient.' He quickly described how he would open the chest, saw through the breastbone and then clamp back the ribcage to expose the heart. 'After gaining access to the coronary arteries, the ones which supply the blood-flow to the heart muscle, I will flush them out with an ice cold salt solution containing drugs that will paralyse the heart muscle. By stopping all heart activity and cooling it to about ten degrees centigrade the metabolic demand is reduced. The heart muscle can then survive without oxygen for several hours.'

'You have to transport it over a thousand kilometres to Cape Town. How will you do that?' The Minister's interest was now fully aroused. His politician's mind told him that what they were talking about would not meet with popular approval, but the human drama of moving a living heart from one end of the country to the other had gripped him.

'Once chilled and paralysed, the heart will be removed from the body, put in a sterile plastic bag, placed in a bed of crushed ice in a sterile container for transport. After that it's just a matter of ensuring air transport is standing by. Within three hours of donor death the heart will be in the operating theatre where the patient will be prepared and ready to receive the transplant.'

Ben Voos had lived through many changes in his country. He had seen his fellow Afrikaners replace the English ascendancy which had ruled it for a century and a half. He himself had moved from being a back-country farmer to one of the highest offices in the land. He still didn't quite believe it. He knew, too, deep in his bones, that the upsurge in black aspirations would one day topple his administration.

But certain immutables would never change. He had a different view of the human heart from this eager young doctor, who was prying into things which even he admitted he still didn't understand. Looking into Barnes's eyes he asked, 'How do you think your patient will react when he finds out that he's now living with the heart of a murderer?'

A hypothetical question meant the interview was over. Barely able to conceal his satisfaction, Barnes smiled and rose to shake the Minister's hand. 'Evil deeds are not planned and executed by the heart whether white or black, evil or good,' he said. 'The heart is just a pump.'

CHAPTER 2

The evening flight back to Cape Town was a commuter sardine can, packed with business travellers. A tired cabin crew slopped the coffee, interested only in reaching the end of a long hard day. Barnes barely noticed. His head buzzed with what he had come to think of as the time problem. How could he shorten the time between the execution and removal of the heart from the body?

True, the visit to the prison had only been a dry run. Next time he hoped to be carrying a donor heart. But if removal from the body had to follow the letter of the law there was a sure chance that the heart could be seriously injured. He was still turning the problem over in his mind when he picked up his car in the airport car park and headed for home. What he needed desperately was a hot shower and eight hours' sleep.

Home was an eighteenth-floor apartment in a beach-front tower block on the northern shores of Table Bay. Like his car, it was an expensive bachelor indulgence. The security barrier to the basement car park acknowledged his card with a bleep and raised itself clear. He coasted to a halt in his reserved parking bay, dropped the key on the service pillar and headed for the elevators. By morning the night staff would have ensured that his car was serviced, valeted and gleaming, reflecting Barnes's lifestyle in which there was a place for everything, and everything not only had a place but was also in perfect condition and operated to maximum efficiency. Nursing staff at the hospital had cause to know that. Operating theatre staff in particular were drilled to perfection, preferring Barnes's bark of thanks to his bite of reprimand.

Subdued lighting glowed in the serviced apartment. Muted Vivaldi ghosted through the sound system. Silver gleamed against polished wood on a table laid for one. A cold buffet with crisp salads waited under covers in the kitchen, next to a slightly chilled bottle of Cape Riesling in a cooler. It was a shy-bearing variety, from a private estate. A grateful patient had sent him a case and Barnes had been savouring it slowly over several months.

As usual, he noted, Valmai had done a superb job, except for the music. He frowned. Vivaldi was for morning listening. He selected a disc of Bartók, dropped it on the changer and felt the modern rhythms wash over him. He looked around. His African maid had taken on his need for perfection and had added a few touches of her own. She also seemed to operate on the invisibility principle, with an uncanny ability to come and go without being seen.

He showered, enjoying the needle-sharp sting of the water and feeling it massage away the tension. Afterwards he changed into a towelling robe and poured himself a glass of Riesling. It tasted like silk. The aromatic bite on his palate sang of well-tended vineyards, sunny slopes and eternal summer. It complemented the food perfectly, and he felt himself drift off into a pleasant haze. If Nirvana existed, this was it.

The phone buzzed, a soft insistent sound. Barnes reached for the receiver standing on the bookshelf and gave a one-word answer: 'Barnes!'

It was Kapinsky. The slightly Germanic voice sounded irritated. Barnes realized guiltily that he had promised to ring him as soon as he got back from Pretoria. He looked at his watch. That was three hours ago. He smiled. His research fellow was the classic workaholic – a man driven by the hands of the clock, each minute of his waking day allotted its place.

'You have permission? We can go ahead? When do we start?' It was a typical Kapinsky opening – shorn of courtesies, direct and to the point.

'The answers are yes, no and I don't know,' said Barnes. He

sketched his trip to Pretoria. Kapinsky interjected the odd *ja* but offered no comment.

Not for the first time Barnes thought that, in the five years they had worked together, he knew little about Louis Kapinsky. Apart from a fierce commitment to solve the donor program, he kept to himself. He never socialized, never appeared at medical school or hospital parties. Hospital security reported to Barnes that they often found him at the research laboratory in the early hours of the morning, talking to the animals. But whatever his lack of charisma, Kapinsky had a solid postgraduate research record with a first-class degree from a leading British medical school.

'We have to overcome the time problem, Louis. Unless we do that, I don't think we can get the heart down here without serious damage to the myocardium.'

There was a silence. Barnes could almost see Kapinsky frowning as he considered the problem.

'How about we try the heterotopic position? You remember about two months ago we transplanted a donor heart that had several episodes of cardiac arrest? For twenty-four hours after the transplant the test showed it was doing very little but with the assistance of the patient's own heart it gradually recovered and within forty-eight hours had almost taken over the circulation.'

Barnes remembered the operation in detail. He had transplanted the donor heart against his better judgement and only because the patient had no other option. The seriously ill man had only days to live. The donor organ matched perfectly but had been damaged by poor circulation. Transplanting it into the heterotopic or 'piggy-back' position – where it was attached to the patient's own heart in a helping or support capacity – was a calculated risk that had paid off. 'Louis, you may be right. But I'd hate to take that chance, especially with the first heart we get from the prison. We're going to collect enough negative publicity without the added jibe that it was all for nothing.'

'*Ja*, you worry too much, Professor.' Use of his academic title was Kapinsky's way of saying that the matter was closed.

'Louis, I'm tired. I'm going to hit the sack. We'll talk tomorrow.'

Kapinsky grunted and hung up. A brilliant researcher, Barnes thought, but he would never win prizes for diplomacy.

He slept restlessly and awoke to a feeling of unease. A shower and two cups of coffee later it was still with him.

He took his second cup, as was his morning ritual, standing on the balcony overlooking the beach. The outlook was usually breathtaking: Africa Face, the towering cliff fronting Table Mountain, was clearly visible across the sparkling waters of Table Bay. Behind it, the sun was rising in a blaze of red, outlining the flat table-top and breaking up the city haze, but this morning a cold front had moved in across the ocean. Squalls of rain obscured one of the world's great skylines.

Later, as he swung his car into the morning traffic, Barnes found himself thinking again about Kapinsky, the man who had been at the core of the donor program since its inception. At least he could be trusted to be unemotional about transplants, and a staunch supporter in the endless battles with the Ethics Committee. He caught a glimpse of himself in the rear-view mirror. He was frowning: the thought of that bunch of ageing doctors who made up the committee was enough to set his teeth on edge.

He was willing to bet they'd never had an original thought in their heads throughout their long and safely organized medical careers. Given a new research project they could always come up with ten good reasons why it would not work. If it did, they had ten more to prove it would have no scientific value. He wondered what their reaction would be if they had known about the idea that had come to him during the night and resulted in such a fretful sleep: a baboon with a human heart, loping blithely about its cage, mightn't fit their geriatric ideas but it would go a long way to providing some vital answers.

Particularly the ability to protect the heart muscle cut off from its blood supply for prolonged periods of time. What next? he wondered, grinning. A baboon with a human brain? We already had humans with the brain of a baboon but they were all in Parliament. He chortled at the cheeky-schoolboy thought.

He joined the stream of traffic from the city's northern suburbs and settled down to thread his way into position for the turn-off to the hospital.

Unbidden, the thought came to him: Why was that man executed yesterday? He hadn't even bothered to ask. How strange that he, who had spent so many years learning how to ward off death, should have had such a profound curiosity about a hanging. He had actually gone there to see a man die. Perhaps it was because there was nothing he could have done to stop it. Perhaps that's what made it so easy to watch. He shrugged off the morbid thought. Death had been waiting for the guy at the end of the rope and it mattered not whether he, Rodney Barnes MD, was there or not. It would have been interesting to open the man's skull and see what damage the fall had done to the spine and midbrain.

Barnes angled his car onto the hospital lane and coasted up the incline to the flyover. A shy sun slanted bright rays across the city. He halted at the intersection and waited for the lights to change. The little black boy selling the morning newspaper had cut open the side of a plastic bag and used this as a hood and a jacket to protect him from the rain. When he spotted Barnes looking at him, he tried to tempt him to buy a paper by showing him the front page.

Banner headlines blasted: Transplant Surgeon in Secret Jail Visit.

Christ! Somebody must have seen him leaving the prison, or worse, perhaps there was an informer on his staff. Cheque-book journalism opened many doors. He mentally ran through the list of people likely to know where he'd been yesterday. It was an extremely short list. Apart from Kapinsky and his secretary there was no one else. He frowned. Even his secretary knew only that he had gone to Pretoria but not the purpose of his visit.

The car behind him hooted, an irritated double blast. He'd missed the light change. The jowly red-faced driver he glimpsed in the mirror was almost visibly steaming. Unappeased by Barnes's apologetic wave he tooted again.

Blood pressure, Barnes guessed. Some people woke up with it.

The thought of the informer worried him. Kapinsky was the only person he'd discussed it with, apart from the Minister and the prison doctor. However, his face was well known – too much television and tabloid exposure. Transplant surgery was still a focus of media interest. Somebody must have seen him leave the jail.

Instead of taking his usual spot in the office car park Barnes headed for the hospital. It would be more difficult for the reporters to find him there. He avoided the consultants' parking bays, drove into the surgical interns' area and switched off. He needed time to think. The Minister had warned him that the issue was sensitive and advised against any press release. Now here it was, or at least a good guesstimate, on the front page.

Shit! If it became public that he and Kapinsky were planning to use organs from executed felons there'd be an international outcry. At the very least it would put a crimp in his plans for a supply of healthy organs and there could even be a backlash from patients. There were enough Jekyll and Hyde scare stories doing the rounds without this new angle on transplant psychosis.

With antennae on high for any sign of a reporter or a camera he headed for the general ward.

CHAPTER 3

'Dr Barnes!' The staff nurse poked her head out of her office cubicle as he entered the general ward and waved a slip of paper. He wasn't surprised to find it was a message from Fiona asking him to contact her urgently on the 'red phone' – her unlisted office number. As a secretary, Fiona had few equals. She had alerted every department in the hospital with the same message, keeping the press hounds at bay while she pinpointed his whereabouts.

Barnes was good copy for the tabloids. Swinging bachelors of any age were an easy mark but his profile – film-star good looks, a charismatic public speaker, unmarried at thirty-eight, at the forefront of cardiac research, in demand by the glitterati and a seemingly endless supply of what an American reporter called 'classy broads' – made him a constant target. And if the story didn't have enough punch then few reporters agonized over adding the odd piece of fiction to make it good faction – a story not altogether true but more readable.

He crushed the note as if it were a dangerous insect and reached for the phone, pushing down his irritation as he dialled Fiona's number. The hospital switchboard leaked like a sieve when it came to newsy information and it made good sense to use a direct line.

She didn't mince words. 'I don't know what you did yesterday but the place is crawling with cameras. Where are you?'

He told her and listened closely to a list of messages from which the press requests had been carefully filtered out. The lab tests on three patients had arrived. He had been invited to an international conference on cardiac surgery, and a major drug company was interested in funding a student research project.

He put down the phone and looked around the ward. There was no sign of the medical staff. Clearly ward rounds had already started.

The nurse answered his unspoken question, 'The doctors are all in the intensive care unit – with the new admission.' He opened his mouth to correct her and then said nothing, following as she led the way. Referring to patients by their symptoms or position in the ward – 'the new admission, bed three, the cardiac myopathy' – might be helpful to staff but did little for a patients' sense of self. It was a growing trend to talk about patients in this way and he made a mental note to bring it up at the next hospital board meeting. Somebody was either teaching this kind of approach or failing to correct it, and it led to treatment of the disease rather than the person.

There was only one patient in the unit, his face hidden by an oxygen mask and his bed surrounded by a knot of medics and nursing staff. Barnes noted he was in severe heart failure, breathing rapidly and coughing.

'Good morning, sir,' the knot chorused, opening a space to make room for their chief at the bedside.

Barnes acknowledged the greeting and glanced at the record card. It described an eighteen-year-old, David Rhodes from an up-country rural town – talented sportsman, good scholastic record, son of a wealthy farmer, who had played first-team rugby until three months before when he had developed a flu-like illness with chest pain.

'The history points to rapid development of left heart failure followed by right heart failure,' said Alex Hobbs, the junior surgeon. Conscientious Alex would have arrived already at a diagnosis, Barnes thought, and now would be ready to defend it to the death.

'What treatment has he had?' The houseman, Jan Snyman, looked at his notes and back at Barnes. 'Yes, Dr Snyman?' Snyman was a good student who knew his medicine but often needed prompting.

Snyman looked back at his notes. 'His local doctor did all the right things – bed rest, diuretics to keep down water retention, and afterload reduction medication.'

'Thank you, Dr Snyman.'

The youth in the bed coughed again and struggled for air, sucking hard in great gasps to penetrate his waterlogged lungs.

One of the registrars pushed the chest X-ray forward.

'Thank you, Dr Louw.' Barnes took the X-ray but didn't look at it. 'I'd like to examine the patient first.' He tried to keep the sarcasm out of his voice. Des Louw was the hospital know-it-all, most often right but wrong often enough to be dangerous. The team knew Barnes's basic rule: examination before tests. But then, as he often reflected, medicine wasn't the only field where it was possible to put the cart before the horse.

The nurse pulled down the sheet to expose the patient's chest and handed Barnes his stethoscope. He slipped the earpieces around his neck and took David's right hand. The pulse was soft and fast and there was a bluish tint to the fingernails. A look at the swollen feet showed skin peeling from the soles – an indicator that the patient hadn't walked for some time. The ankle pulse was absent. Cold and mottled skin spelt out the warning signs of a collapsing circulation. A glance at the neck showed the veins standing out and pulsating, even though the patient was sitting almost upright.

Barnes put his hand on the swollen abdomen. The liver was enlarged at least five fingers width below the ribline. He looked at Alex Hobbs. 'Urine?'

'Passing very little but we did manage to get a specimen. It tested strongly positive for albumin and bile pigments.'

It was a grim picture. The blood was damming back in the body as the weakening heart failed to pump it around the circulation, causing the legs and feet to swell and congesting the liver and kidneys. Without intervention, the boy was marked for death. Barnes put the stethoscope on the heaving chest. Wet lungs crackled in the earpieces as they struggled to pass oxygen into the blood. All the signs were there of a grossly enlarged and dying heart.

As he straightened up Barnes realized that the patient's eyes were following his every move. His irritation with the day disappeared. Gently, he took the mask off the youth's face. When he spoke his voice was gentle. 'I'm Dr Barnes. I won't ask you how you feel but I promise we'll soon have you back on your feet again.'

The patient gave a twisted smile. It was as much as he could manage between gasps but he seemed naïvely certain that their skills would return him to health.

Barnes nodded and replaced the mask. Trust in the doctor was often the missing factor in patient recovery. Without it, a patient's chances were very much reduced.

He took the X-ray to the viewing screen where they could talk out of earshot of the patient. It showed nothing that his examination had not already revealed. A look at the echocardiograph only served to confirm it – the pumping chambers of the enlarged heart were barely functioning. He could hear the dry Scots voice of the professor of cardiology back in his student days: 'Lab tests can only confirm what ye already know from yer physical examination. If ye do a thorough physical yer lab tests canna add much.'

Barnes looked around. 'Have you had a chance to have his blood chemistry analysed?'

'Yes, sir.' It was Des Louw who replied. 'The sodium is very low and the blood urea raised.'

'Potassium?'

'I gave him a gram intravenously as his blood level for this was low and he had several extra beats when admitted.'

Barnes swung firmly into control. 'Take a sample of his arterial blood and analyse the gases. With his poor circulation he may be acidotic.'

There was silence. Hobbs hesitated, and said, 'Where do we go from here?'

'First, let's make a diagnosis.' Barnes heard the lecturing tone creep into his voice and suppressed it, consciously trying for face-to-face contact with the small group. He fervently hoped he wasn't developing into a boring old fart like some of his predecessors in med school. He went on, 'The patient is suffering from a cardiac myopathy. The murmurs produced by the leaking mitral and tricuspid valves are caused by dilation of the left and right chambers. It is not a result of rheumatic fever.' He indicated the enlarged heart on the X-ray. 'The flu-like illness and very short history suggest the pathology is the result of infection – a viral infection. He has viral myocarditis or, in layman's terms, inflammation of the heart muscle.'

All three doctors looked surprised. As Barnes suspected, they had talked the case over before his arrival and, with Alex Hobbs leading the discussion, had concluded with a different diagnosis. In their view, the failure was due to what Hobbs regarded as 'disease of the heart muscle of unknown origin – the so-called idiopathic cardiac myopathy'.

Barnes handed his stethoscope back to the nurse.

'The treatment, sir?' Des Louw was at the forefront again.

'Normally, strict bed rest and medication. We have cases on record of spontaneous recovery, given enough time for the immune system to suppress the virus. In this case the situation is too far gone. The heart has little hope of recovery without assistance – and that means a heterotopic transplant.'

Eyebrows went up all the way round. 'A piggy-back?' It was Jan Snyman who spoke, the words bursting out in surprise.

'Yes, Dr Snyman. As you put it, a piggy-back – a donor heart placed in parallel with the damaged heart and linked to the circulation system. We have no better way available to rest his heart,' Barnes replied, moving to the door. 'It is the only totally implantable device that can assist the heart and buy time for the recovery. If the worst comes to the worst and the patient's heart packs up, the piggy-back heart can take over the total circulation.'

Alex Hobbs, already mentally crossing the bridges, frowned but said nothing.

Barnes added, 'With help, the immune system will deal with the virus. But the indicators here are that the circulation is collapsing. The heart is now too weakened to recover spontaneously. It needs help.'

A fit of coughing drew attention back to the bed where the nurse was adjusting the patient's oxygen mask.

Louw looked at Hobbs. Both looked at Barnes. The team was ready to move.

It was time to inform the patient. This was Alex Hobbs's job. As the junior surgeon he had most to do with the preparation of the operation.

Barnes stopped at the door. 'Dr Hobbs, I want you to go and sit down with David. Make sure he understands the need for a transplant. As he is a minor we will need permission from his next of kin. Dr Louw, please inform the neuro-surgeons and the transplant co-ordinator. We can start looking for a donor immediately.' He hesitated. 'By the way, what's the patient's blood group?'

Des Louw looked apologetic. 'I'm sorry, sir. We haven't had time to type him but I'll send a blood sample to the lab right away.'

Barnes nodded and left. He hoped it wasn't one of the rarer groups. It would make it more difficult to find a suitable donor.

Leaving his car in the car park, Barnes opted to walk the five hundred metres to his office in the surgical block. It was only a few minutes' stroll to his office in the administration block but it would give him time to think of an explanation for his trip to Pretoria that would get the reporters off his back, satisfy the hospital mandarins and not alarm the Ethics Committee.

Stepping out of the elevator he decided to bluff it out. The door to the reception area was wide open. He strode past Fiona's desk with a cheery good morning, every inch the capable head of department without a worry in the world.

Fiona, a tall lithe blonde who looked more like a catwalk model than a top-flight secretary with a business brain and a keen grasp of medical politics, looked up. Picking up her message folder, she followed him into his office and watched as he stretched full length in his swivel chair, clasped his hands casually behind his head and raised his eyebrows at her. 'What's the panic?'

Fiona wasn't fooled. Five years in the office hot seat – fending off the time wasters and the opportunists who wanted an audience with the country's top heart surgeon – had taught her that Barnes had most to hide when he was at his most disarming.

'Every newspaper in the country, the hospital administrator and the head of the Division of Surgery. Which would you like to see first?'

'None of the above. How about a cuppa?'

Fiona switched on what Barnes called her dumb-blonde look, fluttered her eyelashes and said, 'Certainly, doctor. Tea or coffee?'

He grinned and felt the tension ease. He had seen too many reporters, medical reps, pushy academics and fussy admin types fall for this routine as they tried to penetrate her efficient visitor-screening process. The leak could not have come from her. Apart from having too much to lose, Fiona simply didn't fit the profile of the alienated office personality. A back-stabber she wasn't.

J. J. Kemble, head of the medical school's Division of Surgery, had his office only ten paces down the passage from Rodney Barnes. He was mad as hell, looking for Barnes and, most of all, looking for an explanation as to why his day had been taken up by a flood of press calls all wanting to know why his top cardiac surgeon had been visiting the country's largest prison.

It was unfortunate that he was a head smaller than Fiona, which meant that for a second he appeared to be staring at her breasts, which were just centimetres from his nose as he tried to squeeze past her into Barnes's office. He mumbled an apology and stood aside. Fiona smiled wickedly and sashayed out of the door unfazed, leaving him to collect his wits. Barnes rose immediately and offered a chair.

Like many small men, JJ had a short fuse. He brushed aside the usual courtesies and came to the point. 'What the blazes is going on? I hear you have a transplant planned? What's this about your visiting Pretoria Central Prison?'

JJ was not only a fine surgeon and teacher, he was also an able administrator who knew to the last detail what was going on in his department, and in most others in the medical school too. He had been well informed. The decision to transplant had been taken barely a half-hour earlier. What else did he know?

Barnes waited until the flow of questions ended. JJ had always given him a free hand and, like all good administrators, operated on the 'if it ain't broke don't fix it' philosophy. He had only once raised his eyebrows when Barnes had invited him to the research lab to see Kapinsky's two-headed dog experiment. There had been no scientific base for the experiment but Kapinsky had persuaded him that it was important to know if it was technically possible to transplant a second head onto a healthy dog without damage to the donor animal's brain. Kapinsky had been excited by the success of the operation. The animal had walked about with two heads, both conscious of their surroundings, and both had lapped up milk when it had been offered.

JJ didn't share the enthusiasm. He had looked at the dog for a few minutes without speaking. Then, quietly, he had turned to Barnes and said, 'You are in charge of this department. This is your responsibility. I think you should stop these experiments.' Then he had left. That was all. He never enquired whether Barnes had destroyed the animal or what was happening to the program.

Barnes remembered the experiment as a turning point, which had sharpened his interest in what he had come to call cardio-neurology: the influence of the nervous system and particularly the brain on heart function. Early transplants had treated the heart as just a pump – a self-acting organ with its own power source which needed only a blood supply to keep working.

From then on he had read avidly, combing scientific publications for research on states of consciousness, sleep, coma and general brain function. Often he had lain awake into the night, pondering brain action. How, he wondered, was it possible for a person to memorize an entire piano concerto, then, at will, recall every note and chord, and translate these into hand and finger movements to reproduce the sounds on the keyboard? Once, during his musings, he had recalled the full text of a poem learned at school almost a quarter-century before. Where had it been stored for all that time, and what was it that triggered the memory?

'Bugger it, Rod. What's going on?' JJ had calmed down and was now hunting through his pockets for a cigarette packet.

Barnes automatically moved to open a window. JJ had already lost a large section of his stomach to an ulcer and still persisted in the habit. 'Give it up, Professor. You'll stunt your growth.'

The old joke eased the tension. JJ grinned, found a packet, lit up, wreathed himself in smoke and looked hard at the other man. 'Let's hear it. Is there something you want to tell me?'

Barnes considered giving him the full story and then thought better of it. JJ was old guard, steeped in the medical ethics of an earlier age when the frontiers of knowledge were more fixed, more certain. A time when it was easier to tell right from wrong, who was the good guy and who the bad. Today there were no limits to knowledge, not even a discernible frontier. All the sciences had begun to run together. Questions answered raised even more questions and some of these challenged even the ability to understand the question let alone the answer. JJ's world was a secure one where following the rule book made everything seem simple. A humane man, he had passed his values on to several generations of students. Barnes had been one of them.

Barnes suddenly felt isolated. It was lonely out there beyond the limits set by his mentor. He cleared his throat. 'Nothing very much. The usual case-load.' Even to his own ears it sounded a bit lame.

'You made a trip to Pretoria – to see a patient?'

'That's right.' It was possible to think of the executed man as a patient – not that he'd had any hope of treating him, Barnes thought.

'And who was this patient and what was wrong with him?'

Barnes shifted in his chair so that he wasn't looking directly at JJ. 'Sorry, Prof. I can't break patient confidence. You know that.'

He could see the veins come up on JJ's forehead. The older man took a breath. 'Dammit, Rod. I've never interfered with your activities. Time and time again I've defended you at Senate and Faculty meetings when your public image was taking a beating in the press.' He leaned forward. 'This isn't the time to play games. I can smell a problem. What the hell is it? Is Kapinsky up to some half-arsed experiment?'

The man was incredible. He had a mind like a razor and the knack of getting to the heart of an issue with a few simple questions.

'Professor, I appreciate your support. But at this stage I can't say much –'

'Can't?' JJ cut him short. 'You can't trust me?'

This was getting too confrontational. 'No, sir. It is not a matter of trust but a matter of ethics. I'd be grateful if you would just accept my explanation that I went to see a patient in Pretoria Central Prison.'

The appeal struck a chord. Like all his generation, JJ lived by a code of ethics. He understood the constraints of ethical behaviour. To him, Barnes was bound by the same code. He stood up, leaving a smouldering stub in Barnes's pen stand. It was a small price to pay for the end of what could have been an awkward interrogation. 'Thank you, Rodney. I don't think the press will be as easy on you. But before you make any statements, just make sure the Administrator knows.' He walked out past the studiously busy Fiona, wished her a very good morning and was gone, mollified if not informed.

I'm over the first hurdle, thought Barnes. The Administrator would be even easier – tell him that everything had been explained to the head of the Division of Surgery. A phone call would be sufficient. After that, a short press statement. It was a doddle.

As he sat back in his chair his eyes fell on the photostat copies of articles strewn all over his desk. 'The Vicious Gene', 'The Gene Hunt', 'Cloning', 'Where do we draw the line?' and many more. Why don't they just leave me alone to do my work? Then his eyes fell on an editorial in the Vatican's *L'Osservatore Romano*. 'Such procedures could lead humanity down a tunnel of madness.' Is that where I am going?

CHAPTER 4

Barnes left his office and took the elevator down to street level. He walked briskly past the pathology building to the research block. He heard people shouting in the animal house but could not make out Kapinsky's voice so he took the elevator to the man's laboratory on the third floor.

Louis Kapinsky was a short, stocky man with a mop of black hair and a thick moustache. As Barnes entered he was bent over a double-barrelled microscope, oblivious to all else. His senior assistant, Dr Susan Bates, acknowledged Barnes with a nod.

Junior lab assistant Nat Ferreira – the ink on the brand new Bachelor of Medicine and Surgery degrees barely dry, and proudly displayed on the door of his locker – smiled and stood up, eager to be of service to the country's top surgeon. Barnes smiled back and shook his head. Ferreira was a nice youngster who would go far in his field, he thought. Being eager to please was a trait in short supply in the world of top-level medicine, and Barnes felt himself warm to him.

Dr Bates, who ran the lab the way she ran her life – clinically, coldly and efficiently – was a different story. As if to show that life was not only grim but earnest she wore her hair scraped back from classically good features and tied into a tight bun at the back of her neck. She respected Dr Barnes the academic and surgeon but did not approve of Rodney the playboy. Not for the first time Barnes wondered what she would be like in bed. Would that bun of hair cascade easily down around her shoulders or would she demand a clinical inspection of an ardent lover before she opened her legs? Come to think of it, the legs showing under her white lab coat looked spectacular.

'Yes, Dr Barnes?' She had swivelled in her chair to face him, and he realized that he had been staring. Staring and fantasizing, he thought.

'Sorry, Dr Bates. I was thinking of something else. I came in to see Dr Kapinsky.'

Kapinsky was hunched over in a familiar posture, engrossed in what he was viewing. He could shut out all distractions and concentrate single-mindedly on the work in hand.

Barnes knew little about his background except that he had been born in Poland. Both parents had died in the Communist takeover at the end of the Second World War. Brought up by an uncle and aunt who had managed to immigrate to England, he showed a keen interest in medicine and sailed through a top English medical school. After gaining fellowship of the Royal College of Surgeons he had made a name for himself, not as a surgeon but as a geneticist at Guy's Hospital. Impressed by a paper Kapinsky delivered at a conference, Barnes had made it his business to research the man's medical background and soon persuaded him to join the heart research unit in Cape Town.

'Rod – you've been here long?' Kapinsky's voice still retained the staccato consonants of his European upbringing. He looked pleased to see Barnes, stood up and extended his hand. 'Let's talk in my office.'

Kapinsky's 'office' was a wooden cubicle without a window in the corner of the lab. The desk looked as if a hurricane had struck it. Built into shelving against one wall was his latest toy, a computer he claimed could outperform the university mainframe, housed in an air-conditioned chamber under the mathematics block. Barnes could believe it. After all, as head of department he had authorized the expenditure – an amount that still made him blink even in retrospect.

'I see you've made the headlines again?' The statement was pitched like a question.

'Yes. Bugger it, Louis, we've got a leak somewhere. Somebody tipped off the press . . .' Barnes sat down on the only chair in the office and felt his irritation rise again at the thought of an informer on his staff.

Kapinsky shook his head sympathetically but said nothing, listening without comment as Barnes told him of the visit, the execution and the possibilities in this new source of donors. 'The time delay between brain death and the cessation of heart-beat is a problem. Every minute counts. If we could reduce the time difference it would give us an organ in better shape to survive a transplant.'

Kapinsky pushed back his shock of black hair and scratched at his jowls. Meticulous in everything else, he seemed not to notice that his heavy growth of stubble never appeared clean-shaven. 'You worry too much, Rod. We've already shown in our experiments that the heterotopic position reduces the total loading on both the patient's own heart and the donor heart. Any damage to the myocardium caused by the delay will recover within forty-eight hours of transplant.'

'I agree, but I'd hate to take that chance with the first heart we get from the prison. There'll be enough criticism as it is. We cannot risk losing the patient as well.'

Kapinsky gestured with one hand, as if waving away the problem. Clinical work had never been his major interest and Barnes knew that his strength lay in his grasp of genetics – increasingly a field towards which their research seemed to be moving.

Suddenly Barnes had an idea. 'The tolerant baboons, how far have you got?'

Kapinsky picked up a thick pile of notes and hefted it. 'Nowhere.'

'Jesus, Louis!' Barnes couldn't help showing his exasperation. 'Three years and thousands of rands later, and you tell me we're still floundering?'

Kapinsky was the epitome of the single-minded researcher. Nothing mattered beyond the goal, certainly not budgets or angry heads of department. These were just barriers to be navigated or, better still, ignored. 'I have a new approach I'd like to try.'

'What's that?' Barnes was immediately focused. The baboon line of research had swallowed many hours of time and effort. He was beginning to wonder if they were in a blind alley.

'We are going to introduce tolerance into a baboon foetus.'

Barnes's face reflected his excitement. The curse of transplants – rejection of the donor tissue by a recipient's immune system – had only been partially solved and then at tremendous cost. Even with tissue matching, which ensured that the donor heart matched the recipient's as closely as possible, a complicated treatment regime was still needed, the equivalent of chemical warfare to hammer the recipient's immune system into tolerating the transplanted organ. What was needed were donor tissues which matched the recipient so completely that rejection was a non-starter or, alternatively, some means of fooling the immune system into accepting the donor heart. Three years ago they had embarked on a project to breed baboons with an immune system that was non-responsive to human antigens. A clue lay in the way in which animals and humans reproduced themselves. One of the mysteries of reproduction is why the mother's uterus doesn't reject the foetus: it has, after all, inherited half of the father's genes, which are normally incompatible with those of the mother. Once the baby is born, however, the mother's body rejects any organ or tissue transplanted back into her body from her child, even though that child had been successfully carried and nourished within her uterus. Kapinsky had theorized that a gene in the foetus was switched off thus masking its incompatibility, 'a disguised invader', he called it, which fooled the mother's immune system into accepting it as part of her own tissues. After birth the gene switched on and any tissue transplanted back would be rejected.

'You've found the gene?' Barnes could hardly contain his excitement.

Kapinsky's reply was sobering, a simple head-shake. He had been cloning the baboon foetus to produce two identical embryos: one embryo was stored in liquid nitrogen and the other reimplanted in the baboon foetus to reach maturity. When this was born, the one that was stored was planted back in the uterus but not allowed to reach full term. Removing it at the foetal stage gave Kapinsky a set of identical twins, one of which was still a foetus. If his theory was correct, the foetus would carry the gene in a 'switched-off' state, while in the older but still identical twin the same gene would be switched on.

'So where are we?' Barnes kept his voice calm. He and Kapinsky were different animals. While he focused on the goal, Kapinsky enjoyed the detail and could happily immerse himself in an obscure technical problem which to Barnes was irrelevant and boring.

'Not much further but we have a new line of enquiry.' A 'line of enquiry' was Kapinsky's lifeblood and could mean anything from repairing a lab meter to original research.

Barnes contained his impatience and resisted the temptation to speak.

Kapinsky sensed his mood and spoke placatingly. 'Rod, I told you at the beginning it would be a long job. Remember that it's not just a matter of extracting DNA from each animal and comparing them to find the difference. Analysing the cell structure or the DNA message means looking at literally millions of combinations. You yourself are fond of telling your students that if the DNA in all the cells of a baboon were aligned in a single strand they'd stretch about 8,000 times to the moon and back.'

'Christ, Louis, get to the point!' But even as he spoke, Barnes recalled Kapinsky's warning when they had first embarked on the search for what he had come to think of as the reluctant gene. It had all stemmed from Kapinsky's request for a six-month research period at the George Washington State University where lab workers had first cloned the human embryo. Ever after he had referred to his spell there as his 'tour of duty on the Clone Frontier', while busily perfecting the technique in the research lab.

The American experiments had attracted world attention and fierce debate on the ethics of what the Right to Life advocates referred to as 'baby farming' and 'human spare-part sales'. This was followed by accusations of murder against researchers who discarded defective embryos. Once the debate entered Cloud Cuckoo Land, as Kapinsky called it, they kept their research well away from the public gaze, issued no press releases, resisted all invitations to publish findings, and when visited by members of the Ethics Committee, gave little more than the routine cup of coffee and an innocuous summary of research.

For all the furore, the cloning technique was fairly straight-forward. It involved little more than fertilizing a human ovum, or egg, in a glass dish and incubating it in a nutrient solution until it divided into two. The two-cell embryo was then treated with an enzyme to remove its envelope and expose the nuclei. Each nucleus was then given a coating of gel; one was placed in cold storage while the other was implanted back into the mother to develop to maturity.

Barnes remembered thinking that the technique opened up all sorts of possibilities, from the plain wacky, such as a woman being able to give birth to her own twins, to clone banks that would ensure against the loss of the original child and even provide a source of 'mail-order' children. This last was Kapinsky's idea. It was basically a catalogue of photographs of children born from a clone embryo, giving their intellectual and psychological profiles. Childless women would be able to choose from the catalogue, order a coded embryo from the clone bank, have it implanted and give birth to the exact genetic duplicate of the child of their choice. Kapinsky's ultimate goal was not to clone the embryo but genetic material from the adult. Unlike Barnes, he believed in the power of the computer to crack the genetic code and give him the key to genetic manipulation.

The subject engrossed him. He would sit for hours, long into the night at the keyboard of his little computer. One day, he believed, he would decode the genetic instructions from a mature cell that would enable science to clone an identical animal. The complexities excited him.

That was the first time Barnes had felt doubts about Kapinsky. The man had almost capered around the laboratory as he enlarged on his vision. 'Think of it, Rodney,' he had said. 'Each of the body's hundred trillion cells have these instructions in DNA code in the nucleus. So far, worldwide, we have deciphered only a fraction of the human genome which has a hundred thousand genes. Each gene is a DNA sentence that instructs the cell to make one specific protein – and each sentence has up to a hundred and fifty thousand letters or bases.'

Barnes remembered how Kapinsky had got more and more excited as he warmed to his subject. 'In the human being the genetic sentences are about three billion letters long. We will one day read them and even rewrite them to build the kind of genes we need . . .'

That was when he went off into a long harangue that made Barnes wonder to just what kind of man he had given charge of his research program: 'The world and its oceans have reached their biological limits to house and feed the overpopulated planet. That's why every pregnant woman must be able to determine the genetic profile of her unborn child. All genetic misfits, with hereditary disorders or predispositions to cancer, heart diseases and other weaknesses, must be aborted. We can no longer afford to have babies that will be a burden on society.' With growing distaste, Barnes had realized that he was listening to old-fashioned Nazism dressed up as science. Something must have shown in his face. Kapinsky had abruptly changed the subject and the idea had never been mentioned again.

Barnes shook off the memory and saw that Kapinsky was looking at him as if he expected an answer. He hadn't heard the question so he stalled for time. 'Yes, go on?'

'There may be a simpler way. I don't know why I didn't think of it before.' Kapinsky's face reflected his excitement. 'Acquired immunological tolerance – we inject cells from the donor into the baboon foetus and then allow it to be born. You remember MacFarlane's work, way back in the sixties?'

'Yes, with Medawar. What did they do again? I can remember the picture of a white mouse with a patch of black skin, or was it a black mouse with a patch of white skin?'

Kapinsky chuckled. 'I see you know more immunology than most surgeons.'

Barnes ignored the jibe. 'What's the implication here?'

Kapinsky savoured the moment. 'MacFarlane introduced what became known as acquired immunological tolerance by injecting cells from a black mouse into the foetus of a white mouse. When the injected mouse was born it accepted skin grafts from the donor without rejection. In other words, it tolerated the antigens from the donor without an immune response.'

Barnes jumped up, knocking over his chair in excitement. 'Louis, if you bred a baboon tolerant to human organs we would have a wonderful way to test the viability of the heart removed from the executed prisoner.'

'Would you do that?' Kapinsky asked, eyes gleaming.

'Do what?' Barnes appeared ignorant.

'Transplant the heart of a murderer into a baboon.'

'If it would eventually lead to a steady supply of donor hearts, why not?'

The excitement stayed with Barnes throughout the day. It looked as if the three-year research program had reached a breakthrough. With donor hearts available virtually on request, there was no reason why the heart transplant unit would need to turn away patients. Better still, there was every possibility of expanding their work, making their hospital an international centre for heart transplants – a kind of medical Camelot where hearts came to be healed.

The mood was still with him as he arrived home. The sun was setting across Table Bay and the north-wester was still blowing, chopping the sea into orderly rows of white horses that stretched to the horizon.

Valmai had come and gone, leaving the apartment spotless.

The dining table was laid as smartly as for a dinner party although tonight there would again be only one diner. A bottle of Cape White stood ready in the cooler with corkscrew beside it.

Barnes felt a sudden sense of loss, of disappointment, as if an expected guest had failed to arrive. Here was peace and tranquillity, comfortable living surrounded by a scenic paradise, and no one to share it. He shook himself: he had a lot of thinking to do and some priorities to set. Uncorking the bottle he filled a glass and took it out to the balcony. Africa Face blazed red in the setting sun. Behind it the land shimmered in the fading light. All nature was putting on a display. He raised his glass and sipped, savouring the smoothness of the wine: he was drinking pure Cape sunshine and this was paradise.

The phone buzzed softly. It was Alex Hobbs. 'Just had a call from Casualty, sir. It looks as if we have a donor for David Rhodes, only eighteen, male suicide case. Mrs van der Walt is talking to the parents to get permission to use the heart. She has also arranged for tissue matching. We should have a full report from the lab first thing tomorrow. Do you have any special requirements?'

Barnes thanked him and asked him to run through the transplant checklist to ensure that medical and technical staff, and theatre equipment, were in position so that they could get going as soon as the parents had signed the necessary forms. 'Oh, and don't forget the bumf,' he added, as an afterthought. The 'bumf' was the blizzard of paper which surrounded all transplants, made up of forms and notifications to various hospital departments and medical authorities so that, as Barnes saw it, the kudos went to the administration while the buck stayed with the transplant team.

He hung up and looked out across the bay. The wind had dropped and the sea was calm. Africa Face still glowed red but the shadows had deepened. Now it appeared forbidding, brooding, threatening. A trick of the light, thought Barnes. A few minutes ago it was paradise, now it looked like a scene from hell.

His mood was getting worse. This was ridiculous. He shrugged off his depression and refilled his glass. He had a nearly full bottle of Cape sunshine and, if that wasn't enough, there were another half-dozen in the liquor cabinet.

Barnes had often wondered why an ostensibly healthy young person would wish to take their own life. He remembered meeting one of his colleagues in hospital and being surprised to see her dressed in a gown and slippers. He asked what she was doing there. 'Oh, I was stupid! I tried to commit suicide, but I am OK now,' she had replied. Barnes had known her well and felt he could ask his old classmate how she had felt before she attempted to take her life. 'You know, Rodney, you reach a stage where you don't want to live a minute longer and will do anything to end your existence.'

Her reply and the look in her eyes conveyed the sense of urgent finality that the death-wish brings – *now*! With no time to waste in contemplating how best to achieve the peace that death would bring. This explained why some people used the weirdest ways to kill themselves: he remembered reading about a woman who went to her husband's workshop in the basement, switched on the electrical circular saw and put her neck on it.

'Are you sure that you're rid of this insane idea?' he had asked.

'Yes,' she had replied. 'I realize there's still a lot to live for.'

Three months later she had killed herself.

What had made her do this? Here had been a brilliant and successful gynaecologist with a big private practice and in good physical health.

Barnes took his drink and walked out onto the balcony. The light had gone. Africa Face was lined and black against the starlit evening sky. The wine tasted bitter. Perhaps, he thought, we should be thankful for the happy blend of nature and nurture that gives us the strength to cope with the trials and tribulations of life; to accept the responsibilities that society imposes. Sad are those who evade the problems that confront them and even sadder the unfortunate souls who find pleasure and relief from the stress of living in the altered view that drugs provide. Barnes shook his head, and turned his mind to the more demanding and less elusive problem of the moment.

CHAPTER 5

Several quick telephone calls set the transplant machine in motion. One was to David Rhodes's parents to inform them that a possible donor had been found, and the second to Casualty to check on the donor's condition. Karen wasn't surprised to find that once the neurosurgeons had certified brain-death they had considered the body no more than a corpse and, apart from hooking up the respiratory system, had left things to run their course.

She repressed her irritation. This was medical politics, played not with pawns but with human lives. It wouldn't be the first time that a donor body had been handed over in poor condition. The neuros weren't members of the heart transplant team and didn't feel it incumbent on themselves to help the 'glory boys' to get some media attention. From a neurological point of view, their patient couldn't be saved so why spend a sleepless night earning Brownie points for somebody else?

Quick intervention could still salvage usable organs, and Karen arranged for transfer of the body to the heart team's intensive care unit where more sophisticated life-support systems were available. Calls to the Medical Administrator and the State Pathologist alerted both to the need for legal consent and after that arrangements had to be made for blood grouping, tissue typing and virology tests to exclude the possibility of hepatitis or the AIDS virus. Tissue matching results would be available within an hour, after which staff could begin to prepare both patient and donor for the operating theatre. If there were no snags the operations – in several departments – could begin in a few hours' time.

Now for the tough part, gaining permission from the next of kin to take the organs. Karen's stomach contracted at the thought. She had never yet been able to master the sense of involvement when faced with relatives of a possible donor. She knew what they were feeling because she had been there herself. She closed her eyes. The images played again into her brain. Time is a great healer, they had told her. It was a lie. Time had healed nothing. The loss still ached like an open wound.

She could remember every detail of the policeman's face. He had been young, embarrassed by his task, unaccustomed to speaking English. She had just put Kimberley, then an eighteen-month-old handful, to bed. The table was set for two, Johan would be home in a few minutes and they were going to have a quiet celebration – their second wedding anniversary.

Two years of wedded bliss. She remembered thinking the cliché funny – like an old-fashioned soap opera where model wives waited at home for model husbands. But no soap-opera perfection could ever match what she and Johan shared. They had met in London where, as Karen Jones, she was senior nurse in charge of the intensive care cardio-thoracic unit at world-famous Guy's Hospital. Johan van der Walt, like so many young South African doctors, was there to complete his training for registration as a fellow of the Royal College of Surgeons.

It hadn't been so much love at first sight as passion at first touch. A career nurse, holding down a demanding job in a top hospital, Karen had felt fulfilled until the day Dr van der Walt had appeared in the intensive care unit. He stood out among the other surgical registrars – a head taller, tanned and muscular, with a ready smile. Male attention was no novelty to Karen but he had awakened feelings in her that at first she hadn't wanted to examine. She had found the best defence was to adopt a coolly professional air, an attitude that had drawn him even more strongly.

Any male would have found it hard not to notice the high-breasted, leggy brunette who ran a competent nursing team, but for Johan it was more than that. Always a focused doctor, he had found that she filled his thoughts almost to the exclusion of his studies.

They had surprised themselves when they ended up in bed on their first date, but it had been the start of a relationship that began in passion and deepened into mutual need. Soon they had become a recognized couple among the hospital fraternity.

Some months later Karen had been horrified to find she was pregnant. This wasn't part of her life plan. At first, fearful of losing this handsome, outgoing South African who had so changed her very English life-style, she had considered an abortion, but almost immediately Johan had picked up her mental stress and had gently drawn out the fact that he was to be a father.

He had been elated – and for the first time in her adult life Karen had allowed someone else to make the decisions. An abortion was out of the question. She would go back to South Africa with him, where domestic help was cheaply available. They would get married and have their baby. Within weeks they had made a nest in a little cottage in a suburb of Cape Town and Johan had a post as a registrar in the heart unit at Groote Schuur Hospital. 'Bliss' was the word that exactly described their life together, and it had been heightened by the arrival of Kimberley – until the knock on the door that had brought paradise to an end.

'Mrs van der Walt?' The policeman's heavily accented Afrikaans voice had been nervous. A police car had stood at the kerb with a second policeman at the wheel.

She could never remember what he said next, something about a car accident. She knew only that her world had died as he talked.

After that things were hazy. She remembered driving to the hospital in a dream, through a world drained of colour, suddenly switching to brilliant clarity when she had found herself in the neurosurgery unit.

Johan was lying on his back, unattended. His head injuries

were massive. A mechanical ventilator had clicked rhythmically, while the regular beep of a monitor indicated that his heart was still beating. His eyes had stared at the ceiling, pupils fixed and dilated, seeing nothing. She had known with awful certainty that he would never see again, never again hold her in his muscular arms.

Dr Johan van der Walt was brain-dead.

Instinctively she had taken his right arm and had felt for the radial pulse. His hand had been warm to the touch and his heart-beat strong and regular. But her training had told her the signs were meaningless. The heart was there only to sustain the brain, and the brain was gone.

'We are deeply sorry, Mrs van der Walt, there was nothing the neurosurgeons could do . . .'

It had been Alex Hobbs, one of Johan's colleagues on the heart team. Several others were there. One by one they had murmured condolences. She had looked at the familiar faces and seen them as strangers. But these men had celebrated team successes with Johan and together mourned failures. They and their wives and girlfriends had shared meals with Karen and Johan at the little cottage, and laughed and talked and loved the world. Now there was nothing, just a group of strangers around a hospital bed. A hand had touched her arm. It was Des Louw, a friend of Johan's since their student days. 'A cup of tea?'

At least it had been a neutral question, one she could answer. Karen had nodded and he had guided her out of the unit into the doctors' office. The rest of the team had not followed, leaving her and Des Louw alone in the room where – only hours before – her husband had worked as an enthusiastic young surgeon. Louw had pulled out a chair from behind a desk. Karen had sat down as if sleepwalking.

After a few minutes she had become aware that Louw was speaking. She had heard the sounds but the words hadn't made sense.

A knock on the door, she had thought. That's all it took. A single knock that had changed her life for ever. Before she had opened the door on that policeman her life had been secure, happy, even idyllic. Now . . .

'Karen?' Louw had been looking at her, expecting an answer. She had no recall of anything he had said. But whatever it had been it would have made no difference to that feeling of sheer numb misery.

'Karen, do you understand? Johan has been declared dead by two neurosurgeons. He is a potential donor.'

The words had sliced cruelly into her consciousness, shocking her wide awake. She had felt sudden anger: how could this colleague of Johan's be so insensitive? The body was still warm and here he was hanging around more like a ghoul than a friend. He had just told her that she had lost her husband and, almost in the same breath, had asked her permission to invade his body, pluck out his organs, cause even more destruction to that wonderful being who had shared her life . . .

'I know it's a very difficult decision.'

Des Louw's voice had been sombre. He had watched the conflicting emotions flash across her face. It hadn't been easy for him: he had known how dreadful it was for her even to think about the possibility.

'Your husband died as a result of a car accident. In the eyes of the law this is not a natural cause of death. That means the authorities will insist on a post-mortem.'

She had wanted to scream at him, to plead with him to stop harassing her, to tell her it wasn't true, to say there was some hope – anything but this awful choice he was forcing on her.

'If you give permission we'll start the post-mortem here in the operating theatre. The difference is that the organs we remove will not be burned or buried afterwards. Instead they will be used to alleviate human suffering and perhaps save a life.'

Louw had paused, his own grief for his dead friend near to surfacing but he had had a professional job to do, and professional distance from the tragedy was what would help both of them best. This was his friend's wife. He had so much wanted to hug this woman who was suffering so much. But it was the

44

wrong moment. She needed space to move and time to think, to allow the import of his messages to sink in.

He had waited. She had swallowed hard and stared at him in unseeing misery.

'Karen, you've been involved in this work. You know how many people can benefit from a single donor.'

She had closed her eyes and said a silent prayer: Please, God, give me the strength to do the right thing.

'Two from the eyes, one from the heart, two from the lungs, one from the liver and two from the kidneys – eight people in all.'

If only she had Johan to guide her, she had thought, but that was silly, these were his organs they were asking for.

Louw's voice had become even softer, almost reflective, as if he were musing to himself. 'Johan often sat in this very room, making the same request of relatives of loved ones who had just died.' He had stood up and looked out of the window. He could see hospital staff bustling in and out of the ward. When he turned round she was staring at him.

'Karen, your husband must have believed in the transplant program. Otherwise he wouldn't have been able to do that.'

She had felt as if her throat was constricted and had swallowed again, hoping the words would come. What would Johan have done if the situation was reversed and she was the prospective donor? Somehow it was always much easier to tell others how to behave, how to put aside fear, how to trust. When you are personally involved it is quite a different matter.

She had remembered then how, as a nurse in the heart unit at Guy's, she had told anxious parents not to worry. Everything would be OK, she had said. She'd felt so confident. Yet when it came to a minor ear operation for her own child she had been unable to find words of comfort for herself. She had remained fearful throughout the operation and for days afterwards.

Des Louw had turned from the window: it was clear that Karen needed to put the problem at a distance before she could answer. 'Don't try to decide now. Take time to think about it.'

The cottage had been a blaze of lights when she arrived home. Grace, her African maid, and Kimberley had been sitting on the carpet surrounded by dolls and toys. Grace had looked up, her usually smiling face sombre. 'Kimberley awoke when the policemen came. I picked her up . . .' She had searched Karen's face for some message of comfort, some hope that the police had got it wrong.

Karen had waved away the explanation. A volcano of emotion was building up inside, needing only a trigger to cause it to explode. The trigger had been right there in front of her. A table, set for two. On it, a single red rose in a silver vase, in the oven a meal, now cold. Tears had welled and flowed, scalding her cheeks. Grace read the signs and stood up, hugged her close and then pulled her down to the carpet next to the child. Kimberley caught a glimpse of her mother's face and screamed in alarm.

There on the floor – the blonde child in one arm and Karen enveloped in the other – Grace held them both, rocking slowly in an age-old rhythm of comfort.

With the tears had come the words, the questions, the bargaining, the pleading. We didn't deserve this. Why did it happen? Why didn't he come home earlier? Why us, why me . . .? If she could just explain how unfair it all was perhaps some kind fate would change it all back.

The three had clung to each other, the child dry-eyed and wondering, Karen crazed with grief, Grace comforting both. In the early hours the sobs had turned to a dry racking, lungs heaving without sound. Grace, carrying the sleeping Kimberley, had led Karen to bed and tucked her in with her child.

Karen had woken to bright sunlight and a terrible sense of decision. Without disturbing Kimberley, she slid out from under the covers. In Johan's tiny study she picked up the phone.

Reception put her straight through to the senior sister in charge of the unit. 'Sister? Karen van der Walt speaking. Please tell Dr Louw I'll be there in an hour to sign the consent papers.'

She had sensed her body calming as she put down the phone.

She had taken the decision and with it achieved some kind of peace. It was a long time before she felt whole again but the wound had started then to heal. Purpose began to form. There were things to do, arrangements to make and a final good-bye to be said. Somewhere ahead she had a life to lead and a child to bring up but for now she must cope with the rawness of grief.

Years later, Karen remembered that moment as the turning point. She never regretted her decision. It was as if part of Johan was still alive and advancing what he believed in as the goal of medicine: improvement of the quality of life.

Some months after his death, she had been sorting through his personal papers, including a few recent medical journals that continued to arrive until their annual subscriptions ran out. One carried an advertisement for the post of Transplant Co-ordinator at Groote Schuur Hospital. She had applied immediately and been accepted.

That was six years ago now. They had been fruitful years of responsible, competent work. She had watched Kimberley grow into a tall happy child, blonde locks and ready smile reminding her so much of Johan. They had been years of quiet satisfaction but they failed to touch the dead area where her dreams and hopes were buried. Nor did they much help in steeling her to carry out the gut-wrenching job of talking to donor relatives. She'd often thought it might have been better if she had been less personally involved in the transplant program.

Now, she quickly completed the blizzard of legal and administrative paperwork that, more than in any other field of medicine, had grown up around organ transplants. It was such an emotive action to take parts of one person's body and transfer them to another that the issue had gone from being simply a medical decision to one of legal and religious importance. Ruefully she reflected that legal and medical authorities worldwide had hedged the process around with so many checks and balances that doctors often joked that if they could charge for

47

form-filling they could give up surgery and live on the clerical work alone.

The phone rang. Reception reported that the parents of the young suicide, a Mr and Mrs Jooste, were waiting for her in Casualty. The wheel had again turned full circle. It was time to face the Joostes, explain to them that their son was dead and then ask them to consider donating his still living organs to the hospital for use by others.

Although she had never met the couple before she spotted them immediately when she walked into the reception area. The pair huddled forlornly together, the man unshaven and the woman's face swollen with weeping, could be none other than the Joostes. Working-class whites from their appearance, they nodded without speaking as Karen introduced herself and led them to the interview room.

'It's not true, is it, nurse, what the doctor said?' The man searched her face as she spoke, looking for some sign of hope. Before she could reply he said challengingly, 'If he's dead, why does he have all the wires and tubes in him?'

They remained uncomprehending and silent as she told them that their son's condition was terminal but that his body was being held on a life-support system pending their permission to donate his organs. The woman began to shake her head and sob quietly, as if she feared disturbing the hushed atmosphere of the hospital. Her husband held her tightly and looked desperately at Karen. The words came with a rush. Jerry was their only child. This couldn't be true. They had always been good parents. Why had this happened? What could they have done to avoid this terrible thing? Was there another doctor they could see . . .?

Karen let him work his way through the pleading, the anger, the guilt, the explanations until at last his flow of words slowed.

The receptionist was watching them through the office window, awaiting the signal. Karen nodded and she immediately picked up the ever-ready tray of tea and brought it in. Dumbly, almost as if out of polite convention, the woman accepted a cup. It was a diversion from the awful reality that had entered their lives.

Then Karen explained in simple terms the condition of brain-death and how it was that although their son was dead his organs were still alive. And also how temporary this was and that soon they, too, would die. 'Those organs are needed. We did what we could for your son but it was not enough to save him. Now we need your help in saving others.'

Through their pain, the couple were now listening. The woman had clutched her thick hospital cup in both hands, feeling the heat and grateful for it.

'We have patients whose own organs are diseased. People with damaged kidneys, people who are blind but who could see again if they could only have part of an eye, people with lung trouble who can no longer breathe properly, heart patients who have but a short time to live . . .'

The couple looked at each other. The husband kept one large gnarled hand on his wife's shoulder. She put down her cup and patted his hand. Karen could see the authority passing from one to the other as the woman visibly took on the full tragic burden.

Karen kept a tight grip on her professional calm. Buried deep inside her a small voice was screaming but she refused to listen, forcing her attention to remain on the couple. She spoke slowly and deliberately, looking at both in turn. 'We do not have artificial organs to replace the heart, liver, lungs, kidneys, the cornea of the eye . . . We are also unable to use the organs of animals.' She could see acceptance in their eyes. What was it about the working class and the poor, she wondered, that made them so willing to give up the little they had to help others? She added, 'We depend on the love and understanding of people such as yourselves. Mr and Mrs Jooste, I am asking you to give the hospital permission to use the organs from your son's body to help other people to live.'

It was the man who replied, 'OK,' and he choked up. His emotions took over.

Karen went over to the parents, put her arms round them and wept with them.

In the intensive care unit, Des Louw was going through the check-list with the houseman, Jan Snyman, to ensure that the young donor who had just arrived was properly monitored. The body's internal environment was no longer under the control of the brain. It had to be carefully watched and artificially maintained in as near normal condition as possible.

Half talking to himself he ran down the list: 'Yes, ventilation adequate. Urinary catheter in place. Large bore intravenous line for administration of fluids, blood and drugs. Also CVP and arterial lines. Rectal temperature low, warming blanket in place.' He looked at Snyman. 'What's the position with blood tests?'

Conscientious as ever, the houseman listed the test samples: 'Astrup, urea, electrolytes, glucose and blood cross match. The results should be back shortly.' Forestalling the next question, he added, 'I've also arranged for two units of blood on stand-by.'

Louw nodded, approvingly. Apart from students, housemen were low on the hospital totem pole but this one showed promise, he thought.

Without glancing at his list, Snyman went on, 'I have also confirmed with the co-ordinator that blood has been sent for tissue typing, hepatitis B and C, CMV titre VDRL and HIV tests.'

'Blood culture?'

'Yes, doctor. We also have the chest X-ray and ECG. The cardiologist will be here shortly to check the heart.'

Louw picked up the treatment chart. 'I see you started the donor on a dopamine drip.'

Snyman looked up from adjusting the drip counter. 'Yes, doctor. I couldn't get the blood pressure above sixty on vasopressin and T_3.'

Louw looked back at the chart. 'You gave him Kefzol and Solu-Cortef, also insulin and blood. Good.'

This was praise indeed from an up-and-coming transplant surgeon. Snyman felt emboldened to point out the wavering arterial pressure. 'I'm worried,' he said. 'For some reason the donor is very unstable.'

Des Louw interrupted his train of thought: 'Stay with it, doctor. Do what you can to keep the donor going until we're ready to transplant.'

'Why not take the donor to theatre, remove the heart and keep it on ice until then?'

Louw was already on his way out of the small ward, replying over his shoulder as he pushed his way through the swing doors, 'I'll suggest it to Dr Barnes.'

Alex Hobbs was standing by David Rhodes's bedside when Des Louw arrived. Two nurses had just completed the morning checks. The atmosphere was electric. Within days of his arrival this determined youngster had won the admiration of nursing staff with his refusal to accept that his heart was dying. Hour after hour, day after day, fighting for every breath through half-drowned lungs, he had never stopped believing in the heart team's ability to pull him through. And day after day, as his condition worsened, the nursing staff had watched him slowly slip away. The chance of a transplant gave hope that he would live. They must not let him down. It showed in the body language of the staff as they moved quickly and smiled often.

In the operating theatre just across the corridor there was an air of purpose. Nurses were setting up the equipment and the perfusionists busied themselves on the heart-lung machine, which would keep the patient's blood in circulation and his brain oxygenated during the critical part of the operation.

Alex Hobbs nodded to Louw as he entered and continued checking the results of the lab tests on David's blood chemistry. He had already scrutinized the X-rays and electrocardiograph reading, and ordered azathioprine to be given by mouth with the premedication. There would be no need to wait the usual six hours for the patient's stomach to empty. The youngster had eaten virtually nothing for days.

Hobbs looked up at Louw. 'It looks like all systems go. Have his parents been notified?'

'Yes, they're here already. In fact, they've asked to wait in the corridor to see David just before he goes into theatre.'

'Any problems?'

Des Louw hesitated. 'No, not really. I spoke to them briefly as I came in here. They're beside themselves with relief. As far as they're concerned it's a foregone conclusion.'

He looked uncomfortable. Hobbs raised an eyebrow. Louw opened his mouth, thought better of it and shook his head.

'Come on,' Hobbs urged.

'Well, it's the attitude, the difference. They look upon us supermen as if we were their gods . . .'

Hobbs felt a shiver run down his spine and immediately shook it off, but not before a childhood superstition had surfaced in his mind. Somebody, somewhere, had just walked over his grave.

CHAPTER 6

Kapinsky was in the operating room of the research block, brow furrowed, peering through a laparoscope into the pelvis of a female baboon.

In spite of what the administrative plan showed, Rodney Barnes didn't figure large down here except as a means of getting the equipment Kapinsky needed to reach his goal. And when that day came the tail would wag the dog. The thought of the English saying made Kapinsky laugh out loud, a sudden bark of hilarity that set the caged baboons around him gibbering.

The problem he was trying to resolve, of induced immunological tolerance making the recipient's immune system blind to the presence of the donor organ, needed a steady supply of pregnant baboons on which to experiment. Kapinsky had discussed it with a lab technician in the department of gynaecology. Between them they agreed that the easiest way was to remove mature eggs from female baboons, fertilize them outside the body with male baboon sperm, and intubate the cells to embryo level, at which stage they could be stored at low temperatures. Given such a back-up supply, he reasoned, it should be possible to induce tolerance by first implanting an embryo into a female baboon then, a few weeks later, injecting the resulting foetus with antigens of the donor. But, first, he had to obtain the eggs, which the gynae lab technician didn't seem to think so difficult.

Kapinsky had already placed the baboon in the Trendelenberg position – body low, legs and pelvis raised. The abdomen was filled with carbon dioxide gas, forcing the bowel back into the upper abdomen and giving him a clear view of the pelvic structures. He was surprised at how easy it was to identify the uterus and the finger-like fimbria which guide the ovum into the Fallopian tubes where it can be fertilized by the spermatozoa. Both ovaries were readily identified. Kapinsky felt a leap of excitement as he noted the little bubble on the left ovary, which carried the maturing ovum.

This was his target.

He allowed the gas to escape from the abdominal cavity before he withdrew the laparoscope and stitched the short incision through which it had been inserted in the baboon.

Satisfied that he could get the eggs he needed, Kapinsky went back to his desk and again checked the protocol of the experiment. Super-ovulation, to increase the number of ova, could be stimulated with drugs such as Clomid and HMG (human menopausal gonadatrophin). It was relatively straightforward to monitor follicle growth by regular ultra-sound examination of the ovaries. When they matured, the ova could be removed by puncturing one follicle and aspirating its content into a glass tube containing culture medium at 37 degrees Celsius.

Kapinsky frowned at his notes. The harvested eggs should be incubated for six hours at a steady temperature and in a balanced atmosphere that most resembled their natural habitat. This prepared them for the semen, taken from a male baboon by masturbation one or two hours before insemination. Careful treatment of the ejaculate, which included washing and storage in a culture medium, would enable him to collect up to a hundred thousand mobile sperm. More than enough, he smiled, to ensure that the ovum was well fertilized. The embryo – or embryos, no reason why he couldn't have as many as he wished – could be stored in sealed glass containers and supercooled in liquid nitrogen. He looked up at the lab clock. The transplant would be almost finished.

It had been disaster almost from the start. With David Rhodes already in the operating theatre and lying on the table, Dr

Ohlsen, the anaesthetist, was running a final check on his equipment before beginning to anaesthetize his patient when he was asked by the senior nursing sister to delay.

'What?' he asked, irritably. He had been seconds away from the induction. But she had already gone, leaving him with the junior theatre aide.

He heard the sound of a trolley being rushed past, then the doors of the next theatre were flung open. A flurry of action was happening in there. He picked up odd words, something about the donor being unstable. He walked through to offer help. When they had been getting ready to transfer the donor from the ICU to the operating room, he developed frequent extra heart-beats and periods when the heart raced at high speed. Jan Snyman had resorted to hormonal therapy, giving hourly intravenous doses of insulin, cortisol and thyroid hormone, and achieved a temporary improvement – until a few minutes before they were to move the donor to the theatre next to where David was waiting with the anaesthetist. Barnes joined Snyman to check on the donor; he left nothing to chance.

'He's fibrillating,' the nurse shouted. Barnes and Snyman looked at the monitor as it screamed up in pitch and frequency. Rapid waves flickered across the screen. It was a dance of death. The heart was trembling but not pumping blood.

'Get the defib,' Barnes yelled as he jumped with both knees onto the bed and began cardiac massage.

Jan Snyman was about to question the action. What was the use of keeping up the circulation if the brain was already dead and couldn't be damaged any further? He opened his mouth and closed it again as he realized that blood-flow had to be maintained to the heart muscle which, once damaged, would be difficult to start again.

'Okay, defibrillator paddles on.' It was Barnes's voice, quiet and clear, as he applied the electrodes from the defibrillator, one to the donor's breastbone and the other slightly to one side. He slid off the bed and nodded.

Alex Hobbs, who had just joined them, pushed the button.

The body arched as several thousand volts shocked it rigid. The flat line on the electrocardiogram screen showed a single heartbeat, then another, then shivered back to the familiar fibrillation pattern.

Barnes started cardiac massage again, hands thrusting hard into the yielding flesh while he desperately tried to recall what the lab studies in brain-death had indicated. Des Louw's paper on brain function leapt into his mind. The research, undertaken during Louw's two-year registrarship while training as a cardiovascular surgeon, covered vital changes that occur just before and after death. Carried out on laboratory animals, it involved inflating a small balloon inside the skull of an anaesthetized baboon to induce brain-death. Changes in heart-rate, circulation pressure and blood hormone levels were monitored. Louw had reported that the anesthetized animal responded as it would have if conscious and faced with a major life threat such as an attack by a leopard. The body's hormonal system poured out an increased level of hormones to prepare for the emergency, galvanizing the muscles for sudden movement and heightening all body responses. Known as the 'sympathetic storm', it was a survival action that occurred in all living animals to meet impending catastrophe. An unfortunate side effect was an excessive delivery of hormones to the heart muscle, which forced it to perform well beyond its normal range. After death the animal's heart had been dissected and displayed on glass slides. With horror, Barnes remembered that each slide had showed massive heart muscle damage.

Beneath him, the donor's body lay, unresponsive, air whooshing from his lungs at each thrust of Barnes's hands. 'Defibrillator,' he yelled again. Everyone stood back as the paddles were placed and the current discharged. The screen gave a single blip and settled down again to the thin wiggling line.

Barnes forced himself to breathe more slowly. He had faced this situation before, a donor heart that had been extensively damaged and couldn't be restarted. The transplant had been cancelled. But this one was different. This was David Rhodes's last chance.

Think, he ordered his mind. *Think!* There had to be something else, something he had missed.

Suddenly he realized that the room was silent. Everyone was staring at him. He had to stop massaging the heart. The decision was his. Keep it up? Call it a day? Abandon the donor and, almost certainly, the patient? 'Let's get him to the operating room, connect him to the heart-lung machine and perfuse the heart muscle with some warm, oxygenated blood. It will restart.' Even to himself the words sounded hollow.

The donor's limp body jerked and twisted as Barnes – on his knees beside him on the table, hands flat on his breastbone – straight-armed with his full weight in an urgent cardiac massage. He barked as he pumped while gowned figures milled about. Then he stopped the massage and moved away so that the team could prepare the operating field and hand out the plastic tubing which would connect the patient's circulation to the heart-lung machine.

'Knife please.'

David opened his eyes as the whining sound of the surgical saw drifted through from the next room. Des Louw was slicing through the exact centre of the donor's breastbone, a cut that would run neatly from top to bottom and allow him to pull the ribcage apart to expose the heart.

'They're looking at your new heart,' Ohlsen encouraged his patient.

Back in the donor theatre, Barnes stood at the head of the table, looking over the green linen screen erected by the scrub nurse when she had draped the body. He hadn't said a word while Alex Hobbs opened the chest.

Hobbs expertly fitted the retractors and pulled the ribcage open. He held out a gloved hand. 'Scissors,' he requested.

The scrub nurse slapped them into his palm. Hobbs eased the blades into the sac that enclosed the heart and slit it wide open. The doctors looked at the flabby grey muscular pump. It lay there without any evidence of life.

'Arterial catheter.' Hobbs's voice wrenched Barnes back.

With the dexterity of a gifted surgeon, Hobbs placed the catheter into the aorta – the large heart artery – and a second catheter into the right atrium. The body's circulation system was now in circuit with the heart-lung machine.

'Pump on, start rewarming the patient. Temperature?'

'Just about thirty-one,' the pump technician responded.

'The heart is picking up.' It was Jan Snyman's voice.

Barnes noted the improvement but experience told him it was far too early to expect major change. There were several hurdles to cross. First the heart had to be defibrillated and placed on a regular sinus rhythm before it could be taken off the machine. That would be the crunch point. This was going to take some time and it might be better to send David back to the ward.

Barnes walked through the connecting door. He found David sitting upright on the operating able, an oxygen mask covering his mouth and nose. Every breath was a tortured rasp.

Dr Ohlsen looked up and caught Barnes's eye. 'The pre-medication has worn off,' he explained. 'It's impossible for him to lie flat. His lungs have to work harder to pull in air and he gets acutely distressed. I think the best would be to intubate him and connect him to the ventilator – it's the only way he'll get enough air.'

David was alert enough to follow the conversation. He looked at Barnes and attempted a smile, which came out as more a grimace. He hadn't the energy to speak but his supreme confidence in his consultant surgeon shone like a beacon.

Barnes patted his hand and nodded in agreement with Ohlsen. 'Even if he has to go back to the ICU it would be better to intubate him. It will improve his oxygen intake and reduce the load on the heart. Will it be necessary to anaesthetize him?'

Ohlsen looked at his patient. 'Yes, he'll tolerate the introduction of the tube into the windpipe better if he's sedated.'

'Thank you, doctor. Go ahead.' Turning to David, Barnes

gave a reassuring smile. In his head he could hear a dry, rasping Scots burr: 'If yer patient has no faith in ye, ye canna help him.' Making his voice warm and reassuring, speaking strongly over the sound of the boy's breathing, he promised, 'When you wake up you'll have a new heart,' and returned to the donor room.

There, only the whining of the heart-lung pumps could be heard. No beep from the monitor and no unnecessary conversation. Each member of the team was concentrating on the job in hand.

'What about the Astrup and electrolytes?' Barnes asked, peering over the screen.

'Astrup is spot on and we've given some more potassium,' said Snyman.

Alex Hobbs sensed the strain in Barnes. 'Things are looking good,' he assured him. 'Every minute the heart becomes more and more active and soon we can defibrillate.'

Barnes looked back at the heart. Muscle tone had returned and it was fibrillating actively.

'The Administrator is on the phone.' He hadn't noticed the nurse who had just entered the room. She began to retreat as soon as he looked at her.

'What does he want?' Barnes couldn't keep the irritation out of his voice.

'I don't know, sir. He said it was urgent and that he wanted to speak to you personally.' She was clearly eager to put distance between herself and this tense, angry doctor, her eyes large above the mask.

'Stop all stimulants and start some lignocaine. Wait till I get back before you try to defibrillate,' he snapped over his shoulder as he headed for the doctors' office.

The telephone receiver was lying on the desk. He picked it up. 'Yes?'

'Sorry to disturb you, Dr Barnes.' Administrator Webber sounded unsure. 'I know you're having some trouble but the newspapers have been on the phone all morning. They want to know if the transplant has been successful.'

'How the hell do they know we're operating at all?' The informer again, Barnes thought.

Webber heard the tension in his voice and spoke soothingly. 'Rod, you know the patient has an outstanding sports record and his family are well known in the area. I've got an army of reporters and photographers here.'

Barnes briefly considered telling the press to get stuffed but knew that, as an old journalist had once advised, 'It's better to feed the crocodile than risk getting bitten on the arse.'

'Tell them we haven't started yet. We're having some technical problems. The operation will be finished in about three to four hours.'

He put down the receiver without waiting to hear the Administrator's 'But . . .' Why could he not be left alone to focus his energies on the patient?

'OK, let's try and defibrillate the heart,' he ordered, as he walked through the door of the donor room.

Hobbs took up the paddles again. Barnes reset the voltage and activated the machine. The charge again arched the body high off the table. He peered over the drape. Fibrillation had stopped. Everyone was waiting for the first co-ordinated contraction of the muscle fibres.

The heart remained static. What the hell could be wrong *now*?

'Touch it with the forceps,' he instructed Hobbs.

Hobbs gave the heart a gentle prod. It contracted.

'Again,' Barnes said. Again it contracted.

The nerve centre of the heart, the 'pacemaker', wasn't firing, he thought. It must have been paralysed by some injury. Nerve tissue was always more susceptible to oxygen starvation than muscle. The next step was to attach electrodes to the outside of the heart and pace it.

It was like fighting an unseen enemy that was taking over one position after another. He and his team were falling back to weaker and weaker positions.

'What do you think, Dr Barnes?' said Hobbs, producing another contraction with the forceps.

'There's more to brain-death than we know,' Barnes replied, and immediately wished he hadn't. He had sounded worried. He was spooking his colleagues. They were all experts in their field but a fall in morale could wreck the teamwork and even cause elementary errors – mistakes that could cost life.

Suddenly Barnes felt dog tired. He had taken all the steps. He spoke aloud: 'The donor is well ventilated. Blood volume, electrolytes and Astrup are within normal range . . .'

'And I gave insulin, cortisol and thyroid hormone every hour.' It was the houseman's voice, with a slight overtone of pride. Jan Snyman knew how fortunate he was to be in on a surgical procedure such as this. In his first year as a fully fledged doctor, here he was on the frontiers of medicine.

'We took all the precautions to prevent depletion of the heart muscle energy stores,' Alex Hobbs added, still stimulating the heart to contract.

'OK, let's pace it.' As Barnes spoke, the scrub nurse moved to pick up the electrodes. He looked around. 'Where's Dr Louw?'

'Getting ready to open the patient,' said the floor nurse.

'Ask him to come here, please. We need an opinion.' She nodded and, keeping her gloved hands clear, shouldered her way through the intervening doors.

Hobbs took the proffered electrodes from the scrub nurse and looked at Barnes. 'Shall we pace the atria or the ventricles?'

'I think it would be safer to pace the ventricles in case it develops a heart block later. The nerve connections picking up the impulses from the upper chambers may also be affected.'

Using a 3.0 stitch, Hobbs attached two metal discs to the surfaces of the ventricles, connected them to the ends of the lead and handed the leads out. 'Set at a hundred beats a minute. Pacemaker on.'

There was no response.

'Voltage up.' Barnes tried to keep his voice from rising.

'It's beating.' Hobbs's relief was obvious.

Barnes looked at the screen. Yes, the heart was contracting at a hundred beats to the minute. They had retaken one position from the enemy and gained ground. At that moment he became aware that Des Louw was standing next to him. 'Dr Louw, you've put in some good lab work on this problem. What do you think?'

Louw looked over the screen. 'I see you're pacing the heart.'

'Yes, it's in complete standstill.'

Both stared at the heart as if they could find the answer written on it.

'I'd say an excessive release of catecholamines on brain-death must have caused extensive heart muscle damage. In the lab we've observed remarkable rises in hormones such as epi-nephrine, nor-epinephrine and dopamine within minutes of brain-death.' He pursed his lips and added, 'We can send a biopsy of the heart for frozen section and ask the pathologist to determine the extent of the damage but I personally think it's too late.'

He was pronouncing a death sentence. Both for this donor heart and the young man lying next door.

'I'm sure we'll find extensive histo-pathological damage, such as contraction bands, focal necroses, myocytolysis with oedema and cell infiltration.'

He was describing the cell changes in a dead heart. Barnes had a wild urge to tell him to shut up, but stayed quiet.

Suddenly the beep of the monitor became irregular. God, was the heart going into fibrillation again?

'Dr Barnes, its own beats are coming through,' Alex Hobbs shouted. 'Turn the pacemaker down.'

Barnes responded immediately, counting off, 'ninety, eighty, seventy.' With a sigh of relief he said, 'It's keeping the rate up.'

Louw peered over the screen. There was no doubt, each atrial contraction was being followed by a ventricular response.

They had taken another position, Barnes thought. Now for the final assault. Would the heart maintain adequate circulation when the support of the heart-lung machine was withdrawn?

He turned to the technician and instructed, 'Lower the flow.'

There was an instant change in the pitch of the motor driving the pumps. 'What's the pressure, Dr Louw?'

'Dropping. A hundred, seventy-five, eighty, eighty . . . keeping at eighty.'

Barnes watched the heart closely, looking for evidence of overload. No, it appeared to empty well with each contraction. He walked back to the heart-lung machine and this time carefully slowed the pumps himself. Artificial support continued to drop until it was barely a quarter of the circulation.

'Too low,' Hobbs and Louw shouted together. The heart was distending and faltering.

Barnes increased the flow again.

'Heart recovering, pressure rising.' Hobbs kept his eyes glued to the struggling organ.

'Maybe we're in too much of a hurry. Let's give the heart more time to recover.' Barnes looked through the window at the theatre clock. The donor heart had been on circulatory support for forty-five minutes. 'I'm going next door for a moment. Hold things steady as they are.'

Dr Ohlsen was injecting something into the venous line when he arrived. David was lying on his back fully sedated, chest moving up and down with the ventilator.

Barnes immediately noted that both arterial and venous pressures were within normal limits. What disturbed him was that extra beats were coming from the lower chambers of the heart. 'His heart is quite irritable,' he remarked.

Ohlsen looked up. 'Yes, I've just given him some potassium and started the lignocaine again. How are things progressing next door?'

'Slowly winning. The next few minutes will tell. I'll be back shortly.' He headed back towards the donor room. He was about to make one of the most difficult decisions of his life. This was crunch point.

He squared his shoulders and strode back to the heart team, again taking over the controls of the heart-lung machine. 'OK, let's try again,' he said, hoping he sounded more casual than he felt. 'Ready? I'm slowing the pumps. Watch the blood pressure and the heart.' He read off the level: 'Seventy-five per cent, sixty, fifty, twenty-five.'

'The BP's falling,' said Louw.

'Heart faltering,' came from Hobbs.

'I don't think the heart will recover in a hurry, if it recovers at all,' Louw concluded as Barnes increased the support again.

Maybe this heart needs a brain to recover completely, Barnes thought. They were in unknown territory here. There must be some factor governed by the living brain that they knew nothing about, an essential something that maintained the health of the vital organs. But the brain was gone. No one spoke.

'Dr Barnes?' The technician had asked him a question and was now clearly expecting an answer.

He blinked hard and felt himself swim back out of the mists of uncertainty.

A thought jolted him. David's brain! David had a body and a reason to live. His brain had that factor, that will to survive. If he piggy-backed this heart onto David's then his brain could begin the healing process and give both hearts a chance.

He turned to Louw. 'Get David ready. I'll be along in a minute and we can open the chest.'

Louw hesitated, paused as if he were about to say something, muttered a quick 'Certainly, sir,' and left.

'What was that again?' he snapped at the heart-pump technician, then nodded at the flow reading he was passed and turned to Hobbs. 'Dr Hobbs, cool the patient, arrest the heart by flushing the muscle with the paralysing solution. When it is absolutely quiet and cold, remove it and place it in an ice saline solution.'

'Yes, sir.' Like everyone else, Alex Hobbs had noted Barnes's change of manner. Gone were the worried frown, the defensive answers. Now he barked orders and looked confident, assured.

Barnes started to walk away from the table then turned to the surprised group. 'I'm going ahead. We'll do a heterotopic transplant.'

CHAPTER 7

'I tell you, they're up to no good.' Red-faced, veins protruding, Professor Thomas, who had come from the pathology building, almost shouted the words as he burst into Professor Kemble's office. JJ, ever courteous, stood up to greet him.

'I'm sorry, sir. He didn't give me a chance, he just went right past me.' It was JJ's secretary, pushing in behind him. Not often caught off-guard, she was enraged, glaring up at Thomas almost as if she were about to throw him out.

JJ repressed a sudden urge to laugh at the sight of the tiny woman, fists clenched and bristling, challenging the bulky professor of pathology. He always preferred women shorter than himself and Betty Lloyd was no exception. She had run his office quietly and efficiently for twenty-five years shielding his privacy and driving off anyone without an appointment, students and staff alike.

'Thank you, Betty. I'll handle it.'

She glared an over-my-dead-body look at Thomas, and left.

'They're up to something and I'm damn well going to find out what.' Thomas almost choked on the words, his broad English Midlands accent making him almost unintelligible.

JJ considered him, his surgeon's eye noting the high colour, the sheen of sweat across the fleshy upper lip, the overweight body and shortage of breath. If the hospital's professor of pathology kept up this lethal combination of high stress and low fitness levels it wouldn't be too long before he became one of his own interesting cases on a slab. He kept his face neutral, which was difficult enough in present circumstances but more so when it was Professor St John Thomas, lay preacher, self-appointed moralist, most active member of the Ethics Committee and right royal pain in the arse.

He'd often wondered how a man with such a poor research record and minimal forensic skills could have been appointed head of pathology at one of the world's great teaching hospitals. He had seen his CV, noted the short list of published papers – none in mainstream journals – and the lukewarm praise from various medical and academic references in Britain. Perhaps it had more to do with the fact that doctors were leaving South Africa in droves, fleeing the apartheid policy, leaving top posts to be filled by second-raters. Maybe what counted in his favour were his religious pretensions, smiled on by the Afrikaner medical bureaucrats of the appointments board.

'Good morning, Professor. Have a seat. What can I do for you?' JJ indicated the chair opposite. Thomas immediately sat down with a whoosh of breath and wiped his forehead.

JJ's simple courtesy had given him control of the situation, as he knew it would. Whatever dance Thomas did now it would be to JJ's tune.

'They're collecting baboon embryos. There's a great evil being planned here, I'm warning you, a great evil.' Thomas's voice became lay-preacher sonorous, speaking to some great invisible audience.

JJ pushed down his dislike. The sanctimonious bastard was on to something. It was high time he paid another visit to Barnes's lab: whatever he was up to JJ was sure it was within ethical parameters. Barnes seldom consulted him about his work but he published regularly, spoke at international conferences and – right up until the academic boycott began to bite – pulled in a steady flow of research funds from international drug companies and medical institutions. Added to that he was not only the country's top heart surgeon, he was world famous, while this jumped-up hypocrite spent his time spouting religion and blocking useful research. Not for the first time JJ cursed the politics that had saddled the medical school with such an

66

unbalanced man. He looked straight at him and lied with a straight face, 'Yes, I know.'

Thomas looked thunderstruck. 'You know, and you're doing nothing about it?'

JJ was enjoying this. He offered a cigarette to Thomas, who shook his head. Then he took his time lighting up, sat back in his chair, sucked in a deep draw and expelled a cloud of smoke above Thomas's head. The man visibly tensed further, if that was possible.

'Professor Thomas, my department is responsible for at least thirty publications every year. What's more, they all appear in top research journals. How many papers do you publish annually?'

It put Thomas on the defensive. JJ knew he had been criticized at Faculty meetings for the lack of research in the department of pathology.

'I'd rather have no papers, no publications, than allow the evil practices that are going on in your laboratories in the name of research.' Thomas heaved himself out of the chair and stuck a finger in JJ's face, his own features alight with fervour. He was an Emissary of the Lord, come to warn of sin and the retribution to follow. 'Kemble, you're being led astray. For evil to succeed it is sufficient for good men to do nothing. But ignorance is no excuse.' A slight froth gathered in the corners of his mouth as he spoke, his words booming around the small room and bringing Betty bustling protectively through the door. Thomas pushed past her, turning only to deliver a parting shot. 'Mark my words. One of these days you'll see female baboons giving birth to God knows what, perhaps even human babies. Whatever they're doing, I'll stop them. *I will stop them.*'

He was gone, his voice ringing back from the corridor where a couple of startled clerks side-stepped him as he puffed past.

JJ raised his eyebrows at Betty, nodded at her offer of tea and sat back to consider Thomas's outburst.

Jesus! Baboons giving birth to humans? The creep must have

picked up some lab gossip which, like all scuttlebutt, grew in the telling. Nevertheless, it might be good politics just to pay Barnes and that funny bugger Kapinsky a courtesy visit.

But it was Thomas who got there first. Kapinsky was surprised to look through the open door of his office and find the Ethics Committee member staring down at him. He had heard that Thomas had been snooping around and making enquiries from the technicians about the research animals. Fortunately the sensitive areas were under lock and key.

'Good morning, Professor Thomas. What can I do for you?' said Kapinsky, keeping his voice friendly and unwittingly mimicking JJ's earlier greeting.

Thomas barely noticed. He had come here primed to fire and little was going to stop him. He launched straight into his harangue. 'You must stop this work. God will not allow you to continue.'

Kapinsky was genuinely puzzled. 'I do not know what you are talking about.'

'Don't lie, Dr Kapinsky. Those human embryos you're going to implant in female baboons.'

Kapinsky's voice chilled. 'And may I ask what gives you that idea, Professor?'

Thomas felt himself on safer ground here. Kapinsky! What kind of name was that? Polish? German? It didn't matter. These middle-European types were all the same. They only needed to be spoken to firmly, show them who's master. They soon came to heel.

'I know you've been consulting your friend in the department of gynaecology for weeks now. Don't try to fool me. I demand to see your notes and also that you destroy all experimental animals used in this abuse of God's creation. This abomination will be brought to an end today.'

Scheisse! For a moment, Kapinsky was shocked back to childhood expletives. This bastard was dangerous. He knew a hell of a lot more than most of his own lab staff did. He could ruin everything. Right now the important thing was to get him the hell out of here.

Something crystallized in his mind. Suddenly he knew that he had a mission, a project to fulfil. Nobody, but nobody, and that meant the whole Ethics Committee if necessary – let alone this Bible-quoting bigot – was going to harm the project. He stood up. 'Professor. You have no right to be in this laboratory without permission. What is more, you have no right to tell me what I can or cannot do.' Raising his voice, and taking a step nearer, he added, 'So get out of here before I throw you out.'

Thomas had heard of Kapinsky's violent temper. The look on his adversary's face convinced him he would carry out the threat. In chapel, on Sunday morning duty as a lay preacher, he felt invincible, surrounded by the armies of the Lord. Here, facing this angry man, things were a bit different. Kapinsky, with a barrel chest and forearms like hams, looked capable of anything.

'Dr Kapinsky, if Dr Barnes cannot control you and Professor Kemble will not stop you, I will,' he said, and stormed out of the door.

Kapinsky leaned both hands on the specimen table, bowed his head and forced himself to stay calm. At the far end of the lab, staff fussed as if they had heard and seen nothing. The fool had given him an idea. Speaking to himself, he said, almost in a whisper, 'I have killed before. If you get in the way, you bastard, I will kill you. Nothing and nobody gets in the way of the Project.'

In the heart unit's operating theatre Barnes had reached a crucial part of the transplant. With Des Louw assisting he opened David's chest in minutes, splitting the breastbone down the middle and pulling the ribcage apart with a retractor.

The inflamed heart was now clearly visible, struggling to keep up circulation and calling for help with every beat. Sure fingers working quickly, he opened the right pleural cavity and turned down the right side of the sac that enclosed the heart.

This created a space the size of a man's fist where the assisting heart could be placed, comfortably, without compressing the lung.

'Should be enough room here,' Barnes muttered, standing back.

Louw watched the procedure, admiring the dexterity and seeing the textbook being virtually rewritten on the table. Never before had he seen this surgical procedure. This was why he had come here, from a lucrative general practice, to spend two years as a lowly registrar; an apprentice who did what he was told, watching the master at work and noting every move.

When Barnes had decided, some months previously, to use the donor heart as an assist device, he had found that researchers in this field had, for some unknown reason, always positioned the donor's heart in the left chest where there was not enough room. This forced them to resect a portion of the left lung. If, he had reasoned, the donor heart was to be placed on the right side, where there was ample space, there would be no need to cut away part of the lung. Moreover, if the transplanted donor heart failed it could be removed leaving the patient no worse off. The appropriate experiments soon convinced Barnes that his reasoning had been correct. The technique was introduced in the treatment of patients with excellent results.

He nodded to Des Louw, who moved to assist with connecting the patient's circulation to the heart-lung machine. Barnes felt himself approving the other man's confident procedures. A bumptious young bugger, he thought, but he'll go places. Perhaps they would have a place for him in the heart team at the end of his term.

At a signal, the machine took over David's circulation.

'Tell Dr Hobbs we're ready,' Barnes said to the floor nurse.

Alex Hobbs, who had been awaiting the summons, appeared in seconds, carrying the donor heart in a stainless steel dish. He placed it on the instrument table next to Barnes, who turned and lifted it out of the ice-cold saline.

It was soft and flabby, and had the greyish brown tinge of death. The cold hand of uncertainty choked him. Will this heart ever start again? He set his teeth and focused hard, forcing himself to become mentally as ice cold as the saline. Somewhere in this lump of muscle and tissue there was a spark of life that would start firing as soon as he could give it warm, oxygenated blood.

To make the procedure technically easier, David's heart was also briefly stopped. There were now two bodies in adjoining rooms without a heart-beat. It was a crucial cross-over point in the operation, a psychological Rubicon, Barnes thought, a moment that could easily become one of self-doubt and trepidation. He had always warned his registrars to be aware of this point and to guard against any hesitation.

'Let's get it hooked up,' he said, firmly. Again Des Louw was there. With a continuous stitch they joined the left upper chambers of the two hearts so that there was a free flow of blood between, then the same for the two right upper chambers. The end of the donor's artery that led to the lungs was joined to the side of David's lung artery. This meant that both right lower chambers could now pump blood to his lungs.

'Aorta!'

Both moved in unison to work on the large vessel carrying blood to the brain and the rest of the body.

'I'll do this with a side clamp,' said Barnes. 'Release the clamp on David's aorta so that his heart can get some blood.' Apart from brief instructions, the team spoke little. Barnes didn't encourage idle chatter during his theatre work.

'Clamp off,' Louw informed his chief.

Immediately the heart turned pink and became tense. A few seconds later it showed signs of life by going into fibrillation. Barnes put a side clamp on to the aorta so as not to obstruct the blood to the coronary arteries. Then he made an opening large enough to fit the donor aorta and joined the two, end to side, with a neat row of stitches.

'Side clamp off!'

For the first time since the donor heart had been removed two hours before it received life-giving blood.

'Start warming,' Barnes instructed the technician. This was the moment of truth. He would soon know whether he had made the right decision.

Nobody spoke, each occupied with their own thoughts, but all sent up a silent prayer that David's heart was now fibrillating with vigour. Barnes was tempted to start it immediately so that at least one heart would be pumping blood.

'What's the temperature?' he asked of no one in particular.

'Thirty-four,' a voice replied.

Then, as if cued by a conductor's baton, they all cried, 'It's beating!'

David's heart had started to beat spontaneously, as if the few minutes' rest it had received during surgery had helped.

For how long? Barnes wondered, but shrugged the negative thought aside. He looked at the donor heart: it had also changed to a more healthy colour, and was no longer the flabby sac he had stitched in parallel with David's heart. The upper chambers had started to contract urgently but the lower chambers seemed deaf to their call.

'Temperature?'

'Now thirty-six,' came the reply.

'Astrup?'

'Spot on this time,' Ohlsen answered.

'Give some isoprenaline followed by the third dose of cortisone.'

A new enemy had entered the battle: rejection. David's immune system had already detected the presence of the donor heart. It would be recognized as non-self, an invader, in the same way as live bacteria or viruses would be recognized and destroyed.

The new heart would soon be under attack. David had received drug treatment during the operation to reduce the intensity of the immune response, but it would be constantly there to a greater or lesser extent.

'Isoprenaline started,' said Ohlsen.

The heart did not react. Normally it would have showed a muscle movement in response to the stimulant.

'Let's pace it.'

Ohlsen reacted immediately. 'Pacemaker on.'

The heart did not respond to the electrical stimuli pulsed out through the electrodes still in position on the ventricular wall.

'Not pacing.' Barnes's voice was calm but he felt a cold fear clutch at him. 'Turn up the voltage.'

'I have already,' said Ohlsen, observing the situation and anticipating the move.

'Up more.' Barnes hoped the desperation he felt did not sound in his voice. It looked as if the heart muscle was too far gone to sense the electrical shocks from the pacemaker.

A sense of hopelessness welled – sudden, unexpected, paralysing. He had no one to turn to for advice. They were out on the frontiers of medicine here and there were no signposts.

'Sir, it looks as if the heart is dead.' Louw was his sombre self. 'I think you should take it out. The non-contracting chambers will interfere with the circulation and there is a great danger that the blood will clot in them.'

Barnes knew it was a decision only he could make. 'Let's see what happens when we reduce the flow. Dr Ohlsen, start inflating the lungs.'

The two hearts moved up and down in unison with the ventilator. Barnes checked the chest. 'His right lung is still down, could you inflate it fully?'

Ohlsen increased ventilator pressure.

'That's better. Now start decreasing extra-corporeal support.' The whine of the electric motors fell to a hum. David's heart started to fill and showed no signs of faltering.

'Venous pressure?'

'Barely three and the patient's heart is pumping. I can see it on the arterial tracing.' Ohlsen sounded relieved.

Barnes made the decision. 'The donor heart stays in.' He felt he owed his team an explanation. 'Some of you may remember Mr Moore, our worst rejection case?'

Des Louw nodded.

'Rejection was so bad that the transplanted heart fibrillated, yet the patient's own damaged heart kept him going until we had the rejection under control. We defibrillated the heart on the fifth day.'

'Yes,' said Louw. But this heart is not rejecting, he thought. This heart is dead.

Barnes went on, as much to convince himself as his registrar, 'Mr Moore is still alive today. We had no problems with blood clots and the donor heart is now working better than his own.'

He looked again at the donor heart in David's chest. The pumping chambers were in standstill, with no sign of contraction. It hung there next to the patient's own sick heart, as useless as a broken crutch.

Barnes inspected the suture lines for bleeding. Satisfied, he took the final step. 'Stop bypass.' The whine of the motors died. The only sound was the whoosh and sigh of the ventilator.

'He's keeping a mean pressure of thirty,' said Ohlsen.

'What's the venous?'

'Only five.'

'Give blood from the pump and let's see how he responds to an increase in the preload.'

Barnes turned to see the venous pressure for himself. It was creeping up, slowly – six, seven, eight, nine, ten.

'OK, hold it there,' he told the technician.

'Arterial eighty.' Ohlsen's pleasure at the strength of the reading was unmistakable.

Barnes had already noted the improvement in circulation as the blood volume increased. 'Get the heparin neutralized so that the blood can clot again. Give the protamine please, Dr Ohlsen.'

'He's starting to pass urine,' the technician said.

Barnes suddenly felt drained, mentally and physically. A great weariness weighed him down. He turned to the scrub nurse. 'Ask Dr Snyman to scrub.' She nodded. He looked at Des Louw. There was no mistaking the eager light in the eyes above the mask. The man was itching to take over.

'Dr Louw, do you mind taking out the venous and arterial catheters and closing the chest for me? I'll be in the doctors' room. Call me if there is any change in his condition.'

In the washroom he stripped off his gloves, dropped the mask from his face and headed for the medics' rest room. He was dying for a cigarette. Strange how the craving came back. He'd stopped smoking years ago yet there was still that urge for nicotine after periods of high stress.

He resisted the temptation to bum a cigarette off one of the orderlies and instead asked for a cup of tea, a more potent drug. He felt his body relax into the easy chair after the first swallow, the slightly tannic tang refreshing mouth and throat. Tiredly, he considered the options facing him. If his theory was correct, David's own heart would have already begun to assist the donor heart to recovery while the X-factor from his brain would be healing the wounds inflicted by the death of the donor brain. Again a part of his mind noted the detachment of the word 'donor'. The young man who had been called Jerry Jooste no longer existed. What he had to deal with here was a donor organ, a mass of tissue useful only in the context of heart surgery.

A movement at the door caught his eye. It was one of the junior nurses to say the Administrator was on the phone again. 'Thank you, nurse. Ask Exchange to put the call through here.'

She nodded and scurried away, only too anxious to put distance between herself and this gowned figure with the deep frown.

The telephone rang. It was, as he had expected, a press query. Was the transplant a success?

Barnes was tempted to say the transplanted heart was not functioning but that the operation had been a success. 'We're just closing up, Dr Webber. Everything has gone well but it's too early to say when we're going to get full donor heart function.' Webber thanked him and rang off with a word of encouragement. Nice old bugger, Barnes thought idly. He ran a tight ship. A major hospital administrative post wasn't the easiest of jobs and he supposed he wasn't the easiest of doctors to deal with.

Christ, I *must* be tired. He grinned at his reflection in the window. Now he was feeling sorry for the Administrator. He drained the cup, slipped on his mask and walked back into the theatre.

David's breastbone had been wired together and Des Louw was suturing the skin, a neat row of continuous stitches beginning just under the throat. Without comment, Barnes noted urinary output, venous and arterial pressures. The boy was holding his own – for now.

Barnes knew that, without assistance, David's overworked heart could collapse at any moment. A sour thought came to mind: all this could have been avoided if his budget hadn't been cut. If he had been allowed to buy a mechanical circulatory assistance device, now almost standard equipment in any good American heart clinic, there would be no question mark hanging over David's chances of survival. The heart assistance devices were designed to sustain patients awaiting a donor. He remembered reading a paper in an American medical journal which described how one patient had been kept alive for over three months before he received a transplant.

In his mind he went through the surgical connection routine. It was not difficult. Blood was drained from the ailing heart's left pumping chamber, and the oxygenated blood was then pumped back into the body through the aorta. The device not only assisted the circulation, it also reduced the workload of the heart's left pumping chamber. In turn this reduced the load on the lungs, which decreased the work of the right pumping chamber. He remembered that the prototype required the patient to be connected by tubes to a console holding the pumps.

Now the devices were electrically operated and so small that they could be implanted in the patient's abdomen, allowing more mobility and faster recovery.

'Where will the money come from?' had been the Board's response when he had confronted them with his request. That bloody fool Thomas had asked the question.

The Government had reduced the subsidy to the provincial hospital service by 15 per cent this year and his sorely needed machine was one of many that had come under the axe. Yet there always seemed to be enough money to satisfy the apartheid monster, always enough to pour into the vast bureaucracies which operated the system. And nobody asked where the money was coming from when the Army and Air Force decided to launch another of their attacks on the Communist spook operating from neighbouring black states. For all the good they did they might as well pour the money into a hole in the ground.

He felt increasingly bitter as he walked back to the doctors' room. Thank God that at least his research program was well financed: the money could never have come out of the miserable budget allocated. Kapinsky's anonymous and obviously wealthy supporter had seen to that. Curious, the way he had suddenly popped up just when it looked as if the whole program was about to fall over. He repeatedly asked Kapinsky to set up a meeting with their benefactor but the man never seemed to be available. Barnes supposed that with that kind of money there was plenty to keep him occupied . . . He heard the operating room door slam open, pulled himself out of his reverie and walked into the passageway.

David was in his bed and on his way back to the intensive care unit. The ventilator was attached to the head frame of the bed. Three bottles with IV lines attached were suspended from stands clamped to the side frame. The boy lay unmoving, without sign of life.

'I'm going to keep him sedated,' Ohlsen told Barnes. 'We'll bring him up slowly to avoid any patient stress or anxiety, and keep the workload down on the heart.'

Yes, thought Barnes, ease the heart and hope for a miracle. What was needed now was time. Time for the donor heart to recover, if it was ever going to.

Louw came out of the operating theatre, mask down and stripping off his gloves. 'His blood pressure has come down to seventy, sir, but the venous is also down so I think he needs a little more blood.' He looked wound up, ready for another punishing few hours in surgery and almost elated.

Perhaps I'm getting past this kind of thing, Barnes thought. He was surprised at how tired he felt, as if he had climbed a mountain or run a marathon. His body ached and his head felt dull and heavy. Time to take charge again. 'Dr Louw, will you stay with David in the intensive care unit for the night please? I'm going down to the lab but I'll be in to see him before I go home. Thank you for a good piece of surgery. Well done, doctor.' Without waiting for a reply he headed for the change room.

CHAPTER 8

Kapinsky was sitting at his desk, scowling at the jumble of journals, the odd pieces of lab equipment, microscope slides and the syringe tray that littered its chaotic surface. He turned when Barnes entered and launched without greeting into a tirade.

'This Thomas bastard has been snooping around again. You have to stop him, Rod, he's going to create a lot of problems for us.'

'Such as?' Barnes enquired, innocently. He was not afraid of Thomas. JJ would see that the silly old bugger stayed out of his hair. But it was funny to see Kapinsky lose his cool like this.

'He's been picking up gossip around the medical school, and putting two and two together and getting five. Now he's all fired up to bring the Ethics Committee here for an inspection. That's what.'

Barnes had never seen Kapinsky so upset. 'I'll handle that, Louis. Leave it to me.' He kept his voice assured, calm, hoping to defuse Kapinsky's anger. He needed to bounce some ideas off him and it didn't help to have him fulminating about something as unimportant as the preacher.

'Christ, Rod, you're not taking this Bible-toting shit seriously enough. I tell you he is determined to stop our work. According to him, we're interfering with the work of God.' Kapinsky gave a blow-by-blow account of Thomas's visit and how close he had come to throwing him out.

Barnes whistled quietly. This was worse than he'd thought. High time to see JJ and have the man put to rights. 'I'm sorry, Louis. I'll have a talk to Professor Kemble –'

'Not bloody good enough,' Kapinsky interrupted, his face reddening. 'We'll have to get rid of him. I'll put the bugger down if I have to. Nobody, *nobody* is going to get in the way –' He stopped suddenly, realizing that Barnes was staring at him in concern. 'Sorry, Rod. He gets to me. What was it you wanted to talk about? Let's go to my office and have a cup of tea.'

It was a remarkable turnaround, almost as if Kapinsky had pressed a button. Barnes had seen this once before: towering anger that suddenly gave way to calm and reason. That had been two years before when a baboon had escaped from the animal room into the lab and chewed up several computer discs. Kapinsky had put it down with a dart gun. *Put it down?* What was that he'd said about Thomas?

But Kapinsky was the genial host, pouring tea and indicating a plate of biscuits. Barnes had opened his mouth to ask him to repeat it and then thought again. What the hell? Angry talk, hot air – there were more important things to talk about.

He related the drama of the morning. Kapinsky listened carefully, asking a question here and there, closely following the course of events. 'So at this stage the donor heart is not functioning?' He was half talking to himself.

'No, it's not. When we closed the chest the atria were contracting but the ventricles were not responding. There was complete ventricular standstill.' Barnes looked at his watch. Time to make a first check on the patient. 'Excuse me while I phone the unit.'

Kapinsky passed the telephone across the desk and Barnes punched in the intensive care unit code. The nurse passed him to Des Louw almost immediately.

The registrar sounded alert, efficient, almost as if he was starting the day. Barnes envied his youth and energy.

'Dr Louw, how is your patient?' He listened without comment then asked Louw to keep him informed of any change.

'What's happening?' Kapinsky asked.

'From the ECG and arterial pulse tracings it appears the

donor heart has not recovered. There has also been a deterioration in the patient's circulation.'

He stared at the wall, speaking half in thought, 'Maybe I was wrong. I should have removed the donor heart.'

Kapinsky said, brusquely, 'I don't know why you feel you must save every patient. This one was clearly too far gone. There's a time to give up and just let them go. God knows there are enough humans destroying the Earth.' He looked almost sorrowful.

'Louis, we're different doctors. You are a research scientist. It's your job to keep your distance from your subject, to be objective, even cold and calculating. I am a medical doctor who works with people. This patient is my responsibility and I must do all in my power to improve the quality of his life.'

'So why are you running a laboratory and encouraging me to do the work of the devil, as your friend Thomas labelled it?' Kapinsky had never had much time for doctors who got emotionally involved with their patients and this was a side of Barnes he had seen all too often.

'For the ultimate goal. So that I can use the knowledge we gain here to better serve my patients.'

'Bullshit, Rod. You can be as cold a scientist as I am. Remember when we tested the alkalinity tolerance of those embryos to see how soon it would take for half the test group to die? I'll tell you what are you, Rod. You're a bloody Jekyll and Hyde.'

Barnes fought to keep his temper. The jibe about the embryos had caught him on the raw. After all, they were test-tube cultured . . . He cut off the defensive thought and swallowed hard. It was pointless to argue. He needed some expert advice here and this spat about nothing was taking up time.

'Let's leave it at that, Louis. I need to know something about Louw's hormone theory – you remember the work he did on brain-death?'

'Yes, of course. He was almost obsessed with the idea that donors should be treated with hormones. He also considered that thyroid hormone was the magic potion that would go far to solving donor-heart problems.'

Barnes nodded. 'Yes, and since we've made use of his suggestions there has been a significant improvement in our ability to manage the donors.'

'So why are you in trouble now?' Kapinsky asked, a tinge of sarcasm in his voice.

'That's what I don't know and what I want to find an answer to. There are still many aspects of brain-death that we don't understand.'

'You're damn right!'

Barnes ignored the remark and added, 'We do know the brain is also an endocrine organ which secretes certain hormones. There may be a hormone we have not yet identified that is essential to the survival of organs such as the kidney, liver and heart. You must find this hormone, Louis.'

Kapinsky, ever the scientist, looked intrigued but sceptical. 'Let's first see whether your hypothesis is right and whether the heart in your patient recovers. Somehow I doubt it very much. Let's see.' He walked to the shelf where the books and journals were stacked in disarray and took down a dozen or more of the latest issues of *Current Contents*, a weekly list of all recent important medical literature. Within a few minutes he was running his finger down lists of journal articles on the topic, stopping occasionally for a quick look, marking the item and moving on.

Barnes had lost him. If he knew Kapinsky he would be there all night, and by morning, he would have a list of all the articles dealing with brain hormones over the last ten years. He left quietly and headed for his office.

When he walked in, Fiona took a look at his face and knew immediately that the transplant hadn't gone well. His mail was on his desk, sorted into urgent and non-urgent items. He found it therapeutic to deal with the administrative quibbles and queries that came his way as head of the heart team and he felt himself relax as he worked his way through the pile. These decisions were simple. All they required was a straightforward yes or no. There were none of the uncertainties, the stressful demands for judgement that took such a toll at the bedside. Occasionally he heard the telephone ring and Fiona's voice, sweet reason itself, deflecting the enquiries and listing those that needed to be answered. Some time later she appeared at his office door, eyebrow raised, local restaurant menu in hand. He realized he hadn't eaten since breakfast, which had consisted only of a cup of coffee.

Over a snack, he scanned the journals, returned his calls, dictated several letters, and by the time the sun was slanting through the curtains he had finished the OB – office bullshit, as Fiona termed it. He decided to call at the hospital on the way home. It had been a tough day that he wouldn't forget in a hurry, one of uncertainties – and decisions from which there might be no return.

Barnes put on a gown and mask and washed his hands before entering the intensive care unit where David was being nursed under sterile conditions. With his immune system suppressed to prevent rejection of the donor heart, his body was easy prey for disease organisms.

Alex Hobbs, Des Louw and Jan Snyman were standing at the bedside. Barnes could see they were not happy, and a brief examination of the patient told him why. The patient's feet were cold and his urinary flow had slowed. Blood pressure was being maintained at sixty-five but the venous pressure was up to fifteen. He was holding his own, but only just.

Barnes asked for an arterial and ECG tracing. A glance showed him that the transplanted heart was not contributing to the circulation. The doctors waited for his verdict.

'What did the last Astrup show?' He directed the question at Alex Hobbs.

'The Po $_2$ is ninety-five per cent and he's not developing acidosis, so it must be adequate. However, as you noticed, his circulation is poor.'

'Has he been awake?'

'Yes, but Dr Ohlsen recommended we keep him sedated. He prescribed morphine.'

'Thank you, Dr Hobbs.' Barnes turned towards the door and hesitated. 'We don't expect miracles. It may take days for the donor heart to recover.' If it recovers at all, he almost added but stopped himself just in time. A negative attitude was no help either to staff or patient, he thought, and wondered why he was being plagued with self-doubt. Normally he would be forward-looking and positive. He shook off the gloomy thoughts and smiled at the group. 'I'm going home now, Dr Louw. I want you and Dr Snyman to monitor the patient tonight and call me if things change.'

In the corridor he found David's parents, anxiously waiting for news. He recognized them immediately. They were unmistakably wealthy Eastern Cape farming stock. Danie Rhodes, in hacking jacket and cavalry twill slacks, had a handshake like a vice.

'You must be tired, doctor,' was his first remark.

Mrs Rhodes, in a blouse buttoned to the top and a severely cut suit, clutched her shoulder-bag tighter and came straight to the point. 'How is David, Dr Barnes?'

He looked at them. They had been waiting for hours and the strain showed. A believer in open communication with patients and their relatives, he never exaggerated or tried to disguise problems with medical jargon. 'Dr Hobbs did explain the situation to you, did he not?'

Both nodded, but clearly they wanted to hear it from him. Mrs Rhodes was leaning forward, lips slightly apart, eager for any word of hope. Behind her, her husband stood, feet apart, hands thrust in jacket pockets, body balanced against the blow he feared.

'He said you put in the second heart, but it was not working . . .?' The last word rose in pitch. It was both a question and a plea.

'That's correct. It isn't working now but we believe that by tomorrow or the day after it will have recovered enough to start beating and gradually get stronger.'

'You're sure of this, doctor?' Mrs Rhodes was anxious, almost prompting, in her hope that he would tell them good news.

'One can never be completely sure. We're into unexplored territory here but I assure you this is David's best hope. I would not have carried out the operation if I hadn't rated the heart's chances of recovery highly.'

'How is he now, doctor?' Danie Rhodes, not normally a hesitant man, spoke as if he didn't want an answer.

Barnes ignored his dragging feeling of depression, straightened his sagging shoulders and smiled. 'The remarkable thing is that his own heart took over immediately after the operation and is keeping up a satisfactory circulation.' He gave them an abbreviated account of the operation and saw the couple relax. Information was power. Good or bad, it gave people power over their own decision-making. It made them feel part of the decision. He reminded himself to make the point at the next staff briefing. Informed people were better able to take the news, good or bad, and reduced the stress levels that always surrounded a family illness. Lower stress meant a better treatment environment and that, in turn, led to better healing.

'Thank you, Dr Barnes. We won't keep you any longer but we would like your permission to stay the night.'

Barnes didn't usually encourage relatives to stay at the hospital. They tended to interfere with the management of the patient, but this couple were such stolid characters that their presence could be a plus. 'Yes, of course. I'll ask the nursing staff to see you have something to eat and find a comfortable spot for you to relax. Good night. When I see you in the morning I hope we'll have better news for you.'

Barnes slept fitfully, with recurrent troubled dreams of botched surgery and dying patients. In one the transplanted heart became gangrenous and ruptured, then large blood clots were forming in it and breaking off into the circulation.

Twice he was awakened by calls from Des Louw. It was

obvious he and Alex Hobbs were not taking any decisions on their own. With each change in David's condition, Barnes was consulted. Could they give some fresh frozen plasma as he was bleeding slightly? No, not actively bleeding. His venous pressure was down to five, was it in order to give some more blood? These were run-of-the-mill decisions that in normal circumstances they would have taken without reference to him. But this case was different and, though they didn't say it, was not being handled as they would have wished. It had also taken on a high profile in the media and the press was following each slight change in condition, with statements issued every twelve hours by the hospital administrator.

It had affected the intensive care unit staff. Several of the day team felt they were deserting their patient when it came to the end of the shift and stayed on duty throughout the night, their presence lending support to the others.

Barnes was dead to the world, though, when his alarm sounded. He woke groggily. Accustomed to surviving on little sleep, this time he felt as if he had been awake all night. He was glad the night was over but unwilling to face the day. That feeling had barely surfaced before he shrugged it off and reached for the telephone.

The patient had stabilized but disturbingly the donor heart still showed no sign of life. Barnes was immediately wide awake but his nightmare followed him into the shower where he opened up the cold tap and turned his face to the stinging spray. He knew it would be impossible to concentrate on any other work until this case was resolved.

After the shower he adopted his normal routine to order his racing thoughts, shaving carefully, selecting a suit and tie, and dressing slowly. Good grooming wasn't just for horses, Barnes believed. It set the standards for the day, told the world you were serious about what you were doing, reassured staff and reminded students that patients took them at face value. 'Hobo school is over there,' he had once told an unshaven, dirty-shirted first-year student in scuffed sneakers, pointing to the exit. 'This is medical school. Here we dress for success, not failure. Come back when you've made up your mind.'

He was savouring his second cup of coffee when the phone rang. His pulse heightened. They never ring urgently for good news, he thought, reaching for the receiver.

'Barnes!' he barked.

'Good morning, Dr Barnes. This is Vorster from the *Times* speaking.'

Christ! The bloody press never gave up. He had changed his unlisted number twice in three months and still they got through. There *had* to be a leak on the hospital switchboard.

'Yes, Mr Vorster?' He was sorely tempted to hang up but kept his voice cool.

'Sorry to disturb you so early in the morning.' If he was so goddamn sorry why had he rung?

'We have information that you transplanted a dead heart into David Rhodes yesterday.'

His nightmare was growing worse. Now the press were getting into it. This kind of misreporting was enough to bring the whole Ethics Committee down round his ears, slash his funding, such as it was, and cut off the supply of donors. He'd had a long row to hoe with the medical establishment in trying to assure them that transplants were a useful and viable part of surgical treatment. Many remained unconvinced and formed a vocal group on the Medical Council. This kind of crap would have them screaming for his head on a plate.

'Where do you get this kind of information from?' Stay calm. Sound slightly amused. Whatever you do, don't sound defensive.

'Sorry, Dr Barnes, the news editor didn't give his source but assures me it is very reliable.'

It must be that fucker Thomas! He had access to all the information and was the only one with an axe to grind. Anything to put Barnes and his team in a bad light.

'Dr Barnes? It is true that you used a dead heart? Is this a new kind of approach in transplant surgery? Is there a proven research background for this procedure?' Vorster was no fool. He worked the medical beat, read the journals and had made it his business to know as much about heart transplants as it was possible for any layman to know. He was probably better informed on the subject than most general practitioners.

'Mr Vorster, it depends on what your editor's idea is of a dead heart. If he means one that is not beating then all my patients who have undergone transplants have had dead hearts. To answer your question, there is nothing new in the procedure.'

'What do you mean by that, doctor?' Vorster always played dumb, asking apparently simple questions and seeming too thick to understand a simple answer.

'If you don't know that the heart is routinely stopped during surgery, and for obvious reasons, then perhaps you should get somebody who knows something about medicine to do the story.' Despite himself, Barnes knew he was losing his cool and could hear the sarcasm in his own voice. Better to put down the receiver and kill it here and now.

Too late. Vorster jumped in quickly, 'Doctor, I've come to you to get the correct information. If you don't want to talk to me then I'm forced to go elsewhere, in which case it may be to your disadvantage if the details are not correct. I prefer to get the story right in the first place.'

He was doing his job, and doing it well. It was true that the press would publish any update on the story, even if the reporter had to suck it out of his thumb.

'Mr Vorster, the donor heart was not beating when it was connected to the patient's circulation but you can take it from me it was not dead and I have every reason to believe it will recover. Does that answer your question?'

'Yes, doctor, but . . .' It was time to be forceful. Crocodile-feeding time was over.

'Mr Vorster, I have better things to do this morning than give you a lesson in surgery. I have answered your question. I have patients to care for. Goodbye,' he said, above Vorster's protests.

Bugger it! This was all he needed right now. A full-blown scare story, no doubt front page. He could just imagine the headlines, which would almost certainly feature the words 'dead heart'.

The drive to the hospital was sombre. As he wove his way through the morning traffic, he sought desperately to understand the donor heart's malfunction. Had there been some technical slip? He went through a mental check-list to ensure that every step of the operation had been properly completed. In his mind's eye he could see it all. From the first excision of the donor heart to the last stitch required to attach it to David's own, it had been perfect. All the checks had been properly made. All the answers came back positive.

The hormone therapy? This was the only part he had not supervised personally. But Jan Snyman knew the procedure backwards. He had been an outstanding medical student, graduating *summa cum laude* with honours in surgery. That's why he was here. Barnes accepted only the best into his heart team, and Snyman was that year's cream of the crop. So far, his houseman year had been exemplary.

Des Louw's work on brain hormones? The X-factor? That was it! The donor's brain had been almost destroyed by the bullet. What he had had was a dead heart that had been deprived of the X-factor because the brain itself had gone. Perhaps the neuro-surgeons had been right: no point in keeping a body alive when there was no brain.

This was damn silly. He was going around in circles. Start with the facts and look for the odd one, the one that didn't fit.

Suddenly he visualized himself cutting away the sac surrounding the donor's heart. At that moment he'd had to force himself to think only of the work in hand, to discipline his thoughts and concentrate on the surgical technicalities. But there had been something, a kind of frisson of energy which pulsed through his fingers as his gloved hand touched the heart. What does a brain do when it faces the last catastrophe? Even when consciousness goes, is there still some elemental form of cerebral awareness of the whole body which persists until the brain is truly dead? Does the brain, as a last dying gesture, close down all its circuits and kill even those organs which are still 'viable', or worse . . . does the body recognize and reject the hands of the healer, which have now become the hands of a killer? Hands that carve away at the basis of life itself? With a shock Barnes saw he was in his own numbered bay in the hospital car park with the engine still running and not the slightest recollection of the twenty-minute drive from his home. He switched off and sat there, gathering his thoughts. Good surgery, the kind that he and the team had carried out in the past twenty-four hours, always gave him a high. This time he had felt nothing except a dragging sense of depression and anxiety.

Was there more than just blood and bone and nervous tissue? Put them all together and the sum was more than the parts: a personality. But where did the personality go when the parts were separated? What happened to the soul?

Talk of the soul had always made him smile but even psychologists recognized a special something, a driving force in all human endeavour. Perhaps it was time surgeons took another look at what they were doing. Transplants had pushed the limits of human knowledge well past the ignorance barrier, riding on the back of technically advanced surgery. But until now little attention had been paid to the psyche. When you carve up the body do you also slice away at the soul?

He laughed aloud at the thought and suddenly felt better. He was a surgeon, not a witch-doctor. Superstition and theology were not subjects for scientific enquiry. If it could be measured, quantified and tested, and if the tests could be repeated by others, then it was science. No doubt there were other forms of knowledge, but until they were scientifically examined they could only cloud the issue.

He hurled himself out of his car, braced his shoulders and headed for the intensive care unit. Come what may, he was ready to face the day.

CHAPTER 9

As soon as he entered the doctors' office Barnes could feel a change in the atmosphere. The smile on the face of the charge nurse alone told him volumes. Dr Louw had gone home for a shower and clean clothes, she said, but Dr Snyman was with the patient.

The change in David Rhodes's condition was obvious. His colour had improved. The monitor showed mean arterial pressure above eighty and venous pressure at six. When Jan Snyman saw Barnes he straightened up and grinned. In spite of his all-night session he looked brimful of energy. Adrenaline, Barnes thought. Maybe we should market the stuff.

'It's all good news, sir,' said Snyman, standing up. 'Since six o'clock this morning his circulation has been steadily improving. And in the last two hours he has passed two litres of urine.' Obviously delighted to be the bearer of good news, Snyman rushed on, 'His extremities are getting reasonable circulation and his toes are much warmer to the touch. I can also feel the pulses. They're faint, but they're there.' He frowned, looked at the chart and back at Barnes. 'It's possible that the inflammation in his own heart has been countered by the steroids and has now subsided.'

Barnes felt the mood of the unit wash over him. He felt warmed by Snyman's obvious pleasure. Not for the first time he noticed how his supposedly professional staff were affected by patient outcomes. Snyman had worked almost round the clock yet here he was, bubbling with vitality. Last night staff had been facing defeat, reaching into themselves for the ultimate effort and carried along by discipline alone. This morning the picture had changed completely. Victory was in the air. He read through the chart, noting how the vital signs had changed, coinciding with the dawn. The eternal rhythms, he thought, daylight and dark, the body's low and high points.

'There appears to be some interference with the heart monitor, some extra beats,' Snyman could not stop talking. 'Maybe the donor heart isn't needed now.'

Barnes glanced across at the monitor. 'Did you turn on the pacemaker?' he asked. 'That would show on the screen.'

'No, sir, we haven't touched it since the operation.'

'We need some hard copy as a check, Dr Snyman. Please run an arterial pressure tracing.'

Snyman adjusted the recorder, triggered the tracing needle, waited for the graph paper to emerge, tore it off the printer and handed it to Barnes, who studied it, not quite daring to believe what he saw. There were now two distinct wave forms, each quite separate from the other. He felt like hugging the houseman. The 'interference' was the tracing of the second heart, now strong enough to make a distinct pulse of its own in the circulation of the blood.

At that moment Des Louw walked in, looking as refreshed as if he'd had a full night's sleep. Barnes slapped Snyman's shoulder and beamed at Louw. 'Congratulations, gentlemen. The donor heart is generating a pulse.'

Louw gave a whoop, which brought in the charge nurse. They crowded around Barnes while he pointed out his proof. 'Look, here's the QRS of David's own heart and there is the smaller one of the donor heart. Your "interference", Dr Snyman, is the donor heart chiming in.'

'Jesus. Sorry I didn't spot that.'

'You've done a hell of a good job. All of you. Thank you. Without your all-out effort we might not have reached this stage.' Barnes felt himself on the edge of burbling. Strange how this one case had so affected his usually professional calm.

He carried out several more checks to test the level of donor-heart activity. Although the transplanted heart was not contributing much to cardiac output it was acting to take some of the load from David's own heart, which appeared to be strengthening. As young Snyman had astutely observed, the steroids were at last getting on top of the inflammation. Barnes ordered a chest X-ray on the portable machine and spent the rest of the day on a high, spreading it like a wave wherever he went on his ward rounds. A brief stop at the research block found Kapinsky, as usual, with his nose deep in journals. As Barnes entered his office, he looked up, his eyes darkly circled and jowls unshaven.

'Christ, Louis, you look like an unmade bed. What's going on?'

Kapinsky grinned crookedly. He had been working alone in the laboratory most of the night, slept briefly on his office couch, shocked himself awake on hot coffee and was back at work before dawn. He had scented a line of enquiry and was single-mindedly pursuing it.

'Morning, Rod. There's so many bloody interruptions here during the day,' he said, raising an eyebrow sardonically, 'that I have to catch up on my reading at night.' There was also his secret project that even Barnes didn't know about, work that could only be done when no one else was around. But he would bide his time on that until he had the kind of results that even Barnes couldn't get shirty about.

Kapinsky had given Barnes's idea much thought. The concept of an X-factor excited him. It would explain so much that he had observed in the behaviour of transplanted organs in animals. During the night he remembered an observation made when he had still experimented with hormones. For no special reason, they had performed a piggy-back transplant into one of his brain-dead baboons. The heart never recovered despite the circulatory support it had received from the recipient's own heart. Both he and Des Louw had concluded that the donor had been a bad choice. Later, he had reprimanded himself never to assume anything but to find some explanation. This had been an important observation, which should have been followed through.

He had to search for the X-factor. It would mean extensive biochemical work, fairly complicated test procedures and certainly wasn't in his line. Some sophisticated equipment would be required. And that meant money. He also needed first-hand contact with leading researchers – reading published research work could only take him so far. He had to talk to prime movers in the game, people ahead of the rest of the world and probably too engrossed to publish.

'I have some ideas on your X-factor,' he said, looking straight at Barnes.

'That's good to hear, Louis. In fact, it's good news all round today. The donor heart is generating a pulse and picking up by the hour. What can you add to that?'

Kapinsky grinned and shook his head. 'Congratulations. I hear it was a marathon session. I can't give you anything definite on the X-factor and I have to talk to a few people first in case I start up any false hares.'

Barnes mock-groaned. Seeing 'a few people' meant overseas travel, which never came cheaply. Kapinsky was obviously about to tap him for more funds, and JJ had already warned him he was over budget and into emergency funding. 'Tell me the bad news, Louis.'

'I want to visit Professor Volkov in Petrograd. Despite being the world's foremost authority on genetics Volkov has never published because of Russia's scientific isolation, but I know from my last visit that he has made some dramatic advances in genetic engineering. And in case you're thinking it's just a matter of a couple of air fares, and a few hotel bills and some pieces of new equipment that would be required. When I come back I'm sure I'll be able to think of a few more bits and pieces we need just to get started.'

Barnes looked hard at him and realized he was serious. And if he was serious then he certainly wasn't talking about a few hotel bills. He was talking telephone numbers. 'Louis, I won't promise anything I can't deliver. JJ will throw me out of his office if I ask for anything like the kind of money you have in mind. But what about our friendly fund-raiser? Let's both talk to him – maybe this is my chance to meet him at last.'

Startled and off-guard, Kapinsky stared at him, cleared his throat and mumbled, 'He's, uh, overseas right now.' Barnes looked disappointed. Kapinsky added, 'But I suppose I can put in a call and see what can be done.'

Barnes looked intrigued, frowned for a moment then said, 'Do you realize, Louis, that your benefactor has already shovelled about two hundred thousand American dollars into our little venture and yet I've never had a conversation with him? What's his line of work? What motivates him? Why should he be so interested in what we're doing? He's not fronting for some big drug company, is he?'

'Drugs!' Kapinsky jumped as if he had been stung. 'No, nothing like that. He's in retailing – supermarkets, I think. Yes, he made his money in retailing.' He again nodded vigorously, as if agreeing with himself.

Barnes was even more interested. 'Retailing? That's a bit far from medicine. Why is he interested in us?'

'Shit, Rodney, how the hell do I know?' Kapinsky looked irritated. 'Maybe he lost a relative or something in a transplant. All I know is that he called at my hotel after I delivered the first baboon paper at the Los Angeles conference. He told me he wanted to back our kind of research. You know the rest – that's where all this stuff came from.' He gestured at his well-equipped lab shelves.

Barnes immediately regretted his probing. Kapinsky was doing a fine job. He was motivated. He had been up all night chasing after one of Barnes's half-arsed ideas. He had every reason to be irritable. If some American millionaire wanted to off-load some of his ill-gotten gains in the cause of medicine, well and good. 'When do you want to go, and for how long?'

'Not right away. I still have to wait for the results of a few experiments and do some more reading on these elusive brain hormones.' Kapinsky was suddenly as excited as a schoolboy about to get time off school.

'Done. Drop a note to Fiona. I take it the Iron Lady will supervise your staff in your absence?' It was a hypothetical question. There was no doubt that the unbending Dr Susan Bates would rule the lab like Genghis Khan.

Kapinsky looked pained. He wished Barnes would bugger off and stop making childish jokes.

They went through a few housekeeping items, then Barnes wished him luck with the trip and left, pausing only to admonish him, 'And for Christ's sake get some sleep.'

A couple of hours clearing the OB and occasionally back-chatting Fiona, who was pleased to see her boss in fine form, took Barnes into the late afternoon. Hourly checks with the intensive care unit showed that David was continuing to progress, and Barnes called a quick staff conference in the doctors' room.

He arrived to find the heart team assembled. The latest lab results, X-rays and chart notes on David's condition were tabled. From this point they had to decide how the case would be managed.

Like Des Louw and the staff nurses, Jan Snyman had gone home briefly and slept for a few hours. He was at the conference, looking rested and ready to do it all again. Barnes looked round the shining faces of his staff and wondered again at the rejuvenating effect of good news. Youth, some writer had once said, was wasted on the young. He should have met this bunch before writing that kind of crap, Barnes reflected.

He went through the main points of the case, going back to the original diagnosis, adding his reasoning for each decision taken, and asking for input from each team member. Each gave their own summary, with Louw looking unusually contrite.

'My apologies, sir,' he said. 'I have to tell you that I really doubted the viability of the donor heart. But you were right.'

'As usual,' chimed in Alex Hobbs, raising grins all round.

'Thank you, boys. You all contributed to this happy outcome but before we form a mutual admiration society I should warn you there's a long way to go.' He looked around the table. 'Management from here on. I suggest we leave it to the intensive care staff for the night.'

'No, sir, with respect to the staff, we'd like to take the patient through his second post-operative night.' It was Jan Snyman, looking determined.

'We?' Barnes asked.

'Yes, sir. Myself and Dr Louw. We've already discussed this. He'll be on duty for the first half of the night and I'll take over until morning.'

Des Louw nodded. Both looked at each other and back at Barnes.

'OK, that's settled. I don't think we should try to wean him off the ventilator until tomorrow morning. We can call Dr Ohlsen to assess the situation. Agreed?' They all nodded. 'Good. The rest of the treatment program remains as is. I don't believe in making changes during the night.'

'Sir, what about the cases for surgery tomorrow? Are you going to operate?'

It was the ever-ready Alex Hobbs again, looking ahead to the next goal. The routine work of the hospital had to go on.

'Yes,' said Barnes. 'Mr Smith is scheduled for a double valve replacement. Put him on first. Then we have four other cases. It'll be a busy slate.' Hobbs agreed and scribbled notes as Barnes went on, 'Well, I think that covers everything. No other points?' He looked at each face. 'Thank you again. I don't know about the rest of you but I'm about to hit the sack.'

It wasn't quite everything. In the corridor the Rhodes parents were waiting. Barnes wondered briefly whether they'd gone home since the night before. They were watching his face carefully as he approached and relaxed visibly when they saw his smile.

Always signal ahead, he thought. Old McKenzie had trotted that one out year after year in lectures, driving home the point

97

that people get the message as much from your body language as from what you say to them. In this case he couldn't help but smile. It was a wonderful feeling to pass on good news to the family. The other thing that McKenzie had hammered home to his students was a three-word commandment: 'Follow yer instincts.' Barnes did just that. Before Mrs Rhodes knew what was happening he had flung his arms around her, gripped her in a bear-hug and begun a soft-shoe shuffle around the floor. Mr Rhodes stood back for a second, unsure, then jumped into the huddle, huge farmer's hands clapping Barnes's back.

'Good news. David has had a good night and an even better day,' was as much as he could manage before Mr Rhodes's thumps knocked his breath out.

They continued to waltz around and beam at each other, Mrs Rhodes with tears streaming down her face. When they broke apart, each parent took one of Barnes's hands, squeezing in gratitude.

Quietly he explained the full sequence of events, pointing out that the transplanted heart had recovered and was now helping their son's own heart, which was strengthening as the infection faded.

Mrs Rhodes raised his hand and kissed it. 'Thank you, Dr Barnes. God has answered our prayers. Thank you, thank you.' Her husband added his thanks, tears brimming in his eyes. It had been a hard time for the Rhodes family. They had carried the strain well but now the dam was breaking. He ushered both parents into the unit's reception office, briefly explained the need for sterile conditions during this crucial phase of the treatment and signalled to the charge nurse. He added that she would find gowns and masks for them and they would have a few minutes to view their boy through the ward observation window.

On the drive home he was floating high on the sheer joy of living, yet only hours before he had been in the depths. Of such was the stuff of manic-depression made, he thought, and laughed – a deep belly laugh that shook his body until he had to grip hard on the steering wheel. He had been in hell. Now he was in heaven. What more could a man ask? The poster at the traffic lights read: 'Dead Boy's Heart Beats in Man's Chest.' It was a masterpiece of newspaper brevity and told the whole story. It could have been worse. They had obviously given up the dead heart angle.

Over the next few days David made an uneventful recovery. On day two they were able to take him off the ventilator. Twice he tried to speak, throat hoarse and aching from the ventilator tube. At last he croaked, 'I can breathe. It's wonderful. I can breathe again.'

Hour by hour the fluid level in his lungs fell steadily as his circulation improved. As the blood pulsed stronger in his vessels the ruddy colour of life chased the purple tinge from his cheeks.

On the fourth day the IV lines and his catheter were removed, and he was allowed to sit out of bed for a few minutes. Startled to find how weak he was, his mood changed quickly from one of desperately wanting to get out of bed to being glad to sink painfully back again. For the first time he noticed his wasted muscles, starved of circulation by his failing heart and lack of activity, and was appalled. When the physiotherapist arrived to begin a program of gentle exercise, he was an enthusiastic and willing patient.

Seven days after the operation he again found himself facing Dr Ohlsen's sedation needle. It was time to find out whether or not the anti-rejection drugs were doing the job, how successful they had been in controlling the attack by his immune system on his transplanted heart. Des Louw, with Alex Hobbs assisting, punctured a vein in David's neck and slowly fed in a thin, wire-like catheter through the needle. The vein led directly to the right pumping chamber of the donor heart. Slowly and carefully, pausing to check on the X-ray screen, Louw threaded the catheter down until it reached the heart. Next, a pair of minute wire-operated forceps were passed down the catheter and used to remove three slivers of muscle from the donor heart.

Barnes waited in his office for the call from the pathology lab, forcing himself through the OB routine and refusing to speculate on the outcome.

'Dr Lee from the path. lab on line two.' Fiona's voice on the intercom startled him. He picked up the telephone.

'Dr Barnes?' He grunted some reply, throat too dry to speak. 'Dr Lee here. You'll be pleased to know your sample of donor-heart muscle showed only minimal lymphocyte infiltration. No further signs of rejection.'

He breathed a long sigh. They could now start slowly reducing the immunosuppressive drugs and begin returning David to a normal life. He murmured his thanks, put down the receiver quietly and looked out of the window. With surprise he noticed that the sun was shining. It had been a week that began with tragedy and ended in this small triumph.

The team was dead-beat. They had kept themselves at peak performance for days and nights on end. It was time to relax. He asked Fiona to book a table for twelve at Gino's. They had earned an evening out. Six of the nurses and Karen van der Walt accepted immediately. Ohlsen was unable to make it. Hobbs, Louw and Snyman would be late but would be there. Even Kapinsky, never keen to attend a dinner party, agreed to come. The group enjoyed getting together socially and none more so than Barnes. He had succeeded in building a disciplined team and loved finding a reason to celebrate their every success – a habit frowned on by other departments at the hospital.

Barnes couldn't care a damn what other departments thought. He saw himself as a team coach, a motivator and, above all, an achiever. From his point of view his methods worked. Top people scrambled to be part of his success. He could take his pick of nursing and medical staff in his field, and did so without compunction. If other departments were saddled with the also-rans, so be it.

As always, he had prepared for the meal carefully, detouring on the way home to discuss the menu with Gino. They had settled on fresh seafood – anything from the freezer was banned – and a selection of Western Cape dry whites, Barnes's own choice. As far as he was concerned, South Africa produced top-rated wines and nowhere more so than in the Western Cape. Here, less than an hour's drive from Cape Town, a superb climate had combined with centuries of wine-growing expertise to create some of the world's great wines. Among them were Barnes's favourites, the estate wines, the trade's best kept secrets made in quantities too small to export but greatly sought after by the initiated.

The restaurant, one of the most popular local Italian nightspots, was a blaze of light when he arrived. Heads turned as he entered and a camera flashed. The bloody press were everywhere, he thought. There must be a factory somewhere turning them out by the hundreds. He switched off the thought and smiled widely. Tonight belonged to the team and nothing was going to interfere with that. Gino met him at the door and, anxious to avoid any press clash, steered him to his table in an alcove off the main dining room.

He found the nurses already there. They stood up when he arrived but he laughed and waved them back to their seats. 'We aren't playing doctors and nurses tonight, this is a team party. Gino, how about those icebreakers you promised us?'

This was a different Barnes from the driven, grim-faced, ultra professional, who for the past week had directed their every step. This was the team coach they knew, ready with a smile and a word of encouragement, a man who set goals and achieved them, taking everybody with him along the way.

Gino reappeared with a flourish, bearing a magnum of Veuve Clicquot. To a round of applause from the nurses he stylishly two-handed the huge bottle and filled each glass to the brim.

By the time the doctors had arrived, Barnes had already had three glasses of champagne and most of the girls at least two.

The conversation had become much less inhibited. Barnes changed the seating arrangements, so that nurses and doctors were now intermingled. He placed Karen van der Walt next to himself. He knew that Kapinsky would not discuss his work, but the other doctors habitually dominated the conversation with 'shop' talk. He warned them as soon as they were all settled with a drink that there was to be none of that tonight.

The food was excellent and the conversation lively but relaxed. Snyman, whose father was a game ranger in the Kruger Park, entertained the group with stories about the bushveld. Barnes soon realized that some of the stories were not his own, to say the least, but they were recounted with such enthusiasm and conviction that he did not question their validity. The most exciting events in the bush, Snyman said, could be seen simply by sitting down next to a water-hole and waiting. Take, for example, the time he saw an impala ram approach the water and start to drink. Suddenly the surface was turned into foam by the thrashing tail of a crocodile that grabbed the unfortunate little buck in his jaws and started to drag it in. But before the crocodile could pull the impala under, a hippopotamus appeared. Its charge frightened the crocodile and it released the impala and fled.

The hippopotamus, heavier by hundreds of kilos than the little buck, then attempted a rescue by nudging the little animal out of the water with its massive head. When it considered the little buck was safely out of danger on the river bank, it stopped and stayed with the patient, helping it onto its feet every time it collapsed as a result of the vicious wounds inflicted by the crocodile. After about fifteen minutes the sun became too hot for the hippo, which abandoned its charge and returned to the water. The crocodile had been observing this scene from a safe distance and, when the hippo left, decided to retrieve its prey. It crawled up the embankment and pulled the defenceless buck back into the water.

Barnes knew that this was a true story because he had seen it on a video. He knew, too, that Snyman had not been given any credit for the photography! He kept quiet, however, because he did not want to hurt Snyman's pride, and spoil the evening.

Karen, who had come to the restaurant with the nurses in their crowded small car, gratefully accepted Barnes's offer of a lift home. They were both quiet as he drove along the foot of Table Mountain to her little cottage. She sat admiring the lights of the city below while he had to concentrate on the road after all the alcohol he had drunk. As soon as they stopped in front of the gate Barnes hopped out, walked round the car and opened the door for his companion, but she stayed in her seat. It seemed she wanted to say something. She remained silent, appeared to think better of it, then got out. Barnes accompanied her to the front door. She unlocked it and then turned round. She was so close to him that he could smell her perfume.

'That was a splendid evening, thank you. Would you like a final drink?' she asked.

'Thank you, but no. I have surgery in the morning,' he replied, retreating to his car.

'Well, thank you again for a wonderful evening.'

She opened the door and disappeared.

As he drove home Barnes discovered that she had awakened something in him.

'Damn!' he murmured softly to himself. With a wry smile he shrugged it off.

CHAPTER 10

Since his discussion with Barnes about the possible existence of a factor from the living brain that was essential for the health of vital organs and the miraculous recovery of the donor heart placed in David Rhodes, Kapinsky had spent many hours in the medical library. Neurophysiology was not within the realms of his expertise. He had to resort to textbooks and medical journals for some insight as to how this problem could be tackled in the laboratory.

After several days of searching he was convinced that it was not the neural disconnection in the brain-dead patients that led to the deterioration in the function of vital organs, but rather the cessation of secretion of chemical messengers by the brain.

It has been known since 1930 that the neurosecretory cells of the brain release hormones into the circulation. These have a wide-ranging effect on distant target cells whose secretions, in turn, are essential for the vital metabolic functions in organs such as the heart, liver and kidney. Dr Louw's work had given some insight into the importance of this secretory function of the brain, in that hormonal substitution had led to a significant improvement in survival of donor organs. A number of these pharmacologically active neuropeptides had already been reported and new ones were discovered virtually every month.

Kapinsky could find no references to such work having been done on brain-dead animals. His task would be to compare the concentration of each peptide, first in the donor and then in the living animal. In this way he could determine which chemical messengers were either missing or present in low concentrations in the brain-dead patient. Fortunately technological advances had made this possible. Two techniques most commonly used were radioimmunoassay and immunocytochemistry. Both techniques make use of the same immunological principle: an antibody will only bind with a specific antigen. In other words, an antibody for antigen A will not bind with antigen B or C. The neuropeptides being short-chain amino-acid molecules behave as antigens, so if a labelled antibody specific for a particular neuropeptide is injected, the peptide and its concentration can be detected in the cells and body fluids.

Kapinsky looked at the notes he had taken over the last few days. There must be an easier way, he thought, a way that was more in the line of his research.

Following the party, Barnes enjoyed spending time at the hospital. There was a lot of routine surgery to catch up with – the cases had piled up during his nearly full-time involvement with David Rhodes. The cardiologists complained that more deserving cases than transplants were being neglected.

But Barnes's frequent visits to the hospital stemmed from another reason. He liked meeting up with Karen van der Walt and he was trying to find the courage to ask her out to dinner again – this time without the other members of the team.

One morning after the ward round he decided to go to the lab to find out when Kapinsky was leaving for Russia. He had not had any calls from him for several days. Normally they met or talked on the phone every day. Yet, despite their close academic association they rarely met socially and Kapinsky never spoke about his childhood or parents. All Barnes knew was that he had grown up in Poland during the war and that his parents had been slaughtered by the Bolsheviks. It was as if Kapinsky wanted to forget about that period of his life and Barnes could understand that. It must have been hell to grow up during the Nazi occupation of Poland. Barnes once asked Kapinsky whether as a child he had been aware of the atrocities that took place in the concentration camps. His colleague's reaction had been strange. It was as if his memories had taken him back to a different world, a world that was interesting and enjoyable – and then suddenly came the fierce denial and the unmistakable indication that he did not want to discuss this any further. Barnes knew that children who grew up in those times and under those circumstances must have been psychologically maimed, and he never brought up the subject again. He was fortunate to have grown up in South Africa where they hardly realized that a war was on. Everything happened so far away. Death and destruction were never at their doorstep.

When Barnes went to the laboratory that morning he saw straight away that his colleague was in a bad mood.

Kapinsky exploded, 'Rodney, you are trying to do the impossible. The brain, unlike the heart, has many more than one function. We know very little of what it really does and even less on how it does it. To find your missing factors is the work of a neurophysiologist and biochemist. It is not for a little surgeon like you.'

Barnes ignored the sarcasm. 'But that is why I have you. You're not just a little surgeon.'

'Nor do I specialize in the brain.'

Undeterred, Barnes continued, 'You have successfully tackled several problems that one cannot classify as surgical.'

Kapinsky saw it was no use to try to bully Barnes so he related to his friend what he had learnt in the library. He ended, 'So you see, Rodney, it will be like looking for a needle in a haystack.'

'What do you think our chances are of finding that needle?' Barnes enquired.

'Well, the techniques for finding a specific neuropeptide are not that difficult. I think our technicians will master it in a few weeks' time.'

'Louis, just think what it will mean if we can keep a donor alive.'

Kapinsky chuckled. 'That will not be possible.'

'Ah, you know what I mean. I can have a ward full of human

beings with dead brains, but with their vital organs very much alive and healthy.'

Kapinsky heard the excitement in his friend's voice. 'Slow down, Rodney. We have a long way to go before you will have the ward with the living dead.' He suddenly stopped and a blank look transformed his face.

'What's wrong with you, Louis? Are you feeling sick?'

Kapinsky shook his head. 'No, I was just thinking of the scientific possibilities.'

'Yes!' Barnes took off again. 'We'll have a living bank of human organs and tissue. There could be no objection to studies such as the effect of drugs and irradiation, and new surgical procedures could be attempted and performed on living humans.'

'Do you think the Ethics Committee will allow this?'

'I don't see how they can object, as long as the relatives of the donors agree. After all, they're dead and we cannot harm them any further.'

Kapinsky again had that strange look but responded immediately, 'I agree. What is the difference between cutting up the body in the post-mortem room or working on it when it's still alive?'

'Come on, Louis, it's not really alive. These patients will be nothing more than living corpses.'

Wilhelm Kapisius, the eldest son of a hospital orderly, was born in Berlin. His father was a religious man and described himself as a strict Catholic. Wilhelm, or Willy as he was more commonly called, used the more favoured Nazi category and on all official forms identified himself as a 'believer in God'.

Because of his father's hospital contacts Willy was often invited to accompany him during weekends and he assisted in taking patients from the wards to the X-ray department, for physiotherapy, and, what he enjoyed most, to the laboratory for blood tests. It was no wonder that after matriculating he went to study as a doctor at the medical school in Munich. Here he soon came under the influence of a right-wing student body and became an enthusiastic supporter of the Nazi movement. He joined the SA in 1934 and applied for party membership in 1937. The next year he became a member of the SS.

While studying in Munich he was honoured to meet high-ranking Nazis such as Alfred Rosenberg and Himmler. Once he even had a glimpse of Hitler while attending a street parade. Meetings addressed by SS doctors who worked in the concentration camps were popular events for young Willy.

He qualified as a doctor and considered himself lucky to be appointed as a registrar at the university hospital in Munich. He was neither brilliant nor stupid, neither inherently evil nor particularly ethically sensitive. Part of the training of these young doctors was a rotation over three months in Dachau as research fellows. Here they took part not only in the experiments on the inmates but also in the healing by killing. They were told that just as one could not kill someone already dead one could do no harm by mutilating their bodies. Wilhelm believed unequivocally in the principle enunciated by Bethmann-Hollweg in 1914, that 'necessity knows no law'.

In late 1941 and early 1942 annihilation camps had sprung up all over the German-occupied territory and especially in Poland: Chelmo, Belsen, Sobibor, Treblinka, Majdaneck and Auschwitz. It was to Auschwitz that Dr Wilhelm Kapisius, now promoted to captain in the SS, and his wife and son, Lodewick, were transferred. Dr Josef Mengele became his friend and tutor.

The Jews were considered 'the eternal blood suckers', 'vampires', 'germ carriers', 'people's parasites', and 'maggots in the rotting corpse'. The cure had to be radical to cut out the cancer of decay. The Final Solution.

Wilhelm's son was now a boy of fourteen and he was proud of his father. It was with intense interest that he listened to his father talk about some of the work he was doing in the camp. During the day, he looked up with pride at the smoke belching from the chimneys: the flames inside those crematoria were purifying the German soul.

One day he asked his father whether it would be possible for him to accompany him on one of his shifts in the camp. He was overjoyed when his father told him that the Commandant had given permission and that that evening he could attend a Ramp Selection session.

They always arrived at night. Wooden trucks each with two slit-like openings high up, with criss-crossed barbed wire. When the train stopped the doors were slid open and the guards, armed with machine guns and dogs, started screaming and whistling, 'Out! Out! *Raus! Raus! Raus!*' The bewildered contents of the railcars poured out onto the ground clutching the worldly possessions that they had saved. There were women, children, men, young and old. They were surrounded and herded by SS men. Then the command came, 'Throw everything down.' They parted with all they possessed.

A rough line was formed and, slowly, around fifteen hundred people filed past Dr Mengele and the boy's father to where the selection was made: 'You to the truck, you walk.'

After a while Dr Mengele turned to the boy. 'Would you like to take over for a while?'

He grabbed this opportunity, and for five minutes he could decide who would die and who would live – for a while.

After the selection, young Lodewick got into the ambulance with his father and Dr Mengele and they followed those selected for special treatment. Arriving at their final destination they were told to undress so that they could have a shower after the long journey. Their clothes would be disinfected. The naked bodies were then chased into the shower rooms with whips and lashes. The boy could hear the horrible screams of these people as the doors closed and as his father introduced the pellets through a tube next to the peep-hole. The doctor moved away and allowed his son to watch in fascination through the peep-hole as one inmate after the other fell over.

After that night the boy was a regular visitor, helping his father with his medical experiments until 8 June 1945 when Russian troops overran the camp. His father was captured and his mother rounded up a few hours later, although she had never participated in camp activities.

They were both hanged without trial. He could still hear the last words of his father before the wooden box on which he stood with a rope around his neck was kicked out. 'I die as a German officer who served his Fatherland! *Heil Hitler!*'

After his parents' execution, an uncle smuggled the boy out of Poland to London where he was educated as a Polish refugee and took the name of Louis Kapinsky. Those who knew of his past and that his father Wilhelm Kapisius had been an SS doctor were all dead now. He never discussed his German background with anyone. He told his friends he was an orphan who had escaped the Russian reign of terror, and that he had managed to become educated by working part-time in the laboratories of the Hammersmith hospital.

On his way to visit Volkov in Russia, Kapinsky had stopped off in Poland to visit the camp-site he remembered. He didn't visit the museum or look at the display of photographs. There were no family or friends to visit, nobody with whom he could share his memories. What he wanted to find wasn't there. There were no graves or tombstones for his father or mother. It was as if they had never existed. There were plaques and lists of names of camp inmates but no mention of German dead, except in reference to war crimes.

Only the losers were criminals. If these monuments were to be believed, the victors, the Allies, were guiltless. Yet, as a boy, he had witnessed atrocities committed by Russian troops: gang-rape of young girls had been common, and theft of food from starving families, to feed the victorious Russian Army, a daily occurrence. Homes were looted. Plunder, rape and starvation for the losers; medals, monuments and the spoils of war for the winners.

Young German boys had answered the call of their Fatherland and obeyed the commands of their superiors, yet they were now criminals. Criminals because they didn't win.

How different it would have been, thought Kapinsky, if Hitler had conquered Russia. Stalin's campaign of terror against his captured population would not have taken place. The great German nation would have civilized Russia and turned it into an efficient, industrious Western nation.

The man standing alone as he relived his childhood days with secrets deep in his heart turned round and walked away from the watch-towers and barbed wire still attached by insulators to the concrete poles. I must be successful, vowed Kapinsky. I must be a winner in memory of my father and mother, and of the German race.

'We will be landing shortly at Moscow's Sheremet-Yevo airport. Please ensure your seat belts are fastened and all hand luggage is safely in the racks above your heads.' The intercom chimed once and went silent. There was a flurry of clicks as passengers prepared for landing.

Professor Volkov would understand the need for success, thought Kapinsky – Volkov, who had spent so many years of his life as a Russian geneticist appearing to follow the Party line while despising everything Communist. 'We do what we have to do. That way, we get time to do what we want to do,' he had told Kapinsky. What a waste it was for this genius to be hidden away in his Moscow laboratory with little exposure to the world of Western science. In Kapinsky's eyes he was the greatest living geneticist, years ahead of his Western colleagues. Kapinsky, now on his third visit to the great man's laboratory, felt privileged to be one of the few Westerners to meet him. It was a shame that Volkov did not have normal access to Western research. Science worked best when ideas were cross-fertilized. Worldwide, researchers studied each other's work and added little bits of information, all the while testing the theory against the practice. Volkov's work received little exposure in Western journals. The opposite was true, too, Kapinsky thought. One's own ideas were not redirected along the well-worn path taken by others.

The airport was as he remembered it from his last visit, empty but for transit passengers with hardly a Russian in sight. No sight-seeing groups of Mum, Dad and the kids wandering around eating fast food, no bookshops, no Western magazines or newspapers for sale, nothing except an expensive coffee room with poor service and queues, and a duty-free shop with only Western goods. And always the loudspeakers with their interminable announcements and patriotic music. The Russians were told constantly by their radio, television and newspapers that they'd never had it so good. They had no notion of what was happening outside their borders. Keep out Western influences, ran the official line, and what the eye doesn't see, the heart won't grieve for.

Even Volkov's lab appeared to be afflicted by the unchanging, dreary sameness. Obsolete apparatus that had been there for years, odd fittings repaired with wire and string, throwaway commercial containers in place of proper equipment. Volkov delighted in watching visitors' faces, seeing disbelief followed by disappointment, followed by Western politeness and pretence not to have noticed anything unusual.

Kapinsky now knew that Volkov sometimes played the 'poor Communist' card. The charade always elicited an offer to donate the latest scientific gadget or piece of equipment, always courteously accepted. After recounting one of these incidents, Volkov added, 'What they do not realize is that we are not in the laboratory business, we are in the people business. The most important apparatus in the laboratory are the people who work there.'

On his arrival Volkov welcomed Kapinsky cordially and told him he was grateful for the batch of baboons he had sent from South Africa, a statement that made Kapinsky wary. He had cause to be – Volkov's gratitude was always expressed with vodka. On his last visit, two years before, Volkov had arranged for him to speak at a major teaching hospital, the Vashevsky Institute. The day had started harmlessly enough. A car arrived at his hotel two hours before the talk was due to start at noon. It carried an interpreter who told him she was there to help out as Professor Vashevsky, the head of the Institute, spoke only Russian.

The Institute was a very old building, dating from before the Revolution, Kapinsky guessed. The corridors were wide enough to be streets and the ceilings over four metres high. There were no private wards. Males and females were treated in one general ward. With great pride, Professor Vashevsky hosted Kapinsky on a tour of inspection, talking continuously of his achievements and successes. About an hour before Kapinsky's talk was due he ushered him into his office. It was sparsely furnished with a small round table in the centre and three chairs. On the table were glasses, snacks and a bottle of colourless liquid. The Professor offered Kapinsky a chair and then went to sit opposite him. The interpreter took her place to one side. Vashevsky offered him a drink but before Kapinsky could reply he filled two glasses from the bottle. Clearly the interpreter was not included in the party.

Vashevsky said something in Russian and knocked back his glass in one quick gulp. 'Your good health,' said the interpreter. Kapinsky replied appropriately but decided to sip rather than quaff the vodka. It was a good move: one sip and his throat was on fire. The liquid burned all the way down his gullet.

Vashevsky spoke to the interpreter and she explained to Kapinsky that the correct way to drink was to drain the contents of the glass in a single swallow. He did just that and wondered why the chair rocked. When the tears cleared he found Professor Vashevsky had filled his glass again and he was off on another toast, again in Russian. Kapinsky obliged. By the fourth toast neither man needed the interpreter.

Vashevsky explained that he had to carry out an operation just before the lecture but that he would be there on time. In the meantime, Kapinsky could stay and finish the bottle.

Kapinsky felt as though his face had been anaesthetized. He was sure that if someone put a pin through his cheek he wouldn't feel it. He asked the interpreter if they could walk around outside for some fresh air. The last thing he remembered was walking out of the office and down some steps into the sunshine.

When he regained consciousness he was lying on his back in the centre of his double bed at his hotel. It was dark outside and he had a splitting headache. He spent the night sleepless, unable to remember the Russian word for aspirin. Early next morning his phone rang. It was his interpreter to say that Professor Vashevsky apologized for the cancellation of the lecture as the operation had taken longer than he thought.

He never told Volkov of the experience and Volkov never asked about the lecture. But he did tell Kapinsky that, because funds for entertainment of guests were almost non-existent, they often served alcohol from the dispensary as vodka. Kapinsky resolved to take it easy with any future offer of 'vodka'.

'Vodka?' said Volkov, holding up a bottle. When he saw the hesitation on Kapinsky's face he smiled and turned it round to show a Western label. 'Your baboons gave me the experimental material I needed. I have much to tell you,' Volkov said, pouring each of them a glass. 'Here's to your success too,' he added.

They both drank. Kapinsky savoured the smoothness of the real vodka and waited.

'I have made what I think to be a very significant finding,' said Volkov. He looked closely at his glass; it was half empty and he refilled it. Kapinsky waved away the bottle when it was offered to him.

Lighting a cigarette from the stub of another, Volkov went on, 'Until now we have always believed that rejection of organs transplanted from baboons to humans would be hyperacute due to the presence of anti-baboon antibodies in humans. Thanks to your baboons, we know now that is not so.'

Kapinsky changed his mind and decided to have another drink. Volkov waited for him to fill his glass.

'I have been able to show that skin grafts from baboons to

114

human volunteers are not always automatically hyperacutely rejected. Some of the baboon grafts were more compatible to humans than others. The rejection of the skin was not antibody mediated but, rather, was caused by rapid cellular response.'

Kapinsky said nothing. Volkov liked to complete his explanation before answering any questions.

'We know there are three kinds of rejection,' he said, beginning to pace up and down as he did when facing a lecture room of students. 'The hyperacute condition occurs within minutes due to the presence of antibodies. The acute cellular response is a little slower but occurs within hours. Subacute cellular responses may take days to occur.'

Kapinsky wrinkled his brow and sampled more vodka. Volkov would tell it his way and take his time over it.

A severe coughing spell interrupted Volkov's flow of words. He leaned with both hands on his desk, while his lungs heaved, to clear his throat. He spat the phlegm into the laboratory sink, had another swallow of vodka, smiled at Kapinsky and continued, 'Let's use a military model. Let's say the baboon antigens are soldiers from an invading army and that the immune response of the patient is the army of the defenders.'

Kapinsky nodded.

'The defending soldiers can be mobilized in three ways. First, they can lie waiting in ambush and when the invaders appear there is an immediate response. This is our hyperacute rejection due to the presence of defending soldiers already in the battlefield. You follow?'

'Yes,' said Kapinsky. 'In this case the soldiers being the human antibodies.'

'Exactly,' said Volkov, lighting another cigarette. 'The second response follows when the soldiers are in the vicinity but not immediately aware of the presence of the invaders. They will only respond once a messenger has carried the news to them.'

'Yes, I follow,' said Kapinsky. 'That's why the response takes a little more time.'

'But the important point here is that there must be a messenger, just like the third response where the soldiers are still in their barracks. In that case the time taken to initiate a response is even longer.'

Kapinsky put down his glass. That was it! That was the key to the problem. If it was possible to stop the messenger then there would be no response, no rejection. His excitement showed. 'Professor, if what you say is correct, all that is needed is first to select baboons who conform best to the second option, then block the messenger and transplants can take place without rejection.'

'Theoretically yes,' said Volkov. 'But remember that theory and practice are different ends of the stick. I have not taken my animal experiments to the stage where I can make any definitive statements but the indications are there.'

Kapinsky could have kissed him. All the loose ends were coming together. Volkov's 'messenger' and Barnes's X-factor pointed to chemically mediated triggers which caused various body responses.

Together Kapinsky and Volkov spent hours in Volkov's laboratory where they examined tissue samples from the baboons and also human volunteers. They ranged over the hormonal functions of the brain and the vital role these played in keeping the body going, and they concluded that the search for the chemical messengers made good science but bad strategy.

Kapinsky, Volkov pointed out, simply didn't have the time to explore all the avenues and blind alleys implied by such a research program.

It was then that Kapinsky revealed his secret dream. Volkov listened carefully without comment, stubbed out his cigarette, stood up and growled, '*Kom*, we have work to do.'

For the next three days they never left the laboratory, subsisting only on food sent in by Volkov's landlady. Kapinsky swallowed the fatty foods that Volkov loved, and wondered how the man could remain so skinny on such a diet.

*

Kapinsky felt his body being pressed back into his seat as the powerful turbo-prop engines of the Tupulev accelerated Aerovlot flight 207 down the runway of Sheremet-Yevo airport. He was leaving Russia, not without mixed feelings. Relieved to get out of the depressing atmosphere of a socialist state where the individual was seen as subordinate to the community, he was sad to say goodbye to Ivor Volkov, his friend and mentor. It could well have been their last meeting. Volkov, now in his seventies, was a hard drinker and chain smoker who cared little for his health.

The seats of the converted bomber did not recline and there was little of the luxury to be found in Western aircraft. Kapinsky decided he had better follow the Russian example and anaesthetize himself. He signalled to a stewardess as she paraded past and ordered a vodka and ice, in English. Apart from a muttered '*Da*' to show she had heard him, the woman's expression did not change. She looked as if she would have been more at home as a prison warder.

The vodka did the trick. The upright seat seemed much more comfortable and Kapinsky settled back and dozed off . . .

It was young Ferreira who woke him, tugging urgently at his sleeve. 'Dr Kapinsky, there's a problem in the animal room. One of the cleaners in the laboratory has just phoned.'

Kapinsky was instantly awake. 'What does he want?'

'He says the baboons are savaging each other.'

Please God the experimental baboon is not harmed, Kapinsky thought, as he headed for the elevator. Born after intra-uterine exposure to human antigens it was tolerant to human tissue. That had been the point of yesterday's operation, to implant a donor heart from an executed prisoner and monitor the rejection rate. Barnes would be livid if the project went astray at this stage. He had gone to great lengths to bring a heart by air from Pretoria and had delivered it in perfect condition. The operation had gone well and there were no indications of any complications.

Metallic bangs, rattles and baboon screams came from the

animal room as he rang the bell for admittance. The cleaner, his black skin glistening with sweat and eyes staring out of his head, opened the heavy steel door. 'Boss, it is the young one with the new heart. He has killed the other two.'

Kapinsky took in the scene at a glance and felt a rush of relief. The experimental animal with the heart of an executed murderer had recovered sufficiently to strangle its two cage mates and was now shaking the bars. The transformation was frightening. The animal, meek and mild before the operation, now looked incredibly vicious as it bared its teeth and frothed at the mouth.

'Why have you not removed the bodies?'

'Jesus, boss, I have never seen anything like this. This baboon was as tame as a lamb, now I can't get anywhere near him.'

'He's probably in pain. Give him a sedative and call me,' said Kapinsky.

He heard nothing for the rest of the day. That evening he decided to go and see what had happened, although things must have been sorted out.

The staff had gone home and Kapinsky was alone as he entered the research block. From the corridor he could hear a baboon chattering but that wasn't unusual. At least it wasn't screaming. The room was in darkness. He took the emergency torch from its hook by the door and as he did so his foot struck something. He switched on the beam and looked down. The shaft of light fell on the black body: the eyes bulged from their sockets and the protruding tongue was blue and swollen. He fitted the description Barnes had given him of someone who had been hanged. There were no signs of rope around the neck but vivid claw marks stood out on the throat.

Suddenly, something grabbed him by the arm. Kapinsky gave a startled yell.

The stewardess let go his arm and stepped back. 'Sorry, sir, we're about to land at Heathrow. Please fasten your seat belt.' Embarrassed, Kapinsky buckled up immediately then looked at his watch. He had two hours to connect with the direct flight to Cape Town. Two passengers nearby grinned sympathetically. He stared out of the window at the cloudy English skies and wondered if his subconscious was trying to tell him something.

'Maybe Rodney is wrong. Maybe the heart is more than just a pump,' he whispered to himself.

CHAPTER II

When he arrived back in Cape Town, Kapinsky went straight to the research block. Pausing in his office only to pull on a white lab coat and grunt acknowledgement of greetings from wary staff, he headed for the animal room.

He went down the passage to the operating theatre and surprised Samuel Mbeki, in mask and gown, bending over an anaesthetized baboon on the operating table. Nat Ferreira was on the other side of the table.

'What the hell are you doing operating?' he yelled at Samuel, who, after a few years in the laboratory, had become used to Kapinsky's outbursts and simply looked at him. The tag colour on the animal's wrist told Kapinsky it was part of Barnes's experimental batch.

'Welcome back, Louis, and simmer down.' It was Barnes, dressed for surgery and holding his gloved hands clear as he shouldered through the swing doors. 'I asked him to open the thorax and do the transplant. I will be assisting him. You will be pleased to know that since we promoted Boots from cleaner to lab assistant he has acquired considerable surgical skills.'

The black man did not look up but kept quite still. This was a matter between white men and there was nothing he could do or say that would alter it. Dr Kapinsky was a very angry white boss who did not like black people. He walked like a *skollie*, always looking for trouble, and he was almost as dangerous.

Just as a man could not say whether a *tsotsi* would attack or let you pass without harm, so it was not possible to know whether this white boss would curse him or ignore him.

'What next? Do we train the baboons to hold a scalpel?' Kapinsky asked Barnes while glaring at Samuel.

Barnes moved in to defuse the situation. Clearly Kapinsky wasn't about to be placated. 'Thanks, Boots, let's get on with the job.'

The black man's hurt was visible in his eyes above the mask but he nodded and stood aside. Ferreira was clearly unimpressed by Kapinsky's behaviour and showed it, turning his back and busying himself with the anaesthetic machine.

'Good to see you, Louis. Can we get together after lunch? There's a mass of data collected over the past ten days that you'll find very interesting.' Barnes was trying hard to make it easy for Kapinsky to leave without losing face.

He picked up the vibe, grunted agreement and was gone, leaving the theatre doors swinging behind him. He fumed all the way back to the lab. The so-called liberals were everywhere. They'd fucked up England and America and now they were fucking up South Africa.

After the operation, they gave the baboon a new drug that the pharmaceutical industry was crowing about to check its immunosuppressive action. Barnes asked Samuel to close the chest and to 'keep an eye on Dr Ferreira to make sure he doesn't kill off our friend on the table here'. This jocular note finally dispelled the tension and Barnes was gratified to see the relaxed sense of mutual respect that Ferreira and Boots had for each other. Boots knew more practical surgery than any new registrar and Ferreira was a likeable youngster who showed a bent for anaesthetics. They made a good team, Barnes thought as he left to look for Kapinsky.

Ferreira helped place the baboon in the recovery cage and left a still troubled Samuel. The black man thought long and hard. He must walk softly when Dr Kapinsky was around. This was white man's work he was doing and it could be dangerous for him if Dr Kapinsky wanted to shout about it. Who knew why white bosses like Dr Kapinsky were always angry with black men? It was not a question that could be answered. His father had once told him that a man should leave a space so that the angry men might have room to walk. He would leave much space for Dr Kapinsky and all would be well. The thought, like a heavy hand on his shoulder, stayed with him throughout the day. But it was good that his head was making him think about this thing. He, Samuel Mbeki, had not come this far from his tribal land without learning that white people were like the wind that harmed you only if you did not bow to it.

Barnes was glad to get home that evening. It had been difficult to stop the bleeding while redoing the triple bypass. Gratefully, he now sank back into his pillows. These few moments were his 'think-time'. He used the time between getting into bed and the onset of sleep to plan the work of the next day. He found it especially valuable to do this when several patients were slated for the operating table. In his mind he would go over each operation, even the most routine, mentally working step by step from the first skin incision to the last stitch. His mental preparation complete, he would close his eyes and would be asleep in seconds. The habit had never failed him, not even when, occasionally, the diagnosis had been wrong and he had found a completely different pathology on opening a chest. A quick reassessment and he could carry on, leaving his assistants marvelling. Respect was high among housemen and registrars for the Barnes ability to change tack almost in mid-incision.

'Barnes can think on his feet,' Ohlsen reassured a visiting surgeon.

Barnes had never forgotten the day he opened the heart of a child diagnosed with a single upper chamber. He had planned to reconstruct the upper chamber with a partition to create two chambers, only to find that the lower chambers also were not partitioned.

How was he to reconstruct a heart with only one chamber?

He remembered staring at the single-chambered heart and recalling an exchange with Manzu, the Italian sculptor. Visiting his studio, Barnes had noted a number of blocks of marble lining the driveway and asked why they had been left untouched. 'Because I cannot yet see what is inside them,' the sculptor had replied. As he held the ineffectual, malformed organ, Barnes felt that rush of revelation that had eluded the sculptor. Vividly, almost as if he were looking at a projected image, Barnes saw what he needed to do and set to work. His excitement grew as he saw the reconstructed heart emerge from the mass of useless tissue. Like the slaves of Michelangelo, he thought, having once seen the master's work in Florence.

But tomorrow he expected no surprises, even though he intended to try a new surgical technique he had never used before. Again he visualized the patient's heart and thought back through the procedure. Obstructions to the outflow of the right and left lower chambers are conditions that often confront surgeons. If the resistance to blood-flow from the ventricles is due to a narrow valve the surgeon has one of two choices: cut out the valve and replace it with a prosthesis, or sculpture the existing valve tissue to relieve the narrowing. But when, in addition to the abnormal valve, the ring to which the valve is attached is also underdeveloped, relief of the obstruction becomes more complicated. Then the surgeon has a choice of cutting across the ring and sewing it open with a plastic gusset – as was often done on the right side – or excising the fibrous obstruction and replacing it with a suitably sized graft.

Barnes decided on the second approach. Cutting across an aortic valve ring and sewing in a roof was more difficult on the left side due to the more complicated anatomy and that the coronary arteries – the fuel lines of the heart muscle – originate from this area of the aorta. The decision to replace the outflow with a homograft was to ensure that, after completion of the operation, there would be no further obstruction. The woman had given them a second chance – it was unlikely there would be a third. His last thought as sleep enveloped him, was that attachment of the two coronary arteries to the graft could be tricky. He had practised this process on cadavers and found that when a small cuff of aorta was left around the openings of the arteries the stitching was much easier.

He was awake at dawn, his body already abuzz with adrenaline. He often experienced this feeling just before a major operation and found it energized him throughout the day. A brisk run on the beach was indicated, he thought.

As he stepped outside, a warm, oppressive *berg* wind was blowing, leaving the air hot and uncomfortable. Gathering its heat from the interior of the country, it could blow for days, turning the city into an oven. Barnes decided to abandon his run in favour of a cold shower, but not even the mountain wind could affect his rising excitement at the day ahead.

The drive to the city was fast and enjoyable; a mirror of his eagerness to face the surgical problem that awaited him.

In the ward he found that Dr Ohlsen had already taken the patient to the operating theatre.

Jan Snyman was connecting an intravenous line. 'Good morning, sir,' he said, wearily. His eyes were ringed with dark circles.

'Have they started surgery on Mrs Felini?' Barnes asked.

Snyman stopped work to answer. 'I don't know, sir, but the patient was taken to the operating room about half an hour ago and Doctors Louw and Hobbs left about fifteen minutes ago with the two Italian doctors.'

'I'd better join them,' said Barnes. He hesitated a moment, looked more closely at Snyman and asked, 'Any problems?'

'We had a hell of a night, sir. Things went wild again in Langa. We had to admit three patients with gunshot wounds to the chest. Another four were dead on arrival.'

Barnes threw up his arms in despair and left without comment. His first thoughts were for Samuel Mbeki. Poor bugger. How could anyone sleep in the black townships where wars were fought every night?

He donned gown and mask and entered the theatre. The Italian doctors recognized him behind the mask, nodded a greeting and moved away from the screen that separated the anaesthetist from the surgical field.

Barnes peered over the screen. The patient was completely draped. Alex Hobbs was about to make the skin incision down the middle of the breastbone. He paused and looked up at his boss. 'You want me to excise the scar?' he asked.

'I think so. We can probably leave her with a nicer-looking trademark,' said Barnes, his eyes smiling. He looked at Ohlsen. 'Everything OK?'

'If I could get near to the patient I'd be able to tell you,' said Ohlsen with a chuckle, indicating the visiting surgeons with a lift of the eyebrow.

'I'm going to have a quick cuppa and then I'll scrub,' Barnes said. 'Call me if you run into any problems.' Opening the chest after previous surgery could be tricky, he recalled. He had once seen a surgeon slice into the right ventricle with a sternal saw because the heart had adhered to the back of the breastbone. However, Hobbs was an old hand at this game and aware of the pitfalls.

Before heading for the tea room, though, Barnes looked in the specimen fridge to check on the homografts. The previous week they had removed five grafts of various sizes from cadavers. These were being held in an antibiotic solution. They looked in good condition. Three were from females and should be an appropriate size for his patient. One of the problems encountered with biological valves was the need for an accurate fit. If too large they could cause an obstruction and if too small there was a chance of blood leakage.

He swallowed a cup of tea and slipped his mask back into place. As he entered the scrub room he could hear the high whine of the saw as Hobbs cut through Mrs Felini's breastbone. Meticulously he scrubbed both hands and forearms with antiseptic soap, dried them with a sterile towel and slipped on a fresh gown and gloves. He took up a position next to Des Louw on the right of the patient.

'We were fortunate they closed the pericardial sac after the previous operation,' Alex Hobbs remarked.

Barnes gazed into the woman's chest. The sac around the heart was open and dissected free from the organ it surrounded.

'The adhesions were not so bad,' Des Louw observed.

'Probably because the last operation was only about three months ago,' Hobbs added.

Barnes picked up the scissors in his right hand and the dissecting forceps in his left. Silence fell over the room, punctuated only by his requests to the theatre sister. 'Needle holder ... three nil stitch ... scissors ... heparin ... arterial catheter.'

Fascinated, the visitors watched Barnes's flawless technique as the aorta was exposed, coronary arteries identified, arterial and venous catheters inserted and bypass started. The low hum of the arterial and venous pumps filled the room.

'Full flow,' the technician said loudly.

'Start cooling,' Barnes responded.

The heart began to slow as cooled blood started to flow through the coronary arteries into the heart muscle.

Barnes lifted the heart out of the sac and placed the small vent through the apex into the left pumping chamber. 'I need a clear view of the aortic root,' he said crisply. 'Get the coronary catheters ready please, Dr Louw.'

'Fibrillating,' Ohlsen called.

The co-ordinated contraction of thousands of heart-muscle fibres had changed into chaotic activity – the rhythm of death.

Barnes clamped across the aorta below the insertion of the arterial cannula and opened the vessel down to its root. He identified the openings of the left and right coronary arteries and then detached each in turn, leaving a cuff of about five millimetres of aortic wall around the openings. Working carefully, he cannulated each artery with a small catheter and secured it with a snare. 'OK,' he announced. 'Start perfusing the coronaries.'

The pump murmur changed slightly as it began to supply the heart muscle with oxygenated blood from the heart-lung machine. This was to protect it from damage while the coronaries were not fed from the aorta.

Working precisely and with confidence, Barnes excised the narrow aortic root and about four centimetres of the vessel, leaving a huge opening on the top of the outflow of the left pumping chamber.

'Let's see which of the grafts will fit best.' He gauged the size of the graft against the measuring rings. 'I think twenty-eight will do nicely,' he decided.

Jan Snyman left the room and returned with the homograft. He carefully opened the container and held it steady as the scrub nurse used sterile forceps to remove the contents. She washed the graft thoroughly in saline to remove the antibiotic solution, placed it in a kidney dish and offered it to Barnes.

'Four nil suture,' said Barnes, lowering the graft into the wound.

Ohlsen looked at the visitors. Even behind the masks he could detect admiration as Barnes's evenly placed sutures set-tled the graft snugly into the outflow of the left ventricle.

After five minutes of intense concentration Barnes looked up. 'Now to reimplant the coronaries.' With small scissors he made a five millimetre opening in front of the graft for the right coronary artery, then moved to the left side and made a similar-sized opening. 'Five nil suture. Stop the flow to the right coron-ary artery.'

Silently the team complied.

With skill and speed, Barnes removed the catheter from the vessel and attached the right coronary artery to its graft. 'Stop the left.'

Within a few minutes the left coronary was in place. The heart muscle had now been without blood for at least half an hour.

Using another five nil suture Barnes joined the upper end of the graft to the lower end of the aorta. After venting the graft with a needle to allow any trapped air to escape, he released the aortic clamp.

He relaxed. Nothing more could be done until warming had been completed. The seconds ticked past. All eyes watched the patient and the monitoring equipment. Five minutes elapsed and Barnes felt a stir of unease.

'What's the temperature?' he asked.

'Warming nicely. Oesophageal temperature thirty-five degrees.'

'Why's the heart so sluggish?' he asked of no one in particular. 'Defib,' he called. The electrodes were placed and a single charge jolted the heart.

The shock brought order to the erratic activity of the muscle fibres but the contractions were weak. Barnes knew that at this level of heart activity he could never wean the patient off the heart-lung machine. Twenty minutes later and his concern had turned to chilling certainty. The heart had been damaged during surgery and would never carry the full circulation load without support. Here was a clear case for a mechanical heart assist. He mentally cursed the hospital authorities for their penny-pinching. His request for a mechanical heart had been rejected twice in three years on the grounds that it was 'beyond the budget'. The bean-counters who ran the hospital clearly knew the price of a dollar but not the value of human life. A few days with a mechanical heart assist would enable this heart to recover full function.

Barnes looked up at the doctors surrounding the table. 'We'll have to do a heterotopic transplant. The alternative would be to have the patient die on the table.'

The two Italian surgeons stood aside as Snyman moved to the head of the table. 'Dr Barnes, I talked to the Transplant Co-ordinator this morning. There is no donor available at present. There was a potential donor last night but the relatives refused permission to remove the organs.'

All eyes were on Barnes.

He didn't hesitate. 'Keep an eye on her. I need a few minutes to talk to Kapinsky.'

His call was answered within two rings. 'Kapinsky!'

'Louis, I need a heart,' said Barnes, without ceremony.

'What . . .?'

Barnes briefly explained the situation, pointing out that the patient was still on the heart-lung machine while her own circulation was unable to take over.

'Rod, I don't see how I can help. We haven't advanced far enough with the transgenic animals to use their organs . . .' His voice trailed off. For the first time Barnes felt despair, but suddenly Kapinsky came back. 'You say your patient needs support for only a few days, enough to allow her own heart to recover?'

'Yes.' He tried to make his voice sound assured.

'Then why not use the heart of one of those two chimpanzees we were given as a gift from the Dutch laboratory? We've been feeding them to no purpose for several months. This place isn't a zoo, you know. It's time they earned their keep.'

Barnes couldn't help a smile. Trust Kapinsky to be completely practical. Trust him also to come up with a sensible solution. 'Do you think it will work?'

He thought of a previous operation in which they had used the heart of a baboon: it had stopped beating within two hours, irreparably damaged by acute rejection.

Kapinsky read his mind. 'I think you'll have a better chance with a chimp than you did with that baboon. The chimpanzee is genetically closer to man. Of course, a gorilla would be better.'

Unaccountably, Barnes felt a chill go down his spine. 'Tell Boots to get the chimp ready. I'll send Dr Louw down. The two of them will manage to remove the heart.'

The phone clicked. Kapinsky didn't waste time on courtesy.

Barnes was suddenly doubtful. Was he doing the right thing? He would have to obtain permission from Mrs Felini's husband.

Back in the theatre he spoke to the Italians and explained the situation. They immediately agreed to act as interpreters. It was an exhausting and emotional fifteen minutes. In tears, the distressed husband eventually agreed, with much gesticulation and arm-waving.

Barnes returned to the operating theatre. There was no

change in the condition of the patient. She had now been on bypass for more than four hours, which could pose problems after the operation. He worried at the dilemma for several minutes. The artificial pumping could damage the elements in the blood responsible for coagulation: if left untreated, her wounds would continue to bleed. 'Arrange for a supply of platelets and fresh-frozen plasma,' he instructed Hobbs, who acknowledged him with a nod.

The phone rang. The heart would be available in five minutes. Barnes quickly scrubbed and gowned again, and put on fresh gloves. As he took up position at the table Des Louw walked in with a plastic bag containing the heart of the chimpanzee. He said he wished to be excused and asked if Snyman could take over. Engrossed in the problem at hand, Barnes did not notice the distress in his colleague's eyes. He waved him away and nodded to Snyman to scrub.

Placing the chimpanzee heart in the heterotopic position was a straightforward procedure. All went like clockwork and when the heart was rewarmed it started immediately with a strong beat. Barnes waited a few minutes and then took his patient off the heart-lung machine. The beating heart continued, strong and sure. Mrs Felini's heart was getting the help it needed. It would recover within days. The only question to be answered was how they could control her immune system's attack on the animal organ long enough for that to happen.

Barnes stripped off his gloves and left the operating room well satisfied. Again he had proved master of the situation. The two Italians showered praise on him and he had to admit to himself that he enjoyed the adulation.

Des Louw met him in the corridor. He looked drawn. 'May I see you in the office?' he asked.

Barnes looked at him quizzically and led the way into the small room.

Louw closed the door behind him and looked at Barnes, his face working. 'What we did today was as close to murder as one could get,' he blurted out.

Barnes was taken aback. 'What? I don't understand . . .'

'Of course you don't understand. How could you? You weren't there to see it.'

Slowly, haltingly, Louw told the story. On arriving at the laboratory Samuel had asked Louw to give him a hand as he could not control the donor animal with the squeeze-back – the device fitted to all the cages which allowed the keepers to hold the experimental animals steady for sedation. The chimpanzee had resisted with all his strength.

Louw followed him to where the two chimpanzees were housed side by side in separate cages. As soon as the men appeared both animals went berserk, leaping about and screaming as if to warn or frighten them off.

'They know what is to happen,' said Samuel. 'That is why they make a noise. They do not want to die.'

'Nonsense, Boots. They're simply unaccustomed to being handled,' Louw said, approaching the cages.

He could not have been more wrong. Normally docile animals, the two chimps had acted as if demented. So violent was their behaviour that Louw feared for his own safety, expecting them to break out of the heavily barred cages at any moment.

At last, using the squeeze-back, he and Samuel had managed to press one animal against the bars and give it the sedative, which acted within minutes. As they dragged its limp body from the cage the other suddenly quietened and began to whimper. He clung to the bars of his cage, never taking his eyes off them, making what sounded like pleading noises.

'My God,' Louw had thought, 'he's asking us to let his mate go.' Suddenly he wasn't dealing with animals any more. These were sensitive, affectionate beings that knew sorrow and hope, happiness and despair. 'I nearly gave in,' said Louw, shaking his head. 'I wish to God now that I had. The operation was a nightmare that I never again want to relive. Killing a wonderful animal and taking its heart . . .' His voice trailed off.

Barnes felt uncomfortable. The idea was ridiculous. True, there had been some research which showed that chimps could be taught a sign vocabulary of up to five hundred words but that didn't make them sentient beings.

'Des, I realize you're upset,' he said, avoiding the other man's eyes. 'But wouldn't you have been more upset if Mrs Felini had died on the operating table? Is it not our duty as doctors to do everything in our power to give our patients a chance for a better life – even if this means the sacrifice of an animal?'

Louw was silent for a moment. Then he said, 'I now know that we do not have the right to do to animals whatever we want and then excuse our actions by claiming that they're for the benefit of the human race. Animals, too, have a right to life. After today, I have my doubts that I'll ever again be able to experiment on an animal – even if my job is on the line.' He turned abruptly and left the office, leaving Barnes staring at the wall.

Time to pay a visit to the animal room, he thought.

He found Samuel sitting in front of the chimp cage with a handful of fruit. The animal looked as if it was seeing nothing. It ignored the fruit and sat at the back of the cage, rocking back and forth. Although it showed no tears, the air of grief was strong. Twice it sat up and stopped, staring at the empty cage where its mate had been held.

Quietly, Barnes turned and left. There was nothing he could do here.

On the fifth day after her operation, Mrs Felini's immune system rejected the chimpanzee heart. She died in the evening.

The next morning Samuel found the other chimpanzee dead in its cage. He picked up one lifeless hand. It felt cold and stiff. Death had come during the night. 'You did not want to live any longer, my friend,' he said, the tears starting.

Samuel felt lonely and confused by the cruelty of those men who could be so nice and yet could kill so callously. This was one of those times when he would have liked to talk to his father.

As a young boy in the Transkei he had seen little of him. Benjamin Mbeki worked on the mines in Egoli, the place of gold, which was so big it was called many names. Some white men called it the Reef, some called it Johannesburg and he had even heard other names but they all meant the place where the mines were.

Benjamin Mbeki was not allowed to take his family there.

Samuel would never forget the times when, once a year, the mine boss allowed his father to come home for three weeks. Then life was good, not only for him but also for his mother and brothers and sisters. Always these holidays from Egoli were good times. One of the oxen from his grandfather's herd of twelve would be slaughtered and every day they would have meat with their porridge. Before bedtime his father would tell the children about the big city where lights burned without fire. His father worked deep in the stomach of the earth, so far down that the rocks were warm to the touch and the air was hot. It was a strange place.

Always, after his father went back to the mines, his mother got sick. The white doctor, who came every week to the medicine room next to the black people's church down in the valley, said it was an illness that his father carried from the dirty women at the mines. He always gave her the same *muti* of little white pills in a box and did good *juju* on her arm by pushing a thin silver stick into her skin. The *muti* cost almost all of the money his father left behind. His mother said they did not need the money as they could grow all the corn they needed on his grandfather's patch of land. There was also milk when the cows were in calf.

When Samuel was old enough his father said he should go to the Catholic school next to the church. There, the nuns taught him to read and write and to count. When he was twelve his father told him that his time had arrived, the days of the testing, after which he would become a man. He had seen this happen to all his brothers and he could not wait for it to happen to him. He and his friends had talked about it often. They knew there was much pain in this thing and sometimes a boy died because he got sick with the pain.

On a day when the winter rains had stopped and the land was green with many flowers the elders gathered his age-group together and set them to building a shelter of reeds. Within the *boma* they would feast for seven days before the testing.

Samuel stood straight and tall, keeping his hands behind his head and staring at the distant hills as the elder took his penis, drew out the foreskin and slashed at it with the blade of the *assegai*. Blood spilled on Samuel's thighs and agony filled his body. He could think of nothing but the pain. It was taking over his mind. All he had to do was pull away from the awful tugging and sawing at his penis and it would stop. *Now!* It had to stop *now.* But it went on and on for what seemed like a lifetime. He saw the hills blur and felt the dizziness rise in his head. He was going to fall down like a woman in front of his friends and, even if he lived, he would never be a man among men.

A hand touched his shoulder. It was his grandfather, speaking softly and leading him into the shade of the *boma*. The cutting of his foreskin was over. He had passed the first test.

His grandfather carefully bandaged his penis with a strip of thin bark, staunching the blood-flow. The bark came from a tree that had healing properties and would keep him free from the sweating sickness that often came with wounds. It was tied with string, leaving an opening through which he could urinate. Another strip of bark was tied around his waist like a belt and his bandaged penis was tied up to his left side so that it would not hang down. It throbbed like fire but Samuel ignored the pain.

On the sixth day he awoke to find the pain had gone. Only a slight itch remained. He removed the bark and, for the first time, examined his circumcised penis. The wound was healing well. It was time to wash off the white clay, which distinguished him as a *mkweta*. Samuel lay in the stream bed, scrubbing his body with river grass until all signs of the white clay had gone. With it went his childhood. The school he attended only went on to standard six. When he reached this milestone his education stopped. The nuns told him that a standard six certificate qualified him to become a teacher. As there were too many children at the school for the nuns to handle, he could start teaching at the beginning of next year.

But Samuel had already decided to go south. He could see there was nothing for him in his tribal homeland but more poverty and backwardness. He wanted more than his father had, his father who now had the breathing sickness that men suffered when they worked under the ground. He had heard that the white people in Cape Town, over a thousand kilometres away, were better to work for than the whites up north where the mines were.

One morning he asked for the blessing of his grandfather, bade his mother farewell, and set off with his few possessions. He had twenty handfuls of mieliemeal wrapped in a cloth, some old clothes his father said they wore in the city, a knife, a spoon, a blanket and his fishing line. The *kraal* was close to the coast and he knew he could live off the sea when his food ran out. He could also earn a few cents diving for crayfish off the rocks and selling them live to white people travelling along the road.

After a few days he met a group of four Xhosas and was pleased to learn that they, too, were on their way to find work in Cape Town. This was a great help as one of the group had made the journey before but had been caught without a passbook and deported back to the homeland. That made him an *amagodukwa*, that is one who went to the city and came back. *Amagodukwas* had status; they were wise. He said they should sneak onto a train at East London, and hide from the ticket collector for the two days and nights it took to reach the big city.

In East London, Samuel spent a few days doing odd jobs to earn cash for food. He and his friends had arranged to meet at the station at the end of the week. Boarding the train without tickets was so simple that it left Samuel wondering. They stood on the dark side of the station until midnight when the train left, and boarded a moving coach like five shadows. They had been warned by the one who had done it before that they enter only coaches with the number three, marked 'Black only'. 'This is the third-class part of the train. Always we look for the number three. There you will find no whites or coloureds or even Indians,' the *amagodukwa* said. And so it proved.

The next day they dodged the white conductor who, in any case, only walked through twice. At night they scrounged something to eat. The *amagodukwa* stole food from sleeping passengers but did not tell Samuel until they had eaten. The food felt strange in his stomach at first but he felt better when the others said the food had been taken from foreigners.

The next day two of the group were caught in the toilet and locked in the guard's van. Samuel was upset about this but the *amagodukwa* said they would not go to jail. The white man who judged people would sentence them to five strokes of the cane, then with bottoms still burning, they would be put on a bus back to the homeland.

He was glad when the train at last steamed into Cape Town and, with his two friends, he could melt into the crowds. When they walked out of the station Samuel remembered his father's stories of the big city. Surely this city was even more wonderful than Egoli? They were on a wide road lined with shops, each with windows packed with all kinds of treasures. Apart from clothes and shoes, some of the shops had good things for which he could not even imagine a use. He felt almost faint with excitement and wanted to linger at each window but the *amagodukwa* said they should not stay too long as this was a place for white people only. As the only blacks in a crowd of whites, they would soon be asked for their passes.

They had to go to the black townships which were just outside the white city. It was a three-hour walk to a place called Langa. They arrived hot, thirsty and tired. Worse, the place was a disappointment. This was no sparkling city but a big *kraal*, much like other places in the homelands except that it had many more huts.

Dirt roads ran between heaps of foul-smelling rubbish and paper, with here and there a pool of stagnant water. There were no patches of maize, and the few goats seemed to graze on the papers blowing around. There were rows and rows of little brick houses with fences around them, and in between were shacks made of tin and wood and cardboard.

Many men sat around and appeared to have no purpose in life. Some played cards and finger stones, others drank and still others seemed to be asleep. The experienced one warned them to keep walking and not to look to one side or the other. Men attacked here at a look or just to get a few cents. Assaults and serious injury happened every day, he said. Samuel felt as if he had lost control over his destiny. He was taken along in the stream, unable to plan his route or where he would eventually end up. The wise one took them to a place called a hostel where men could find food and a bed until they could build their own shack.

Samuel, his dreams of the big city shattered, spent his first night in Cape Town with a hundred and twenty other men in a long, cement-brick dormitory, longing for the open spaces where he had been born and for the comfort of his grass mattress. Each man had room for just a bed and space underneath to keep a few belongings.

Over the next few days, the three men dodged the Bantu inspectors who spent their time stopping black men, asking to see their passbooks. From a group gathered around a shebeen – an illegal grog-shop – they picked up the information that the university was looking for gardeners. A university, Samuel remembered from his talks with the nuns, was another kind of school where people went to get even more learning. Something crystallized in his mind. A place of learning was what he wanted: perhaps he could attend classes and become educated like the white people.

Next morning, he dressed in his father's old suit with shirt and tie. He had no socks but he shined the shoes like glass and was thankful the trouser cuffs did not show his ankles.

They left before dawn because they had been told that it was a long walk to the university, about ten kilometres. They needed to be at the office there at nine o'clock when the white people started arriving in their motor cars for work.

That was where Cecil White, head groundsman at the University of Cape Town, found them. He was not in the best of moods. The morning paper had been running a series of articles on the environment, sarcastically citing the kilometre-long entrance drive to the university as an example of visual pollution. Bloody fine, thought White, if the bastards from the Bantu control inspectorate didn't keep pitching up and scaring away his gardeners. He always seemed to be hiring new green workers who didn't have a clue about anything, let alone holding a spade at the right end.

He surveyed the latest crop of aspirants standing outside his office door. Only three this morning, all young and fit. Not necessarily a good thing as young blacks seldom stayed around long. One of them wore an old shiny suit and a tie. Hardly the kind of gear an experienced gardener would wear. 'You.' He pointed at Samuel. 'What do you know about gardening?' For the first time Samuel was glad that the old white nun at the school had forced him to spend so many hours learning English. He told the fat white man with the red face how he had prepared the land around the hut and planted corn when the rains came. He added that he also had experience with cattle and had helped the cow when it was giving birth to a calf. 'As I thought, no great shakes but you talk as if you're keen which is more important.'

Samuel understood only that the white man hadn't said no. He rushed to answer: 'Yes, sir, I qualified as a teacher.'

White looked up in surprise, thought for a moment and then handed each of the three a piece of paper. 'Go over to that counter and fill it in,' he said.

Samuel looked at his paper. It wanted to know his name, his date of birth, his home address and – his heart stopped – his passbook number. They conferred in the home language. The *amagodukwa* wasn't sure. Samuel pointed out that they didn't know any passbook numbers and if they gave the wrong numbers the white man would know it. It was best to answer all the questions except that one, he said. The other two looked at each other and then at Samuel. They agreed. They went back to the desk of the fat man and handed over their papers. He glanced at them casually, then stopped reading and looked up. 'None of you have passes?'

A little book of four by three inches that stood like a mountain between them and happiness.

'I will give you a letter to say that you are employed as gardeners at the University of Cape Town. Take it to the offices of the Bantu Administration in Langa and ask them to give you a pass. When you have one, come back to me.'

A few minutes later a white woman handed them an important-looking envelope with the university mark on it, addressed to the Bantu Administration. She smiled at them and wished them luck. This Cape Town is a nice place, thought Samuel. They immediately started the long walk back to Langa. It was a good day. They had work.

There was a long queue at the Administration offices when they got there at midday but they patiently took up station at the end. The sun was slanting down when they got to the office door only to be told that it closed at four o'clock and that they would have to come back the next day.

Samuel had a restless night. Twice he woke up to feel for the important envelope under the pillow made by his rolled-up trousers.

Before sun-up the three were on their way again to the Bantu Administration offices. To their surprise, they were not the first to arrive. There, in the darkness, a handful of men and women were already waiting.

Just after nine o'clock a big black car rolled up and a white man with a large beard got out. Samuel's spirits dimmed. The man was clearly a Boer. He had heard that Boers usually wore beards and did not like black people. It was almost mid-morning when at last the three were herded into the office. The man with the beard sat behind a desk with a wooden board on it that said his name was J. van Rooyen.

'What do you three want?' he asked, glowering.

The other two looked at Samuel. He was now their spokes-man. He looked at the board on the desk. Clearly, this was how he wanted to be addressed. 'We have a letter from the university, J. van Rooyen,' he said, holding out the envelope.

The man knocked the envelope from Samuel's hand. His face reddened and the veins stood out on his forehead. 'You cheeky black bastards. I've a good mind to knock your bloody head off your shoulders. My name is Boss van Rooyen. Remember that.'

The three took a step back. 'Yes, Boss van Rooyen,' they chorused.

'Pick it up, you damn fool,' he said to Samuel, who bent down, retrieved the envelope and held it out.

Van Rooyen snatched it with a glare. He looked at the uni-versity crest, curled his lip, ripped open the envelope and scanned the letter. 'So the three of you came here illegally.' They said nothing. Van Rooyen looked back at the letter and said, 'And the idiots at the university gave you work?'

They understood him to say they had a job at the university and nodded.

'You black bastards didn't come here to work. You came to steal, kill and rob. I should really hand you over to the police.'

Samuel was shocked. This man did not understand them at all. They were men who had come to do men's work. 'Please, Boss van Rooyen, we did come here to work. That is why we went to the university.'

'Why the hell don't you do some work in your own home-land?' Clearly, van Rooyen did not expect an answer. He went on, 'That's why it's such a bloody mess. Everybody lies around all day and does bugger all. Now you want to come here and bugger up here too.'

Van Rooyen was in a quandary. He didn't know quite what to do. He would like to call Sergeant Botes at the Langa police sta-tion and ask him to come and pick up these illegal immigrants. But he was wary of their connection with the university. He looked back at the letter. It was signed by some bastard called White, who probably earned three times as much as he did for doing nothing but instigate trouble among the blacks. If he turned these blacks in, he might have the local Communist lawyer on his back – and who knew how far that would go?

'All right, it's your lucky day,' he said to Samuel's surprise. He gave them some forms to fill in, stamped them with the official stamp of the Bantu Administration and signed his name. 'Take these forms back to the Bantu Administration in Umtata, and they will give you a pass.'

Back to Umtata? To the Transkei? They had struggled so hard to get to Cape Town and now they had to go back? The three looked at him in disbelief.

'But we have no money for the train.' It was the *amagodukwa* who spoke.

Samuel said nothing. Something told him that objections would be a waste of time and he was already planning ahead.

'That's your problem. Now get out of my office before I kick you black and blue. Jesus, I forgot, they're already black.' Van Rooyen laughed uproariously and all the clerks joined in. Samuel felt sympathy for them. They worked with this white man all day and owed their jobs to him.

Outside, in the bright sunlight, they found the queue was several hundred long – all resigned to being kept waiting, insulted and laughed at in the hope of getting that coveted passbook, which gave them the right to stay and work in the Cape.

They walked in silence for a while. Then the experienced one stopped, took out his Bantu Administration form and slowly tore it into pieces. The other two said nothing.

Then he spoke. 'I have been here before and I have learned that there are gangs you can join. They live well by robbing people and stealing cars. They sell white man's drink too and the people pay much for it. I am tired. I have walked far. I will not go back to Umtata. I will stay, paper or no paper.'

Samuel said nothing. Both looked at their companion. He also took out his paper and tore it to pieces. They all watched as the wind blew them away.

The two who had made a choice looked at Samuel, but he made no move. They both shrugged and walked off in the direction of the city. He was alone.

CHAPTER 12

The next morning Samuel set out for the university, dressed in his suit and tie. Cecil White was pleased to see him.

'You are Samuel Mbeki?' he asked.

'Yes, boss.'

'Please do not call me boss. My name is Cecil or Mr White, whichever makes you feel comfortable. Where are the other two?'

Samuel smiled. 'They did not come.' He suddenly felt he did not want to tell this man about their decision.

'Did you bring your passbook?'

'No, sir, I have to go to Umtata to get it.'

White's mouth opened and then closed. He shook his head slowly – sadly. 'They do everything possible to make it difficult, Samuel.'

'I do not mind to go to Umtata, but I have no money for the train or bus,' said Samuel. He was deathly afraid that Mr White would change his mind but he felt he had to tell him the truth.

'You're too well dressed to work in the garden anyway. We will give you a return ticket to Umtata, my friend. The bureaucrats will have to do more than that to make us give up.'

Samuel had never heard the word 'bureaucrats' before but he was sure it meant the Bantu Administration.

That was the beginning of his work at the university. When he returned a week later from Umtata, proudly carrying his passbook, he decided to stay at the men's hostel in Langa until he could afford his own quarters. Where he spent his nights mattered little as he felt so weary at day's end that he slept like the dead.

*

Smartly dressed in his blue overall with UCT in bold white letters on his back, he started work in the spacious gardens of the university. It was not strenuous and he enjoyed the pleasant surroundings. Sometimes he drove the machine which cut the grass and that was easy work. What made it a long day were the queues for transport each morning and night. Blacks stood in line for hours to travel from the townships to the city and back again.

His day began at four a.m. to give him time to get to work by seven. He left again at five not reaching the hostel until eight o'clock. Some workers gave up on the transport and walked.

Samuel didn't work on Saturdays or Sundays. He used these days to do his laundry and buy what he needed. But he also knew that weekends were dangerous times in the crowded township, because of the drunkenness and muggings. Blacks used this time to forget the hard reality of the working week. They had nothing to look back on and nothing to look forward to, except the shebeen at the weekend. When the drinking started so did the fighting, and anyone could get drawn into it.

During these early summer days the Cape south-easter seemed to blow constantly, filling the township with dust and sand, driving up the level of aggression on the streets.

On Sundays, if the wind did not blow, Samuel would go to the sea. The fishing was good and from the very small section of the beach that was open for blacks he would often pull out a sizeable meal. Then he would take the long trip back to Langa and feel that life was good. Men coming from the homelands were not allowed to bring their women with them, which raised the sexual tension of hostel-dwellers even higher. Samuel remembered from his childhood the doctor's warnings to his father each time he left for Egoli, and resolved never to touch the shebeen women. He knew all there was to know about sex and would wait for a woman of his own, he thought.

He was awakened one night by a noise from the next bed, to find two men struggling together in the way he remembered his father doing with his mother. He decided to ignore this strange activity but next day talked about it to one of the other black gardeners at the university. The man laughed and said that a man could also have sex with another man and this was one way of getting pleasure when there were no women around. Samuel thought about it for days, and decided that his needs were not that desperate.

The work at the university soon became routine, but Samuel could not understand why the vast area of land around the university, more than a kilometre from the main road, was used as a garden instead of a farmland. He knew it was good soil and there never seemed to be any shortage of water, so it made no sense that they planted only little trees and flowers that nobody could eat. And when the grass was long enough to graze the machines were brought out to mow it back. Often he watched the young white men and women coming and going along the university walkways, carrying their books, laughing and talking as if they had no work or worries. He envied them and wished that he, too, could go to university.

One day he spoke to Mr White about it. He reminded his boss that he was already a teacher and would like to attend some of the classes during his lunch break.

White looked at him for a long time, trying to make up his mind how to say it, then put a hand on his shoulder. 'Samuel, you do not qualify for university. Not because you are black. This is one of the few universities in the land which allows blacks to study here. You do not have enough schooling.'

Patiently, White explained that the level of education for white children was much higher than for blacks. Only a very few blacks had ever reached the level required to get into the university. From that day Samuel tried not to look at the carefree white students walking around the campus. The days, months and years passed but inside a deep resolve formed: that some day he, too, would reach the same heights of education.

One evening, it was already dark when he reached the hostel. Outside, a group of people surged around. He could hear women screaming and men swearing. He checked that his week's pay was tucked safely into his belt. As a rule he did not get involved in these gang wars. They were almost daily occurrences and he found it best to walk a wide circle around them. Then he stopped. A man lay on the ground. Even from this distance Samuel recognized him. A police siren sounded nearby and many of the group fled. Samuel pushed his way through and bent over. It was the *amagodukwa*.

'I see you, Samuel.' The voice choked on a gurgle of blood-stained froth that came from his mouth. Several stab wounds in his chest made sucking noises as he tried to breathe.

'Good day, wise one,' said Samuel.

The *amagodukwa* raised himself on one elbow and put a clenched fist in the air. '*Amandla*,' he said, and fell back into the dirt he would never escape.

The police pushed everyone aside, called an ambulance and grabbed a few people as witnesses. Samuel walked off quietly.

Amandla! It was the slogan of the African National Congress. It meant power. But the wise one had no power. He didn't have the power to change his life, and at the end he didn't even have the power to save it. Samuel had always believed that the wise one had become a gangster but something about the man's dying face would not go away. He asked around among the hostel-dwellers and was told that the *amagodukwa* had been an organizer for the ANC. They told Samuel that his friend had been killed by the hit squad of the South African police.

Life in the townships was a daily struggle for survival, and Samuel counted the days to his annual holidays when he could go home to visit his family. There would inevitably be a smiling group to meet him, and his mother would weep as he embraced her. It would be a time of eating and drinking, with talk of friends and family, and slow relaxation into the age-old rhythms of tribal ways.

On one visit he received bad news. He pieced together the story from talks with his mother and with other family members as they came and went. The news had come a few months before, in a letter from the white people at the mine, which said there had been a 'pressure burst' in a shaft. His father had been crushed by thousands of tons of mud and rock – like a black beetle under the foot of an elephant. His body had been recovered several days later and, as there was no money to bring it to the homeland, he was buried at the Reef with no one to mourn his passing. His mother had a small pension from the mine but it was not enough to feed and care for the family. Samuel immediately agreed to take over the burden of family support. It was the least he could do. It was a sad holiday but which, nevertheless, had a happy outcome: he met Sophie. His memory of the wedding itself was slurred but ever after he remembered that December holiday as one of the happiest times in his life.

All too soon it was back to work and the long months of separation while he sweated for a living in the gardens of the university.

Life in Cape Town was agony. Time dragged. Samuel took to enquiring after overtime work to supplement his wages, and also if there were any other jobs that paid better than gardening. He had to improve his income if he was ever to support his wife and family.

One day he was told to report to Mr White's office. His boss looked up from the mass of papers on his desk as Samuel entered. 'Good afternoon, Samuel.'

Samuel could not make out from the white man's tone whether this was going to be a good meeting or a bad one. 'Good afternoon, sir,' he said, holding his hat with both hands in front of him.

'I think it is time for you to move.'

Samuel felt his heart thump. Was he being asked to look for another job? Perhaps Mr White was tired of his constant requests for more work and extra pay.

'They need cleaners at the medical school animal room. There's quite a pay difference. I recommended you to Clive Warren.'

Samuel couldn't quite take it in. 'Does that mean I will move from here?'

White smiled. He liked this quiet, hard-working man. He had overheard enough gossip from the other gardeners to explain Samuel's sudden dissatisfaction with the job which he had done for years without complaining. Any man who was married needed to improve his income.

Samuel had long given up hope of attending classes at the university and now couldn't see how looking after animals would give him better opportunities. As a child he had enjoyed caring for the goats and cattle but now he was a man with a man's responsibilities. But looking at Cecil White, he knew he could trust this white man. If he thought Samuel should move to the animal house, he would go. Samuel thanked him profusely. This was going to be a good move.

A few days later Samuel was told the job was his. He never enjoyed going from the known to the unknown. Here in the university grounds he knew every tree, shrub and path. He had cared for them from season to season. What would he find in the animal house?

Over the years, as his wages increased, Samuel had reached the stage where he could take the train to work. This gave him an hour's extra sleep. On the first day of the new job he got off the train one station earlier and made his way to the medical school. It was six thirty when he arrived and the buildings were deserted. He headed for the one where the animals were kept and waited. Slowly life returned to the various buildings that made up the complex where young men and women learned to become doctors.

Clive Warren, in charge of the animal room, liked the look of him immediately. Neatly turned out, in clean but worn work clothing, Samuel seemed to be a man who was serious about his work. Warren allocated him, as one of a team of three, to the section that housed the animals belonging to the department of surgical research.

Although work at the animal house started at eight, Samuel

made a point of turning up an hour earlier. He enjoyed the routine and the fact that the cleaners had a small room to themselves where they could change into overalls and gumboots, keep personal property, and also relax during meal breaks.

The animals were not what Samuel had expected. There were no cattle or goats but lots of rats, mice and rabbits. In his section only dogs were kept, bought from the local municipal pound. These were unclaimed animals which, if not bought by the animal room, would have been destroyed. A few young doctors diverted from their clinical duties for three or four hours every week to experiment on these animals.

Samuel began his day by inspecting the holding cages and removing any dogs that had died during the night. The dead animals were taken to a small room on the same floor where the doctor who had operated on the animal did the post-mortem. They told Samuel they did so to find out why the animal had died or what had gone wrong during the experiment. When the doctors had completed their work and taken specimens, Samuel disposed of the bodies in the incinerator at the end of the passage. After that he cleaned all the cages with a hose, washing away excreta and old food, then mopped the floors. He was also responsible for ensuring that fresh water and food was placed in each cage.

Victor, the most senior member of the cleaning staff, had just been promoted to laboratory assistant and spent most of the day helping the doctors with the experiments they carried out in the operating room on the third floor. He and Samuel soon became firm friends. Samuel was fascinated by Victor's tales of the operations performed on the dogs. According to Victor, the chief – Dr Barnes, who had just come back from America – showed them how to cut open a dog's heart, work inside it for hours then stitch it closed again – like the rips and tears that Samuel sometimes repaired in his working trousers – and the dogs lived.

If these stories about Dr Barnes were true then he had greater powers than the witch-doctor and that could not be. He recalled the time when two men had fought in the village over a woman. One had stabbed the other in the heart with a spear and all the efforts of the witch-doctor could not save his life. There were some things that men could not do.

Victor was angry when Samuel expressed his doubts. 'If you think I'm lying why don't you come and have a look for yourself?' he snapped.

'Do you think I can?' He was excited by the prospect of seeing inside the laboratory.

'Well, I don't know. Your job is in the animal room,' Victor replied and marched away.

Samuel remained sitting on the small wooden bench in the animal house, his nostrils filled with the smell of dog excreta and urine. He said aloud, 'My place is not in the animal room. In the Transkei I already have a house and a wife and four healthy sons. I have a herd of twelve cattle and the people respect me. One day they will also respect me in the land of the white man.'

He was Samuel Mbeki. He could do what he wanted to do. The moment seemed to mark a point in his life where things changed.

Next day he took an interest in the post-mortems. Usually he placed the dead animals on the cutting table and came back later to remove the remains. Today he stayed to watch one young doctor, Dr Ferreira, at work and later to help him clean up. This particular doctor had been coming to the animal house more often than the others and was always appreciative of Samuel's help.

Samuel noticed that each dog had been cut down the front of the chest. Inside, the breastbone was split down the middle and the bones had been wired together. He could barely believe his eyes when the doctor showed him where the heart had been opened and stitched closed again. So Victor did not lie. The white doctors *could* open a heart and close it again! Samuel asked how this could be done without causing the animal to bleed to death.

Dr Ferreira, only too pleased to talk about his work, explained how all the blood was diverted from the dog to a machine that breathed air into it and then pumped the blood back into the body. The machine, he said, acted like the heart and lungs of the dog. While this was happening, it was possible to open the heart, which was now still and empty of blood, and carry out whatever operation was required.

Samuel had little sleep that night. Over and over in his mind he followed the action of the machine that breathed and pumped blood for the dog. But something was missing. Suddenly, he realized that the white doctor had not explained how he prevented the soul from escaping when the heart was open. As he lay, tossing and turning, Samuel had a brilliant idea. At first it was so simple that he wondered if perhaps there was something wrong with it. He would go to the medical school library in the morning and ask the white woman behind the desk for a book that would tell him all about the inside of the heart.

He soon discovered that the idea was both simple and unworkable.

'Are you a student?' the white lady asked when he made his request, eyeing his white overalls and gumboots.

'No, missies, but I work in the animal room at the medical school.'

'I'm afraid the books in this library are only for medical students and doctors,' she responded, turning to the next in line.

'But I don't want to take the book away. I will only read it in the animal room,' Samuel insisted, feeling his resolve weaken.

The woman turned back to him, impressed by his persistence. Her face softened. She sounded genuinely sorry as she said, 'I'm sorry but the rules of the library don't allow me to do that.'

Samuel knew that this was as far as he could go and left, vaguely pleased that he had at least stood up for what he wanted.

A few days later he told Dr Ferreira about his disappointment. 'That's no problem,' said the doctor with a smile. 'Tomorrow I will bring you a book with coloured pictures of the inside of the heart. You will be able to read as much as you want about heart surgery.'

That began an engrossing period of night-time reading, interspersed with question-and-answer sessions with Dr Ferreira in the post-mortem room. When the doctor left each day, Samuel would take up the scalpels which had been thrown into the disposal bin and try his hand at dissecting the hearts before putting them in the incinerator.

The other cleaners were at first amused by his interest in surgery, greeting him with 'Good day, Dr Mbeki,' but Samuel was so immersed in his new-found interest that he hardly heard and after a few days they accepted his strange behaviour. After all, wasn't he a teacher turned cleaner?

Samuel persisted until he understood the way the blood was pumped by the heart. This great organ in the chest took in blood on one side and ejected it on the other, constantly pumping it forward and around the body. He found and identified the right upper chamber which received the blood from the upper and lower body through two big veins. He noted how the upper chamber contracted, squeezing the blood through a valve into the right lower chamber where the process was repeated, pumping the blood through another valve along an artery to the two lungs.

Fascinated, he saw then how the blood was oxygenated by the air in the lungs and then returned to the left upper chamber of the heart. From there it was squeezed into the lower chamber and expelled powerfully back to the circulation of the whole body.

When he had a little spare time he would practise stitching on the dead animals, neatly suturing the wounds and tying off in tidy knots just like those used by the young doctor.

One Monday morning, after he had been helping Dr Ferreira for several months, something happened to change everything. Victor was ill and Samuel was called up to the laboratory to assist with an operation on a live animal. When he arrived he found Dr Ferreira with a tall white man in a white coat, who was introduced as Dr Barnes. This was the famous doctor, the one who had taught these young doctors to do more than the witch-doctor could do.

Dr Ferreira was singing Samuel's praises. 'He is remarkable, Dr Barnes. His knowledge of the work is far beyond that of a cleaner.'

They both turned to look at him. He felt shy and, at the same time, proud, and wished his grandfather could hear these words. The young doctor went on to tell the other how Samuel had helped at the post-mortems, read the textbooks, asked questions about the work and could remove and identify organs with proper surgical technique.

Dr Barnes smiled. 'Clearly you're wasted in the animal room, Samuel?' It was spoken like a question but he could think of no answer.

The young doctor jumped in. 'He is not only wasted in the animal room. I think it is a waste that this man never had the opportunity to study medicine. He tells me he is a Bantu Education teacher, but I think he is much more than that. He is a talented natural surgeon.'

From that day, Samuel took on more and more complex work in the experimental heart surgery program. At first he was permitted only to work on dogs, holding retractors and sucking the blood back to the heart-lung machine. Soon he was allowed to demonstrate his skill with stitching and tying off sutures.

From there he progressed to baboons, finding the new layout of body organs a challenge and quickly adapting his routine. Within a few months he was opening the chest, removing the heart and stitching a donor heart in place. 'You can do that better than most young registrars I know,' Dr Barnes said one day, watching him as he moved through the operating procedure with quiet assurance. 'You go in there, boots and all, without a doubt in your head.'

The name stuck. In no time he was known as Boots to staff and doctors alike. He accepted the name for what it was, a compliment.

In the following year he became a regular member of Dr Barnes's operating team, gowned, gloved and masked just like the white doctors who had trained at the medical school. Everyone accepted him at the laboratory – all except the senior doctor there, Dr Kapinsky. Samuel learned never to put on a mask or gown when Dr Kapinsky was around, and had managed to avoid a confrontation until now. It was Dr Barnes who was the unwitting cause of the incident which had triggered off Kapinsky's anger on his return from his trip to Russia.

'Boots, I need ten transplants performed over the next few days,' Dr Barnes had told him, adding, 'We have a full test schedule set up for a new anti-rejection drug and need a hand with the transplant surgery.' And that was how Kapinsky had found him, scalpel poised over the chest of an anaesthetized baboon.

Samuel exhaled a long sigh and stood up from the animal-lab bench. He had been sitting for almost an hour, oblivious to all around while his mind ranged over his whole life. His thighs ached. He was no longer young. He had angered the big white doctor Kapinsky and his job was in danger. He expected no help from the other white doctors. He had seen this before: when a white man grew angry with a black man no other white man would interfere. And so it would be in this case.

He felt himself fill with rage. This time it would be different. This time he would let no white man take away what he had worked so long to achieve. If Dr Kapinsky came for him he would say out loud what he thought in his head. He could not lose.

CHAPTER 13

'How would you like to be a donor?'

David Rhodes looked at Barnes, bright blue eyes widening, and then at Karen van der Walt who had been called in as transplant co-ordinator. They were in the doctors' office on the same floor as the transplant ward.

As Karen listened to Barnes, she remembered all too vividly the moment when – in that same room – she had been asked to donate her husband's organs. It was a fleeting thought, immediately banished.

'You mean, blood?'

'No, I mean your heart,' Barnes answered, and couldn't help chuckling at the expressions chasing each other across the boy's face, beginning with surprise and ending in alarm.

Since his discharge almost a year before, David's progress had been followed carefully by the cardiologists. His rapid rate of recovery and absence of any sign of heart failure or rejection seemed little short of miraculous. What excited Barnes was the final cardiology report. This detailed investigation, completed only a week previously, had used sophisticated techniques. Internal and external examination of both hearts using coronary-angiography, eco-cardiography and radioactive isotope scanning showed each beating strongly and regularly. Biopsy reports on tissue samples taken from each heart showed no permanent damage to David's own heart from the inflammation and no sign of rejection in the donor heart.

The rare event, a total success, Barnes thought. As living proof, David Rhodes stood before him. He was the picture of health, bronzed from the sun, his muscular young body fit and trim.

'You can remove the transplanted heart and throw it away,' the senior cardiologist had remarked to Barnes when he handed over the report. 'It serves no purpose any more and the immunosuppression can only cause problems.'

He was right, Barnes thought. He *would* remove the donor heart – but he had no intention of throwing it away.

'After your operation you may remember I explained to you that I thought the heart failure was due to an inflammation of your heart muscle.'

'Yes, a myocarditis,' said David, keen to show he had picked up some of the medical jargon.

'That is correct,' Barnes replied, smiling. He always enjoyed talking to this intelligent youngster. 'I also said that if we could assist your heart long enough, its function would return once the inflammation subsided.'

David nodded. Karen sat very still, anticipating the next question.

'The tests you underwent during the past few days indicate that the function of your heart has returned to normal. You do not need a second heart any more.'

As he spoke, Barnes saw the excitement grow in David's face. 'So you want the heart back, Dr Barnes,' he said with a smile, making it sound as if they were talking about a borrowed book.

'No, it's not that I want the heart back, but its continued presence in your body is a health hazard.'

'You mean rejection?'

'Yes. If we don't remove the donor heart you will have to remain on immunosuppressive drugs. You know as well as I do the dangers and disadvantages of this treatment.'

David said nothing for a moment, then gazed levelly at Barnes. 'Dr Barnes, I cannot put into words my gratitude and admiration for you and the other doctors and nurses. Of course, my parents and I will do whatever you recommend.' Suddenly impish, he grinned, glanced at Karen and added, 'But I want a pretty girl to ask me for my heart.'

Almost overcome by a rush of emotion, Karen put her arms around him and hugged him.

He smiled, obviously enjoying it, and asked, 'When will you operate, doctor?'

'The tests show the donor heart is still in excellent condition . . .'

'That's because I love that heart too much to allow my immune system to harm it,' David interjected.

They all laughed at the idea, which, Barnes thought, might not be too far off the mark. There was still a lot to be learnt about the workings of the immune system.

'With your permission, I would like to remove the heart as soon as a suitable patient is available,' Barnes said.

'It's yours. That means I'm now officially on stand-by as a donor.' David laughed. 'It must be the first time you've had a healthy, live human donor for a heart.'

'If things go as I hope they will, it won't be the only first. There will eventually be two human beings who can each claim they had the same heart beating in their chests,' Barnes replied.

They celebrated with the hospital stand-by – a cup of tea.

Karen felt a great sense of thankfulness. That was the least stressful donor interview she had ever arranged.

Later, driving back from the hospital to the medical school, Barnes, too, had a sudden rush of gratitude for simply being alive. Both his professional and private life seemed to be back on track. Since the night of the staff dinner party, he had been going out with Karen, first occasionally, then more regularly as they got to know each other. He kept on telling himself it was a platonic friendship, almost as if he didn't want to become involved with another woman. But he'd found himself rethinking many of his long-held views on the professional life and permanent relationships. He had come to accept Karen as the ideal dinner companion for an evening out, but he had never bothered to examine closely how he felt about her until once when her child was ill and she had to turn down his invitation. Disappointment had overwhelmed him.

Their dinner-table talk generally concerned work at the hospital and the laboratory. He had never discussed details of his research program, but both bemoaned the shortage of research funds and Karen agreed with his view of the Ethics Committee. Afterwards, he would drive her home and say goodnight at the door. She never asked him in and he had not thought to invite her to his tower-block apartment for a drink. Until the previous night.

From the outset, things had been different – Karen's appearance for one. She had been dressed in a white top that did little more than gift-wrap the creamy swell of her breasts, set off with a mini-skirt that showed her tanned legs to perfection. Her hair, which was usually massed about her head, had been brushed to a shining jet and left hanging loosely, almost to her waist.

She slid into his car in a subtle breath of perfume with a rush of words. 'Hi, there's no need to be back early for the baby-sitter tonight. I have a friend sleeping over. She and Kimberley get on like a house on fire, so they were only too happy to get rid of me.'

He had felt excitement build in his loins, which stayed with him throughout the meal at Gino's. They seemed to talk of everything but hospitals and medicine, perfectly attuned to each other's mood and often laughing.

After the main course she had excused herself and headed for the ladies' room, threading her way through the restaurant. He had watched the heads swivel after her and had experienced a sudden male sense of possession. This, he admitted to himself for the first time, was his woman.

They drove back in silence but with a heightened awareness of each other. She moved slightly closer to him, and said nothing when he took the coastal turn-off, which led to his apartment. It was as if they had already come to some unspoken agreement.

In the lift they had held hands like teenagers. She had exclaimed with pleasure at the view from the apartment's balcony, giving Barnes a peculiar feeling of pride, almost as if he owned the view. Across the bay the city pulsed with neon. Cars streamed in arrows of light along the freeways while above it all, as if suspended in the warm night air, hung Africa Face bathed in the glow of floodlights. The city was putting on her best display for a special evening.

Wordlessly Karen had turned to him and put her face up to his, lips opening like a flower. She had helped him undress her, shrugging off the white top to reveal thrusting breasts and erect nipples, which throbbed in his mouth. The miniskirt zip had snagged briefly and he had fallen to his knees to free it. Her fingers dug into his hair as he dropped the skirt and slid her panties to her ankles. Insistently, she pushed forward her pubic arch and pressed his face into the warm moistness, moaning.

Her whole body shook as he held her buttocks tight and tongued her clitoris gently. For a moment she stayed rigid as the waves of orgasm peaked, then slowly collapsed over him.

He couldn't remember taking off his clothes or even dragging the rug from the living room to cover the cool tiles of the balcony. There they had coupled, quietly but for Karen's faint moan of pleasure as he parted her thighs and slid into her. She spread her legs wider, lifting them high and locking her ankles across his back. The movement cradled him possessively, inviting deeper penetration. His orgasm racked him. She felt him ejaculate and held him gently.

They surfaced hours later. For the first time in what seemed like years, he was quietly content. Karen remembered with surprise that the long felt ache in her mind had gone, as if a void had been filled. It wasn't just that she felt sexually fulfilled. Orgasm wasn't the goal. She could always achieve that on her own, she thought wryly. It was as if something had been exorcized, a lifting of her spirits.

He drove her home in the early hours, and each felt a bond that filled every part of them.

*

From her window, Fiona saw her boss's car slowly enter the medical school car park, miss a bay, reverse and try again before parking across two spaces. Puzzled, she watched for some minutes while Barnes sat, staring straight ahead at a blank wall. Then he got out, smiling vacuously, headed in the wrong direction, stopped, shook his head and turned back into the entrance below her.

'Good girl, Karen, and about bloody time too,' said Fiona, speaking aloud to the window-pane. Hearing the elevator whine she went back to her desk and waited. As Barnes entered, still grinning inanely, she looked up. 'How about some work around here?'

Faculty meetings were always held on a Friday. The junior lecturers claimed that this was because the heads of department could take off early for whatever recreation they had in mind for the weekend. True or not, few subjects survived the lunchbreak, and woe betide anyone who brought up extra business in the afternoon.

Oblivious to this convention, Thomas waited until Faculty members had run through the agenda and then stood up at the start of general business. 'Mr Chairman, I want a full investigation into the joint project operated by Doctors Barnes and Kapinsky,' he told JJ. 'I have reason to believe that unethical practices are being carried out. As Ethics Committee representative, it is my duty to inform you that I have strong misgivings concerning the laboratory work on animals. Perhaps even more significantly, I have been prevented by senior members of the research group from seeing the work at first hand.'

Jesus, more Thomas bullshit, thought Barnes. He listened without expression as the man recounted his suspicions, his meetings with both Barnes and Kapinsky, and how Kapinsky had threatened him physically.

Professor George Bills, head of Cardiology, looked out of the window. The sky was cloudless. By four o'clock the tees would be crowded. He looked back at Thomas. The bigoted old bastard looked as if he could go on all day. He sighed. Please, God, let Barnes demolish him in short order and let's get the hell out of here.

'Thank you, Professor,' JJ cut in as Thomas began to reiterate his views. 'Dr Barnes, would you like to comment?'

Barnes stood up. He looked around and sensed the mood of the Faculty. Thomas was out on a limb here. He had chosen the wrong end of the meeting to launch his attack.

'Sir, I appreciate Professor Thomas's impatience with us but we have discussed the project at length with him, the Ethics Committee has the protocol on file and this is the first time that anyone has queried our rationale.'

JJ could recognize a long slow curve when he saw one but he was in no mood to cut any slack for Thomas. The man was an academic cipher and a research-shy time-server. He looked back at the man enquiringly. 'Professor?'

'Mr Chairman, I would like the Faculty to appoint a sub-committee to investigate and report back. I will be happy to serve on it.'

Even to Barnes it sounded a reasonable request. Out of the corner of his eye he saw Cherrington of Obstetrics change position impatiently. Bills had stopped staring out of the window. Other Faculty members had perked up.

'Sir, Dr Kapinsky is running a program with a number of severely immunosuppressed animals. He needs to keep to the strictest quarantine levels and a single unnecessary visitor could compromise the project, on which we have already spent a lot of money.' He looked around. Faculty members were showing interest. Time to put in the boot. 'Dr Kapinsky is a dedicated research scientist with an impeccable record. His work is internationally respected. This very expensive research program has reached a critical phase. So much so that Dr Kapinsky does even the most menial cleaning work on his own for fear of cross-infection. With respect to Professor Thomas, none of these basic laboratory procedures appear to carry any weight with him. He insists on entry even at risk of the entire project . . .'

It was all over bar the shouting and Thomas did plenty of that. 'This isn't the last you'll hear of it. The Medical Council will be interested in what I have to say!' he yelled as he stormed out.

Well, at least I've won this round, thought Barnes. But what the hell was Kapinsky up to? High time he took another look, quarantine or no. He hadn't been down to the lab for the past few weeks but gossip drifting up sounded a bit odd. Kapinsky was looking stressed and Security reported that he had taken to sleeping overnight at the lab. Perhaps the bugger was really getting paranoid.

Although the onset had been insidious several members of the medical staff, and especially those working closely with Dr Kapinsky, noticed how the German doctor had changed. He had became gradually more withdrawn, and now kept much to himself. He started working late in the laboratory, often until the early hours of the morning, and had brought in a bed so that he could sleep there. The room next to the lab was fitted out with two rows of cages and the area was out of bounds to everybody. He cleaned the cages in this section himself and also saw to the food and water and medication of the animals in 'isolation'.

When Barnes visited him, several days after the Faculty meeting, he immediately saw that although his colleague was pale and unshaven his eyes glowed like coals.

'Hi, Louis. Sorry I haven't been able to get to see you lately but there's been a lot on my plate.' Barnes sounded inane, even to himself. It was his own bloody department, for Chrissake! He didn't have to explain his comings and goings.

'Yes, I noticed. I hear the plate is mostly at Gino's.'

Barnes did not rise. Kapinsky was clearly spoiling for an argument whereas what he wanted was co-operation. He grinned. 'Report time. What news of our baboons?'

Kapinsky slid a few sheets of paper across his desk. 'It's all here. Take it with you,' he said, and looked back at his printout.

This wasn't going to be easy. He persevered, 'Thanks, Louis. In a few words, where are we?'

Kapinsky underwent one of his startling mood changes, smiled, sat back and launched into an unstoppable flow of words. 'As I told you some months ago, I was able to collect a number of ova from female baboons by aspirating the follicles through a laparoscope. The ova obtained were stored in liquid nitrogen. The next step was to take one ovum at a time, thaw it, fertilize it and incubate the resulting embryo until it had divided to reach the sixteen-cell stage. The clear envelope that surrounded the cells and the glue that held them together were dissolved with an enzyme, and there I had them: sixteen identical single cells from each fertilized ovum and each cell capable of forming a new embryo with the same genetic material.'

He was in full flight and stood up, face alive with excitement. 'I encapsulated each cell in a covering of seaweed gel and then implanted it into the uterus of a female baboon that had been treated with hormones to come on heat at the same time.'

'Did it work?' Barnes could not help interrupting.

'Yes, in actual fact I successfully impregnated thirty females, but seven of them aborted,' Kapinsky proclaimed, looking pleased with himself. 'I've already injected the foetuses of the remaining twenty-three with human antigens.'

'Does that mean your baboons will eventually be capable of accepting human organs without rejection? Shouldn't you have used tissue from a specific donor for each foetus?'

Kapinsky snorted. 'And how will that work in practice? It would take at least two years to raise an adult baboon in this way. We do not have donors so far ahead in time, do we?'

'Hmm, I can see your point. With executed prisoners we can plan an organ supply ahead of time but not that far,' Barnes conceded. Yet he was intrigued. 'How did you solve the problem?'

Kapinsky looked thoughtful. 'I do not know whether I have the complete answer but by using the cells of a mixed lymphocyte culture I did expose the baboon foetuses to a wide variety of human antigens.'

'You used cells from several individuals?'

'Yes. I took blood from sixteen members of the lab staff. That should give us a good range of human antigens.'

'How did you manage to inject the tiny foetus? Did you open the uterus?'

'No, no, no.' Kapinsky looked outraged. 'They would all have aborted.'

'So how did you do it?' Barnes, the surgeon, visualized the delicacy of the surgical work.

'We monitored the pregnant female baboons with ultrasound screening until I could detect the foetus in each case. Dr Louw then helped me expose the pregnant uterus through a small abdominal incision. By palpation, the foetus was located and injected through the uterine wall.'

'And when do our baboon mothers reach full term?'

'Since baboons carry five months . . .' Kapinsky counted on his fingers, 'that makes it about a month from now.'

No wonder the poor bugger looks shagged out, thought Barnes. He's been nursing the baboons day and night. He felt guilty about his proposed inspection of the animal room and decided to forget it. He well knew that one extra visitor could result in a major outbreak of infection. Things were too far advanced to rock the boat just because some bloody madman was shouting accusations.

He had an idea. 'It's going to be an exciting and demanding time for you. If you need extra help, why not ask Boots? He's become a skilled surgeon, you know.'

Kapinsky did not respond but his resentment showed. Barnes saw it had been an unwise suggestion.

Kapinsky stood up. 'Sorry, Rod, but you'll have to excuse me. I have to attend to the animals now,' he said.

Barnes said nothing but watched in surprise as Kapinsky unlocked the door that led to the animal room. A lock on the door? Across it in bolder letters were the words: STRICT ISOLA-

TION. NO ENTRY. Clearly Kapinsky was taking his quarantine seriously.

Without a backward glance Kapinsky closed the door behind him with a clang and Barnes heard a bolt slide home on the other side. He hesitated for a second and then left the laboratory. He would have to take a look at the animal room soon but right now was not the time. When Kapinsky had cooled down a bit, they would talk again. Bugger Thomas!

As Kapinsky entered the room, there was a sudden restlessness among the animals, who anticipated food. He walked to a cage in the middle, which housed a large female baboon. She sat quietly and watched him approach.

'I see your breasts are starting to swell, Mrs Kapinsky,' he said, taking an apple out of his coat pocket. The baboon stuck a paw through the bars and Kapinsky dropped the fruit into the open palm. 'One of these days you will give birth to our child.'

She ignored him, crunching steadily at the apple.

'No one will know our secret, darling. Not a soul,' crooned Kapinsky, staying out of the animal's reach. The baboon looked back at him and bared her teeth.

Another nearby screeched, gripped the bars and rocked its cage. 'What do you want, you ugly bitch?' said Kapinsky, causing the screeching to intensify.

All ten animals showed signs of advanced pregnancy.

Kapinsky spent the next two hours cleaning each cage and providing the baboons with fresh vegetables and water – taking special pains with 'Mrs Kapinsky'.

Then he sat down at the table in a corner of the room, unlocked the wall cupboard and took out a clipboard with a heavy sheaf of notes. Listing every detail, he wrote up his assessment of each animal's condition. Mrs Kapinsky worried him. Her belly was so much larger than that of the others that she might not be able to give birth naturally. She might need a Caesarean. What the hell was he going to do if that arose? He hadn't carried out any surgery for years and, even at his best, had been a mediocre surgeon. Perhaps Barnes was right, the nigger could do it. At least he would be able to keep him quiet.

Kapinsky flipped through his notes. A thought struck him. He rubbed the stubble on his chin. During the past few months he had been transplanting baboon skin onto human volunteers from the laboratory staff. He had found nine baboons for whom skin grafts were not hyperacutely rejected. According to Professor Volkov the organs of these animals would be rejected slowly by the human recipients.

This meant he had time to kill the messenger.

Alternatively he could use some way of disguising the foreign tissue. Volkov had suggested that this second way would be the best approach and had supplied him with a solution of several human genes. These genes, he claimed, would code for the glycoproteins which cover the surface of every cell in the body. During his last visit to the medical library he had unearthed an article by a researcher who had imaginatively likened this monitoring of the body to a spy satellite scanning the earth below for enemy troop movement. The satellite can distinguish between friendly and enemy forces by the difference in uniforms and insignia. When the enemy moves onto satellite territory, it sends a signal to defence headquarters to mount an attack. The enemy could avoid detection in two ways: by deception or camouflage, or by destroying the satellite and blocking the signal. Deception is what you have to achieve, Volkov told Kapinsky. Change the proteins on the surface of the cells of the baboon to resemble that of the human. The immune system would not then be able to detect the presence of baboon organs when transplanted.

He had gone a long way to achieving that goal since bringing his precious vial of DNA from Russia. A clear liquid that looked like water, it could provide the camouflage net that would fool the immune system. All he had to do was somehow to integrate it into the baboon genome.

The standard technique with mammals was to inject the gene directly into the nucleus of the fertilized ovum, and re-implant into the mother or a foster mother. The second method, known as biolistics and used mainly on plant cells, was to bombard them with micro-projectiles that had been coated with DNA. Both techniques required special equipment and expertise, neither of which he had, Kapinsky realized.

He had spent weeks studying the problem until, almost in despair, his computer turned up an article on integrating DNA with spermatozoa. The authors showed that sperm are capable of capturing DNA molecules when they are added to the sperm suspension, the ejaculate in which the sperm swim. When these transformed sperm are used to fertilize the ovum the foreign DNA is integrated into the nucleus of the new embryo.

He knew he was on the right track when, using some of his precious DNA source which had been labelled, he found rapid association with baboon sperm cells.

It had taken many nights of painstaking effort to ensure that his nine baboons had been impregnated with the fertilized ova carrying the human genes. And there they were, healthy mothers about to produce offspring with human proteins, the camouflage that would hide their baboon origins from the human immune system. Volkov's voice rang in his head: 'Deception, that is the answer. Those human donors will never know that their body functions are regulated by chemical messengers from the baboon brain.'

An exciting few weeks lay ahead. He had prepared well. The black cleaning staff – Victor, Boots and the others – had been ejected from their locker room. The buggers could change in the feed room – they never washed anyway, he reasoned. Their room was a place where he could shower and shave, and also keep some spare clothes. He planned to move in full time just before the baboons went into labour. He could always get a midday meal from the cafeteria and bring in sandwiches for the rest.

How to deliver Mrs Kapinsky was still a nightmare. He would have to approach that jumped-up *kaffer* who thought he was a heart surgeon. But he would have to be careful, and there had to be some way to ensure his secrecy. Like all *kaffers*, he was shit scared of losing his job so that could be a good lever. If not? Kapinsky grinned at his stubbled face in the locker mirror. He would have to meet with an 'accident'. Barnes would be bloody upset, of course, but he was determined to let nothing stand in the way of his ultimate goal. To create a super race? That had been the Führer's goal before he was thwarted by the Communist monster. But Kapinsky knew that the new techniques could improve on nature. He leaned his head against the bare brick, feeling the rough texture cool on his brow. 'I long for the arrival of my child,' he whispered to himself.

CHAPTER 14

Alex Hobbs had already opened David Rhodes's chest and had begun to dissect the two hearts free from the surrounding tissues when Barnes entered the operating theatre.

'How far are you, Dr Hobbs?' he asked the busy surgeon.

'Not as far as I'd like. We've got remarkable adhesion to the chest wall,' he replied.

'I can't believe so much tissue involvement has built up since the transplant. It's been barely a year,' said Barnes, peering over the screen that separated the surgeon from the anaesthesiologist. With each respiration he could see David's own heart and the donor heart move up and down.

'I don't suppose it will be necessary to dissect the patient's own heart free completely, will it, sir?'

'Hmm. Can't say at this stage. We'll have to vent it and get the air out before we start it again.'

Barnes had spent some considerable time in preparing for this operation and had decided to remove the heart while David was on a heart-lung machine. The less complicated way was to use side clamps only, but then he would have had to leave too much of the donor heart's upper chambers behind. He reviewed his decision. The severe tissue adhesion was certainly a complication but nothing that a good surgeon like Hobbs couldn't handle. And if too much muscle from the donor heart's upper chambers was removed it would cause major surgical difficulties when retransplanted.

'How much time do we have before we go on by-pass?' he asked.

'Oh, say about fifteen minutes,' said Hobbs, cutting delicately at the adhering tissues.

In the next-door operating theatre Des Louw was at the same stage, freeing the ill patient's heart from the pericardium, or surrounding sac of membrane. The recipient was a forty-year-old man who, four years earlier, had had a triple by-pass after a severe heart attack. Now Barnes observed closely, keen to know how his by-pass had served the patient, who had been unable to understand why he'd had the attack. 'My sport is road running,' he had told Barnes. 'I gave up the marathon two years ago but I still keep fit. I'm a non-smoker, watch my diet carefully and always thought I was in good physical shape.'

Barnes had explained that the cause of the disease which was clogging his arteries was not clearly understood. 'We know there are certain risk factors, some of which you have just mentioned. If you avoid them the chances of a heart attack are greatly reduced but not totally eliminated,' he told him.

The patient grinned wryly. 'I can't help feeling it should have happened to somebody else, like a drinker or a glutton.'

'I suppose it all depends on your philosophy of life. The *que será será* principle – whatever will be, will be – gets a lot of people by on the basis that the quality of life is more important than the quantity.'

'And what is your philosophy of life, doctor?' he asked.

The question had thrown Barnes for a few seconds. Then he had said, 'I believe the quality of life is important but, as a surgeon, I cannot just stand still and accept that whatever will be, will be. I have to do all in my power to add quality to the lives of patients or at least maintain an acceptable level of quality. That is why I have suggested you have a heart transplant.'

'Does that mean a second heart?' The man was suddenly concerned. 'I've read that with the piggy-back operation your old heart will help the new heart if anything goes wrong with it.'

'In your case, no. You've had several heart attacks. With each one a part of the heart muscle died and was replaced by scar tissue which cannot contract like muscle and can't help in the pumping of blood,' Barnes explained.

'But why didn't I develop heart failure after the first attack?'

'The heart has a lot of reserve. It can lose a considerable amount of muscle before its pumping ability is reduced to the stage where failure will set in.'

Des Louw cut away the last of the pericardium and revealed the diseased heart. Barnes could see that the left pumping chamber had become a dilated, fibrous bag. Through it ran thin strings of muscle, feebly contracting. Unlike David's, this heart would never again recover full function. Leaving it in place had no advantage and could only give rise to complications later, he thought. He would do an orthotopic transplant – complete removal and replacement with the donor heart that had served David so well.

Louw severed an artery, the last link that the patient's heart had with the circulation, and lifted it out of the sac where it had been housed since it first started beating forty years before.

Barnes stared down into the empty cavity. Only the two cuffs of the upper chambers and the stumps of the two arteries were left. The heart was gone. Here was a human being, alive, without a heart in his chest. He always felt a tug of anxiety at this stage of the operation.

But action always dispelled doubts. Alex Hobbs had already brought in the donor heart in a bowl of cold saline. Barnes checked the edges of the severed tissues, lifted it from the bowl, briefly drained off the saline and lowered it into the patient's chest. Expertly locating the chambers with the cuff and arteries, he began the slow, laborious work of connecting it to the body's circulation.

He had just finished the last sutures in the aorta when a theatre nurse came in with a message from Hobbs that David was off the heart-lung machine. His heart had taken over strongly and was maintaining good circulation. It was good news, particularly at this stage of the transplant.

Barnes removed the aortic clamp and allowed warm, oxygenated blood to flow into the donor heart. 'Let's see how you behave,' he said to himself.

The muscle immediately regained its tone and began to fibrillate. 'Electrolytes and Astrup spot on,' Ohlsen announced, anticipating Barnes's next question.

He nodded but said nothing. Under his breath he continued his conversation with the donor heart: 'Are you going to be as stubborn as last time? Are you going to refuse to beat?'

After what seemed like an eternity, but which the theatre clock said was less than three minutes, the heart suddenly came to life. Barnes could see that it was in sinus rhythm – each contraction of the upper chambers was followed a split second later by a contraction of the lower. 'Start ventilating and slow down the heart-lung machine,' he ordered. He watched the heart strengthen. What a magnificent pump! It had an inbuilt need to beat and pump blood without any nervous connection to the brain. All it wanted was a supply of oxygenated blood at the right temperature.

But for its continued survival it needed an essential chemical message that could only be supplied by a living brain. David's brain had served that purpose well.

The change-over from the heart-lung machine went without incident. Des Louw closed the chest. Checks showed both patients in excellent post-operative condition. Intensive care unit staff took over and the weary heart team headed for the dressing rooms.

Within hours it had hit the headlines. The city's morning paper decided to steal a march on its rival by running a late special with a front page that screamed, ONE HEART KEPT THREE ALIVE. Not to be outdone, the afternoon paper came out with, DRAMATIC TRANSPLANT BREAKTHROUGH, and a reasonably accurate report of how one heart had been the life support for three different people.

Unbelievably, on the same page, it ran a picture of Barnes and Karen leaving Gino's and asked who was the 'mystery woman'.

Fiona took full advantage. 'I have a mystery woman on the line,' she told Barnes. 'Do you want to take the call?'

He fell for it. 'Ask her name and business. It's probably a reporter.'

'I have her name. She says it's Karen and her business is you.' She put Karen through before he could think of a reply.

David Rhodes and the heart recipient were discharged on the same day, barely two weeks after surgery. It was a triumph for heart surgery and the hospital. JJ was the first to call. 'Congratulations, Rodney. While the Board is still smiling why not put your equipment request list through?' It was the old campaigner at his best, expertly setting up the bureaucrats to relieve them of their tightly held budget.

Barnes thanked him and put down the receiver. His proposals for new equipment had been knocked back so often that he held little hope for another attempt but decided to go through the motions one more time. He spent most of the afternoon poring through lists of possibilities. The pumps on the heart-lung machine had been in service for six years. They had already packed up once during surgery and almost cost the life of a patient. The maintenance department had done a good job of keeping them serviceable but warned him there were no more spares to be had. The monitoring equipment was worse. All electronic machinery was notoriously fragile and doubly so where it was hauled from patient to patient. The information it gave was vital but no longer trustworthy, too often wiped out by electrical interference from elsewhere in the building. And there was so much more: sterile air-conditioning units, surgical instruments, isolation tents, spares for the anaesthesiology equipment, it went on for pages.

Groote Schuur was a state hospital. That meant it was funded by the taxpayer while the bureaucrats held the purse strings, thought Barnes. He hurled the pages back on his desk. The exercise was pointless. Only last month the Administrator, tired of being the target of Barnes's anger, had brought the Assistant

Secretary for Health in person to tell him that no funds were available.

No funds available? True, there were none for saving lives and alleviating suffering but always plenty for killing and maiming. While the Assistant Secretary was talking, there had been a newspaper on Barnes's desk with a report of an air strike on 'terrorist' positions just across the border. He had asked the Assistant Secretary how much a rocket cost and how much fuel half a dozen jet bombers could burn in an hour. The conversation had ended there, with the Administrator ushering his political VIP away. A good thing too, Barnes decided, as he had been about to ask a few questions about the cost of the vast bureaucracy that operated the apartheid system. Working quickly, he cobbled together his previous submissions, drafted another covering letter, thanked the Assistant Secretary for his good wishes on behalf of the heart team, walked through to Fiona's office and dropped it all on her blotter.

She looked up. 'Again?'

'Hope springs eternal. We're the flavour of the month since the double transplant and JJ feels we should cash in. Four copies, please, one for ourselves and three for the bureaucrats. Have them on my desk by no later than yesterday.'

'Yes, sir,' said Fiona, throwing a mock salute.

The phone rang. It was Dave Johnson of Cardiology to ask if Barnes could see a patient urgently. He said he'd be there in minutes, handed the receiver to Fiona and headed for the elevator, strangely hopeful that perhaps, this time, he could prise some funds loose from the state cashbox.

It was almost dark when Barnes's car stopped at Karen's cottage. She saw the headlights flash as he turned into the little tree-lined cul-de-sac and ran to open the door. He embraced her without a word. She felt his tension and looked at him enquiringly as they drove off.

His smile was somewhat crooked but he patted her knee and said, 'Let's have a drink first.'

This was serious, she thought. Summer was ending, so was their relationship also over? It had been a marvellous time, not only for her but for Kimberley too. The little girl, now seven and with no memory of her father, was a joy. Kimberley and Rodney had hit it off from the first moment of meeting, and summer for Karen was a long parade of memories, happy hours on the beach, playing in the surf, long walks with Kimberley skipping ahead, the salt taste of lips after a day in the sun. Nights, too, his body on hers . . . She sighed, and realized the car had stopped.

He was looking at her with amusement. 'Hey, we're here. Where are you?'

She laughed and squeezed his hand as they entered the restaurant. Gino gave them their favourite corner table and Barnes ordered a bottle of dry white. Even Gino thought this unusual: Barnes was an informed wine buff who took care over his choice. He queried it with a raised eyebrow but was waved away.

He returned with Barnes's favourite chardonnay. Barnes didn't bother to taste it but took the bottle, splashed himself a full glass, filled Karen's and toasted, 'Here's to us,' before draining his glass.

Karen blinked as he refilled and downed a second. She took a sip of the wine. It was too cold and sent a chill through her as she swallowed. It was time to hear the worst. 'Rodney, you look as if you're stressed out of your skull. What's the problem?'

For the first time he relaxed, laughed, had another drink, held it up, squinted at the pale gold fluid and looked suddenly serious. 'I'm sorry, Karen. You're owed an explanation. I have two problems. One a colleague, the other a patient – and the first is Dr Kapinsky.'

What a relief. She wasn't the colleague or the patient. Their relationship was not under discussion here. Curiously, her relief was tinged with disappointment. They would have to talk about it soon and if he didn't bring it up she would.

'Go on,' she prompted.

'Kapinsky worries me. It isn't just that Thomas has been

jumping up and down about him. He's also been behaving strangely of late. More and more I get the feeling that as far as the research program goes I'm not getting the whole picture.'

She agreed and said that odd rumours of Kapinsky's idiosyncrasies were floating around the hospital and medical school and had even reached her ears. 'The technicians claim he's taken to sleeping in the laboratory and they've heard him talk to the baboons in the room where he houses some of his animals.'

'There's nothing wrong with talking to animals. At least, it's a step up from talking to yourself. It's what he's hearing back that bothers me.'

'What do you mean?' asked Karen, puzzled.

'Voices.' Barnes grinned. 'Thanks, Karen. Now that I've reduced the whole thing to absurdity I feel better. Of course Kapinsky isn't hearing voices. He's simply nearing the end of a very long and stressful research program and is feeling the tension. He's put a lot of time and effort into those animals and if sleeping in the laboratory is what it takes to ensure their safety and progress . . .' He didn't finish and his grin disappeared.

Karen put a hand on his arm. 'There's something else, Rodney. Is it the patient?'

He looked into his glass for a long moment. When he spoke, his voice sounded tired, flat. 'Some doctors believe they are infallible, invincible. They think death must be fought all the way. They consider death their greatest adversary and that losing a patient is a kind of failure.' He put down his glass, spread both hands on the table and looked at them. 'Please God, I never become one of those doctors.'

She placed her hand in one of his and squeezed it. He covered it with the other, looked at the wall and spoke as if the words were written there. 'Never let me forget that sometimes death is the best medical treatment.'

In spite of herself she was shocked and showed it, before quickly suppressing her expression. Barnes appeared not to notice. 'How can you say that?' she asked, keeping her voice carefully neutral.

'Because there are times when death can put an end to suffering when the medical profession with all its technology cannot,' he answered. He thought for a moment and added, 'What they haven't realized is that the real goal of medicine is not to prolong but to improve the quality of life.'

She was genuinely puzzled. 'But you do prolong life, don't you?'

'Yes, of course. Through our efforts to improve the quality of life we often prolong it, but this must be of secondary importance.'

She took both his hands. He kept looking at the wall. She pulled slightly to get his attention and said sharply, 'Rodney, look at me.' He turned to her, eyes focusing back to the present. 'Tell me, what brought this on? What happened today?'

He picked up his glass, took another sip and sat back. When he began to speak it was as if a dam had burst. At one point Gino arrived with the menu but Karen shook her head, anxious not to stop the flow.

'I was called to see a patient today. He was seventy-eight years old and had widespread bone secondaries from a carcinoma of the prostate. The surgeons had already carried out a bilateral orchidectomy, removal of both testicles, and he had received radiation therapy for some of the bone deposits. According to the case history, he showed signs of compression of the spinal cord in the lower back about six months ago. Indications were that this was caused by the spread of cancer secondaries.' He threw up his hands in exasperation. 'You won't believe this but the orthopaedic surgeons did a bone graft to stabilize the lesion. How the hell can you stabilize a cancerous growth with surgery, I ask you?'

Karen said nothing. In her mind's eye she had already formed a horrifying picture of the unfortunate patient.

'He now has very little sensation in the lower body, suffers from large bedsores, is incontinent, and the cancer has eaten him to a living skeleton.'

Gino returned once more with the menu and presented it to Karen. She gave another faint head-shake.

'Now comes the worst,' Barnes began again. 'This afternoon his body decided to give up the struggle and he developed a cardiac arrest.'

Suddenly Karen had a feeling she didn't want to hear this story but he went on, relentlessly. He leaned forward. 'Would you believe that the insensitive bastards who call themselves doctors put out an alert for the resuscitation team?' He ran his fingers through his hair as if trying to clear the memory. 'These goons, promptly and without enquiring what it was all about, jumped on a living skeleton and started external massage, incubated him and connected him to a ventilator.' His voice dropped to a whisper, as if he didn't quite believe what he was saying. 'They massaged, pumped and started the poor man's heart. They also broke three of his ribs while doing so.'

'How could they have done that?' asked Karen, stunned.

'The ribs were most likely weakened from the cancer secondaries or perhaps bone loss due to ageing. But that's not all . . .'

Karen wanted to put her hands over her ears. But Barnes clearly needed to talk.

'By the time I was called to see him he had developed acute left-heart failure and a leaking mitral valve, probably due to a ruptured papillary muscle.'

'Don't tell me they wanted you to operate?' she almost shouted.

'Damn right. When I saw him I realized that, unluckily, the resuscitation team had been so efficient that he had not developed brain damage from the fairly lengthy heart arrest. He was wide awake. They had him sedated enough to stop him fighting the ventilator but his eyes were open and searching the room for some way out of this hell.' He almost choked on the words. Karen waited. 'I told Dave I'd never seen such evil use of medical treatment in my life and said the proper treatment was a sufficiently large dose of morphine to allow the patient to die in peace and dignity. He was offended and I pointed out that it was nice to be able to afford the luxury of being offended while torturing another human being.' He grimaced at the memory. He was sure that Professor Bills would not have had second thoughts about what was right and wrong in this case. 'Dave Johnson said he was a God-fearing man who lived by the Commandments and then scolded me for playing God by wanting to end a life. I asked him if he wasn't playing God by causing the patient's heart to be restarted and putting another human being into a living hell.' He savoured the moment. 'He didn't like that but by then I was past caring. He came back with the old story about it being our duty to respect life and preserve it. He's a fine cardiologist but I don't think he can speak for God.'

Barnes twirled his glass and put it down again. 'I don't speak for God. I can speak only for Rodney Barnes. But I know in my bones that God considers life to be more than just the presence of a heart-beat and movements of the chest. It doesn't have much to do with the kind of life we create with medical technology. I'm as certain as I sit here that the life God gave that man has already ended. All that we, as doctors, are doing is maintaining a cruel parody.'

'So what did you decide, Rodney?'

'I refused to operate and discussed the position with the family. They agreed. His wife told me how upset she was when they restarted her husband's heart, only to let him endure another day of agony.'

Gino came, this time bustling and determined. They ordered but neither had much appetite and, much to Gino's dismay, only picked at the meal. Both were tired, as if they had just completed a long journey. What felt good was that the tension had gone.

Barnes ordered coffee and smiled at her. He leaned across the table, kissed her lightly on the nose and said, 'I've just realized something.'

The statement prompted a question. 'What?' Karen felt weary but also safe and secure.

'We ask ourselves questions about life while the answers are under our noses. This is life. This is living. Just being with someone you love – and I do so love you, my darling.'

It was the first time that he had stated his love so openly. Afterwards, in the car on the way home, she marvelled at how a meal which had started out so disastrously could have ended with such a bonus.

Next morning as soon as she reached her desk, she called the cancer unit to ask about the patient. 'I'm afraid we lost him during the night,' the day nurse told her. 'Strange story too. He was transferred to a single room and was on ventilation and monitor survey. He was being checked at regular intervals by the nursing staff but somehow in the early hours of the morning he managed to reach his ventilator and switch it off.'

Karen put down the phone. Rodney was right, she thought. Death was not the enemy. The real enemy was inhumanity.

CHAPTER 15

The man at the back of the little church hall looked out of place. He was dressed in civilian clothes while the others were proudly strutting around in boots and uniforms that varied from plain khaki to camouflage khaki. Among the crowd were about forty members of the Iron Fist Battalion, a right-wing paramilitary group. The hat pulled down over his eyes was out of keeping with the forage caps worn by the others but his thick black moustache fitted well with the apparent hirsute demands of this aggressive and militant occasion for a variety of moustaches and beards surrounded him.

He looked with interest at the bearded, truculent faces and at the flags decorating the stage. There were black flags and red ones, each with a single white circle in which the numeral seven was repeated in a pattern which pointed the stems inward. The result closely resembled the swastika of the German Nazi Party. The walls were decorated with the old four-colour flag of the Transvaal Boer Republic.

The man felt a rising excitement as, suddenly, the hall fell silent and men in black formed a guard of honour along the centre aisle. A voice shouted, 'Be standing for your Leader in Chief.'

All jumped to their feet and looked towards the door. A group of men strode through the entrance. The man in the centre, overweight with a sagging beer belly, was dressed in camouflage trousers and matching bush jacket. His hat brim up-turned on one side, sprouted a white ostrich feather. Flanked by four bodyguards dressed in black, with side arms prominent on their hips, he moved briskly to the front. The group mounted the steps to the stage amid thunderous applause. The man with the ostrich feather in his hat walked to the podium and raised both hands like a preacher about to pronounce a benediction. There was immediate silence. Enunciating each word clearly, he spoke in a booming voice, beginning with a quotation from *The Great Boer War*, by Sir Arthur Conan Doyle.

'"Take a community of Dutchmen of the type of those who defended themselves for fifty years against all the power of Spain, at a time when Spain was the greatest power in the world. Intermix them with a strain of those inflexible French Huguenots who gave up home and fortune and left their country for ever at the time of the revocation of the Edict of Nantes."' His listeners were gripped both by the words and the voice. Eyes aglow with fervour, the leader paused for effect, and went on. '"The product must obviously be one of the most rugged, virile, unconquerable races ever to grace the earth. Take this formidable people and train them for seven generations in constant warfare against savage peoples and ferocious beasts, in circumstances in which no weakling could survive, place them so that they acquire exceptional skill with weapons and horsemanship, give them a country which is eminently suited to the tactics of the huntsman, the marksman and the rider. Then, temper their military qualities by a dour fatalistic Old Testament religion and an ardent and consuming patriotism."' The leader looked around the hall. The man in black felt his body tingling and wondered just how it felt to be an Afrikaner and listen to this. '"Combine all these qualities and all these impulses in the one individual, and you have the modern Boer – the most formidable antagonist who ever crossed the path of Imperial Britain."'

A roar of approval went up. The leader raised his hand and stilled his audience at a gesture.

'These words were written at the beginning of this century as a warning to the British Empire not to underestimate the ability, skill and determination of a handful of Boers. Now, more than half a century later, I would like to repeat this warning to the

Communist alliance. Do not try to take away from the Boer what he has sweated, toiled and bled for.' He stopped and looked around, almost as if searching each individual face. The silence was almost palpable.

Then he raised his clenched fist and shouted, 'Freedom is worth more than peace.'

This time the noise almost raised the roof. The man in black, like the rest of the audience, was gripped.

The leader wiped his face with a large white handkerchief and went on. 'I want to ask Joe Slovo and his Communist followers why South Africa is so far in advance of the rest of Africa in every conceivable aspect.'

He paused.

'There are those who will say it is because you have cheap labour.'

The audience waited for the punch-line.

'If that is so, I would like to ask them, does the rest of Africa have expensive labour?'

A shout of laughter and 'Hear, hear' rocked the building.

He held up a hand for silence and lowered his voice. The audience strained to hear.

'No,' he answered himself. 'It is because of the know-how of the Boer. The Boer made the southern part of Africa what it is today. He fought the savages and the colonial powers. He tilled the soil and dug the mines. He produced food to fill the bellies of the so-called majority. He erected the most modern economy and the soundest infrastructure in Africa. If we did not have the Boer in Southern Africa, chaos and civil strife would have flourished.' He had reached a crucial point of his argument. He had to be sure it was driven home. 'Now that everything our forefathers toiled and died for must be handed over to the majority, it seems our suffering and sacrifices do not count. The thousands of women and children who died in the English concentration camps mean nothing to the Communist masters. Must the supreme sacrifice of the twenty-five thousand burghers be forgotten?' Then, in a voice which rang to the rafters, he said,

'No. We will not forget, nor will we capitulate.' The audience leapt to its feet, in tumultuous acclaim.

He stilled them again. 'Our history may have no meaning for the disciples of Satan. It may seem to them that it is no obstacle in their drive to create chaos under Communist rule in the land of our fathers.' He was in full flight. 'They talk about the Boer as oppressor. They say they want freedom and a government of the people elected on a one-man, one-vote system.' He paused again. Then, 'Yes,' he shouted. 'One man, one vote ... once only! Freedom as they know it in Cuba. Freedom as they enjoy it in Albania, in Romania and in Mother Russia.'

He paused to wipe his brow again. The heat in the packed hall was rising, not all of it due to body temperature.

'They say they will intensify their armed struggle if we do not heed their demands. Armed struggle against whom? Against women and children? Against lonely old couples on their farms?'

His eyes roamed the audience as if expecting answers. 'What do you think will happen when our army faces up to this riff-raff in battle?' He punched the air, yelling, '*Hulle sal vrek* – they will die like animals.'

The audience answered, like a congregation giving a refrain, '*Hulle sal vrek* – they will die like animals.'

Hoarse but still yelling, the leader was unstoppable now. 'Blood will flow as it did on December the sixteenth, more than one and a half centuries ago. As it did when the black hordes dared to test the courage of the Boers.'

The audience went wild. It was the perennial appeal to remember the battle of Blood River in Natal when a small group of migrating Boers drew their covered wagons into a circle, took on ten thousand Zulu warriors and defeated them in an afternoon.

The man in black had no difficulty in deciding whose side he was on. He slipped unnoticed out of the hall. Behind him the leader's voice boomed: 'Our right to our own Fatherland is not negotiable.'

*

As Kapinsky walked into the laboratory, Susan Bates looked up and caught his eye. Her classic features with the tightly drawn hair were tense. She looked first at Nat Ferreira, who had his back to her, engrossed in the contents of a Petri dish, then jerked her head towards Kapinsky's office.

Kapinsky felt his loins tighten. She was prowling again.

She followed him into the office, closed the door and turned to face him. 'You need my services, Doctor?'

She was right. God, how he needed her. She had an uncanny ability to know when he was reaching break-point. The tension had been building for weeks as he watched Mrs Kapinsky's belly swell and her time to deliver came nearer.

'Tonight, at my house, the usual time.' Her voice was staccato, firing out the words in short bursts.

He nodded, unable to speak. His legs had turned to water, his mind filled with images of her jutting breasts and thrusting hips. She turned and left. He sat for long minutes, a delicious anticipation tingling in his belly.

A reminder he had written to himself lay on his desk. It caught his eye and brought him back to reality. Samuel Mbeki's name and a question mark; that was all there was.

Of course, the *kaffer* – it was time to use the black bastard. It shouldn't be too difficult to ensure he kept his mouth shut. All blacks were superstitious and those who were semi-educated were even more so. He remembered Kemble complaining in the staff lunch room that his housemaid insisted on raising her bed with bricks placed under each leg to ward off the *tokkolossie* – a vindictive spirit in the shape of a little man who came at night to cast a spell on his victim. The remedy, the witch-doctor had told her, was to raise her bed so that the *tokkolossie* couldn't reach her.

That story sparked off a flood of anecdotes from other staff to do with spells, wizards, belief in the witch-doctor and his *muti* – medicine. A doctor who had spent time at a mission station claimed that the local witch-doctor could dismiss visiting medics simply by telling black patients to stay away. 'If you don't get the nod from the witch-doctor, you're history,' the doctor said.

'And you, too, will be bloody history if you don't keep your black mouth shut,' Kapinsky said, under his breath, glaring at Samuel's name on the note.

Samuel felt a chill go down his spine when Victor told him Dr Kapinsky wanted to see him in his office. This was the moment he had dreaded. The white doctor was going to punish him in some way for doing white man's work. Never before had Dr Kapinsky taken any notice of him, except to give a curt order and show that he did not like black people. The other white doctors laughed and talked a lot, but this man carried a great anger inside him. He worked as if he had a devil driving him.

When Samuel came into the room, Kapinsky was sitting at his desk, dressed in the blue overall of a cleaner. His hair stood up in tufts, his jowls were unshaven and he looked as if he had not slept for many nights. At first he did not see Samuel. He was staring at a dead computer screen with glazed eyes. Clearly he was somewhere else, Samuel thought, perhaps with the animals behind the door that he now kept locked.

'You want to see me, boss?' Samuel announced his presence softly. Kapinsky turned to face him but there was no sign of recognition on his face, only a blank stare. Samuel felt a great sense of danger. Once, in his boyhood while he had been herding goats, a mamba had slid out from under a bush and showed its fangs at him. Now he had the same feeling.

He was about to retreat when Kapinsky suddenly smiled. The change of expression made him look even more threatening. Samuel felt frozen, unable to move.

'Hello, Boots,' Kapinsky croaked. He cleared his throat and tried again. 'I need you to help me. If you do good work it will go well with you. It might even mean a senior cleaner's job.'

Samuel couldn't believe he had heard correctly. This white doctor who disliked him so much was offering him a chance of a better job. Why would he do that? What did he want from him? The feeling of danger was even stronger. He must be on the alert and not be taken by surprise as he had been the day the mamba appeared.

'What is it you want me to do, boss?'

Kapinsky hated this conversation. Talking to *kaffers* was just a pain in the arse. They were so bloody thick that everything had to be explained half a dozen times and even then they got it wrong. He suppressed his dislike and smiled again. 'I want you to do a Caesarean section on one of my baboons. Can you do a Caesarean section?'

Samuel did not want to show this man that he didn't know what he was talking about. He sensed that such an admission would send Kapinsky into a rage. This needed a careful answer. 'Boss, I have never done one but I can learn quickly.'

Jesus Christ, how the hell can he learn in time? thought Kapinsky. There was only a week to go. He himself had to handle the anaesthetics and he needed this black bastard to do the delivery.

As if reading Kapinsky's thoughts, Samuel added, 'Maybe Dr Louw can teach me how to do the . . .' He hesitated, afraid to mispronounce the word he had just heard.

Kapinsky leapt out of his chair so suddenly that Samuel began to back away. 'No, no. I do not want them to know about the operation.'

Samuel looked even more alarmed.

Shit, that didn't come out right, thought Kapinsky. 'I do not trust them,' he said. 'That is why I have asked you. They want to steal my ideas but I know you will not do that, will you, Boots?'

'No, boss. I will never steal anything.' That sounded like a safe answer. Kapinsky relaxed visibly and Samuel felt emboldened to ask a question. He was eager to know about this section thing. It was obviously some kind of operation and he felt his interest quicken. 'Does boss have a text-book? I can learn from the text-book.'

Why not? thought Kapinsky. Why not give the *kaffer* a book?

He was already regarded as handy with a knife and this was a simpler job than some of the surgery he was supposed to have carried out – if he could believe the crap that Barnes talked about him.

'Yes, Boots. I will see you get the information you need. But you must move in here. There's not enough time left and I don't want you wasting valuable time travelling back and forward to the township. Bring spare clothes and bedding. We will work day and night and I will teach you the procedure.'

Samuel felt excitement override the danger. He still did not like Dr Kapinsky but, whatever his reasons were, this boss was offering him a great opportunity. Everybody wanted to know what was going on behind those closed doors and only he, Samuel Mbeki, was being offered the chance to find out. He left the laboratory, walking on air.

For the first time in days Kapinsky went home to his apartment near the hospital. He prepared carefully for the meeting with Susan Bates, showering slowly, his body thrilling with anticipation. He shaved off several days' growth and dressed in a shirt and slacks. He would not be wearing them for long, he thought, with a leer.

Dr Susan Bates lived luxuriously with her wealthy lesbian lover, Carol, in an upmarket suburb near the university. The house was on three levels above a glittering pool. Carol – nobody seemed to use her surname – ensured that her two gardeners kept the grounds manicured to perfection while the housekeeper, whom she had headhunted from one of the world's top hotels, saw to it that the staff of coloured maids ran the house like clockwork. Flame-haired Carol had astutely amassed a fortune while on the super-model circuit and had retired at the height of her career. Now she entertained in style, revelling in publicity and running what amounted to a *salon* for visiting celebrities and the city's glitterati. She had other tastes. Susan Bates was one of them. But only a select few, including Kapinsky, knew the whole score.

A dozen or more cars were parked here and there under trees when Kapinsky arrived on foot. Couples strolled around the terrace and several bodies splashed in the pool. One of Carol's *soirées* was in full swing, he thought. He recognized a top civil servant, talking earnestly to a well-known Member of Parliament.

The bitch really enjoyed playing close to the edge.

The housekeeper opened the door and greeted him. 'Good evening, Dr Kapinsky. Dr Bates and Miss Carol are waiting for you in the suite.' He handed her his laden briefcase. It would be waiting for him when he left, its contents exchanged for top denomination notes. By tomorrow, the lab funds in his five clandestine bank accounts would grow by at least a quarter of a million. Barnes would explode if he knew where his research funds were coming from. But then he was a bloody liberal wet who thought himself a nice guy. 'And nice guys come second,' said Kapinsky under his breath.

He smiled as he imagined Barnes learning that a sectioned-off corner of his lab was now a factory for designer drugs. And what would he say if he knew that his cardiac research laboratory had given birth to the three methyl-fentanyl derivatives of basic acetone, the stuff that lay around the hospital stores in fifty-litre drums?

This compound was no garbage drug. It was more powerful than morphine, it gave a high that was indistinguishable from heroin's rush, and – this was the part that made Kapinsky almost hug himself with glee – it was street legal. As it was not a recognized pharmacological product, no law had ever been drafted to ban it. Better still, it was undetectable in users. He knew he had exposed himself to major risk in isolating it at such high strength – death or disablement were likely results of accidental ingestion – but he had taken stringent precautions.

The suite was on the top floor, far removed from the rest of the house. Built with tinted windows and, as Kapinsky knew, fully soundproofed, it was Carol's pleasure centre. The door was open. He walked into the small hallway and stopped, waiting for orders.

'Shut the door,' Susan's voice shouted, harsh and peremptory. He did as he was told.

'Come here!' Again it was a sharp command.

He walked into the large room, his heart thumping and that jellylike sensation of pleasure oozing up from his loins.

Susan, in riding boots and skin-tight black leather shorts, was naked to the waist. Long blonde hair fell to her shoulders. Chains around her neck and waist were linked between her oiled breasts. Her lipstick nipples stood out firm and taut. Next to her was Carol, lying back in an armchair in a very plain, very expensive, body-fitting black dress and no underwear. He knew she had no underwear because the dress was up around her waist and her legs were parted.

The reason why her legs were parted was that a beautiful young girl – small-breasted, hair cropped short, and stark naked but for a bright red fake fur glove on each hand – was stroking her crotch.

He stared, licking dry lips, knowing as certainly as if he had written the script what was going to happen next.

Susan's voice came on cue. 'Take your eyes off me, you filthy bastard.'

He dropped them to the floor. The sheer *frisson* of hearing her voice of command brought him close to orgasm but he knew he had to hold out. There was still the pain to come and that was the most delicious of all. Without the pain he would never feel the relief. And without the relief, he would go mad.

For years, it had been this way. First the guilt at losing his parents, then the fear that someone would find out, the need of a woman who would beat him until he acknowledged his sins, and the blessed relief that would keep him sane until the next time.

He and Susan had discovered each other at the same gay club. Delighted at finding he was into sado-masochistic sex she had brought him home to Carol. Together they had used him and abused him, each serving the other's needs. Once they had gone too far by beating him unconscious. He had not been able to work for nearly two weeks until the more visible cuts and weals had healed. The young girl was a new element in their usual threesome. She looked high on something, probably amphetamines. But he was close to relief and past caring how many new variations they had introduced.

'Fetch it! On your knees!' Susan barked.

He crawled to the coffee table, picked up a thin metal harness in his teeth and crawled back to her. Carol suddenly moaned, body jerking in orgasm, and the girl kissed her on the mouth.

'Toni!' The girl turned to Susan. 'Take the bastard's clothes off and harness him up.'

The girl pulled off her gloves, stripped him expertly and clipped the metal harness around him, caging his upper body. As she worked, she rubbed her crotch against his thighs. Susan picked up the light whip next to her and laid a thin red stripe across Toni's naked buttocks. She cried out and thrust herself harder against Kapinsky. Susan struck again but Toni ignored the whip, taking her orgasm against Kapinsky's thigh and exhaling a long breath.

Susan felt the sense of power. It began in her belly and spread through her body, filling her with warm delight. She had administered pain and pleasure in the same stroke and her victims wanted more.

A thin wire ran from the harness to the coffee table. Susan plugged another wire onto the end of her whip and lightly lashed Kapinsky across his back. He screamed. The high voltage shock, his own creation, jerked his body rigid.

Carol rose, slid out of her dress, caught Toni from behind by one small breast, pulled her to the floor and forked legs with her, falling into a slow rhythm.

Leaving no mark and causing no flesh damage, the electric whip gave Kapinsky his pain. He and Susan had worked out the details in the lab after that earlier near-disastrous session. As she lashed him she cursed him, driving him in small circles around the coupling pair on the floor. He screamed with every blow until he could take no more and collapsed to the floor, all passion spent and tension gone.

But Susan had yet to reach her climax. She had reserved that for Carol. 'Fuck off,' she said over her shoulder to Kapinsky, who had raised himself on one elbow and was watching. He did as he was told, unstrapping the harness and picking up his clothes. He dressed quickly in the hallway and closed the door behind him as Carol uttered a loud, piercing cry, and then began to moan.

CHAPTER 16

The shaving mirror conversation isn't turning out the way it should, Barnes thought, grimacing at his reflection, which of course grimaced back.

'Let's start again,' he said, aloud. 'You are Rodney Barnes, MD. You are nearly forty years old, healthy and fit, at the peak of your chosen career, financially secure, and happy. And happy?' he repeated to the mirror.

There was no reply.

'You *are* bloody happy, aren't you?' he added, peering closer and putting on a pugnacious expression. The mirror glared back.

'Your problem,' he said, with sudden insight, 'is that you are rapidly solidifying into a self-satisfied bachelor who doesn't want to change. You're set in your ways. Soon you'll be just like a bloody old woman.' The mirror was silent. 'Worse. You talk to yourself. You've lived on your own for so long that you think talking to yourself is normal. And now that you have a woman who wants you, you're afraid. Of what? That she'll change things? Of course she will.' He looked around the bathroom. 'Designer towels, for Chrissake. And clinically clean, not a pawmark or a hand-print anywhere.'

He walked out into the living room, shaver still in hand, and stared at the furnishings as if seeing them for the first time. Everything colour co-ordinated, understated and expensive, he thought, set off with carefully selected modern art pieces. He could have been describing a museum. 'Take a good look, Rodney. This is your life. Face it, you're just an ageing yuppy who's getting prissier as he gets older. Soon you'll be that abomination to all mankind – an old bachelor!'

He had felt this mood coming on for days, as though triggered by his declaration of love to Karen. In the past week he had made several excuses not to see her, rushing back at night to hide in this apartment like a return to the womb. 'Grow up, you bloody fool,' he told himself. 'Stop confusing the woman you love. Take her away on holiday – somewhere you can be alone together – and just let things happen.'

Immediately after ward rounds he called Karen from his office. Her voice was warm and welcoming. She accepted an invitation to a quiet dinner at his apartment. He put the phone down and looked up to see Fiona standing in the doorway.

'Second thoughts, huh?' she said, sounding sympathetic.

'The problem with secretaries is that they are too damn nosy. I don't accept that they can also read minds so where do you get this idea from?'

'We don't have to read minds. Body language is good enough. You've been walking backwards for the past week.'

He smiled and relaxed, suddenly feeling his mood lift. 'Thanks, Fiona. I needed that. Now if you can also conjure up a cuppa the miracle would be complete.'

'Yassuh,' she said, and sashayed off, leaving him with the morning mail and with his mind on the evening ahead.

Barnes and Karen were companionably quiet throughout the meal, neither feeling the need to speak. Afterwards they took their drinks to the balcony and watched the sunlight go from Table Bay, followed by the mountain's incredible light show. Both knew they had reached a commitment stage in their relationship, a time for openness and honesty on both sides. Karen felt secure enough to say simply that she loved him, that she needed a man in her life, and that he was the man. Barnes still found it difficult to speak easily about his feelings and said so. She hugged him. 'Rod, your body tells me,' she said. 'That's all I need to know.' They made love on the open balcony – a quiet unhurried meeting of bodies under the light of the rising moon.

Afterwards they sat close in the warm night air, watching the moon sketch a silver trail across the water towards them.

He suggested they should take a few days' leave and go to the bushveld together. They could visit his parents and then spend some time watching game in the Kruger Park.

The heart unit was unusually quiet – three convalescents due for discharge and no waiting transplant patients. Barnes delegated all his work to Des Louw, reminded JJ to chase up the capital expenditure proposals, shelved what administrative work he could and passed the rest to a strangely dewy-eyed Fiona.

'What?' he asked, puzzled.

'Oh, bugger off. If you hang around here any longer I'll have to retouch my eye-liner.'

They left at dawn, excited as teenagers, and drove throughout the day, watching the soft pastures of the Cape give way to the foothills of the Karoo escarpment and then on into the empty vastness of the Karoo itself. It had been an unusually wet season and the normally bare landscape was a carpet of wild flowers, vast splashes of colour which ran to the horizon. They drove leisurely, drinking in the beauty of the plains. Here and there a rock-capped lone hill stood like a sentinel, standing out against the centuries of natural erosion.

Karen looked at the blooming semi-desert and saw it as a symbol of her own life – an emotionless desert until a year ago and now blossoming with promise. As a child, when delighted with something, she had had a habit of hugging herself and shivering with joy. She did it now, almost involuntarily crossing her arms and holding herself tight as her body gave a shudder of sheer delight.

Barnes looked across and smiled, taking one hand off the wheel to touch her. If there was a paradise, she thought, it could wait.

They lunched at a roadside café, smiling at the truck drivers' menu. 'Enough cholesterol to kill a horse,' Barnes remarked as she tackled a huge hamburger dripping with sauces and dressing.

The afternoon was a haze of contented cruising through a slowly unrolling vista of great scenic beauty, rimmed on the horizon with low hills. Here and there, a bush-fringed stream meandered its way through the landscape. Karen spotted a jackal that Barnes laughingly dismissed as a stray farm dog. Far from the road, the occasional lonely farmhouse shimmered in the heat. At times she wanted to doze off, but Barnes kept her eyes open with his enthusiastic discussion of the research in progress in his laboratory.

'There is a need somehow to take over the function of the brain in the donor so that the rest of the body can continue to live after death,' he said, staring at the straight road ahead, which led on, endlessly, it seemed, through the flat countryside of the Free State. 'Think of it, Karen, a ward full of living dead – an abundant supply of donor organs.' She was glad he did not wait for her answer. He talked on, oblivious to the effect of his words. She wondered how she would feel if Johan was lying somewhere, unable to communicate but with his liver, heart, kidneys and various other organs still alive. The thought was too macabre and she pushed it away.

Suddenly, as if he had become aware of what his words were doing to her, he stopped. 'That's enough shop! After all, we're on holiday.' He leaned over and kissed her cheek.

They reached Bloemfontein in the late afternoon and headed for the Holiday Inn. 'Dr – suddenly prudish – Barnes,' Karen said, 'we'll have one room. I have plans for you.'

'What if we're recognized?'

'All the better. They can come and watch.'

'Seriously . . .' said Barnes, slightly scandalized.

She kissed his mouth closed and the matter was settled.

The desk clerk summed them up in a glance. Obviously honeymooners, trying hard to look blasé. He smiled, called a bell-hop to take the luggage and handed them the room key. 'Your room overlooks the park and the city, and is well away from the traffic so the noise won't disturb you,' he said, smiling at them.

They had an early dinner and a short stroll through the city park. Then, as the desk clerk had predicted to himself, the 'honeymooners' headed for bed. Karen surprised herself and Rodney too. She was aroused to the extent that she needed only his touch for multicoloured waves of delight to shoot through her body. Barnes, who saw himself as a disciplined lover, was dismayed to find he couldn't hold back and was drained in seconds. This had never happened to him before. He began to mumble words of apology but she hushed him and began a slow, sinuous rhythm with her breasts along his body. With rising pleasure she felt herself become aroused again, needing only the touch of his skin to climax at will. As she shuddered against him he was immediately potent and moved to mount her. 'Hold it, lover. It's my party too,' she said in his ear, and pressed him back to the bed.

Afterwards, they lay close, drenched in perspiration and sated. Barnes closed his eyes briefly and she felt his body jerk in the sleep reflex.

The next morning, they had a leisurely breakfast in a world filled with delight. Whatever they ate or drank or touched seemed to give pleasure. Conversation sparkled. Karen's skin glowed and Barnes thought he had never seen her look so lovely and said so.

'Testosterone, darling,' she said, and smirked archly.

They both broke into laughter and the rest of the dining room looked up, wondering what the handsome couple at the corner table found so amusing.

Later they drove to Barnes's parents' home just outside Pretoria. His father would have everyone believe that the frequent droughts in the Western Transvaal had driven him crazy so he had sold the farm and bought a house in Pretoria. He had scarcely been there a year when he found the inactive city life unbearable so he had sold his house and bought three acres of ground a few miles out of town. He realized that to live is to function; stop the functioning and you stop living. Here old Mr Barnes could spend most of the day in the garden, growing vegetables, which he sold to a shop in the town, while his wife kept herself busy looking after the flowers.

Karen felt her anxiety surface as they drove through the white pillars that marked the entrance to the property. She had dressed conservatively with little make-up, anxious to make a good first impression. Rodney was their only child and she wondered how they would react to her.

As they approached the house she felt her heart thump and her palms turn wet. Very unlike me, she thought, but dammit, this is so important.

Barnes sensed her nervousness and gave her hand a reassuring squeeze. The car rounded a bend and stopped in front of a single storey dwelling, built highveld style with a stone chimney and a verandah around three sides. Flowering gums on the north shaded the building while climbing roses almost completely covered two sides of the verandah.

A lean-to carport housed a four-wheel drive army-style jeep and a well-polished old classic Mercedes. Two dogs rose from the shade and barked threateningly for a few seconds but when Barnes said their names, they welcomed him with an avalanche of snorts, squeals and wagging tails. Karen began to relax even before she stepped out of the car. The atmosphere told her that happy people lived here. The garden spoke of caring hands as the flower-beds showed many hours of well-spent gardening time.

And so it proved. Mr and Mrs Barnes were from the old school. Survivors of the Depression, they had built themselves a quality lifestyle based on hard work, thrifty living and strong family values. Now in their retirement years, they lived simply but well. Rodney and Karen relaxed visibly in the family atmosphere. The conversation wandered from his work and Karen's duty in the team to the good rains they had had in the Western Transvaal.

'I'm still glad I sold up, Rodney. Even though it was hard to leave the old farm that had been in our family for three generations, the droughts we had during those years would have ruined us.'

Barnes knew that that was not the real reason. The old man had sold because there was no Barnes to continue when he died.

Inevitably during the evening the conversation turned to politics. Old Mr Barnes was a religious man and could never reconcile apartheid with the teachings of the Bible. 'Rodney,' he began, 'how can people who proclaim to be Christians go along with this blatant discrimination? The most important Commandment is that you must love your neighbour as yourself. There is no way that you can obey these laws of the Nationalist Government and pretend that you love your neighbour as yourself.'

'But they don't consider the blacks as their neighbours,' Rodney pointed out. 'In fact, some of the fanatics don't even believe that the blacks are human.'

The old farmer sat back in his chair and, after a few minutes in which nobody spoke, he pronounced, 'They will know one day! That I'm as sure of as I'm sure the sun will rise tomorrow.' Then, raising his voice, he said, 'Wait and see. The blacks will one day rule over them.'

That night Karen and Barnes slept in separate rooms.

They left the next morning for the Kruger National Park and since this was Karen's first visit to the game park, Barnes explained the basic rules: no getting out of the car at any time between the rest camps and no open windows if any of the 'big five' were around: elephant, lion, rhinoceros, buffalo and leopard. He proved an informed guide, thanks to the many happy holidays spent in the bush with his father. He knew which water-holes were popular with which animals and at what time, and they spotted four of the big five in the first two days. They saw herds of all kinds of buck and a family of wild dogs; they heard the jackals calling after dark and once they spotted a hyena slinking away in the bush. They didn't see a hippo save an impala, as Jan Snyman had claimed to have seen, but on the morning of their last day, they spotted a leopard in the fork of a large tree. Using the glasses, Barnes could see that the animal was devouring an impala it had caught the previous night and dragged up the tree where it would be safe from other predators such as the lion and the hyena.

Although the game viewing was exciting, Karen looked forward to the evenings. The serviced rest camps were almost luxury accommodation, with thatched rondavels grouped around a communal barbecue site. Other eager park visitors gathered at night to exchange sightings and enjoy the mutual feeling of living in the wilds.

They fell into a pattern of eating late, after sunset, enjoying the barbecued meat and red wine. 'Income food,' as Barnes termed it. He looked around at the knots of diners, all tucking into their steaks. 'The wine opens their arteries and the meat clogs them. Then they pay me to open them again.' He raised his wine glass and squinted through it. 'Who will heal the physician?' he asked, and tossed back the wine.

Karen felt a sudden chill, drew on a jersey and – and then realized the night was quite warm. 'Let's talk about us,' she said, changing the subject. Here in the bush, away from places and faces they knew, it was somehow easier to talk about plans and dreams.

She was surprised when Barnes almost immediately brought up the question of marriage. It must have been the effect of the last few days together, she reckoned. This was the first time that they had lived together, spending both days and nights in each other's company.

'I don't think we should wait too long before having a child, either,' he remarked, first staring up at the blaze of stars in the night sky, and then at the stars in her eyes.

Their lovemaking during the nights in the bush was gentle and unhurried, almost as if they had adopted the eternal rhythms of nature. Afterwards she would lie listening to the sounds of the bush and hear him breathing quietly beside her. Outside was the law of the jungle – survival of the fittest, beast killing beast – while here she was warm and secure with her mate.

It was an idyllic holiday which ended all too quickly. They drove back, staying one night with Barnes's parents. The next morning they left when it was still dark. Barnes was now in a hurry to get back to work. They covered the 1,200 miles in thirteen hours, stopping only briefly to fill the tank with petrol and to buy cold drinks and snacks.

It was exactly five o'clock in the afternoon when he stopped in front of Karen's cottage.

'Won't you come in for coffee?' she asked, when they had off-loaded the luggage.

'No thank you, darling, I'm keen to find out what's happened in the laboratory during the time that we were playing Tarzan and Jane.'

When he got to work, he found that Kapinsky appeared to be having some kind of crisis with the baboons, something to do with an abnormal pregnancy. He was being more peculiar than usual and Barnes felt worried.

Both he and Karen had a backlog of work and, by mutual consent, they did not see much of each other – that is, until she received a call from the laboratory technician. Then it became important for her to spend some time with him alone, soon. But when?

Suddenly, the opportunity presented itself.

Karen was sitting with one of the staff nurses in the canteen telling her of the wonderful few days she and Barnes had spent with nature and bemoaning the fact that she had hardly seen him since. Then, out of the blue, the nurse offered her cottage to the two of them for the weekend. 'It won't be like the bush but it's cosy enough, built against the mountain overlooking Hout Bay. You won't see lions or elephants, but you may get a visit from a troop of baboons.'

'Are you sure we won't be imposing on you?' Karen asked, hardly able to hide her excitement.

'Not at all. I'd planned, in any event, to visit my parents and I hate to leave the cottage unattended.'

The two got up and began to walk out of the canteen. 'I'll let you know as soon as I've spoken to Rodney. You are a darling!' Karen said as they parted.

She immediately phoned him. He was delighted at the idea: 'Pick you up on Friday at six if nothing gets in the way,' he suggested, and rang off. For twenty-four hours she prayed that no emergencies would cloud this stolen weekend. Her ever-helpful baby-sitter arranged to move in at a moment's notice to look after Kimberley but right up until the moment that Barnes's car arrived at her door she felt like holding her breath.

He was twenty minutes late and seemed preoccupied. 'Sorry,' he said, dropping a kiss on her nose. 'The bloody lab is under pressure – our baboons are about to pop and Kapinsky's falling apart at the seams.'

She was so relieved to see him that she hardly listened to the explanation. Their drive along the coast road, a winding scenic route, was bliss. The cottage was everything she had ever imagined, built in the dunes and separated from the beach only by a narrow one-way road. Inside, picture windows brought the seascape almost into the bedroom, wood-panelled ceilings gave a relaxed feel and a bar fronting an open-plan kitchen spoke of convivial sunny afternoons and wine-soaked evenings.

After dinner they sat at the table, and watched the last rays of the sun fade from the hills. It was a magic place. She resolved that one day they would have a bolt-hole just like this. There was just one thing that would make it complete.

'Rodney, I'm pregnant,' she said, wondering why the words sounded so ordinary. Shouldn't there be a blast of trumpets or something? Even a swirl of violins would do. It was a secret she had been hugging for over a month, hardly daring to believe it true.

'What?' His face looked startled, uncomprehending, like that of a small boy asked a difficult question in class. For a second he looked vulnerable, so different from the image of the talented doctor and skilled surgeon that she wanted to smile, to put her arms around him and reassure him.

'Darling, I'm pregnant,' she repeated. 'We're going to have a baby.'

He leapt from his chair, knocking over his glass of wine. He ignored the red stains spreading across the tablecloth and grabbed her by the shoulders, pulling her upright. He crushed her to him wordlessly for a moment and then suddenly began to whirl her around the floor in a clumsy dance, chanting, 'A baby, a baby, we're going to have a baby.' Laughing, she joined him in the chant until they both tripped and fell in a heap, breathless.

Barnes held her for a long moment and then drew back, looking deep into her eyes as if searching for something. He felt his heart would burst with love for this woman who, in a split second, had made his life complete. He had never imagined himself a father. Now his mind raced ahead to life with a growing child. Hell, with children – why stop at one?

'This is a very special moment. It calls for a toast,' he told her. Then, with exaggerated solicitude, he picked her up and placed her gently in the armchair.

He emerged from the kitchen a few minutes later waving a bottle of French champagne. 'I saw you put it in the fridge and wasn't sure what you intended to celebrate, you little devil.' The cork came out with a resounding pop and the wine bubbled into her glass. 'Here's to the three of us,' he said, holding up an overflowing glass. It was beautifully chilled and Karen felt she had never in her life tasted anything as exhilarating.

Suddenly Barnes's smile faded. He looked serious. Karen could have mistaken a number of signs for pregnancy. Women often did, as he had found during his short spell in general practice. 'Darling, are you *sure* you're pregnant?' he asked.

A slow smile spread over Karen's face. She had never looked more beautiful. 'Absolutely,' she said, her smile widening. 'Unless the pregnancy test can tell a lie.'

'So you had a blood test,' Barnes chipped in.

'Yes. On our return I asked Dr Snyman to do one. I spun him a yarn about feeling tired all the time, and that I thought I might be anaemic!'

'And you sent the sample to the laboratory under a false name?' Barnes burst out laughing.

That night they made love gently, aware that a whole new dimension had entered their lives. Afterwards they slept, dreamlessly, each secure in the knowledge of the other's love.

Barnes was awakened by the sun shining through the ivy on the overgrown window. From her regular breathing he realized that Karen was still asleep next to him, so he slid out of bed and headed for the kitchen. Karen didn't stir. It wasn't often he was let loose in the food sector, he thought. Now for a breakfast fit for a king, or for a queen, come to think of it.

He cracked a couple of eggs into a bowl, added a little milk, stirred it well and poured the mixture into sizzling butter in the frying pan. Then he popped two slices of wholewheat bread into the toaster and set up the coffee filter. Within minutes the cottage was filled with delicious smells. 'Breakfast in bed, madam?'

Karen slowly surfaced to find him standing next to her holding the breakfast tray. Golden yellow scrambled egg decorated each slice of toast and the steaming coffee smelt divine. She wanted to hug him but, at the risk of getting her breakfast in her lap, she settled for a cup of coffee. Barnes sat on the bed next to her. The pregnancy raised a number of questions which they mulled over as they ate the simple breakfast.

'I think we should get married sooner rather than later,' he said, as he poured a second cup of coffee.

Karen put a spoonful of sugar into her coffee and stirred it well before replying. 'There's no hurry, darling. We could even get married after the baby's born. These days that's quite acceptable for two people living together.'

'I don't know,' said Barnes doubtfully. 'My parents might find that hard to take. They still hold the conservative Afrikaner view, which wouldn't be too happy with you being pregnant at all before marriage.' He frowned at the thought, and added, 'No, we must get married in church as soon as possible.'

Karen suppressed a smile. She thought it quite funny. After all, if they loved each other what the hell did it matter if she became pregnant? Was marriage merely a licence to begin a sex life?

To him she said, 'I'm happy to get married as soon as you like. But won't it be difficult for you with all the new patients awaiting surgery?'

'We can get married over a weekend. You won't mind if the honeymoon's delayed for a while, will you?' He sounded apologetic.

'As far as I'm concerned the first honeymoon was in the Kruger Park, the second honeymoon is this weekend and the third can wait,' she said, making a move to get out of bed.

'Just a minute, Mrs Barnes,' he said, gently restraining her. 'What do you think our child will be – a boy or a girl?'

'It doesn't matter, as long as it's healthy,' she said, sitting up-right, breasts jutting. Rodney tried to keep his train of thought steady, but failed. He grabbed her by the shoulders and brushed his unshaven morning chin against her nipples. She shrieked and pulled him close to her body, rolling quickly on top to straddle him.

Empty breakfast plates clattered to the floor. The hot sun, blazing a trail across the carpet and onto the bed, awakened them an hour later.

They showered slowly, soaping each other in lazy afterplay. They knew they had a whole lifetime together. Time to love and be loved, and to love again.

'I have a wonderful idea. It's such a lovely day and I know some beautiful mountain trails. Let's go down to the riding school and hire two horses. We can spend the morning giving our baby some fresh clean mountain air.'

Karen started laughing. 'Darling, you forget I wasn't brought up on a farm like you. I've never been on a horse in my life.'

Barnes kissed her lightly on the forehead. 'You've given me a few riding lessons so now it's my turn. I'll get you the tamest old mare they have and we'll never go faster than a slow walk. It'll be like going up the mountain in a rocking chair.'

But although Karen badly wanted to please her lover, she was suddenly afraid. 'Don't you think I'd better stay and cook us a nice lunch while you go for a ride?'

'It won't be fun without you,' he persisted.

'Then let's both forget about it. We can go down to the village and buy some groceries then you can read the medical journals I saw in your briefcase and I'll have the opportunity to show off my culinary skills.'

But Barnes would not be persuaded. 'Don't be such a stick-in-the-mud,' he accused her.

'But won't the bumping on the horse make me lose the baby?'

He burst out laughing. 'If horse-riding caused abortions the roads would be choked with women on horseback! Come on, put on some jeans and a sweater. You'll see how much you enjoy it.'

Karen gave up and started to dress.

'We use this old girl to teach the children to ride. She's as meek as a lamb,' Mr Hill, the owner of the riding school, informed them as the two horses, now saddled, were led out of the yard next to the stables. 'You have nothing to fear, Mrs Barnes, she'll walk all the way. It's only when you return and she gets near her home that she may get a little lively.'

Karen scrambled inexpertly onto the horse. The owner made some adjustments to the stirrups and they started to move away. 'I shouldn't really let you ride without head protection,' Mr Hill remarked, 'but you say you'll only walk the horse.'

'Don't worry,' Barnes shouted over his shoulder, 'we'll be careful.' Then, turning to Karen, 'On the farm as kids we never wore helmets and I've fallen off more horses than I can remember without any serious injuries.'

After five minutes the old horse's gentle motion enabled

Karen to relax. It was not as bad as she had thought it might be. She started to enjoy herself and even looked around at the beautiful flowers and bushes growing on the slopes of the mountain. Rodney was right.

After half an hour during which they had spoken little, only enjoying the mountain and each other's presence, Karen called, 'My bum's starting to hurt. Can we turn back now?'

'Seeing you were such a sport, I agree,' Barnes replied turning his horse round. The old mare followed without any command from Karen. Slowly they followed the trail back, Barnes in front and Karen behind. About three hundred metres from the stables he turned in his saddle and called back to her, 'Darling, I'm going to gallop down to the gate. You keep going at the same pace.'

Without waiting for a reply he kicked his horse in the flanks with both heels and gave it slack on the rein. The big animal jumped away like a racehorse from a starting gate. Karen's old mare thought this was a signal for her to follow and set off too at a lumbering gallop. This sudden increase in speed caught her completely unawares and she could only stop herself from being thrown off by letting go of the reins and grabbing the saddle with both hands. She now had no control over her mount.

As Rodney reached the gate he pulled his horse to a halt, wheeled it round and looked back up the track. He immediately realized what had happened. Karen's feet were out of the stirrups and she was bouncing around in the saddle with each stride. Her hair was streaming in the wind and the terror was clearly visible on her face.

'Hold on, darling,' he yelled. 'She'll stop as soon as she gets to the gate.'

Which was exactly what the old mare did. For ever Barnes remembered the next seconds in slow motion. The sudden deceleration catapulted Karen out of the saddle and she sailed over the horse's head in a flailing curve. The scream only stopped when her head hit the gatepost with a sickening thud.

Barnes jumped off his horse and was at her side immediately. She lay face down, blood seeping from the corner of her mouth. He was used to crises when he was able to push aside emotion and methodically assess the situation, but now he was at a loss what to do next. A cloud came over the sun and the shadow fell over the two pathetic figures on the ground next to the gate.

He could only hear Karen's earlier plea not to go on the ride. Why, oh why, had he insisted?

He became aware of the man kneeling next to him. 'Is she badly hurt?' The riding-school owner's voice suddenly brought Barnes out of the trance. Clarity of thought returned and he assessed Karen's condition. She was unconscious, but still breathing. Her pulse was rapid, but strong enough to maintain an adequate circulation.

Suddenly, though, her breathing became more laboured. Soon she would need respiratory assistance. He could not wait for an ambulance which would take half an hour or more to arrive.

He looked up. 'Mr Hill, my keys are still in the car. Can you please go and fetch it – hurry.'

When the Mercedes arrived the man parked it beside Karen and opened both rear doors. Then, carefully supporting her head to avoid any further injuries, the two men placed her on the back seat, bending her legs so that she could lie flat. Barnes moved the front passenger seat forward as far as it would go, and then crouched on the floor beside Karen. Holding her head in a fixed position, he shouted to Mr Hill to drive as fast as he could to Groote Schuur hospital.

Barnes remembered little about the race to the hospital, only that Karen stopped breathing twice and that he had to give her the kiss of life.

At last the car stopped. They were at the entrance to Casualty. The hospital porters moved Karen off the back seat onto the stretcher and wheeled her into reception. Barnes walked alongside and was immediately recognized by an intern. The young doctor said something but he didn't hear. All he was aware of was his own voice, pleading, bargaining. 'Please God, don't let her die.' His guilt was suffocating him. 'Please let her live and let my child live too.'

CHAPTER 17

I n the sectioned-off area of the animal room an excited Kapinsky prepared for the birth of his child. He remembered vividly the feeling of achievement when the scan showed that the
tenth female baboon he called Mrs Kapinsky was pregnant –
the foetus a product of a baboon ovum fertilized by his own
sperm. He spent many hours pondering the outcome. The offspring would probably have some features resembling a human
and some inherited from the mother. He hoped it would have
the intelligence of a human and the physique of an ape.

Mrs Kapinsky was now near term and showing signs of restlessness. Yesterday she had bared her fangs at him. The delivery
would need to be effected within the next twenty-four hours.
He had already alerted Samuel, who now lived with him in the
cleaners' room and was available around the clock.

'It will be a beautiful child, Mrs Kapinsky,' he crooned to the
hugely swollen baboon. She grunted, put a paw through the
bars of the cage and waited, making small chirruping sounds.
'Clever too, my darling,' said Kapinsky, and put an apple in her
paw. She snatched it through the bars and moved to the back of
the cage. 'But I'm afraid you won't be seeing much of our baby.
I will have to take it away.'

The baboon munched the apple and stared unblinkingly back
at Kapinsky.

'Yes, Mrs Kapinsky. We will have to foster your child. I know
baboons are good mothers but I can't risk an accident.'

Although he was sure the baboon was fairly docile, Kapinsky
had read mountains of material on the species and knew that
they often killed offspring which showed any unusual features

or behaved differently. He couldn't take that chance with his precious baboon child.

He looked around. Every possible precaution had been taken. A complete nursery stood ready in one corner of the animal room, fully equipped with an incubator, crib, nappies, clothing, and facilities to sterilize the bottles and prepare the feed. A world expert on primates from the Frankfurt zoo had given him the best milk formula to feed the infant. He had altered it slightly in a way he hoped would take care of the human component of this child. His wide reading in the care of Caesarean-born and premature infants had identified the most likely problems and he felt he could cope with most of them. Mrs Kapinsky had refused to allow him near enough to listen to the foetal heart-beat but all the signs were good. It was time for Samuel to do the job.

Samuel had had mixed feelings when he had first moved into the cleaners' room. His strong feelings of dislike and fear of Kapinsky were tempered by his desire to learn more of surgery. If he knew enough of the white men's medicine he could become as powerful as the witch-doctor. He could go back to the homeland and live among his people and be rich.

During the day he carried out his normal work for Dr Barnes but in the evening, when the other staff had left, he and Kapinsky would surround themselves with textbooks and illustrations of what had to be done. He remembered how surprised he was when he learned that the operation was used to deliver a baby through an opening in the abdomen. He had never operated there before but it looked easier than opening a chest. Using the animals which came to the post-mortem room, he practised the techniques outlined in the textbooks. The incision was made between the two long ropes of muscle which ran down either side of the abdomen. Surprisingly little skill was needed for the rest of the operation, which consisted of cutting into the uterus and pulling out the foetus. Kapinsky had warned him that he would be doing this part of the operation alone as he himself would be fully occupied with the anaesthetic. It was apparently very tricky to keep a baboon just sufficiently sedated to allow the operation to take place without depressing its vital functions to a level which would threaten the life of the baby.

For Samuel, the day started like any other. The routine work of the animal room kept him and the other cleaners occupied until after lunch when Dr Kapinsky had called to inform him that it had to be performed tonight.

'Good grief, Boots!'

He was jerked back to attention by an irritated exclamation from Dr Louw, who drew his attention to the blood obscuring the operative field.

'Swab it out, Boots, and wake up. You're miles away, man. Pay attention,' Dr Louw added.

He mumbled an apology and tried to concentrate but his mind was on the evening ahead.

For Kapinsky, time dragged. There was no possibility of using the animal room for delivery during daylight hours when the cleaning and medical staff were around. Worse still, there was some wretched problem with that day's transplant, which was holding things up. He cursed and went to see for himself.

It was just after five o'clock. Surgery was complete but the animal was still on the table. Its condition was not stable and there was a problem with bleeding. This was a nightmare. Mrs Kapinsky couldn't possibly last more than a few hours before going into labour. There was no doubt that the foetus was too large for the pelvic opening and, if the uterus was not relieved of its burden, foetal distress would set in. In animals, this period was often short and the foetus might die before delivery.

He looked at the baboon lying on the table, still connected to the anaesthetic machine while being ventilated with a mixture of oxygen and nitrous oxide to keep it unconscious. No one was in attendance. He desperately needed to get this animal out of here and back to the recovery cage – or anywhere but here, where it was threatening to wreck his carefully planned Caesarean on Mrs Kapinsky. A quick fiddle with the machine should do it.

He turned off the oxygen, turned up the flow of nitrous oxide and left the room, leaving the door open to the animal room so that he could hear the heart monitor. It seemed to take an age before the increase in the rate of beeps signalled the lack of oxygen. After another minute it became irregular. It couldn't possibly last much longer, Kapinsky thought. But it was two full agonizing minutes before the sound changed dramatically and he realized the heart had gone into fibrillation. Then he heard a rush of footsteps. Some nosy bastard had noticed and was now in the operating room. Oh, God, they were probably trying to restart the heart . . .

'What's going on? I heard the monitor!' he yelled, and rushed into the operating room.

Victor stood there, looking worried. 'Doctor, the baboon that Dr Louw operated on is in trouble, the heart is not beating. I cannot see what is wrong . . .' He was looking anxiously at the monitor screen.

Good, the stupid bastard hadn't noticed that no oxygen was flowing. 'Hand me an ambour bag. I'll ventilate by hand,' said Kapinsky loudly – the louder you spoke the more flustered these buggers got.

Victor rushed to a cupboard while Kapinsky disconnected the air tube from the machine. Victor handed him the bag. Leisurely he examined it, connected it to the end of the air line and began to compress it. Each pump inflated the lungs – but it also took up more precious time and might resuscitate this bloody animal. He had to make sure that the heart did not restart.

At that moment Samuel came in, looking surprised to see Kapinsky there.

'Boots! Good man, just in time. Take over here,' said Kapinsky, handing Samuel the bag. He took it without thinking, wondering why this white doctor should be so pleased to see him. 'Pump, man, pump,' said Kapinsky, and looked around the room in desperation. The anaesthetics tray? It had to have a potassium supply. Yes, there it was and thank God it was ready and waiting in a syringe. 'Probably low potassium,' he said to Victor.

He took the syringe from the tray, connected it to the intravenous line and emptied the contents into the baboon's circulation.

Within a few seconds the heart went quiet. Kapinsky felt a leap of hope. It was a large enough dose to paralyse the heart muscle and now there was no way they could restart it.

'Quickly, get the defibrillator,' he shouted. Victor dashed past the bemused Samuel and wheeled it to the table. Samuel had seen the potassium go in and knew what it could do. Why, he thought, would Dr Kapinsky want to kill one of Dr Barnes's experimental animals? And why do it after they had worked all afternoon on a tricky heart transplant? It didn't make sense – but, then, so much about this doctor was strange. After nearly five minutes of repeated shocks and several injections Dr Kapinsky eventually put down the defibrillator pads and looked defeated. 'It's no use. The animal's brain is already dead. Victor, you and the other men can go. You've had a long day. Boots and I will clear up here.'

Glad to be off after a long day, Victor and his two cleaning staff pulled off their hospital overalls and left. Samuel Mbeki and this angry white man could do the work now, they joked. They seemed to like living with the animals anyway.

Kapinsky locked the door behind them and then turned to find Samuel still ventilating the dead baboon. 'What the fuck do you think you're doing?' he screeched.

Samuel jumped. He was doing just what he had been told to do and now Dr Kapinsky was angry again.

'The bloody thing is dead. Get it off the table and get it the hell out of here!' shouted Kapinsky, exasperated almost beyond endurance. 'And get that table ready,' he yelled over his shoulder as he headed for his animal room.

Samuel rushed into action. He coiled away the leads of the defibrillator, bundled the bloodstained sheets covering the body into a laundry bag, rolled the surprisingly heavy animal onto the disposal trolley and covered the corpse with a white sheet. Victor and the others would dispose of it in the morning.

He swabbed down the table with an antiseptic fluid, placed a pile of sterile sheets at one end and slid a loaded instrument tray into the sterilizer. His heart was beating hard, whether from fear or excitement he did not know. What he did know was that he was about to do his first Caesarian section on a living animal.

Kapinsky found Mrs Kapinsky lying on the floor of her cage, motionless. He stopped and stared, incredulous, not daring to believe what he saw. Her eyes were closed and there was no sign of chest movement. 'You can't do this to me,' he groaned, his throat hoarse with fear. He scrabbled at the safety bolt, twice failing to undo the spring clip and getting more desperate. His voice grew pleading: 'Our baby, you've got to give birth to our baby.' The bolt slid back and he flung open the cage door. Mrs Kapinsky blinked. Realization flooded back. Of course! He had sedated the animal so that he could anaesthetize her without a struggle. All that bullshit in the operating room had driven it out of his head. She was fine! He checked her pulse. It was slow and strong. She was breathing normally. Mrs Kapinsky was in good condition to deliver a healthy infant. He closed the cage door and rushed back to the operating room. Samuel was mopping the floor.

'I'm almost ready, boss, but the instruments will need another ten minutes in the sterilizer,' he said, anticipating Kapinsky's question.

'Good man, Boots.' Kapinsky felt almost benevolent. 'I will fetch the animal on the trolley. As soon as we have her on the operating table and strapped down you can start scrubbing. I will anaesthetize her and set up the instruments.'

Samuel went through the now familiar routine of scrubbing up and donning gown, mask and gloves. When he was ready he stood next to the table and watched Kapinsky at work. He was surprised by the skill he showed in anaesthetizing and intubating the baboon. He must have had a lot of experience before. Why did he not do the operation too?

The baboon was lying on its back with its legs secured to the bottom of the table. Both arms were extended and strapped to arm boards. Samuel had the sudden notion that it looked as if it had been crucified, its swollen belly even more prominent in that position. He had seen pregnant baboons often in the wild but never one that looked this big.

Kapinsky strapped the drip in place on the baboon's right arm. He smiled at Samuel. 'I will prepare the operating field and then she is yours.' Then, with great care and gentleness, he shaved the abdomen, washed it with an antiseptic preparation, dried it carefully with a sterile towel and painted it with an iodine spirit solution.

Without a word, Samuel placed the sterile drapes to demarcate the operating field. 'I'm ready, boss,' he said.

Kapinsky fussed with a pulse and breathing check, eager to begin but fearful of missing some vital sign. 'OK, just give me a second,' he said. 'I want to give her a little more anaesthetic. She is still very light and may move when you make the skin incision.'

After a few minutes he said, 'OK, you may start.'

Samuel took the scalpel and made a long incision running down the middle of the lower abdomen, cutting expertly through the skin and fat to where the two muscles groups met. With a swab in one hand he mopped away the blood to identify the bleeding points, cauterizing each one carefully as he went. He had gone over each step of this operation at least a hundred times. He knew exactly what to do next but yet felt increasingly anxious as the operation progressed. It was as if he was cutting down towards something evil.

The further he went down to the bloated uterus the stronger the feeling grew. His hands began to tremble.

'What's wrong with you?' said Kapinsky.

Samuel turned to him, sweat standing out in globules on his forehead.

'Here,' Kapinsky said, reaching forward with a rolled hand towel to wipe away the sweat. 'Don't get the jitters on me now.'

Samuel saw that his eyes had gone cold, like a cobra about to strike. This was not something he had seen before. Angry men could be handled but this man's stare meant something more.

He was someone who was set on a path and would not be turned aside.

He returned to concentrate on his operating field. I must finish this work and get out of here, he thought. He was not going to spend another night alone with Kapinsky. He would go back to the township, no matter how late he completed the surgery.

Using dissecting forceps he lifted the sheath from the underlying structures and made a cut through into the peritoneal cavity. With a pair of scissors he enlarged the incision and the gravid uterus appeared.

'Open it,' Kapinsky's voice said. Samuel barely recognized it. The tones were flat, cold, demanding. 'Open it and let's see what we have,' Kapinsky added.

Samuel put in place a self-retaining retractor to keep the incision open. He was engulfed by a sense of increasing horror, a premonition of what he was about to see.

Using wet swabs he packed away the coils of small intestine and carefully made a small incision into the cavity of the distended uterus.

'Open the damn thing,' said the chill voice in his ear.

Obediently he extended the opening with scissors and a jet of amniotic fluid fountained out, followed by a small but perfectly developed human hand.

Samuel shrieked and wanted to run but his legs refused to move. He stood, rooted to the spot, staring at the perfect little hand being pushed further and further out of the uterus by the hairy arm of a baboon.

'Get the head out, you bloody fool,' hissed Kapinsky.

The words broke the spell. Dropping the scissors he ran out of the operating room, ripping off his mask. He blundered down the steps out of the research block and tore through the shadows of the buildings until he cannoned off an unlit light and fell, winded, against a wall of the anatomy block.

For long seconds he gasped for breath in the dark, fearing that the monster in the animal room would follow. He slid down the wall and sat on the pavement, unsure what to do. He could not set off for Langa wearing a surgery gown with only his underwear beneath it. Should he phone Dr Barnes and tell him what he had seen? And tell him, too, that Dr Kapinsky had killed his transplant animal?

No, that would not be a wise thing for a black man to do. Dr Kapinsky had the look of a madman. Samuel had seen his rage before, and he would surely kill him if any whisper of this were to be heard in the hospital. In fact, Kapinsky had said just that several times while they had been living in the animal room. He had thought then that the white man was trying to frighten him, but now he knew that he had meant it.

Thoughts whirled in Samuel's head. If he moved from here in these clothes he would surely be picked up by the police. They would check back with the hospital, and who knew what Dr Kapinsky would say? If he was not put in jail he could certainly lose his job.

He would wait here until daylight, keep out of sight until the day staff arrived and then face whatever the day would bring. Tired, bruised and aching, Samuel dozed.

He awoke to the sound of his name being called. Kapinsky was standing in front of him with the body of the baboon cradled in his massive arms. It was obvious from the way the animal's limbs dangled that she was dead. My end is also near, he thought, and prepared himself for a sudden attack by the mad doctor.

But Kapinsky did not move. Samuel stood up cautiously, ready to flee, and then saw with surprise that Kapinsky was sobbing. Tears were running down his cheeks.

'She's dead.' Kapinsky sobbed out the words. His voice was hoarse, breaking. 'You ran away in the middle of an operation, doctor. You killed her.' There was no anger in the words, just a sad acceptance of the fact.

But Samuel hardly heard. He had called him 'doctor'. A white doctor had addressed him as a *doctor*. This was more than he had ever dared hope for.

Kapinsky let the animal slide slowly out of his arms to the pavement, leaving long streaks of blood on his green surgical gown. 'Samuel, please take her to the incinerator. Let the flames devour her body,' said Kapinsky. Then he turned slowly and walked away into the darkness.

Flooded by remorse, Samuel said nothing. He had been trained to do an important operation. He had been entrusted with the life of a patient and he had fled, leaving the patient bleeding on the table. The animal was dead and it was his fault. He should have known that one person could not handle the operation alone. He had killed the baboon and he had killed Dr Kapinsky's dreams of learning many things from this operation.

Sadly, he shouldered the lifeless carcass of Mrs Kapinsky and trudged back to the incinerator in the animal room. Inside, he placed the body on a table next to the incinerator, turned on the gas and pressed the ignition button.

As the flames sprang to life he noticed the baboon's shaven abdomen. The large incision had been crudely stitched in continuous suture as if to hide its secret for ever. Samuel looked at the tightly stitched wound, stretched across the swollen belly of the dead baboon. So the infant, too, had died. Dr Kapinsky had returned that hideous hand to the cavity of the uterus and had closed the abdomen over his monstrous creation – now, thank God, no more than a lifeless protuberance in the dead belly of his surrogate mother.

But what was it that he had seen emerging from the gashed uterus? Why not take a peep? See what it was that had obsessed Dr Kapinsky these past months. See for himself what this white man with the madman's eyes had created. He picked up the body and carried it to the slab in the post-mortem room. From the instrument cupboard he selected a pair of scissors and dissecting forceps. He snipped the knot and removed the suture with a sharp tug on the untethered end.

The wound parted and something burst out. Samuel jumped back and then realized what it was. In the full glare of the post-mortem lights he was looking at a plastic bag. It had split along one side and was stuffed full of old newspaper. He drew it clear of the abdomen and peered inside, pushing away coils of intestine. There was the incision he had made in the uterus through which protruded a severed umbilical cord. He looked closer.

The womb was empty. Whatever or whoever that hand belonged to was gone.

Back in the laboratory Kapinsky was sitting at his desk, still clad in gloves and gown. Suddenly he burst out laughing. I should have been a bloody actor, he thought. All my worries were unnecessary. Things could not have worked out better. The poor damn fool would think he had destroyed in the incinerator whatever he thought he'd seen on the operating table.

He could not have been more wrong. As Samuel placed the baboon on the rollers and slid it into the flames he made himself a promise. He would find out what creature Dr Kapinsky had created. He was now a doctor, a witch-doctor. He knew about life and death: how to create it and how to destroy it. The knowledge that Dr Kapinsky had discovered was also his to know. After all, he had helped it to live.

Back at the beach cottage, Barnes sat alone at the table, staring at the dirty breakfast plates and cups. After seeing Karen admitted to the hospital he had talked to Professor Anderson, the head of the trauma unit, who assured him everything that could be done was being done. Years of hospital work had convinced him that staff were only hindered by relatives and friends of patients in the first crucial hours of treatment so, assured that Karen was in good hands, he had turned away. He didn't remember the journey back to the cottage but the sight of the unmade bed threw him into a fit of remorse and guilt.

He forced himself once again to assess her injuries. Most ominous was a trickle of clear liquid from one ear, a sign that cerebrospinal fluid was escaping from the brain cavity through a fracture at the base of the skull. Why was she bleeding from her mouth? Only a scan would show the extent of the brain damage.

Remorse overwhelmed him. He had gone over the events of the morning so many times but still couldn't explain why he had persisted with the idea of going for a ride. She told him she had no experience. He should have realized she only agreed to please him. Why did he race away from her near the end of their ride? He should have known that the old mare would follow. He knew Karen couldn't hold the horse if she galloped. Whatever the reason, Karen had paid a terrible price.

Late into the afternoon he sat, reliving their moments together, their lovemaking, her delight at their first 'honeymoon' in the game park. And those evenings around the campfire – the night he had said they shouldn't wait long before having a child.

Now she was fighting for her life – and the life of their child. Just as soon as she recovered they would marry, and build a home for her little daughter and their unborn child. It would be a warm, loving family circle and a perfect environment in which to bring up children.

Twice during the night he rang the trauma unit to enquire about her condition. The next morning a call from a sympathetic receptionist told him that Professor Anderson wanted to see him. He left immediately for the hospital, scarcely daring to hope.

'Sit down, Rodney,' Andy Anderson said. He did as he was told. A night without sleep had left him feeling tired, dull and gritty-eyed. Anderson nodded to someone behind him and a cup of coffee was placed on the desk. 'Milk? Sugar?' Anderson went through the social niceties. Like an automaton, Barnes followed, slowly stirring the milk into his coffee as if it were the most important thing in his life. A sip showed him how much he needed the boost, and the coffee warmed away some of the chill within him.

Anderson waited until he had drained half the cup and then

picked up a green folder. He plunged straight in. 'Rodney, I'm afraid the news is not good. Karen has sustained extensive brain damage and a fracture that extends virtually right across the base of the skull.'

Barnes felt something inside him begin to shrivel. His world was dying as he listened to his colleague give the bare medical facts of Karen's condition. He felt like screaming for help – could someone, anyone, not do something, *anything* to change what he was hearing?

He forced himself to stay calm and ask questions. 'What is the prognosis for brain function? Will she recover consciousness?'

'She will live but I doubt whether she will ever regain consciousness. Her ability to breathe spontaneously has also deteriorated. We had to do a tracheotomy and put her on a ventilator.'

His mind refused to accept the picture of Karen, the base of her neck sliced open and a tube inserted so that a machine could force-fill her lungs with air.

'Her lungs are very wet, we must obviously keep her airway clear.'

Barnes tried to wrench himself away from the anguish that was paralysing him. 'What else, Andy?' he asked.

Anderson watched him with pity. The man was falling apart in front of his eyes. 'I should also tell you that Karen miscarried a few hours after admission.'

Barnes looked down and mumbled something inaudible.

'What was that, Rodney?'

He stared at Anderson with eyes that were pools of agony. 'I would like to see her,' he said.

'Of course, my friend. You can visit her as often as you wish,' said Anderson. 'Come with me.'

Karen was alone in a small single bed ward. Anderson left him and there was no nurse in attendance. The only sound was that of the heart monitor indicating a strong heart-beat, circulating blood to a brain that was barely alive. He had always claimed the heart was there only to keep the brain alive. Once the brain was dead there was no longer a need for that organ in the body. He wondered whether the theory also applied to patients whose brain was not totally dead but damaged to the extent that they would never regain consciousness.

If life is the joy of living, could there be any joy or even life for someone whose consciousness had been switched off for ever?

'Karen?'

There was no response. And why would there be? Wasn't she deeply and irreversibly unconscious? But what if they were wrong? A medical diagnosis was not infallible. What if there was something there that he could reach?

He brushed her cheek with a kiss and began talking, at first sobbing out his regret, turning later to whispered hopes for their future. A nurse came and went several times in the next hour but he barely noticed. He talked on and on, his only response the beep of the monitor and the sigh of the ventilator.

At last the flow of words slowed. Still she lay, eyes closed, unmoving. He took her hand and held it, looking at the carefully manicured fingernails. She had always been well groomed, taking care of her appearance and health. Now this beautiful body would slowly waste away. Lying here in this bed, being turned every few hours by a nurse, with perhaps an occasional visit from a physiotherapist, the muscles would slowly deteriorate and the ligaments tighten. Soon, within weeks, she would begin to cramp into the foetal position, her body curling tightly in upon itself. Worse, unless the nursing care was kept to the highest level, she would develop bed sores – ugly ulcers that would slowly eat her flesh to the bone.

Suddenly, shockingly, Barnes wished she would die. The emotion was so powerful it made him stagger, and only his hold on Karen's hand allowed him to keep his balance. He tucked it carefully under the bedcover and turned away. He could not be in the same room with her and feel these emotions.

He knew only that he could not be inactive. He could not stand by and watch her die. He knew something else, too. His heart felt like a stone.

CHAPTER 18

'It's your fucking fault,' Kapinsky spat, and glared at Barnes. 'You and the black bastard you trained to be a so-called surgeon.'

The violence of Kapinsky's attack was so unexpected that Barnes rocked back on his heels. He opened his mouth but Kapinsky rushed on. 'You said he was good with a knife. Sure he is, but only to stab others in drunken brawls.'

Kapinsky pushed his face close to Barnes's. He looked pale, unkempt as if he had slept in his clothes, his hair wild. 'Your bloody *kaffer*,' he said, speaking slowly, 'killed my animals.'

Barnes suddenly needed to sit down. He had come here to tell Kapinsky of his own tragedy, only to be screamed at as he walked through the door. He felt himself close to breaking-point.

Kapinsky ranted on, detailing the events of the previous night's disaster. Far away, immersed in his own pain, Barnes barely heard.

Kapinsky stopped. Barnes hadn't said a word. Had he fooled him just as he had the nigger surgeon? He looked closer. Barnes was obviously upset about something. Maybe the bloody *kaffer* had already told him. He waited.

Barnes looked up. 'I'm sorry, Louis,' he said quietly. 'I have my own problems. Karen fell from a horse yesterday. She's in the trauma unit with critical brain injuries.'

Kapinsky was shocked. He started to question his friend. It was as if he had opened a floodgate.

Vulnerable and needing support, Barnes poured out his heart. He told of his love for Karen, their closeness, the few days in the game park, his stupid insistence on her going for the ride that had led to her being in a deep coma now.

'And what's the prognosis?' Kapinsky asked.

'Poor, I'm afraid,' said Barnes. 'She's likely to remain unconscious. The awful part is that when I saw her like that I wanted her to die.'

'Perhaps that would be the better outcome. You yourself have always said that death is not the enemy.'

'I suppose it depends which side of the bed you're standing at.'

Kapinsky had no time for this. It was the kind of emotional claptrap that kept incompetent, mentally incapacitated and useless old people alive and eating up the planet's scarce resources. 'Bullshit. A patient is a patient, whether your wife, your child or your enemy. Emotion should have no place in making a judgement as to the best outcome.'

Barnes knew Kapinsky was right, but then he, too, had his emotional side. 'Practise what you preach, Louis,' he said. 'Why are you so upset about the baboon and its foetus? Many animals in your care have died in the past but you didn't react in the way you did today.'

Kapinsky thought quickly. The remark was too close to a risky subject. 'This was different. The animal died because of the stupidity and negligence of the nigger you recommended.'

The remark set Barnes's teeth on edge. 'Do not use the words "nigger" or "*kaffer*". They have no place in this context. It makes you sound like a racist.'

For the first time in the conversation Kapinsky smiled. 'Racist? I am a realist. These people belong to an inferior race. Not their fault, of course. They are just unfortunate in that they have inherited inferior genes.'

'That's what the Nazis thought about the Jews and look where that led.'

Kapinsky felt alarmed at the comparison. They were getting uncomfortably close to his deeply held feelings. He did another of his lightning mood changes. 'Sorry, Rodney.'

'There is more bad news. Karen was pregnant and Anderson has just informed me that she aborted last night.'

'It was only an embryo and, anyway, you didn't want a baby whose mother was in a coma. It is the best thing that could have happened.'

'So you don't see an embryo as life? When does life begin?'

This was an area on which Kapinsky had strong opinions and he had no qualms about voicing them. 'It's not so much a question of when does life begin as when do you begin to have the right to life?'

'The right to life?' asked Barnes, genuinely surprised and drawn into the argument despite his pain.

'Yes, that's the crux of the whole debate. It applies to all living things, *Homo sapiens* included. A living creature has the right to life if it is of value to its own group.'

'You mean the unborn child and the mentally insane have no right to life but your baboon foetus has?'

'Correct.'

'Just like the gypsies and the mongols under the Nazis?' Barnes pursued. He felt he had to dig to the bottom of Kapinsky's attitudes.

But Kapinsky was not going down that road. He had worked hard to conceal his origins and he didn't want some chance remark to endanger his status as a respected, British-trained medical scientist of Polish origin. 'Rodney, I told you my views. What are yours? You keep making judgements. What do you base them on?'

It was the best cop-out he could think of but Barnes took the bait. 'Louis, a life which may be considered at one particular stage to have no value may have the potential to develop into an asset of great value if given the opportunity. An example is the foetus inside the womb of Beethoven's mother. According to your theory it had no right to life yet look what a contribution Beethoven made to music.'

'Yes, and look what happened to the foetus inside the womb of Stalin's mother,' Kapinsky retorted. This was childish debate but he enjoyed it.

Barnes ploughed on. 'That is, unfortunately, a risk society has to take. But you will admit there are more Beethovens than there are Stalins. The unborn foetus has unknown potential and we have no right to decide that it should not be given a chance.'

'You are totally against abortion?'

'No, I am saying the goal of medicine is to improve the quality of life. If it can be shown that continuation of a pregnancy will cause a deterioration in the mother's quality of life, or that the child will be born with little expectation of life quality, then the pregnancy should be terminated – but not because it will spoil a skiing holiday for the parents.'

'Rodney, this discussion is like arguing about the existence of God. You either believe in God or you don't. In this case you either accept abortion or you go pig-headed about the right to life. What about the mother who says: "It's my body and my life, I will decide?"'

'I agree with the mother yet still feel the foetus has a right to life. But you're right in that we are arguing over existential principles. There's no way in which logic can be applied to reach hard and fast rules on which to make a decision in every case.'

Kapinsky looked at his watch. The baby had to be fed in fifteen minutes. Perhaps it was time to inform Barnes of his incredible success at breeding a baboon carrying human genes. He could not resist a last sarcastic jibe.

'You'll be pleased to know that within the next week or so we're expecting the birth of a number of baboons that will be of immeasurable value to society.'

Barnes refused to rise to the bait.

Kapinsky leaned forward confidentially. 'And now I'm going to tell you something of immense importance. It must remain between the two of us. I don't think society is quite ready for this major contribution. Let's talk in the computer room.'

The telephone rang. Kapinsky picked up the receiver, listened for a few seconds and handed it to Rodney. 'It's for you.'

Barnes's face paled as he listened. He closed his eyes as if to shut out what he was hearing. 'I have to go to the hospital,' he said abruptly, and left.

At the trauma unit, Barnes found Professor Anderson in his office. Anderson offered him a chair.

'I'm sorry to tell you this, Rodney, but Karen's condition is deteriorating fast. She is going deeper into a coma.'

Barnes was filled with guilt. Could she have sensed his thoughts? Had she deliberately given up her fight for life to fulfil his wish for her death? *Did he really want her to die?*

The answer flooded in with blinding clarity. *No, he did not!* He would do everything in his power to keep the woman he loved alive, whatever it took.

'Is there anything you want me to do?'

Barnes blinked. He had forgotten where he was.

'Does she have any close relatives?' Anderson persisted.

'Yes, I phoned her parents in London, but there was no reply.' God! He had completely forgotten to try again.

'I think you should phone again and let them know.' He didn't seem in any fit state to answer questions let alone make decisions, thought Anderson, but he needed to know some background about his patient. 'I think you should let them know about the seriousness of her condition.'

'Is she going to die?'

'Rodney, I can't give you a yes or no answer. Where there's life there's hope. A lot of the negative neurological signs could be due to the oedema of the brain. I've given her medication to dehydrate her.'

Where there's life there's hope. It was an old hospital cliché, but Barnes clung to the message. He stood up, suddenly more determined. 'Thank you, Andy. I won't take up more of your time. I'll tell Karen's parents.'

Anderson stared after him. He'd always liked Barnes – a fine surgeon and first-class research scientist. And now he'd discovered another of the man's positive attributes: he could handle strong emotions and still function.

Barnes went to his office, unstaffed at weekends, and

229

rummaged through Fiona's immaculate filing system. He found what he was looking for: Karen's CV and employment details, including her membership of the university pension fund, which listed her parents as next of kin. He phoned straight away and, only after waking her father, realized it was just after midnight in London. He introduced himself and plunged straight in with the bad news.

A retired army major, Gareth Jones quickly took charge of the conversation. He and his wife would travel out on the next possible flight. Barnes could meet them at the airport. They would stay at Karen's cottage and take care of Kimberley. Kimberley? My God, I'd forgotten her, thought Barnes. Major Jones said he would forward details of their arrival time as soon as he had made his arrangements, and rang off.

Barnes looked up. Fiona was standing in the office doorway. Without a word she came round his desk and hugged him. The gesture wrecked his control and he burst into tears. She held him while he wept for Karen, for himself, for the destruction caused in the life of a little girl, and for the awful futility of it all.

Fiona told him that she had heard about the accident on the radio and had come straight to the office. 'Leave Kimberley to me,' she said. 'I'll go out to the cottage right away and talk to Grace. Between the two of us we'll arrange it so that someone will stay there all the time until the grandparents arrive. I'll move in if necessary.'

The heart team and all other staff in the department closed ranks around Barnes. He was almost overwhelmed with the support and sympathy they showed. Des Louw and Alex Hobbs took over the routine surgery while he spent hours at Karen's bedside.

The next two weeks were critical. At one stage it seemed as if the coma was lifting but then Karen had a series of epileptic convulsions, which left her even weaker. Professor Anderson finally controlled them with heavy sedation but this made it difficult to judge the depth of coma.

Major Jones and his wife arrived. To Barnes, they were and remained strangers, never really impacting on his life. After a week of visiting Karen and several meetings with Professor Anderson, they understood that their daughter would not recover. After much discussion, they informed Barnes that they were taking Kimberley back to London. The question arose as to who in future should decide what would happen to their daughter. This was resolved by the old man signing a legal document that put the responsibility on Barnes's shoulders.

It weighed heavily on him. What if Andy recommended they stop all treatment? He would ask Karen. After all, wasn't she responding to his visits by remaining alive when, by all the indicators, she should have been dead?

That realization marked the beginning of a new routine for Barnes, of daily visits to Karen during which he read medical reports to her, talked to her about her treatment, told her she was making good progress and that Kimberley was in good hands. The hospital wards and laboratory work were forgotten.

At first concerned at Barnes's non-appearance, Kapinsky soon discovered he preferred not having to report to anyone. He told himself that Barnes was just a pain in the arse. And if it came to that, this whole goddamn medical school was only a means to an end, a way of advancing his own research and bringing about ultimate benefits to mankind. Samuel was a problem as he was still allowed to operate, now being under the supervision of Dr Louw – but success was almost in Kapinsky's grasp.

His creation was thriving. It had some apelike features but many human ones too. The head was bigger than an ape's and the cranial cavity seemed to have more capacity – an indicator of intelligence, he decided.

More of the baboon females had recently given birth to tolerant foetuses. He would have preferred to keep them under his care but that was impossible so he transferred them to the basement animal house and allowed the mothers to nurse their own offspring. He looked after Josef personally, though. That was the name he had chosen for his own creation, after the man he had admired so much in his boyhood – Dr Josef Mengele, who had carried out medical research on the prisoners in the concentration camps.

During the past few weeks Josef had made amazing progress, and the only aspect of his development that worried Kapinsky was that he cried like a human baby. If the sound was heard outside the special section questions might be asked, particularly if Professor Thomas got to know about it. Josef's physical ability at this tender age was gratifying. He could already stand on his hind legs and grip firmly with his humanlike hands. The project was clearly a success. Now he could go ahead with his aim to create brothers and sisters for Josef.

Samuel could not erase the memory of that hairy arm with the human hand. Try as he might he could not forget the empty womb with the placenta still attached. That and the severed umbilical cord all pointed to the fact that the creature had been delivered. He had no doubt it was still alive somewhere, and the only place in which it could be being kept was the special locked section.

At nights he would dream that the arm came through an opening in the ceiling and slowly reached down for his throat. He would wake and try to scream but be unable to utter a sound. He wanted to leap up and run but his legs refused to move.

What made it worse was that he could talk about it to no one. At first he was frightened of Kapinsky but then gradually he became more frightened of the monster. What would it do to him if he told others about it? Finally Samuel decided to consult Kalolo, a powerful witch-doctor used by everyone in Langa. People said his medicine was very strong. If that was so, perhaps he could ward off the evil. Samuel had heard many stories of Kalolo's powers and how he could punish those who tried to harm his clients.

He thought hard and long. He did not want to harm the

white doctor, Kapinsky, but if that creature was in the animal house somewhere it should be destroyed. He made an appointment to see Kalolo on a Saturday afternoon. When the day came he washed, shaved and put on his best clothes: he must show respect for a man with so much power.

When Samuel arrived at Kalolo's house, a small single-storey dwelling with *muti* signs on the gate, he was met by an old woman who, without a word, showed him into a room where Kalolo was waiting.

Old and frail, the witch-doctor was sitting on his haunches in the middle of the room, dressed in a leopard skin and a hide loin covering. Around his neck hung various bones including the skull of a rock rabbit. He looked up as Samuel entered. The woman signalled to him to sit on the floor opposite Kalolo.

In a croaking voice the witch-doctor chanted strange words for several minutes and then stopped. He looked straight at Samuel and said in Xhosa: 'You are the teacher who cuts up animals for the white doctors and you have brought great evil on yourself.'

Samuel gasped. How did the old man know all these things? Truly he was a great witch-doctor.

'Yes, Wise One, I am the teacher who is now a doctor,' he replied, feeling proud of that word 'doctor'. It would make Kalolo understand that he, too, had status.

'You are troubled by dreams of animals.'

Samuel's eyes showed his fear. This witch-doctor could see inside his head. He knew everything. 'Yes, Kalolo. I am troubled much by this dream. It comes to me always when I sleep. In my dream I am afraid this animal will put its hand on my throat and kill me. I fear the white doctor, too, who made it.'

'It must indeed be a strange animal that attacks like a man.'

Samuel's scalp crawled with fear. The witch-doctor was reading his every thought like a book. He wanted to run but his legs would not work. It was just as it was in the dream.

The croaking voice came again. 'You are surprised that I know all these things.'

'Yes, Wise One.'

'I can see inside your head. But you have not told me what you want. Do you want the creature destroyed and the white doctor also?'

Alarmed, Samuel jumped to his feet. The old man held up a skinny hand and waved him back to the floor. 'What is it you want, my son?'

Samuel wished he had not come. This man was too powerful, more powerful than the creature and the white doctor. He could do Samuel great harm – or perhaps bring him much good? He had to be careful. He did not want Dr Kapinsky destroyed. And the creature? If Dr Kapinsky wanted it so badly, it must be of great value. But for what?

He looked straight at Kalolo. 'I want to know more about the ape that looks like a man.'

Kalolo closed his eyes to hide his surprise. An ape that looked like a man? There was something of great note here. This teacher, Mbeki, that his housekeeper had told him so much about must know that too. Why else would he come here and ask for help?

After several minutes of silence he spoke: 'There are some things the white man can do which may seem difficult to understand. I can tell you more of this when you bring me something that has touched this creature.' He went quiet and dropped his head as if asleep.

The housekeeper came into the room and held out her hand. Samuel paid her and scurried out, glad to be away from the brooding presence of Kalolo. But how could he get something that had touched the ape? Only Kapinsky himself was allowed into the special section.

After nearly two months of sedation, and as Karen's seizures had not returned, Professor Anderson gradually withdrew the sedative. Barnes had watched daily, praying for her to open her eyes. She had begun to waste away slowly, day by day, and her hair had lost its shine, becoming dull and lifeless. The tanned, healthy face was pallid and her skin was flaking. The manicured fingernails had been cropped short for ease of nursing. Today he noticed that she even smelt different: a tinge of antiseptic masked something else. Decay? He cut off the thought. Yet although she had lost her physical attractiveness, Barnes loved her more than ever and could not bear to think of her leaving him. He took her hand in his and squeezed it until the fingers turned white, but there was no response.

He felt a strong need to talk to Kapinsky again. They had not seen each other for weeks and Barnes wanted to discuss Karen's condition with a scientist. He let go of her hand and left for the laboratory.

He found Kapinsky in a jovial mood and, to his surprise, was greeted with a bear hug. Young Ferreira, too, was almost puppy-like in his genuine delight at seeing him and even that ice-cold bitch Susan Bates had a smile for him.

'How is Karen?' Kapinsky asked.

'Not improving, I'm afraid. There's been a steady decline. One of these days Anderson will ask me to turn off the ventilator. This is no longer simply a trauma case and the bed is needed for more urgent cases with potential for a better outcome.'

Kapinsky said nothing. In his mind the seed of an idea began to grow.

'I can't just let her die, Louis, but her brain is going and her body with it.'

Kapinsky looked at him in surprise. This man was no longer thinking rationally. He was obsessed by the bloody woman. 'First things first.' Kapinsky changed the subject. 'You remember when I told you about the baboons that were born after the foetus was exposed to human antigens.' Barnes could feel the man's excitement. 'Well, look at these photographs.' Kapinsky took an envelope out of his desk drawer and spread out the contents.

Barnes studied the pictures, which were all of young baboons, each with a section of white skin, without hair, on the side of their abdomens. He looked up at his colleague. 'I think I know what this is, but it's too fantastic to be true.'

'It's true, my friend. Two weeks ago, I did skin grafts from human donors onto these tolerant baboons and not one of them rejected. What do you think about that?'

Something struck Barnes and he asked, 'You only use white donors?'

'No, it's not what you think. In this experiment there is no race prejudice. I only wanted white skin so that it would show up better.' Kapinsky smiled. 'So now I am ready for the heart. These baboons are still too small to accept an adult heart, but they are growing fast. I am giving them growth hormone injections. We should be ready for the hearts of the convicts in a month's time.'

'You're a shit, but a genius,' Barnes responded, laughing for the first time in days.

Suddenly Kapinsky asked, 'Would you keep her body alive even if there was no possibility of a return to full brain function?'

Barnes nodded as if he had been expecting the question. 'Her physical presence means everything to me.'

Kapinsky felt massive excitement stirring in him. There was no doubt that Barnes was starting to lose touch with reality. He had never come across an example of obsessional thinking before but this matched up with what he remembered from the single course of psychiatry he had done in his student days. But that was Barnes's problem. She must have been an incredible fuck, he thought. The poor sod was still craving her body.

'Rodney, there may be a way,' he said.

Startled, Barnes looked at him. 'The chemical messengers? You've identified them?'

'No. I've gone one better than that. You remember the Eiseman experiment of a few years ago in which a pig liver was used to detoxify the blood of a patient who was suffering from liver failure?'

Barnes nodded, puzzled.

'The point is that the liver was directly connected to the circulation of the patient. There was some initial success but rejection quickly destroyed the liver.'

'Go on.'

'I have an idea for a similar approach in which we could use a brain, this time with no risk of rejection.'

Kapinsky went on to relate his work with Professor Volkov and the creation of a baboon whose organs would be compatible with humans. Barnes, dumbstruck, opened his mouth to remonstrate but Kapinsky held up a hand, undid the buttons of his lab coat and pulled up his shirt to expose an expanse of white belly. In the centre were several patches of dark, hairy skin. Barnes looked at them uncomprehendingly and suddenly realized he was looking at skin grafts – skin taken from baboons and transplanted onto Kapinsky's abdomen. He could see the outline of crude sutures but the grafts were healthy and well healed.

'Christ, Louis! Who did that?'

Kapinsky chuckled. 'I did it myself under local anaesthetic. Not a bad job for a laboratory boffin, eh?'

They both laughed. It felt good.

'What are you trying to tell me, Louis?' Barnes asked, trying to hide his excitement.

'I'm telling you that we are ready to fill up our wards with the living dead. The brains of these baboons will provide the chemical messengers to keep the donor's body alive.'

Barnes found himself caught in the technicalities of such a transplant, how the physical connections could be made, but at the same time he was rejoicing. He was coming alive again. He had begun to think positively.

'Stop, stop. I will answer all your questions.' Kapinsky went to a cupboard, unlocked it and brought out a black box about the size of a human head. 'I have given this a lot of thought. The brain will be housed in this box, cushioned by the same seaweed gel I used to give the nucleus an artificial membrane in the cloning experiments. The box has a thermostatically controlled temperature environment.'

'How would it work in practice?' asked Barnes, intrigued. 'Can we go through the procedures from the beginning?'

The other man produced a clipboard with a thick sheaf of notes. 'This is a brief overview and will need some fine tuning but the essential steps are here.' He flipped over a page. 'Here we are,' he said. 'As soon as the Transplant Co-ordinator informs the lab that a donor is available . . .' Barnes closed his eyes: Karen had been the Transplant Co-ordinator. 'Go on, Louis,' he said.

'We immediately begin preparation of the baboon – anaesthetized, chest opened, connected to the heart-lung machine and cooled. While the cooling is taking place we will expose the carotid arteries and the jugular veins in the neck. All clear so far?' Barnes inclined his head. 'These vessels will be cannulated and connected to a separate perfusion system with a small membrane-oxygenator, so that we can perfuse and cool the brain only. Once we have established brain perfusion the heart-lung machine is stopped, the brain is removed and placed in the black box.'

Barnes stirred. 'If I understand you correctly, the brain, even though it's now at a low temperature, will continue to be perfused with oxygenated blood?'

'Correct. The endocrine system of the brain is susceptible to oxygen deprivation. It is important that optimum levels are maintained.'

Barnes was deeply sceptical. The idea sounded too obvious, too bloody simple. A bit like building with play blocks. 'So now we have the brain positioned in the black box. Where do we go from there?' he asked.

'As already mentioned. Seaweed gel is poured around it to form a protective moulding. The box is closed and locked, leaving only the tubes connecting it to the perfusion system. The idea is that the contents of the box are kept confidential. I don't think the world, and particularly your friend Thomas, is quite ready for this.'

'Go on,' said Barnes.

'The box is taken to the donor. Here the mirror image of the process is carried out. We open the carotid and jugular vessels of the donor, cannulate them and connect them by means of silicon tubes to the brain in the black box, through the tubes already in position.' He glanced at Barnes who nodded agreement. 'The box is now connected to the patient's own circulation. The baboon brain is being oxygenated by the patient and the chemical regulation of the patient's vital organs will be taken care of by the hormones secreted by the baboon brain.'

'What about clotting? A circuit like that will encourage it.'

'Taken care of! The infusion system will inject heparin at the level of the carotid arteries and neutralize the anti-coagulant again as it flows back into the jugular. In this way the patient is never anti-coagulated. Only the blood in the brain.'

Barnes whistled. Kapinsky was a genius. This thing might just bloody well work. But would the hospital authorities and, above all, the Ethics Committee allow him to have a ward filled with the living dead?

CHAPTER 19

The man with the heavy black moustache drew his hat down over his eyes and emerged from the recesses of the medical school, and made his way down to the main road. Keeping to the shadows, he turned left and began to walk briskly. Walking was safer, he thought. His car was known in the area and might be recognized. He couldn't be too careful now that he was a member of the Iron Fist.

The thought filled him with a sense of power. He was an Iron Fist! A fist raised against the Communist menace that was taking over his country. Hearing the leader speak on that incredible evening had clarified a lot of things for him. One thing he was sure of, the whites would have to fight for their survival, and he was not going to be on the sidelines.

It hadn't been all that easy getting into the organization. His contact, who gave his name only as Henk, had questioned him closely.

'I've seen it all before,' he had told Henk. 'These atheists will spread their Communism like a cancer until they have invaded the very soul of the land. The blacks are too stupid to see they are being exploited. Only the hammer and sickle will reap the fruits of their so-called liberation struggle.'

'A nice speech,' Henk said sardonically, when he said he was ready to join the battle against the Communist takeover of South Africa. The Iron Fist would check out his *bona fides*. If there was any doubt . . . He had left the rest of the sentence hanging in the air.

After that, nothing happened for several weeks, but then, all doors opened. 'We had to be careful,' Henk explained. 'It seems crazy but we have enemies in the nation's own police force. There are white policemen who would like to see us destroyed. They have been trying to infiltrate the organization with undercover agents. We discovered three in the past year.'

The man found it hard to believe. How could educated, sane white people in South Africa plan to hand themselves and their children over to a form of Communism which fed on the uneducated black masses?

'It's true, it's happening, and we've given up trying to reason with them. Politics doesn't work. Now we're trying war,' said Henk.

And war, thought the man, remembering an undergraduate course in philosophy, was simply the continuation of politics by another means. This was his sixth meeting. The organization had formed cells throughout the country and he was a valued member of the Observatory cell, named after the white working-class suburb in which it was located. He felt secure, powerful and invulnerable. He, too, had enemies but now that he had the organization behind him he would deal with them as they deserved.

A brisk twenty-minute walk brought him to a street of little terrace houses, each with its wrought-iron railings enclosing a weed-choked patch in front. For several minutes he waited in the shadow of a doorway on the street corner before darting down the alleyway at the rear. He carefully counted seven doors down. At the eighth he gave the agreed three-knock signal. An eye inspected him through a peephole and the door opened just wide enough to allow him to slip through. The doorkeeper, a woman, showed him silently to a rear room.

An open trap door and a flight of steps led down to a small room. Melodramatic, he thought, but effective. The air smelt of damp. The other five cell members rose to greet him with the half Nazi salute. He responded and they sat down around a table.

Each meeting had been held at a different house but it was always the same six who attended; each was dressed inconspicuously, none wore a beard and they were unarmed. 'Dress like everybody else, don't draw attention to yourself, keep your mouth shut and your eyes open,' Jan, the cell leader, had warned them.

It was he who opened the meeting, praised them for their support and solidarity and moved straight into the business of the evening. 'Our next target has been identified. This time he is an enemy of the people.'

The group stirred. This was a big step. So far they had sabotaged township power lines and railway signals, aiming at discouraging black migrants from moving to the urban areas. Now, for the first time, they had a human target.

'His name is Joe Dubofsky, and we will refer to him only as JD.'

Eyes widened. It was a well-known name.

'Yes, he is the lawyer who is always in the news – defending the terrorists who are killing our women and children, and using the courtroom to insult the Boer and paint him as an uneducated buffoon. His cases not only get him a lot of publicity here but also overseas where he is seen as some sort of champion of the underdog.'

'He's as good as dead,' a cell member growled.

'Not so fast, Hannes,' said Jan. 'His death will result in an international outcry. So this party has to be carefully planned. Let's first see what we know about the pig.' Looking down at his notes he told them that JD had been born in Latvia of Jewish parents. The family had somehow survived the pogrom of the thirties and made their way to South Africa, arriving penniless in Johannesburg. JD's father, Sammy, started by peddling fruit and vegetables in a small cart, pushed by hand from house to house. As he went he learned enough English to get by. A born salesman, Sammy Dubofsky became almost a household name in the area. Frugal and hard-working, he saved enough in two years to achieve two ambitions: to send his son Joe to a Jewish school and to open a vegetable stall.

As the years passed he moved into wholesale fruit and vegetables and even built his own cold-storage facility. Soon, a fleet of refrigerated trucks carried fresh produce and the Dubofsky name to every corner of the country.

JD proved a brilliant pupil, winning a scholarship to study law at the University of the Witwatersrand. On campus he showed an interest in politics and quickly became a student leader.

Jan stopped reading and looked around. Everyone was listening attentively. 'It's important to know your enemy, and to do that you have to build up a picture of him in your mind,' he said. 'Our friend JD became president of the student branch of the Communist Party and organized a number of demonstrations in the city in support of black migrants who had been refused work permits. When the Party was banned he carried on his activities under cover.

'After graduation he went into a Jewish law firm, specialized in criminal law and soon became known for his defence of people accused of terrorism. His widely publicized courtroom battles gave him such status that the authorities felt inhibited in taking action.'

'Unbelievable,' said Hannes, stirring restlessly.

'However, from information gathered by the police, his work extended to more than simply being a defence lawyer. There's now no doubt that he was the mastermind behind a number of bomb explosions that had killed women and children.'

'*Die vark moet vrek,*' said Henk, thumping his fist on the table.

'Yes,' said Jan. 'I agree that the pig must die but first we must be sure we know his movements. Karel, you have contacts in the Department of Telecommunications.'

'*Ja*, I can arrange to have his phone tapped,' said Karel.

'The reason the High Command has brought this to our attention is that the police can't gather enough evidence to put him behind bars. They passed the problem on to the organization and it is now in our hands. Any questions?'

'If the police can't deal with this enemy of the Volk then we certainly can,' said the man in the hat. The others growled approvingly and one slapped him on the shoulder.

The meeting moved on to a lesson in the handling and storage of explosives, the problems involved in torching a building and simple time-delay devices that could be made from ordinary household items. The man felt his adrenaline flow as they went through the training routines. This was power as he had never known it before.

Jan closed the meeting in the early hours of the morning. They would meet again in a month's time to analyse the information gathered by Karel. From that they would set a place and time for striking the target.

The man in the hat walked back to the medical school, his head buzzing. It was beyond belief that a murderer like JD could not only walk free but also pose as a respectable professional and appeal for international support. If the members of the World Council of Churches only knew that their Sunday collection money was going to buy plastic explosives for pigs like JD ... He shook off the train of thought. JD was as good as dead.

When he arrived at the medical school he went to his office to change into his normal clothes and prepare himself for his next meeting.

Barnes was the last to arrive at the special meeting of the Ethics Committee, having stopped off at the hospital to visit Karen. He found the others seated and JJ looking at his watch.

'Sorry, Mr Chairman,' Barnes said. JJ grunted his disapproval, but everyone else greeted him as he sat down, except for Professor Thomas, who was looking a bit bleary-eyed. Probably snooping around the laboratory all night in the hope of finding something to raise at this meeting, thought Barnes. He found himself next to Kapinsky who had been invited to present his proposal.

JJ thanked Faculty members for finding time to attend the special meeting, warned that they might find the proposal unusual and asked them to keep an open mind. He turned to Barnes.

'The floor is yours, Dr Barnes.'

Barnes recounted his experience with David Rhodes's heart transplant, the rapid decline in the condition of the donor heart, and his reasons for believing that it was due to the cessation of chemical messengers from the brain. 'Two years ago, Dr Louw researched brain-death and its effect on the production of the thyroid hormone. He showed that a marked change occurred in thyroid output after brain-death and that this in turn led to impaired aerobic metabolism in vital organs. The resulting tissue damage was so severe that the organs were no longer viable.'

Professor Bills stirred. He tried to catch JJ's eye. He had more important things to do with his morning than listen to a lecture on basic body chemistry.

'Gentlemen, the thyroid hormone is only one of what could well be a vast array of chemical messengers yet to be identified. We believe the search for these has only just begun and could well occupy medical science for decades,' Barnes continued.

JJ kept his attention on Barnes and nodded encouragement. He could hear Bills shuffling but refused to look at him. Barnes and Kapinsky were clearly on to something and this could well be one of the more memorable meetings of the Ethics Committee.

Thomas had belatedly noticed that Kapinsky was at the meeting and glared at him. If he could put a spoke in this Polish bastard's wheel today, he would.

'With your permission, Mr Chairman, I would like to ask Dr Kapinsky to speak,' said Barnes.

Bills suddenly lost his irritation. Barnes and Kapinsky didn't exactly toe the bureaucratic line at times, he thought, but, then, which scientist worth his salt did? They had achieved some solid research and whatever they had to say this morning should be worth hearing.

'Certainly, Dr Barnes,' JJ replied. 'Dr Kapinsky, when you're ready.'

Kapinsky stood up and outlined his unsuccessful search for the chemical messengers secreted by the brain. Choosing his words carefully, he omitted any reference to his half-human baboon.

'Eventually, I had to admit that even after extensive reading and some preliminary experimental work, it was still an insurmountable task,' he added.

'I'm not surprised,' Thomas interjected. This was his chance to denigrate Kapinsky and take a swipe at Barnes too. 'You're not a biochemist. Frankly, I'm appalled at how Dr Barnes can permit you to waste research funds in an area about which you know nothing.'

Kapinsky's expression didn't change. He enjoyed the cut and thrust of debate and came back swinging. 'Yes, I can now see my shortcomings in entering a field totally unfamiliar to me. I'm sure you will agree that one should recognize one's ignorance, Professor Thomas.'

It was a bull's-eye. Thomas turned brick red and snorted, the other committee members tried hard to keep straight faces.

Barnes, however, was keen to avoid another verbal brawl. 'Go on, Louis,' he urged.

Kapinsky told of his work with Professor Volkov on the skin test for selecting baboons with a less acute immune response to human antigens. His detailed account of the preparation of the baboon embryo carrying a human gene, which resulted in an animal whose organs could be tolerated in man, caused the committee to sit up and take notice.

Thomas tried several times to interrupt but at last, unable to control his anger, he stood up and pointed at Kapinsky. 'This man is talking complete nonsense. He is trying to distract you from the sinister experiments which are going on in his laboratory.' He faced the committee and raised his voice. 'Nobody, but nobody, can breed baboons whose tissues and organs are not acutely rejected in humans.'

Kapinsky grinned. 'I can and did,' he said.

Thomas swung around to him and yelled, 'You're lying you – you – Communist!'

The epithet was so unexpected and so irrelevant, at least to medical ears, that it caused a guffaw of mirth.

Kapinsky rose slowly. The mirth stopped. Alarmed, Barnes put a hand on his arm but Kapinsky shook it off. Facing down the table towards the committee he raised his shirt. His audience was mesmerized. Most weren't quite sure what they were seeing. 'These are grafts of baboon skin, taken from the animal which Professor Thomas claims does not exist,' said Kapinsky. 'As you can see, the grafts have taken perfectly and coexist with my immune system without any sign of rejection.' He pulled at the long hair growing out of one of the patches, looked at Thomas and added, 'Unless, of course, the Professor has doubts about my humanity?'

Thomas jumped to his feet again and held out his arms towards Kapinsky. 'Heaven forbid. I know the Communists have no respect for God or man, nor for the suffering they inflict on animals, but you, Dr Kapinsky, are not living in Poland now. You are living here in South Africa in a civilized society.'

Kapinsky felt a sudden rush of relief. It was obvious that Thomas did not realize what was happening in the laboratory.

'Professor Thomas?' It was JJ. 'You're out of order. Personal attacks have no place in our discussions. These are serious accusations and you should be aware of the fact that the Communist Party is banned in this country.'

'I'm well aware of that,' said Thomas, 'but that doesn't mean there aren't Communists still walking the streets.'

Incensed, JJ slammed the table with his gavel. 'If you have nothing to contribute on either ethical or scientific grounds, then I must ask you to sit down,' he said sharply. There was a rumble of agreement around the table and Thomas sat, still glaring at Kapinsky. Round one, thought Barnes. If he keeps this up they'll back us just to give him a poke in the eye.

'Carry on, Dr Kapinsky,' said JJ.

'It is common cause that donor organs cannot continue to

function for any viable length of time without brain mediation. This is a clinical reality which poses many problems particularly in the transplant field. Too often we have seen vital organs in donors deteriorate before the recipient is ready to receive them. It is common for surgeons to let donors go because there are no recipients on the waiting list. Even if we remove the organs, there is no long-term means of storage.'

Professor Bills stared out of the window.

Get to the point, Louis, thought Barnes. We're beginning to lose them.

Kapinsky paused until he had the group's full attention. 'Gentlemen, we have overcome these obstacles. We can keep the donor alive using the brain of a transgenic baboon. By that I mean keeping the donor's body alive from the neck down, preserving the organs in a viable state in the body.'

There was a charged silence as each member of the group tried to take in what he had heard. It needed a leap of imagination to grasp its import but nobody there, including Thomas, doubted that they were listening to a report from the frontiers of human knowledge.

'The practical side of this concept is not difficult,' Kapinsky continued. 'When a donor is made available to the transplant team, a baboon brain will be removed from a compatible animal and prepared. The brain will be housed and protected in a special container which we have designed. To keep it alive during transfer, it will be artificially perfused and oxygenated from the time it is removed from the animal until it is connected to the donor circulation.'

'And how will you achieve that?' JJ asked.

'By simple cannulation of the vessels in the neck of the donor.'

'On a point of information, Mr Chairman,' said Barnes.

'Yes?'

'It is important here to make it clear that this project has taken transplant research well beyond anything in the medical literature. For that reason I would ask the committee to hold confidential everything we discuss. We have as yet not written up the work, and have obviously published nothing. For obvious reasons, not least being the availability of funding, we're anxious not to allow premature disclosure before we are in a position to stake our own claim on what you will appreciate is original research.'

There was a chorus of 'Hear, hear,' from all except Thomas, who shook his head.

JJ looked concerned. 'Your view, Professor Thomas?' he asked.

Thomas looked at Kapinsky. 'Don't worry, I will never allow anyone to know that I was privy to this unholy work. I would be too ashamed,' he said.

'I'm glad to know that,' said Kapinsky sarcastically.

'But that does not mean I will give my approval,' said Thomas quickly. He looked around the table. 'Have any of you gentlemen considered the suffering this travesty of science would cause the baboon? Remember, according to Dr Kapinsky, the brain is still alive and can register pain and fear.'

A curly one out of left field, thought Barnes. The old bastard could bring the SPCA in on this one. Every old lady with time on her hands and a thing about animals would be marching in the streets. He had to do something – and quickly.

Thomas felt the mood change and let his eyes travel around the table, directing his words in turn to each member. 'How would this brain react to being locked up in a box without being able to see or hear? Would it register hunger and thirst? What about the memories that lurk in the area where experience is stored?'

Kapinsky saw the funny side of Thomas's words and snorted at the idea of the brain in the box remembering how it once jumped around the lab.

JJ turned an icy stare on him.

Barnes stepped in in response to the temperature drop. 'Mr Chairman, there's no risk that the animal will suffer.'

'And why is that, Dr Barnes?' JJ was giving him the floor but his voice was cool.

Barnes explained the concept of regional heparinization to prevent blood clotting and pointed out that an intravenous anaesthetic would be introduced to the system at the same time to ensure the baboon brain was permanently asleep. He felt the group relax. The next question related to blood group compatibility and he knew Thomas had been fended off.

Another hour of question-and-answer ended with JJ referring the issue to the Professor of Medical Jurisprudence, Dr Leonard Hertz, who had not yet contributed to the discussion but who summed up the situation as having 'no clear legal objections'. 'The reality is that we are out at the limits of human knowledge here,' he said. 'The donors are brain-dead and hence not regarded as legal entities. Research protocols are already in place for experimental animals. If the animals remain fully anaesthetized throughout there can be no objection raised on that aspect. What remains to be spelt out is the ethical position.'

Len Hertz was enjoying his morning. If somebody had told him he would feel stimulated by an Ethics Committee meeting he would have doubted their sanity. But young Barnes and that weird Kapinsky had certainly thrown the cat among the pigeons. This bunch had hoped he would object on legal grounds so that they could all go back to their departments without having to make a decision, but he wasn't going to let them off the hook so easily.

'The question we must answer is what ethical code we are transgressing by allowing donor organs to be maintained by an animal brain. We have in the past authorized research on preservation of donor organs by various means, none of which has been successful. So the principle of artificial maintenance of donor organs has been accepted. What then is the problem here?'

He left the question hanging.

To Barnes's delight, Thomas jumped in to harangue the committee on the need to abstain from the work of the devil. It was the catalyst everybody needed. A show of hands found in favour. Thomas abstained but said nothing. These fools in the Ethics Committee were of no help. Most were academics, godless scientists who supported each other and would agree to anything that brought a few miserable dollars in research funds to the medical school. He would no longer throw pearls before swine. With the power of God behind him he would take his own steps to stop Kapinsky and his satanic project.

JJ announced the majority opinion of the Ethics Committee that the work could proceed. He would ask the Medical Administrator to allow one of the smaller wards to be made available to the research team.

As he and Kapinsky walked back together to the elevator, Barnes suddenly stopped.

'What?' asked Kapinsky.

Barnes waited until they were inside the elevator. He hit the button, watched the doors close and said, in a confidential whisper, 'I've thought about the technical side. There's no reason why we can't use the whole head.'

CHAPTER 20

Samuel was frightened – and not only of the thing that lurked in Kapinsky's laboratory. He was also afraid of Kalolo.

It was more than a month since he'd had his meeting with the witch-doctor and he had not yet found the object that Kalolo wanted. At first, he'd thought he could always get one object the creature had touched out of the rubbish from Kapinsky's animal room. But the flow of food fragments, syringes, swabs and other waste had stopped. For days he had scratched through the department's refuse but to no avail. Kapinsky, he discovered, had installed his own incinerator. He knew, eventually, that he would have to go into the area marked 'Private'. The thought made his stomach churn but there was no other way.

The first problem was that there was only one key to the door and Kapinsky had it. He kept it on his own key-ring which he wore attached to his trouser belt and which, no doubt, he slept with. Maybe Mr Murphy, the caretaker, had a spare. He would go to his house and ask him, but Murphy would want to know why a cleaner needed a key to a place he worked in every day. Samuel decided to bribe the man with a bottle of brandy. Old Murphy always smelt of it and would, surely, be pleased to have more.

One evening, he screwed up his courage and went to the caretaker's house. A small, single-storey dwelling, it stood in its own railed-off garden in a corner of the medical school grounds. The woman who opened the door recognized him as one of the cleaners, so when Samuel asked for Mr Murphy, he was shown into the over-furnished sitting room. The old man was sunk deep into an armchair with an empty bottle next to him. It was clear he'd already had several sun-downers. He looked at Samuel with a bleary eye and slurred as he spoke. 'Whudshuwant?'

Samuel knew that the caretaker was too befuddled to know who he was, which, he reasoned, was a very good thing for Murphy would not remember him in the morning. He reached into the plastic bag he was carrying, took out a bottle of cheap brandy and placed it on the table next to the empty one. The old man focused on it, suddenly coming to life. 'Mr Murphy, I would like to have the key to Dr Kapinsky's animal house,' he said.

Murphy clawed the bottle towards him, twisted off the cap, poured himself some of the amber fluid and downed it at a gulp. He squinted at the glass and said, 'Only Dr Kapinsky has a key to that door.' He looked at Samuel, tried to get him into focus, and gave up. 'Why do you want to go there? Itsha shpooky place, you know. Funny things go on there.'

He filled the glass again while Samuel explained how he had helped Dr Kapinsky with surgery on several animals. All he wanted was to see what progress they were making. He felt some of the animals might be ill during the night and he wanted to satisfy himself that they were all right.

While he talked, Murphy's eyes closed. His head tilted in a light doze. Samuel shook him awake. 'I don't have a key. Only Dr Kapinsky does,' the old man slurred.

'That's a pity,' said Samuel. 'Because if you could help me to see my animals I would give you two bottles of brandy.'

Murphy straightened in his chair. 'I don't have a key but I can help you get in there,' he said.

Samuel poured him another glass. Murphy put out his hand but Samuel held the glass just out of reach. 'How will you do that, Mr Murphy?'

Murphy made a monumental effort, sat up, tried to grab the glass and failed. 'There'sh another entrance, from the cleaners' room.'

Holding up the glass, Samuel drew out of him the information that when Kapinsky turned the cleaners' room into his sleeping quarters he had asked that a door opening into his animal house should be locked and a cupboard put in front of it. Murphy had done that and still had the key. Now Samuel remembered that door: why had he not thought of it before?

'What's on the animal side of this entrance now?' Samuel asked.

'Not sure – think cages for the baboonsh.'

All the cages were on wheels and could be easily pushed aside. 'The key, Mr Murphy. Where is the key?'

Murphy looked at the brimming glass and tried hard to think. 'M' jacket,' he said, pointing to a dust-coat hanging on a peg in the passage.

Carrying the glass with him, Samuel went to it, patted the pockets, took out a ring loaded with keys and handed them to the old man.

Murphy peered closely, then held out one between his thumb and finger. 'Thississit,' he said, triumphantly.

Samuel handed him the glass, twisted off the key and pocketed it. 'Thank you, Mr Murphy,' he said.

'Thassallri'. Don't forget to bring it back – anna 'nother bottle.'

Samuel left the house. He had a key to the secret room and the old man would never remember him when he woke up in the morning.

Barnes quietly entered Karen's ward, where he felt her presence strongly. He sat down next to the bedside and took her hand, noticing again how thin it had become. He was confronted with two difficult choices.

Kapinsky's voice still rang in his ears. 'Make up your mind, Rodney. You have to decide. Either you agree that further treatment will serve no purpose and you should allow her to die, or declare Karen a brain-dead donor and give your signed permission to have her admitted as the first patient in our ward of the living dead.'

They had argued for an hour, Kapinsky at last losing patience.

'Rodney, you claim her physical presence means so much to you. You say the fact that the body is still there to see and touch has become an essential part of your existence. Yet you fail to see she is falling apart in front of your eyes. You talk the talk but you don't walk the walk.'

'What are you saying, Louis?'

'I'm saying you have three choices. You can bury her decently, something to which every human being is entitled. You can embalm her like Stalin or Lenin. Or you can give me a chance.'

'What?'

They had been standing in Kapinsky's office. Kapinsky had reached out, pulled over a chair and pushed Barnes into it. 'Why don't you allow her to be the first human being to stay alive with the help of a baboon brain?'

Barnes had wanted to hit him, but taking a swing from a seated position seemed somehow ridiculous. He had tried to stand up but Kapinsky had pushed him down again.

'Think, Rodney!' he had urged him. 'Think seriously through your options. You're behaving like a bloody lovesick teenager, not a responsible doctor. Remember that doing nothing is not an option.'

Deep down Barnes knew a decision had to be made. Since the meeting of the Ethics Committee a few days ago, he had tried to avoid facing up to it. It would have been no problem with anyone else, but how could he do this to his love, to Karen? His mind refused to accept the image of her lying motionless, connected to a black box.

'Rod!' Kapinsky had gripped him by the shoulders. 'Right now she is dying, cell by cell. Without a brain, her vital organs are deteriorating. Christ, man, you can see it for yourself. Every hour . . . no, every minute you delay takes her closer to the point of no return.'

Now, sitting beside her bed and holding her hand, he realized it was a small, glowing spark of hope. Kapinsky had a point: doing nothing was not an option. That led only to alternatives that were no options at all.

Burying her six feet under the ground meant her body would be eaten by worms. Cremation would turn her into a handful of ashes. He shuddered at his own macabre thoughts.

'What do you want me to do, darling?' he asked Karen.

She opened her large dark eyes and looked at him. Slowly her face broke into a smile. 'I want to be with you, Rodney. I want to have our baby.'

His head whirled. He gave a startled shout, stood up to reach for the alarm bell and then stopped.

Karen lay as always, a shrinking corpse-like figure, with only the blip of the monitor disturbing the silence. Oh God, he had imagined the whole episode. He buried his head in his hands. He was shaking. This was dreadful, he thought. He was an emotional mess, hardly able to control his own mental state let alone care for anyone else.

Something he had read years before about brain-function came into his mind. Someone, he had forgotten who, had carried out experiments to show that experience was stored in the brain not only as a result of electrical impulses but also chemical reactions. If that was the case with memory, why not also with consciousness? Logically, given the right chemical environment, consciousness should return. Perhaps it was based on the chemical messengers secreted by the brain?

Barnes came to a decision. Yes – Karen would be the first patient admitted to the ward of the living dead.

Old Murphy remembered nothing of handing over the key to Samuel, which gave him time to plan his venture. It also saved him having to buy the two bottles of brandy he had promised.

Samuel knew that Kapinsky now rarely left the laboratory. Some days he would go to the medical school cafeteria for lunch, but as he now had his own kitchen facilities in the cleaners' room these excursions became rarer. Sometimes on a Friday evening he would dress in casual clothes and leave the medical school carrying a briefcase. He would stay away about three hours. The visit would therefore have to take place then.

Samuel planned carefully. During the time Dr Kapinsky had stayed on the premises Samuel had noticed that he never locked his living quarters. The only security he was concerned with were the main doors leading to the animal room and the special door to the locked sector. The main doors were not a problem. He already held a key to those, given to him by Dr Barnes so that he could open the buildings when he arrived each morning. Dr Barnes's key would get him into the building, and Murphy's key into the secret place.

Samuel knew his plan was going to be a success and felt pleased with himself – right up to the moment the old woman spoke to him out of the shadows at his door. 'I see you, Samuel Mbeki.'

Trying not to appear startled, he greeted her coolly. 'Good day, old mother.'

'I have a message for you from Kalolo.'

Samuel's scalp prickled and he shivered in the warm summer darkness. 'Yes, old mother? What does the Wise One want from me?'

'He wants you to keep your promise. He says his powers to help you are growing weaker and his anger is growing stronger.'

Oh, sweet Jesus, help me, thought Samuel. That phrase – remembered from a childhood prayer taught by the nuns – kept running through his head. Time had run out. The break-in would have to take place this Friday.

When the old woman left he searched his room from floor to ceiling. If he could find the *doekem* the old woman had left to focus the witch-doctor's powers on him, he still had time. He was looking for a cloth or a stick, perhaps even a piece of shaped clay, a stone or a bone with markings on it.

He found nothing but that didn't mean it wasn't there. It could be invisible, perhaps breathed into the walls. It could be working right now, killing him from inside, making him more and more sick until he died. He could not sleep. There were still two days before he could make the attempt and already he could feel the cold in his bowels. 'Oh, sweet Jesus, help me,' he implored.

The hours dragged until morning. When he tried to eat his usual breakfast of fried bread and coffee he vomited. The coldness grew. Samuel knew his life was in danger. When he reached the medical school his bowels began to run. Kalolo was killing him.

'Boots, you look like death,' said Nat Ferreira, when he arrived for the first surgery session. Samuel jumped at the word. Three times in two hours he had to rush to the lavatory.

At lunchtime he sat in a corner of the animal room, clutching his stomach and lost in misery.

'Here, take this,' said a voice in his ear. He looked up. Ferreira was standing there with a glass of water in one hand and two tiny pills in the other. Obediently, Samuel put the pills in his mouth and swallowed them with the water. They would have no effect against Kalolo's powers but he liked this white doctor and did not want to refuse him. Dr Ferreira meant well but this was not a case for white man's medicine. Samuel would have to face his fate without help. Ferreira told him to lie down for an hour while Victor stood in for him at the operating table.

'Where's Boots?' asked Barnes, when he called in briefly to check on the previous day's surgery.

Ferreira grinned, pointed towards the far end of the animal house and said, 'He came to work with a big dose of the runs. I gave him enough Lomotil to stop the *Titanic*. He's sleeping it off.'

'Just make sure he doesn't dehydrate,' said Barnes. 'And chase him off to the out-patient clinic if he still shows signs when he wakes up,' he added.

Samuel slept like the dead. Ferreira took a look at him once or twice and woke him just before the end of the work shift. Samuel looked around in astonishment. He was still alive. The other cleaners were standing around in a half-circle, grinning. Apart from being ravenous, he had never felt better. He thanked Ferreira and stood up, half embarrassed at being found asleep, and half giddy with relief. Kalolo had only sent a warning. He had another chance. This time he would make sure the old man got what he wanted.

When Friday dawned Samuel took some food with him as he left for the medical school – he might have to stay the night. Public transport to the township stopped running early and it was too dangerous to walk home after dark.

Just before the end of the shift he shouldered his bag, picked up his jacket in one hand and said goodbye to the other staff. Then he went to the washroom and locked himself in a cubicle. He sat on the seat, listening to the building become quiet. The dragging footsteps of old Murphy making a cursory check gave him a few extra heart-beats but then all was quiet.

He jerked awake at a sudden sound and looked at his watch. It was exactly nine p.m. Kapinsky was leaving the building and Samuel was alone with the baboons – and that evil creature. To-night, he would meet the monster. His heart pounded at the thought. He waited half an hour, then quietly opened the door of the cubicle, went out into the passageway and listened. There was no sound from anywhere. Even the animals were asleep.

He did not waste a second. He walked directly to the room where he had spent those uncomfortable nights awaiting the de-livery of the creature. Once there he had no need for lights. He knew the layout of the room and moved confidently to the cupboard. Grasping it with a hand on each side he tried to move it away from the wall.

It didn't budge.

He fought down his panic. He had to move the cupboard, unlock the door behind it and get into the animal room.

He tried again. This time he put his back against one side, braced his feet against the floor and heaved. With a scraping sound that seemed to echo through the entire building the cup-board moved, inch by inch, away from the door.

Samuel stopped to get his breath. He felt around the door-frame in the darkness and discovered that it opened towards him – he wouldn't have to push it against the cages inside. He found the keyhole and inserted the key. It wouldn't turn. Old Murphy had given him the wrong key.

Drenched with perspiration, choking with despair, he finally freed the key and tried again. Finally it clicked round. He pulled on the door, which opened slightly and the warm, familiar smell of the animal room rolled over him.

The room was lit with a single bulb under a metal guard in the ceiling. As Murphy had warned, a cage was blocking the doorway. It was standing on wheels but the bottom tray was high enough off the floor to enable him to crawl through. He was about to do so when he thought of the creature. Better to leave an easier retreat. He pushed at the cage. It moved slowly, silently. He stepped through the door and entered the forbidden place.

As his eyes adjusted to the dim light, he noticed that the floor was immaculately clean. The white doctor must have done all this work himself. It must be important to him to keep people out. He, Samuel Mbeki, was about to find out why.

Suddenly a male baboon barked, loudly. It was a warning to the troop that an enemy was nearby. 'You can call all you want. There's nobody to hear you,' said Samuel, suddenly exultant.

He was wrong. Somebody did hear.

Kapinsky had decided to work late that evening. He was re-designing the black box to accommodate the whole baboon head instead of just the brain. Barnes had been right. Surgically, it was a better approach to disarticulate the complete head of the baboon. It also allowed for an important little endocrine organ, the pituitary gland, to be left intact.

The single bark came clearly to his ears. Kapinsky jerked erect. Was it from one of his animals? He walked to the door of the office and listened. There was the call again. It came from the animal room.

Kapinsky took the key from his belt and quietly unlocked the door. By now most of the other animals had been wakened and had begun to shriek and jump around in their cages. Samuel had to move quickly. But where to look for the creature in this warren of cages? Where to find the creature he had last seen emerging from its mother's womb? He noticed the little row of cots in the nursery area at the rear of the room. That was a likely place to search.

All the animals were awake now and the noise was incredible. Thank God the medical school was deserted at this time of night.

In the nursery, each little animal was tucked into its cot like a human baby. Samuel wanted to see their hands. He bent over the rails of the first cot to lift the blanket away when his head was suddenly held from behind in a vice-like grip. He could not turn to look at his captor, but when he swivelled his eyes down he saw a hairy forearm pinning his arms to his chest. God Almighty, could the creature have grown to this size in a few weeks?

He struggled to free himself from the vice-like grip. The accompanying chorus from the other animals swelled, as if cheering on his attacker and drowning his cries for help.

Slowly the hand and arm clutching his head started to bend him backwards until he could feel the animal's breath. This was a nightmare. A searing pain shot through him. The animal had sunk its teeth into his neck. Samuel felt dizzy and faint. His vision cleared briefly. The struggle had taken them almost the length of the animal room and out of the corner of his eye he saw they were at the door through which he had entered. This powerful beast was squashing his head like a ripe tomato. He had to get out and away or he was a dead man. Out of fear came cunning. He allowed himself to go limp, hanging like a dead weight on the hairy arms. The powerful grip relaxed to take a fresh hold. This was his only opportunity. He jerked his head downwards and felt his forehead skid on the fresh sweat and slip out of the vice. He was free!

Like a sprinter out of the starting block he burst through the door, catapulted himself along the passage and down the fire escape to the basement. There he looked around in the shadows thrown by the street light. An empty laundry basket! He jumped in and pulled the lid closed. Such a creature could move as quietly as a cat, he now knew. It was massively strong and attacked without a sound. He would stay in the basket until morning and hope it would not find him.

Back amid the screaming chorus of the animal room, Kapinsky first checked on the alarmed Josef and then inspected the cages. Nothing amiss. He stood in front of the open door for a few moments and then noticed the key still in the lock. He pulled it closed, locked it, pocketed the key and with a thrust of his powerful arms moved the cupboard back into place. A quick look round. The intruder was gone and had clearly had such a fright he wouldn't be back. Time to go to bed.

Samuel spent a most uncomfortable night, squeezed into the laundry basket and venturing out only when he heard sounds of the day staff moving around. He decided to report sick. Des Louw agreed that he looked under the weather and sent him to the medical clinic, where the doctor thought he might be harbouring a flu virus and sent him home with a small bottle of pills having advised him to stay in bed.

Samuel reached his room at mid-morning. It felt strange to be in the township with only the women and children and the unemployed. He locked his door behind him and lay on the single bed. His neck was burning from the bite he had received. Touching it with his fingers, he could clearly feel the holes made by the canine teeth. His life had become unbearable. He had proved that he could escape from the creature but what about the witch-doctor? He could leave here and go back to live with his wife and children in the homeland. Over the years he had saved enough money to make this possible, but how would that help him evade the witch-doctor?

No, he could not escape Kalolo. The old man could reach him at any distance. He could place a spell on him and his family that would kill them all, slowly. What would his father do?

Samuel sat up on his bed. Whatever his father would have done he would not have been lying here, afraid to open his door.

He swung his feet to the floor. His shirt felt uncomfortable. He drew it over his head and smelt the strange smell. The creature had been in contact with it from the back. He had what Kalolo wanted, something that the apeman had touched. He felt like jumping for joy. He washed and put on a fresh shirt and placed the one he had been wearing in a plastic bag. Then he dressed carefully in his suit and tie and polished shoes. With the sun high overhead he set off for the witch-doctor's house.

The old woman met him at the door. She told him she was glad to see him. The Wise One had expected him many days ago and he did not like to be kept waiting.

Kalolo was sitting in the same position, dressed in the same garments as before. Samuel had a sudden weird thought that the man had not moved since he had last seen him. He squatted on the floor in front of Kalolo and waited.

At last the old man spoke. 'I see you, Samuel Mbeki.'

'Good day, Wise One.'

'You have been long gone, my son. Have you brought the thing I have asked for?'

Samuel pulled his bloodied shirt out of the plastic bag. 'This shirt was touched by the creature,' he said, feeling somehow proud as if telling of some heroic deed. He handed it to the old man.

Kalolo spread the shirt on the floor, took the small leather pouch off his belt, opened it and took out about a dozen small bones. Samuel felt the skin on the back of his neck begin to crawl. Kalolo shook the bones in his cupped hands, mumbled a few words and scattered them across the shirt. He then began to rock backwards and forwards with eyes closed, chanting the strange language. Twice he stopped and looked at Samuel, then started again. At the third attempt he opened his eyes and examined the bones, his face puzzled.

He gazed at the bones for a long time, reached out and touched one with a finger, and then slowly raised his head to look at Samuel with gathering anger. 'You have deceived me,' he said in his dry, whispering voice.

Samuel shook his head. He couldn't believe what he was hearing.

'You have lied to me,' said Kalolo, his voice rising. 'This shirt has only been touched by human flesh.'

'No, no, Wise One,' said Samuel desperately, dragging off his tie and unbuttoning his shirt. He bent forward and showed the wound to Kalolo.

The old man said nothing. He ignored the wound and glared at Samuel. 'Those are the marks of human teeth. You were bitten by no animal. It was a man who did this.'

Samuel protested again.

'Enough,' Kalolo shouted, his voice shockingly loud in that small room. He held up a hand, brought it down slowly and pointed to Samuel. 'The bones never lie. Go and return within a week with what I have asked for. If not, I swear by the soul of your father you will be stricken by a deadly disease, a disease so foul it will drive even your children from you. Heed me, and do as I bid or you will know much pain before you meet your death.'

Samuel scrabbled on the floor in his anxiety to stand up and leave. He found himself in the street with his shirt in one hand and his tie in the other, stared at by curious neighbours.

He walked blindly until, at last, he found himself back in his room. This was the end of his world. He sat on the bed in despair, still holding the shirt. Slowly, he raised it to his nose and sniffed.

Strong and unmistakable, the smell of an animal rose from the fibres.

CHAPTER 21

'You want to keep corpses alive? You're asking me for permission to set up a ward full of living cadavers in this hospital?' The idea seemed so far-fetched that the Medical Administrator, Michael Webber, decided he hadn't heard it properly. He looked at Barnes, brow knitted. 'It's a joke? You're setting me up? Right, Rodney?'

Webber looked so perplexed that Barnes wanted to smile but felt a straight face was the diplomatic option. The Ethics Committee had given the green light to the project but that cut no ice with the hospital administration. This was a state-funded hospital, a place driven by budgets and funding directives going back through layers of bureaucracy to cabinet level. It was like a train – on straight lines that never deviated from the health policy laid down by career civil servants. Like all institutions, it existed as much to serve itself as the powerless patients who poured through it day after day.

'No, it's not a joke,' Barnes answered. 'It's a serious research project which has gone beyond the laboratory stage and can now deliver some worthwhile services to the transplant program.'

This had been a pleasant conversation up until now, thought Webber. He liked Barnes, in spite of all the media publicity generated by the heart team. But publicity was something any civil servant could do without and this latest project would have tabloids worldwide snapping at his heels. A pity JJ hadn't been a bit more informative when he told him the Ethics Committee had given Barnes's donor-pool project the go-ahead. A 'donor pool' sounded fairly conservative and made good sense in terms of transplant surgery but this idea was right off the wall – a ward full of warmed-up corpses? The Department of Health would have his backside on a plate if he let this happen.

After a full hour of discussion, Barnes gradually broke down Webber's resistance and he finally agreed that a section of the old building used during the war, but since deserted, could be used to 'keep corpses alive', as he expressed it. 'But you'll have to renovate and equip it at your own cost,' he stressed.

God knew where the money would come from, Barnes mused. Perhaps Kapinsky's benefactor would see them right.

After the tussle with Webber, the next hurdle was the heart team. Barnes knew he needed their co-operation if the project was to have any chance of success. Obviously he would have to select the information and drip feed it to them. The black box concept shouldn't cause any problems. No need to tell everyone that it contained a baboon brain. It was enough that the Ethics Committee was fully informed.

He called a meeting in his office to discuss staff participation. The meeting was to take place just before lunch. Few people could analyse intellectually on an empty stomach. He wanted agreement, not argument.

The full staff attended, all but Alex Hobbs who was occupied in the intensive care unit. Also invited were Dr Ohlsen and the head of the nursing staff, Sister Julie Meadows. Without the support of Sister Meadows he might as well try to walk on water, thought Barnes.

Time was running out for Karen. He and Kapinsky had to move fast if there was to be any hope of saving her. Without a properly equipped ward and some trained staff they could never hope to keep her on the new brain-support system. This meeting was vital.

Kapinsky sat next to him – keenly observed by the nursing staff who rarely saw him and regarded him as a bit of a mystery. The close quarters and the overcrowding in Barnes's office gave a sense of urgency to the situation. No bad thing, thought Barnes. Medical people tend to respond well to emergencies. He decided to keep it brief and allow questions to come up later when they were already launched on the project. He needn't have worried. It was a walkover. Staff proved so stimulated by the idea of taking a procedure from the realm of pure research into medical practice that they almost clamoured to be included.

From the moment he outlined Kapinsky's initial line of research they were hooked. His description of Kapinsky's 'brain mediation system' caused Des Louw's eyes to light up. When he emphasized the clinical applications, backed up by Kapinsky doing what Barnes called his 'up shirt and flash it' routine, there was a round of applause. This was too good to be true, thought Barnes, and decided it was time to put across the hard part.

'Right at the start, I want to warn you that this will entail extra hours of your time, in addition to the heavy workload you are already carrying.' There were groans all round, followed by grins of acceptance. Next he had expected some objection to the use of the deserted building for ward space but his staff barely blinked. 'We'll occupy the fourth floor and, as seven is my lucky number, our ward will be known as D7, just to give it a title for the bureaucrats to find in their records.' Everyone laughed. In their minds D7 was a reality. All that remained was to impress on them the need for confidentiality.

Each staff member signed an undertaking, witnessed by Barnes, never to divulge information on any aspect of the project. Some eyebrows were raised when he produced a large Bible and asked each staff member to swear an oath never to reveal information on ward D7 or its incumbents.

'Jesus, a bit melodramatic, isn't it?' Kapinsky said in his ear.

'You, too,' Barnes replied, placing Kapinsky's left hand on the book, and raising his other hand. 'Repeat after me. I do solemnly swear . . .'

Nat Ferreira wanted to know how the patients in ward D7 would be fed. Barnes explained that a fine silastic tube would be passed through the nose into the stomach. Such a tube would be well tolerated and cause little or no irritation. The hospital dietician, he told Ferreira, had formulated a special liquid feed that would be dripped continuously into the stomach. It contained all the essential vitamins, minerals, amino acids and calories to prevent the patients from going into catabolic state and burning up their own tissues. 'The dietician has assured me that this feed will allow patients to gain weight rather than wasting away,' said Barnes.

He told them that Dr Ohlsen had volunteered to be in charge of ventilation. As the patients did not have a cough reflex they would be unable to clear secretions from their bronchial tubes in the normal way and regular suction would be part of the duties of nursing staff. 'Dr Ohlsen is in favour of maintaining a soft intratracheal tube through the mouth but it may well be that a tracheostomy would mean fewer complications,' he added.

Although he didn't say so, Barnes hoped that the baboon brain would ensure hormone control of the body to the extent that spontaneous respiration would return.

Sister Meadows voiced her fear that, due to a shortage of trained staff, she could spare only a few nurses for the project and position changes would not be done often enough to prevent bed sores. She looked pleased when Barnes said he had sufficient funds to supply each patient with a computer-controlled water-bed, automatically inflating and deflating in a changing pattern to ensure there were no long-term areas of pressure on the patient's body. 'Nurses will only be needed to suction the patients regularly and wash them once a day,' he told her. 'Oh – I should also tell you that because we have arranged for automatic drug administration, through a computer-related perfusion pump, there is no need for more than one nurse on duty.'

It was a pleased and excited group that eventually broke for lunch, buzzing with ideas and eager to get to grips with this new medical procedure. Barnes felt weary and leaned back in his chair, his eyes closed. He had spent so much of the day pushing his ideas to different people, beginning with Mike Webber, that he felt exhausted.

Kapinsky's voice jerked him to attention. 'You've been so occupied in making sure that your little floozie stays around that you've forgotten we have equally important things to do.' Barnes was instantly angry. The completely unnecessary jibe at his relationship with Karen was typical of Kapinsky in one of his bloody-minded moods. Something must have upset him this morning. Perhaps he hadn't given him enough of the credit when talking to the staff. Bugger it, I'm sick of pandering to his bloody small-boy whims, thought Barnes, and opened his mouth for a blunt reply.

Kapinsky jumped in first. 'I spend a lot of time and energy, and money, producing tolerant baboons at your request. Now it's time you got your side of the act together.'

'What?' Barnes was genuinely puzzled.

'The heart supply, for Chrissake. Have they stopped hanging people?'

The trap doors flew open with a bang and five bodies hurtled down into the room where Barnes, Dr Rood and two warders were waiting. The ropes around their necks jerked them to a sudden halt. Four hung almost motionless but for the swing of the rope. One went into the *danse macabre*, legs scything in little circles, searching for the support that wasn't there.

It was just on a week since Kapinsky had complained they were doing nothing to research his ideas on implanting the hearts of executed prisoners in tolerant baboons to test their ability to protect the heart muscle. Barnes was 'lucky', the chief warder told him when he called. Five healthy young black males were waiting to be hanged. With the permission of the relatives he could have the hearts.

The bodies steadied after the first wild swings. The raw smell of faeces filled the air. These impromptu donors had been in the prime of life, thought Barnes. Now they were paying for doing only what their culture and beliefs demanded of them. Yesterday afternoon he had met the bewildered relatives after they had said farewell to their sons for the last time. At first resenting his request to sign consent papers, they demanded an explanation for their sons' death. Why, they asked, did the white man want to kill their sons for obeying the command of the witch-doctor?

The village headman had become sick, they told him. The witch-doctor had said that the only medicine which could save their chief must come from the fresh liver and heart of a human being. At a village meeting, the elders had selected the five young men for the task of finding the body parts. That afternoon they had set off for another *kraal* where they caught a young boy herding some goats. He was dragged into the bush where his throat was cut, his liver and heart removed, and the organs taken immediately to the waiting witch-doctor. The headman recovered almost immediately. How could that be a bad thing?

A month later the police arrested all five and charged them with murder. Puzzled, the five pleaded not guilty.

The relatives told Barnes that for centuries ritual killings such as this had been a part of tribal life. The victim died a noble death and his spirit would rest with those of his fore-fathers. Because of the boy's sacrifice the headman's life had been saved. Now the white man wanted to hang their sons for doing what the elders had told them to do. Their children, they said, could not refuse such a request from the elders.

Barnes genuinely sympathized with them. The white man, he explained, did not always know black customs and made his laws without asking the black man what he wanted.

The group debated for at least twenty minutes, gesticulating, sometimes all talking at once, sometimes listening to one speaker. At last they stopped and looked at him. The oldest, a frail, grey-haired old man, told him they had decided. None wanted their son's heart removed from his body. How, he asked Barnes, could they go into the other world to meet the ancestors if they had no hearts?

Barnes hadn't hired a private jet and flown all the way to Pretoria just to take no for an answer. 'Consider this,' he told them.

'White people also use the flesh of others to make strong medicine.'

'Hau!' exclaimed the old man, and translated for the others. There were looks of astonishment all round. The difference, Barnes explained, was that whites did not kill people for that purpose. The organs were taken only after death to be used as medicine. 'If you allow me to take the heart of one of your sons I will use it to heal another sick person.' He failed to tell them that it was going to be placed inside the body of a baboon. There was another round of discussion. After a while they informed Barnes that they could not reach a consensus.

He could see that it would not take much more to persuade them. He decided to try once more. 'You told me that the child from whom your sons removed the heart and liver for medicine died a noble death. For this reason his spirit will go to meet his forefathers. Through their noble gift your children will also go to the land where their ancestors are.' The group huddled together again. This time the discussion was much shorter before Barnes was informed that they all agreed.

Fortunately he had with him the forms to be signed so outside the prison with its high red brick walls and heavy wooden gate they made the crosses that gave Barnes the necessary permission.

Samuel was waiting gloved and gowned. It had been a major hurdle getting him to come. Unexpectedly, he hadn't wanted to hear of it. Even when Barnes pointed out that operating on human bodies was his next big step as a doctor, he had seemed almost afraid. He had run through several feeble excuses, unable to tell Barnes he had enough troubles on his mind with Kalolo and the apeman without adding the souls of hanged men.

Barnes had tried his persuasive best, reassuring him that he would not have to see the executions. The covered bodies would be brought into a separate operating room after death and there would be no need even to see the faces. All to no avail. It had looked as if he would be carrying out the work on his own.

Samuel had looked genuinely afraid and Barnes wondered if, perhaps, he was treading on some tribal taboo here. If he twisted the man's arm to make him come along he'd probably be bloody useless anyway. He resigned himself to the inevitable.

'Hmm, I suppose I have to accept your refusal, Boots,' he said. 'I leave on Thursday. Let me know if you change your mind before then – I really do think you'd find the work interesting.'

Samuel had nodded without speaking.

'Dr Kapinsky will oversee the routine work while I'm away,' Barnes had added as he turned to go. 'He also needs some extra help in the animal room. You'll enjoy that.'

Samuel's face had been a study in alarm, eyes standing out of his head. He could not have imagined anything worse. He and Kapinsky had not crossed paths since that terrible night. Now he would be expected to spend time alone with him. Better to go to Pretoria and take his chances with dead murderers.

'Dr Barnes,' he had said, rasping the words out from a dry throat, 'I have heard much about the prison and the hangings. I know that many black men die there. I am afraid to go but I will do this thing for you.'

Barnes had hidden his delight. Clearly Boots's dislike of Kapinsky was stronger than he had thought. He had explained that he could not manage alone without wasting precious time. He would inject the heparin and massage the heart to stop the blood from clotting, all between the time the body was lowered from the rope until the heart was removed. All Boots had to do was to be ready to take out the heart.

Samuel had been both thrilled and fearful: this would indeed be a great step forward in his medical career but was he risking even more by cutting out a newly dead heart from a murderer?

Now here he was, ready to do the work. The awful slamming noise in the room next door left him in no doubt what it was. It meant that five men had just died in there. A shudder jarred him at the thought. He would have fled the building if he had known where to go, but this was a prison and not a place for a black man to be running around in. He was safer staying close to Dr Barnes.

Dr Rood moved a wheeled platform with steps at one end in front of the hanging bodies. All gyrations had stopped and the limbs were still, the bodies just turning slightly on the ropes. Rood mounted the platform and placed his stethoscope on the chest of each body in turn. Barnes felt his impatience grow. Time was his enemy here. Every second counted. Yet the old bugger was doing it by the book, determined to go through this archaic routine, checking for life in a body that was disconnected from its brain.

Rood checked the third body twice, turned to Barnes and said, 'This one is ready for you,' and signalled to the two warders.

Almost immediately the body was lowered and laid out on the platform. At Barnes's request the hood, handcuffs and prison shirt were removed. He found a vein and injected the heparin, then vigorously applied external massage to the heart area to circulate the anti-coagulant. Taking the hood off had been a mistake. Boots would certainly crack if he saw the distorted features of the hanged man, thought Barnes. He tried to close the eyelids but the eyeballs were bulging so far out of the sockets that it was impossible. The swollen tongue, almost blue-black in colour, protruded from the open mouth. There was a burn mark from the noose around the neck which had been stretched to an unnatural length.

A brief word to the warders saw the hood drawn swiftly on again, and the body was lifted onto a trolley and wheeled through double doors to where Samuel was waiting.

His face was blank. He took the little dish of spirits and iodine, clamped a gauze swab into the forceps and was suddenly transformed into a working surgeon interested only in the job at hand. Barnes noted the change immediately. He started to scrub but by the time he had drawn on his gloves, Samuel had already draped the operative field and exposed the chest. He ripped down the centre of the breastbone with the circular saw, clamped it open and slit the pericardial sac containing the heart. Barnes moved in and, working together, they quickly perfused it for five minutes with a cold saline solution, which contained drugs to paralyse the heart muscle and protect it from the effects of lack of oxygen. The heart was removed and placed in a sterile plastic bag and packed in the specially adapted transporter on a bed of ice.

By the time Barnes was ready to leave, Samuel had wired the donor's sternum together and with a continuous suture closed the skin. Barnes felt a flicker of impatience when Samuel insisted they replace the shirt on the corpse. He was working to a tight time schedule.

Dumping their theatre gear and equipment in a heap, he and Samuel left the building almost at a run. On the way they passed the prison chapel. It was full almost to overflowing with relatives and friends of the dead men, voices raised in a hymn. Despite the need for haste, Barnes stopped, transfixed by the singing. Backed by the sonorous tones of an organ, deep male voices harmonized perfectly with the high-pitched sound of the women. It was a haunting requiem for the newly dead.

Samuel touched his arm urgently and Barnes shuddered. He shook himself to get rid of the chill that penetrated his bones.

Carrying the heart in the double-handled transporter the two men climbed into their waiting car, which moved off immediately, behind a police escort. The siren blaring, which caused all other traffic to pull over, they made it in good time to the airport. Pausing only to thank their escort, they boarded the private jet without formalities. As soon as the pilot had gained height and set course, Barnes rang the hospital from his seat phone and asked for Des Louw. 'We'll be there in two hours,' he told him. 'Prep the animal and start cutting in ninety minutes.' He settled back in his seat and looked at his watch. Not bad, he thought. It was exactly forty-five minutes since the executioner's trap door had opened.

Samuel was staring out at the passing cloudscape, his face wreathed in smiles. As a child, the nuns had told him about these machines that could fly without flapping their wings, but he had never – even in his wildest dreams – imagined that one day he would sit in one, and see the clouds below him.

'What?' Barnes asked, wondering what it was that Boots found amusing.

Samuel focused back on him. He couldn't tell Dr Barnes that he felt safe from Kalolo up here above the clouds. 'Very beautiful, the clouds,' he said. He meant it. Somehow they formed a barrier between him and the evil forces that waited for him on the ground.

Barnes grinned. It was nice to see Boots smile. He hadn't been doing much of that lately. 'You're right,' he said. 'This is high living, in more ways than one. Maybe we should do it more often.'

They touched down at Cape Town airport just over an hour and a half later and taxied to where a commercial helicopter waited, blades already turning. Ten minutes later they dropped onto the helipad at the hospital where Kapinsky met them in his car and rushed them to the medical school barely five hundred metres away.

In the lab the baboon was already on the table, chest opened and circulation connected to the heart-lung machine, ready to receive the heart of a man executed three hours before and over a thousand kilometres away.

Samuel scrubbed and gowned himself to help Des Louw. The donor heart was soon expertly stitched into place next to the baboon heart, so that both could share the circulation. As soon as the last sutures were in place the clamps were removed and both hearts beat in perfect rhythm.

'Bloody marvellous,' said Barnes, observing from the head of the table.

'Well, we now know we can restart a heart removed a few hours earlier from a donor in another city, but how are we to determine the extent to which it will carry full circulation?' asked Des Louw, ever cautious.

'Good question,' Kapinsky chipped in.

Barnes felt almost gleeful. It was nice to have the answers for a change. 'I've already thought of that,' he said. Louw wrinkled his brows above the mask and waited. 'You, Dr Louw, will attach two electrodes to the baboon heart and bring the connecting leads out through the skin. In a few weeks' time we will use these electrodes to fibrillate the heart. In that way we can study the output of the donor heart on its own.'

'You mean, we can simply stop the baboon heart at will by applying a current through the electrodes, almost as if we were switching it off?'

'Elementary, Dr Louw,' said Barnes.

They all laughed, including Louw who thought it a brilliant means of monitoring donor heart behaviour.

'In addition, we'll monitor rejection by taking weekly tissue samples from the heart. That way we can put Dr Kapinsky's theory of the tolerant baboon to the test.'

'There will be no rejection. Of that I assure you,' said Kapinsky, looking around the table. 'If this animal did not reject human skin it will certainly not reject a human heart.'

CHAPTER 22

'Rodney, I'm sorry to have to make this call but we cannot keep Karen indefinitely in the trauma unit. You know these wards are for acute cases, and Karen has been here now for nearly three months. Have you made arrangements to accommodate her elsewhere?'

It was the call he'd been dreading. Andy Anderson sounded apologetic but firm. He would move her this week, thought Barnes. The maintenance department had just finished repainting ward D7. Plumbing and electrical wiring had already been checked and the floor-covering would go in tomorrow.

'Thank you, Andy,' said Barnes. 'I have plans to move her this week. I'll be visiting this afternoon and will talk it over with her.'

Professor Anderson put down the phone, not sure that he'd heard correctly. A slip of the tongue, he decided. Surely Barnes had meant he was going to talk it over with *him*.

On arrival at the trauma unit, Barnes went straight to Karen's ward. He found her unattended. Secretions had built up in her upper windpipe and she needed suctioning. He disconnected the ventilator and connected a clean catheter to the suction machine to clear her respiratory passages. Throughout the operation she did not cough or breathe. He reconnected the machine and was suddenly overwhelmed with a feeling of defeat. The elation of the past few days had gone. The successful transplant to the baboon, which had kept him buoyed up until a few moments ago, now tasted like ashes in his mouth. None of it meant anything while the woman he loved was wasting away in this bed.

He stripped off the covers and checked her condition. She

had pressure sores on both heels and a larger area of inflammation just over the sacrum. He so wanted her to return to the beautiful person he once knew yet she was rotting before his eyes.

He replaced the covers and tucked her in, placing the clawlike hands gently under the top sheet. Something was trying to push itself into his consciousness. He resisted it, keeping his mind blank while he fussed around the bed, checking ventilator connections, the drip stand. At last he sat down and allowed the thought to grow in his mind. The ward of the living dead was probably not necessary. The transplanted donor heart so far had shown no sign of rejection and, if this proved a viable option, human organs could be successful stored in Kapinsky's tolerant baboons. Financially, morally and ethically it was preferable to have human organs preserved by a living baboon than a brain-dead human.

Oh, God, if anybody else realized this Karen was doomed! He would have to move her quickly to ward D7 and connect her circulation to the transgenic animal.

He kissed her forehead and left. As he walked away he noticed a faint, vaguely familiar smell. He had reached the connecting passageway to the main hospital before he identified it. It was the factor of the morgue, creeping into his loved one's bedroom and stealing her away from him.

He hurried on. Now, more than ever, she needed to be connected to a living brain so that her system could begin to purify itself. Back in his office he rang Kapinsky and told him he wanted to connect Karen to the brain-mediation system as soon as possible. 'You lucky bastard,' said Kapinsky, sounding cheerful. 'I received the frame for the baboon head only today. It will take a few hours to check the black-box connections and the clamps to fit the baboon head to the frame. By tomorrow morning it should be ready for our first patient. Goodbye.'

The receiver clicked. Barnes called Alex Hobbs and asked him to prepare ward D7 for its first patient, ringing off before the junior surgeon could ask who it was. That evening he sat alone at his dining table. It was set for two, as it had been since the day of Karen's accident. He was expecting a visitor, he always told his maid. He poured two glasses of wine and placed one at the setting opposite him.

'To you, my darling,' he said, holding up his glass. The separation was soon to end. Soon, he knew, Karen would return to him.

The group stood around Karen's bed. Barnes had signed the consent form that would allow the medical staff to disconnect all support systems and declare her legally dead. Professor Arnold de Wet, the head of neurosurgery, and one of his registrars were present to do the examination and check that brain activity had ceased.

A pompous little man with a great sense of his own importance, de Wet was not one of Barnes's favourite people. He insisted on his staff staying a few paces behind him on ward rounds, never answered a phone call personally and saw no one without a set appointment, regardless of urgency. Barnes wondered if he would deign to speak to God without prior notice.

De Wet took a cursory look at Karen. 'Will she be used as a donor?'

The thought hadn't occurred to Barnes. But he knew he couldn't bear to remove the heart of the woman he loved and transplant it into a stranger. 'I'm not sure, Professor. I couldn't really answer that,' he said, almost stuttering.

'Well, if there's any reason to believe that she'll donate organs then members of the transplant team cannot be part of the declaration of death – that is the law,' said de Wet, more pompous than ever.

Barnes was lost for words. This development was so unexpected. What could he say? He was not just a member of the transplant team he was also Karen's guardian and lover.

'Don't be a pain, Arnie,' said Anderson, stepping forward to intercede in what looked like a stand-off. He needed this ward urgently but he could see that Barnes wasn't quite coping with de Wet, whom he privately considered little more than a bullying arsehole. 'Dr Barnes has been deeply involved with this patient and I'm sure he'll ensure that all arrangements are in her best interests,' he added, placatingly.

De Wet said nothing, just looked at Barnes and pushed out his chin. Every department had its damn fool and as far as he was concerned Anderson was one of them. If he didn't understand the law he, Professor Arnold de Wet, the country's top neurosurgeon, was not about to give lessons.

Barnes left the room and went to sit in Anderson's office. Why the hell had de Wet been called in? The only questions this morning were whether supportive therapy was of value and, if not, should it be continued. Surely Anderson was the man qualified to answer them. Fear closed his throat and he could hardly breathe. Before de Wet's arrival this morning, Anderson had said that Karen had passed the point of possible recovery. The best outcome for her, he said, was to disconnect the ventilator and allow her to die.

Barnes's silence made it clear this wasn't the outcome he wanted. In that case, said Andy, the solution was to have her declared brain-dead and notified as a donor. Under such circumstances they could continue ventilation.

Loneliness settled on Barnes like cold mist. He tried to drag his mind from the ward where de Wet would already have disconnected the ventilator. The pompous little bastard would wait the regulation three minutes to ensure she could not breathe on her own. Once satisfied that she had lost the breathing reflex, he would reconnect the ventilator before her heart stopped from lack of oxygen.

He tried to think of happier times, searching for memories of Karen as she once was. Suddenly, wonderfully, she came to him in vivid colour. She was skipping happily in the shallows at the beach, her skirt held high, kicking the foam towards him and urging him to join her. Should he let her go? But only the other day in the ward she had said she wanted to be with him. Death was so final. He felt sure that, once the baboon brain began to secrete hormones into her circulation, consciousness would return. Even if only for a brief moment, he would have a chance to tell her how much he loved her.

'Dr Barnes? Dr Barnes!' She was calling him. That was strange, she had always used his first name. 'Dr Barnes. You're wanted urgently. She has arrested . . . Dr Barnes?' A hand shook him awake. He took in the look on the nurse's face at a glance and leapt up.

A few strides took him down the passageway and through the door into Karen's ward. She was lying face upwards, connected to the ventilator. He looked at the screen above her bed and saw the jagged lines: she had gone into ventricular fibrillation. Her heart was no longer pumping and had lapsed into a quivering mass of muscle fibres, unable to synchronize into a single rhythm.

De Wet and his registrar were standing by, de Wet wearing a look of satisfaction. Anderson was on the other side of the bed, clearly perturbed. Barnes's world went into slow motion. She is dying, he thought, and no one is doing anything to help.

With effort, he took hold of himself. 'Can't you see she's in fibrillation?' he shouted at de Wet. 'Do something. The heart must be started quickly.'

De Wet smiled and said nothing. Something broke in Barnes. Medical rules, professional ethics, procedural agreements went out of the window. He moved towards de Wet. 'You've killed her, you bastard. Get out! *Get out!*' he yelled.

De Wet and his registrar moved quickly to the door where he turned for a last look at Barnes and left.

Suddenly calm and determined, Barnes asked for the defibrillator and began pushing regularly on Karen's breastbone to get the blood moving again in the coronary arteries. 'Give her ten ccs of bicarbonate, please, and put some electrolyte paste on the paddles.'

Anderson and his staff nurse rushed to help. 'Ready,' announced Anderson, holding the paddles.

Barnes stopped massaging, placed one paddle on the side of

Karen's left breast – now withered to little more than a flap of skin – and the other on the front of the heart. 'Ready,' he replied.

The frail body jerked and the back arched as the current slammed into the muscles. Barnes looked at the monitor. The heart began to beat. He knew she wouldn't let him down. It was more proof that she wanted to be with him.

They watched as her circulation improved rapidly. Within a few minutes she was stable. Barnes said, 'Andy, I'd like her transferred immediately to my ward if that's OK with you.'

Anderson nodded. 'She's been declared brain-dead so she's in your care now. Do you want her to go to your intensive care unit?'

'No, to ward D7.'

Anderson looked puzzled. He had never heard of ward D7.

'Don't worry,' said Barnes, reading his thoughts. 'My staff will fetch her. Thank you for all you've done for her, my friend.' He shook Anderson's hand and left him, still puzzled by the heart team's sudden acquisition of a new ward.

That night Barnes hardly slept. Tomorrow, after connection to the brain-mediation system, Karen would be on her way to recovery. He kept seeing mental images of her alive and well, working at her desk, running along the beach, smiling, healthy and happy.

He went over the operation again and again. As they were not going to remove the brain but use the complete head of the baboon, the operation was now much simplified. He would start by exposing the arteries and veins in the animal's neck. The veins would then be cannulated with hollow tubes and connected to the venous inlet of the little portable membrane oxygenator that would be primed with 200 ccs of Karen's own blood. The arterial return would be completed by cannulating the two arteries and connection through a small pump to the arterial well.

Despite his lack of sleep he was up early. After a shower and shave he felt refreshed and eager to start the day. He dressed and took his cup of coffee to the balcony for his morning lift – the sight of Table Mountain appearing out of the dawn mists on the bay.

A little music, he thought. Just what we need to complete this perfect morning, the first day of the rest of our lives together. He switched on a portable radio and found it tuned to a news channel. He was about to retune when he stopped and listened to the announcer.

'Civil rights lawyer Joe Dubofsky was gunned down in front of the Royal Hotel in Cape Town early today. He was in the Mother City to defend two black men charged with the car-bomb explosion outside Parliament last year. Police say the assassination is similar to others carried out by right-wing para-military groups. The getaway car, an old Chevrolet without number plates, was followed by an eye-witness along the main road as far as the University of Cape Town medical school complex where he lost sight of it. Police are appealing to anyone who may have information that would help in the investigation.'

'Kapinsky!' exclaimed Barnes, suddenly overwhelmed by a fear of impending disaster. Who else could it have been but the Pole? He was an extreme racist, never hesitating to show his resentment of liberals, Jews, blacks and anyone else who didn't support his theories of racial superiority.

Barnes's mind raced. Everything fell into place. Kapinsky had isolated himself in his lab where his life could be private. His barring of everyone, including Barnes himself, from his special animal room and his mysterious Friday-night missions. It all added up. He had the perfect set-up to hide weapons, explosives and whatever else was needed for his campaign of murder. It must be Kapinsky, but for God's sake why now? Why prejudice years of research just at the moment when all their work was about to come to fruition? Right now his presence and knowledge were essential. It meant life or death for Karen. And beyond that nothing mattered.

He dropped his coffee cup in the sink, where it shattered, grabbed his briefcase and ran.

The elevator seemed to take for ever to reach the basement garage. He reached his car, hurled his briefcase inside and himself after it. In almost the same movement he switched on the engine and gunned the vehicle out of the building on shrieking tyres, cursing himself for not having taken more notice of Kapinsky's weird behaviour.

If Kapinsky was arrested and locked up, the ward of the living dead was a non-starter. And all the other research projects would come to a stop. Kapinsky's presence was essential. How could he, Barnes, have been so stupid, so trusting? At the very least he should have insisted that Kapinsky train an assistant . . .

He berated himself all the way to the medical school, slowing only to scan a news poster which read: MEDICAL DOCTOR PRIME SUSPECT. How could they suspect a doctor just because his car was last seen near the school? Or did the police know something they hadn't yet disclosed? He put his foot down, his fear growing.

The medical school complex was overrun with police and police vehicles. There was even a car parked in his bay, blue light flashing.

Barnes pulled into Professor Thomas's empty space – he was on a week's leave and unlikely to turn up to claim it. Perhaps just as well, he thought, otherwise the twisted old bastard might be here in person leading the hunt to Kapinsky.

Suddenly the missing piece of the puzzle fell into place. Thomas had been the informer all along. Barnes was sure that, when he had heard the news this morning, Thomas had made an anonymous phone call to the police informing them of Kapinsky's mysterious behaviour during the past few months. That was all they needed to know. The police would have correlated this information with what they may have obtained from other Research Block staff.

But why would Thomas, who had always labelled Kapinsky a Communist, point a finger at him when the man who was assassinated last night had belonged to the South African Communist Party? Barnes decided to go straight to the third floor to see if his suspicions were justified.

He was right. A uniformed policeman stood at the door and a man in plain clothes sat at Kapinsky's desk. There was no sign of Kapinsky himself. The cold hand gripping Barnes's heart suddenly squeezed.

'I am Detective Sergeant Du Toit,' the plain-clothes policeman said, speaking English with a heavy Afrikaans accent.

Barnes decided to bluff it out. 'Yes, Sergeant, what can I do for you?'

'Do you work here?' Du Toit asked.

'I'm Dr Barnes, the head of Cardiac Surgery, and these are my department's research laboratories.'

'Sorry to disturb you, Dr Barnes,' said the sergeant, looking not at all sorry. 'We're looking for Dr Novitsky.'

'There's no Dr Novitsky in this department, Sergeant. You must have made a mistake,' said Barnes, looking levelly at du Toit. The bastards didn't even know Kapinsky's name. Maybe the rest of their information was wrong. His hopes leapt.

At that moment, however, the policeman at the door entered, leading Samuel by the arm. 'This one says there is a Dr *Kapinsky* who is working with the baboons in the animal room next to his laboratory but the door is locked and only he has the key.'

Barnes saw that Boots was terrified.

Du Toit turned to Barnes. 'Dr Barnes, you say you are in charge here. We need to go into that room and speak to the suspect. He could be making a getaway from behind closed doors.'

Barnes had a sudden crazy impulse to laugh at the sergeant's English, but immediately suppressed it. He had to play it straight if he was to talk them out of arresting Kapinsky. 'You can go in if you sign a form that you're doing it at your own risk,' he told Du Toit.

'Risk? Dr Barnes, our job is to protect the public regardless of risk. Signing a form doesn't change the risk,' said Du Toit, looking down his nose at Barnes.

'It does for me, Sergeant Du Toit,' said Barnes. 'It means that you cannot hold us responsible for any deadly disease you may pick up by breathing the air in the animal room.'

Du Toit's expression changed, and he glowered at the policeman with Samuel. 'We can wait, doctor,' he said.

'Does that mean I can go?'

'Yes, but we may need you for questioning. Where can we find you?'

Barnes was about to answer when the door to the animal room opened and Kapinsky came out, locking it behind him. He was wearing the blue overall of a cleaner and showed no reaction when he saw the policemen. Barnes moved in to warn him. 'Good morning, Louis. This is Sergeant Du Toit of the police. He would like to speak to you.'

Kapinsky seemed unworried, asked the sergeant to move from his desk and sat down. 'What do you want to know? I can't give you much time.'

Barnes was nonplussed. Either Kapinsky was a fine actor or he was genuinely unaware of the trouble he was in.

The sergeant gave a brief signal to the uniformed constable, who produced a notebook and took up a stance at the door. Du Toit wasted no time in getting to the point. 'What do you know about the murder of Joe Dubofsky?'

'Who?'

Kapinsky looked puzzled. Barnes's stomach began to uncoil.

'Joe Dubofsky,' Du Toit repeated. 'He was shot early this morning outside the Royal Hotel.'

'Why should I know about it?' said Kapinsky, looking irritated.

'We have reason to believe you could be involved.'

Kapinsky stood up before replying. 'Gentlemen, you are wasting my time and yours. I was in this laboratory the whole night preparing for a very important experiment which we hope to carry out today – that is, if the police will leave us alone.' He moved towards his living quarters.

'Not so fast, doctor. If you were here the whole night, as you claim, then I'm sure you can verify it.'

'No. No one can. I was here alone unless you count the animals and they cannot speak,' said Kapinsky. Under his breath he added, 'Not yet, anyway.'

'That is convenient for you, doctor. Or maybe unfortunate. You say you were in the laboratory the whole night, you sleep here too?'

'Yes, I do.'

'Don't give me that bullshit,' said Du Toit, threateningly.

Kapinsky erupted. 'Who do you think you're talking to, you uneducated buffoon?' he snapped at Du Toit.

Barnes felt it was time to cool things down. 'Sergeant. Dr Kapinsky has told you he was in the laboratory all night and knows nothing about the death of Dubofsky. If you have no further questions then I think you should leave.'

The sergeant picked up his hat from the desk and looked at Kapinsky.

'Yes, I know. Don't leave town,' said Kapinsky sarcastically. 'For your information I'm going nowhere – at least, not until this project is complete and that could take years.'

The sergeant said nothing and left, ushering the uniformed constable ahead of him.

Barnes watched them until they had left the building, then closed the door and turned to Kapinsky. 'Louis, when I heard the news this morning I was worried you might be involved. The getaway car was last seen near the medical school and I suppose that's why the police are turning everything upside down.'

'I have better things to do than shoot a Jewish Commie but whoever did it has done the country a great favour,' said Kapinsky, with a lop-sided grin.

Barnes felt the uncertainty creep back. 'Maybe we should postpone the operation until tomorrow evening,' he suggested, unwilling to probe further.

'I'm ready, Rodney, but if you want to wait that's fine by me.'

'The place is swarming not only with cops but also with

journalists. It might not be the best time to take the head off the baboon. The journalists could be a greater danger than the police. What do you feel like?'

Kapinsky shrugged, clearly annoyed by his exchange with the sergeant. 'Rodney, I'm bloody tired. Do what the hell you like.'

It wasn't the right time to talk strategy with Kapinsky and Barnes decided to defer action. 'Sorry, Louis. Get some sleep if you can. I'll call you after lunch, if we can get the police invasion off the campus.'

Kapinsky grunted and headed for his quarters, and Barnes reckoned it was time for a look at ward D7 and a morning talk to Karen.

The police activity helped Samuel forget his troubles for a few hours. For one wonderful moment he had hoped they were going to take Kapinsky away but the policemen left without arresting him.

'What did you expect? Kapinsky is the wrong colour. They will never arrest a white man,' said Victor, when they sat down for lunch together.

Samuel had ruefully to accept once again that, indeed, white people stuck together. His fears now loomed above him like a shower of *assegai*s about to fall on his head. He had to talk to somebody, but Victor was a coloured, one of the half-breeds classed on a better pay scale than blacks. Most coloureds were better educated and lived under better conditions. If it came to a political showdown most would throw in their lot with the whites, thought Samuel. But if he did not share his fears with someone, he would go mad or kill himself. He could not carry this burden any longer.

'I have a problem, Victor,' he said, not looking up.

Victor liked Samuel. At first he had resented his rapid progress from cleaner to senior laboratory assistant and the obvious preference that Dr Barnes showed for his skills. But Victor had always found him hard-working and honest and, over the years, he had come to look on Samuel as a friend. Their cultures would never mix and he could not visit him in his township home without the risk of a street mugging, but he nevertheless enjoyed their talks together.

'What problem is that, Mr Mbeki?' he said jokingly, using the English Mr to show that Samuel was a surgeon.

'Please, Victor. I have much trouble. I need your help,' said Samuel.

Victor's face shadowed. This sounded serious. He couldn't imagine how a hard-working, thrifty non-drinker like Samuel could be in trouble. He sat down beside him and waited.

Samuel told him of his experiences over the past few months, his strong suspicions that a monster existed in the animal room, omitting only the story of the operation. He also told of his visits to the witch-doctor, the failure to find an article touched by the monster and the awful night when the creature had grabbed him in the animal room.

Victor listened, laughing once or twice, but when Samuel showed him the bite scars on his shoulder he whistled. 'Samuel, I have only heard gossip of something strange in the animal room but this is the first proof that there is something. There is no doubt that Dr Kapinsky speaks to something in there. Some of the other cleaners have heard him. We know there are no other people when he's there and the animals can't speak so it must be something he created, something he is teaching to talk.'

Like most of the Europeans, few coloureds believed in folk medicine, which made Victor sceptical of the witch-doctor. 'I do not believe the old joker can tell you anything by examining something that has been in touch with Kapinsky's creature. But if you have to take something to satisfy him why not a pair of Kapinsky's overalls? Surely when he handles the creature it must touch the overalls in places?'

Samuel jumped up. That was it! He could hardly believe the solution was so simple. He would take one of Kapinsky's overalls to Kalolo that night. He gabbled his thanks to an amused

Victor and rushed off to the laundry box where each day Kapinsky dumped his soiled lab clothes.

He was beside himself with relief when he found an overall he recognized as Kapinsky's amongst various other items. He stuffed it under his coat. Now he had what the old man wanted and he was soon to find out the truth.

Kalolo gave a shriek as the bones fell into a pattern across the overall spread on the floor in front of him. Samuel froze. The witch-doctor had been chanting in a strange language for almost thirty minutes, rocking on his haunches and nodding in rhythm.

Now the movement of his head had stopped and his eyes were fixed on the overall. 'I see it,' he croaked. 'Oh, spirits of the ancestors, protect us from this creation of the evil powers.'

'What do you see, Wise One?' asked Samuel, fearing to hear the answer.

'I see this apeman. He is standing on the feet of a man but the legs of a baboon.'

'His arms and hands. Can you see them too?'

'The hands are those of a man but the arms are those of an ape.'

So the thing that had reached up out of the open uterus had grabbed his head in the animal room, thought Samuel. 'Can you tell me more?' he asked, his fright ebbing.

The old man slowly slumped forward and Samuel had to jump up and stop him from falling on his face among the bones.

The old woman fussed in with a drinking bowl. 'You must leave him. Your questions are taking too much of his strength. Please go and take the evil clothing with you.'

Samuel rolled up the overall, stuffed it into a plastic carrier bag, and left. Even if the Old One had not given him a full description of the monster that Kapinsky was keeping in the laboratory he had at least confirmed his suspicions.

The next evening when Samuel arrived home he found the old woman sitting in front of his door, wailing. When she had calmed down she told him that the witch-doctor had died during the night. She had found him that morning, his body covered with bruises and scratches as if he had been attacked by some large animal.

'Kapinsky!' said Samuel. 'He must be sending his creature to kill everyone that knows of its evil presence.'

He gave the old woman some money and shooed her away. Once inside he locked his door and gave himself up to despair. If the witch-doctor could not protect himself against the creature then his own days were numbered.

CHAPTER 23

Six beds, three on each side, lined ward D7. Karen lay in the one in the far corner. The cup-shaped mattress held her body safely as it tilted slowly from side to side and from top to bottom in long, slow, rolling patterns. At the same time small areas of mattress changed in density, altering her body distribution and making sure that the pressure did not remain localized for too long in one area of her body. The computer-controlled water-beds were an idea that Kapinsky had picked up on one of his numerous visits to the Medical Library. 'I was scrolling through a list of research papers on caring for the unconscious patient and there it was,' he told Barnes. 'A paper by somebody in New Zealand. He got such good results that he handed the idea to a big mattress company and they played around with it. Here's the result – and they think they might be able to refine it even more,' he added, looking pleased. He demonstrated the bed by having Barnes lie in it while he put it through its paces. 'Look. Not only can it be programmed to tilt in any direction or in any pattern, the mattress is also sectioned into little cells each of which can be pressurized or depressurized in any combination you want. They call it the Electronic Nurse.'

Barnes enjoyed seeing Kapinsky in this mood. Always willing to show off a piece of successful research, he particularly enjoyed gadgets and was obviously delighted by the water-bed. 'This is excellent, Louis. It will certainly make all the difference to the care of our patients – but can we afford it? What does one of these things cost?' he asked, sitting up on the bed.

An arm and a leg, thought Kapinsky, but who cares? The addicts are paying. 'Our benefactor came up with the money and gave us the bed as a gift, with another two on order. You can't buy these off the shelf, you know,' he said, punching Barnes good-humouredly on the arm.

'Who is this mystery benefactor of ours?' Catching Kapinsky's mood of pleasure and excitement, Barnes wanted to thank their supporter for his generosity. 'What's his name? Do you have a number? I'd like to talk to him. I think it's time we showed our gratitude in some way . . .'

'Sorry, no can do,' Kapinsky said.

'What?'

'I told you, he wants to remain anonymous. I think he's afraid of ending up as a kind of target for every welfare scheme or request that comes along. He wants to choose his projects and I think we're very fortunate he's chosen us.'

'I can relate to that but I would like to ring him privately and thank him —'

'I've already done that,' Kapinsky cut in. 'He seems happy to leave it in my hands and I'd like to humour him. After all, it's his money and he can throw it around whatever way he chooses.'

'You're right,' said Barnes, feeling vaguely dissatisfied. 'Of course, there's always the problem of the annual hospital asset list. The bureaucrats like to know what's going on and, in particular, how much equipment each department has.'

'Bugger the bureaucrats. That's your job, Rodney. You figure out how to keep them off our backs. Just photocopy last year's list and send it back to them. They wouldn't know the difference even if it came up and bit them on the backside.'

That was the end of the conversation, with Kapinsky going into one of his lightning mood changes and refusing to talk further.

'And that's how we managed to make you so comfortable, my darling,' Barnes told Karen, on his first visit after her transfer from the trauma unit.

He looked around. The contractors had done a helluva job at short notice. The building had been repainted inside and out. Add the roof repairs, window replacements, floor-covering, plumbing and wiring and it must have cost a tidy bundle. Kapinsky had taken it on himself to arrange it all, and had said their philanthropic friend would pay for it. He made a mental note to ask to see the bill.

Karen's condition had improved noticeably. Her circulation and colour were better. There was no doubt she had been neglected in the trauma unit, thought Barnes, written off as a hopeless case and left to die. If it hadn't been for his daily visits and fierce insistence on improved nursing she would have become just another statistic. 'I'll never allow that to happen,' he assured her. He had already given detailed instructions to Des Louw on how this patient was to be treated.

In the corner of the ward, Sister Helen de Villiers sat at a brand new desk and busied herself with the ward's recently acquired computer-based filing system. She wasn't too sure whether the job was quite what she wanted. At first intrigued by what Rodney Barnes had told her, she had volunteered for duty in D7, only to find there was not only little work to do but also these disquieting daily interludes in which the surgeon came along to talk to a deeply unconscious patient.

'Sister!'

She looked up. Dr Barnes wanted her at the woman's bedside. She dropped everything and came immediately.

'Sister, I'd be grateful if you'd turn this bedcover round. It has the pattern running the wrong way and Mrs van der Walt prefers it the other way,' he told her, turning to croon to Karen, 'Don't you, darling?'

Years of nursing training helped Helen de Villiers suppress her puzzlement. If there was any pattern on the new, spotlessly white cover then it was hardly noticeable, and certainly not by a patient in a coma.

Barnes helped her turn the cover and muttered a few more endearments to the body on the bed. Karen was in wonderful pre-operative condition. Tonight he and Kapinsky would connect her to the brain-mediation system and tomorrow would be a turning point in her convalescence. He patted her hand, smiled at Helen and left.

Helen's anxiety intensified. Was something happening that she didn't know about? This patient could not recover but, then, hadn't Dr Barnes said she was part of a research project? Perhaps the one-sided conversation was part of the treatment. Helen shrugged off her uneasiness and went back to her filing.

Barnes decided to make another call at the laboratory to see if there had been any further police activity.

Des Louw, head down and striding out, almost knocked him over as the elevator doors opened. 'Sorry, sir,' he exclaimed.

'Not a problem. We'll get traffic lights fitted here.' Barnes grinned, adding, 'What's the hurry?'

'No hurry, just engrossed, I suppose. Something quite strange about the behaviour of the baboon that received the transplant of the last executed prisoner.'

'Oh, what's that?'

'Good recovery from the anaesthetic and all other signs are OK but there's a high level of agitation. Doesn't appear to be in pain – more emotional stress, if we can call it that. Keeps scrabbling at its neck as if trying to remove something. I gave it a mild sedative. I hope the reaction is transient.'

'Hmm, I'll take a look. Thank you, doctor,' said Barnes, and hurried to the basement where the other animals of the Department of Cardiac Surgery were housed.

He found the baboon sleeping, both forepaws held protectively around its neck. Kapinsky was nowhere to be seen. A glance at the clipboard showed almost perfect recovery and steady progress. He asked Victor to keep the animal under observation and left.

The baboon was carrying the heart of the executed killer, he told himself. That couldn't have any bearing on its present condition. After all, the heart was just a pump. And, anyway, there was nothing that could be done right now. But thoughts of the animal plagued him throughout the day and he couldn't shake off the feeling that he'd missed something. One day he would regret this.

'Why are you so damn nervous tonight?' Kapinsky asked, peering over Barnes's shoulder as he exposed the throat of the anaesthetized baboon and prepared to shave off the surrounding fur. His razor-work was inept and blood welled from several large nicks in the flesh. Kapinsky had selected this baboon as the most promising for the brain-mediation system and was feeling proprietorial.

'Louis, stop clucking around me like a hen. I'm going to cut its fucking head off and that's enough to make me nervous,' said Barnes, surprised at his own vehemence. He immediately tried a grin to make the words sound more in jest. They had been in the animal room theatre for more than an hour, preparing the scene for what he suddenly realized was the world's first brain transplant. It was to be carried out in two stages. The first involved removal of the baboon head, perfusing it with oxygenated blood and mounting it within the black box. The second would take place later when the box, connected to a portable perfusion system, would be installed in ward D7 for final connection to Karen's circulation.

As the minutes passed, he found that while Kapinsky became more intent and calm, he was growing more nervous by the minute. It was almost as if he was suffering from stage-fright. They had decided not to bring in any assistance for the late-night operation on the basis that the fewer people who knew what they were doing the better.

The shaving of the neck complete, Barnes marked his incisions, outlining the sleeve of skin which would be sutured over the stump at the base of the head.

Kapinsky needed no help in anaesthetizing the little baboon and he felt confident that Barnes could cannulate the neck vessels and connect them to the membrane oxygenator.

Taking up the scalpel, Barnes made a circular incision around the lower part of the neck, cutting exactly on the marked outline. He dissected the chosen area of skin off the neck muscle and flipped it back for later use. With blunt dissection, the internal jugular vein and carotid artery were exposed, first on the right and then on the left. The superficial veins were tied off and divided. The two veins were cannulated with thin plastic cannulae and joined with a Y-connector to the plastic tubing which led to the oxygenator. The carotid arteries were similarly treated and the line handed to Kapinsky for connection to the arterial output of the oxygenator.

'Start perfusion. Build it up slowly,' Barnes told him. While this was happening, he stitched the arterial and venous catheters to the deep tissues of the neck to immobilize them.

His next task was to detach the head from the trunk. Carefully dividing each neck muscle, he cauterized every bleeding point before moving on to the next incision. 'You can stop ventilation now. I'm going to cut through the trachea and oesophagus.'

Kapinsky complied. The whooshing of the ventilator stopped. The animal's chest quivered slightly and was still.

Each of the tubes from the windpipe and throat would be brought out through an opening on the skin flap so that secretions could be cleared by a suction pump on the outside of the black box. The cervical spine, cleared of all muscles, was now the only structure holding the head and neck onto the body. Barnes located the space between the lower cervical and upper thoracic vertebrae, and separated the spinal cord at a single cut. The baboon's body jerked as the nervous connection to its brain was severed. Spinal fluid, a straw-coloured clear liquid, immediately began to flow from the spinal column. Bleeding was also evident from the intervertebral arteries.

Barnes stopped the bleeding skilfully with two quick sutures and sewed a muscle flap tightly over the spinal canal to prevent any further leakage of fluid. He took great care, moving slowly from point to point, inspecting and cauterizing all bleeding points on the raw stump of the neck. Only when he was satisfied, did he turn down the flap of skin to cover the wound and suture it neatly into place.

When he finally stood upright and stretched, holding his gloved hands well clear, the operation was over. All that was left on the table was the baboon's head with the stump of the neck from which the venous and arterial catheters emerged. These were connected directly to the perfusion machine humming quietly on a stand. Kapinsky had already removed the headless trunk.

'It's a great pity we can't use the vital organs,' he said, on his return from the incinerator.

Barnes looked up but was too engrossed in a final check of the head to take notice.

'I was thinking, last night, we now have three sources of supply,' mused Kapinsky, half to himself.

'What's that?' Barnes asked, still examining the neck sutures.

'We have three kinds of donor for human recipients.'

Barnes went cold. So Kapinsky had also thought of it. 'What do you mean?' he asked, keeping his face casual while his heart began to thump.

'We have the human organs stored in the tolerant baboon. Then we can use the organs of brain-dead patients, such as Karen, kept in condition by means of the black box, and finally there is the transgenic baboon. The animal donor will be of immeasurable value in supplying organs that match in size for newborn children.' He looked at Rodney, still bent over the baboon head, and nudged him with an elbow. 'Think of it, Rod. We don't really need all that expensive bullshit we're putting into D7 if the other two sources prove cheaper.'

'Organs taken directly from the human donor will always be the best,' said Barnes, straightening and looking back at Kapinsky. It was high time to protect his interests.

'I'm not so sure about that, my friend,' said Kapinsky, warming to this subject. 'Genetic manipulation will eventually prove the answer. Remember, there will be no rejection when the animal organ is completely camouflaged and its presence cannot be detected by the patient's immune system.'

'Let's fix the head into the box,' said Barnes shortly. The Polish bastard was barging into sensitive areas.

Eyes gleaming, Kapinsky placed the black container on the table and removed the hinged door. Inside were a series of needle points, each capable of adjustment. Exactly placed according to measurements taken on the living baboon, each would penetrate to bone just under the skin and hold the head in place. Barnes gingerly supported the head while Kapinsky used a small electric screwdriver to tighten each screw. The eyes in the baboon's head began to blink. 'I think I'd better start the sedation before he bites my finger,' said Kapinsky, laughing.

A removable plastic dish was placed at the bottom of the box to contain the secretions from the trachea and gullet, and Kapinsky had positioned the head so that it faced the hinged door, 'Just in case it wants to look out occasionally,' he joked.

Barnes said nothing. Sometimes Kapinsky's humour was in the worst of taste.

Kapinsky moved the arterial and venous lines so that they exited through a small opening in the bottom of the door and then closed it. 'Now only the two of us know what is inside,' he remarked. He connected the heparin and protamine drips to the perfusion system and then symbolically dusted his gloved hands. 'Stage one complete, Rod. What's your program?'

'I have the operating room ready and the staff on stand-by for an early start tomorrow. Des Louw will have Karen prepped by the time you get the black box there. And that seems to cover everything.'

'Good. That gives us time to do a last-minute check on the head for bleeding or other problems,' replied Kapinsky. 'Any other points?'

'Yes,' said Barnes. 'Coffee – hot and black.'

'In my office. Give me a minute,' Kapinsky said, pulling off his gloves and heading for the animal room. He returned a few minutes later with two cups of coffee and a plate of sandwiches.

'You've got a kitchen in there?' asked Barnes, pointing to the door Kapinsky had locked behind him.

'Yes, I often prepare meals there. And, of course, feeds for the newly born transgenic baboons.'

'What else have you got in there?' Barnes tried to make the question sound casual.

'Nothing that you don't already know about,' said Kapinsky, quickly. 'Why the curiosity?'

Barnes put down his cup and faced Kapinsky. 'Your behaviour over the last few months worries me. You've just about withdrawn from the outside world. You don't allow anyone into the locked section of the animal house, and the rumours are flying thick and fast. Dammit, Louis, you must have noticed that you were the first suspect on the police list of enquiries.'

Kapinsky threw back his head and laughed. 'Firstly, rumours never worry me – particularly when they're generated by the half-wits who staff this building during the day.'

'But why have you become such a loner? It isn't healthy, Louis.'

'They probably said that about Michelangelo when he painted the ceiling of the Sistine Chapel.'

Barnes grinned at the comparison and Kapinsky laughed again. He seemed relaxed and clearly had no worries about the police presence in his laboratory that morning.

'My only weakness, or perhaps it's a strength, is that I do not trust anybody,' said Kapinsky slowly, sipping his coffee and staring into space.

Barnes said nothing, fearful of stopping his flow of thought.

'I moved in here to have more time for work,' added Kapinsky. 'You spend at least an hour a day travelling back and forth to the job, another hour on eating and about eight hours on sleep and bathing. That's ten out of the twenty-four hours in every day.' He paused and sipped his coffee again. 'Now, add that up and you have three thousand six hundred hours a year during which you're not producing anything. That's about a hundred and fifty days a year during which you're idle.'

'Shit, there's more to life than just work,' said Barnes, grinning at this outrageous view of sleep as an idle pastime.

'Not for me. Before the Communists killed my mother and father, I promised them that one day I would take my revenge for their deaths.'

Barnes felt a chill go through him. He put down his cup and looked at a stone-faced Kapinsky. The man clearly meant every word. 'Tell me, Louis. What do you mean by revenge?' he said quietly.

Kapinsky suddenly blinked and turned his attention back to Barnes. He had said too much. 'No, not revenge in the literal sense,' he said quickly. 'I mean revenge in the sense that Kapinsky will be a name that will always be remembered.'

Barnes faced him. His friend looked defiant. 'Tell me, Louis. Did you have anything to do with the death of Joe Dubofsky?'

'Unfortunately not.'

'What the hell does that mean? If you're in trouble, tell me about it. Maybe I can help.'

'I didn't kill Dubofsky and I don't know who did. Nor was I involved in any way. But I think the bastard got what was coming to him. Is that clear enough?' Kapinsky looked at Barnes unblinkingly, staring him in the eye, challenging him until he was forced to turn away. If he was lying he was doing so superbly.

'Do you think somebody at the medical school is involved?' Barnes asked, more to deflect Kapinsky than in the hope that he'd get an answer.

'I was in the laboratory the whole night so I'd be the last to know. Why not ask Thomas? He knows just about everything that goes on around here.'

Barnes realized the conversation was going nowhere. If there was anything sinister in Kapinsky's activities, he wasn't going to find out by asking him questions. 'Let's see how the head is doing,' he suggested.

They walked back to the lab to the operating room where the black box was still on the stand next to the table. Kapinsky opened the little door. The head was asleep. There was no sign of bleeding. He pulled the lip down to explore the gums. They were warm and pink indicating good perfusion and oxygenation.

Kapinsky closed the door, locked it, and put the key in his pocket. 'Just in case somebody in the ward is tempted to open it,' he said, patting his pocket.

'How are you going to move it?' asked Barnes.

Kapinsky had another lightning mood change. With obvious pride he showed how the battery-powered perfusion system fitted together on a metal tray with the black box and was clamped down under webbing for easy transport.

Barnes was again impressed with the man's ingenuity. It seemed endless. He congratulated Kapinsky and saw him glow with delight. It wasn't only his ingenuity that was boundless, thought Barnes. So were his mood swings. 'Well, that's about it, Louis. Let's pack up for a few hours' shut-eye. It'll be an early start tomorrow.'

He left Kapinsky sitting in the laboratory staring at the black box, and headed for the car park. Strange bugger, he thought. Now I understand why he never seems to sleep.

The operation went like a dream. Ohlsen, at Barnes's insistence, kept Karen anaesthetized and a close watch on all the vital signs. The whole team was there observing, with Des Louw assisting. They were clearly fascinated, pumping Kapinsky for details of the black-box circuitry. He waved aside all queries. When pressed, he added, 'You'll read all about it in the literature, very soon.'

Barnes knew that the tracheostomy would present a problem, particularly where the breathing tube entered Karen's windpipe at the base of her throat. This was potentially an infected area. If any bugs from this contaminated the plastic catheters it could pose the risk of life-endangering infection and cause major complications. It would be better to join vein to vein and artery to artery. Technically, this was virtually impossible unless he removed Karen's head. He could not bear even the thought of that but wondered if there would come a time in the project when this would be a routine step.

He carefully exposed the vessels on the right side of her neck, taking care not to get into the tracheostomy area. He cannulated the vein and artery, taking the catheters out through a skin incision, then sewed the muscles over the area where the cannulas emerged from the vessels. He connected a short piece of thin silastic tubing to each catheter and handed the ends to Kapinsky, who disconnected the arterial and venous catheters from the oxygenator. He waited a few seconds for the lines to fill with blood before slipping the tubes over the ends.

'OK, release the clamps,' he instructed Louw. There was a hush as he did so. Karen's heart was in circuit, pumping blood from her body to the baboon brain and drawing it back through the venous system.

'Perfect. All the vital signs are good,' said Ohlsen, from behind the screen.

Barnes's eyes filled with tears. He felt that she was very close to him at this moment, almost as if she were about to open her eyes. Perhaps that would happen as soon as Ohlsen reduced the sedation. 'My darling, this is all for you,' he said to himself. 'The chemical messengers are reaching your body and soon you will recover consciousness.'

'Dr Barnes?' It was Des Louw.

'Sorry. What was that?'

'Do you wish to hold her in the intensive care unit or do we arrange immediate transfer to D7?'

'Take her to D7. Everything is arranged as we discussed. Dr Kapinsky will travel with her as he is in charge of the mediation system.'

Things moved like clockwork. Within minutes, Karen, surrounded by half the heart team and several fascinated nurses, was in the elevator and on her way to the fourth floor and D7. A careful transfer to the water-bed was effected there and Kapin-sky took over. He placed the black box on the wall fitting in-stalled at the head of the bed and made certain that the heparin and sedation drips were connected to the arterial side and the protamine to the venous side. A quick check of the computer program, and the flow of drugs was switched on.

Helen de Villiers watched uncertainly. She wanted to help but did not know where she could be useful. She was one of a team of three who had volunteered to make up a round-the-clock nursing team. As Dr Barnes had pointed out, little physical work was involved but the job demanded constant alertness.

She felt much happier when Dr Barnes arrived. Dr Kapinsky seemed skilled and knowledgeable but there was something about him that troubled her. She couldn't say what it was – per-haps it was the way he seemed to look straight through her when he spoke to her.

She was kept busy for another hour while Dr Barnes fussed around the bed, checking connections to various bits of tubing, talking in that unnerving fashion to the patient and seemingly euphoric. This was clearly a big moment for him, she thought.

Afterwards, when everyone had gone and she was alone in the ward, her doubts returned. This was the worst part of the job, the isolation. The ward's situation on the top floor of this abandoned building was far from the kind of hustle and bustle to be expected in any big hospital.

And then there was this black box. She examined it closely. It had arterial and venous connections and was obviously part of the patient's circulation. But what was inside it?

CHAPTER 24

B arnes sat next to Karen's bedside holding her hand. It was warm and firm. Her fingernails, he noticed, were perfectly manicured. Clearly the nursing staff were following his instructions about Karen's personal grooming. Her dark hair, brushed to a bright sheen, shone with health and her face was lightly made up. She looked as if she had just fallen asleep. Everyone who visited D7 had remarked on how quickly her condition had improved after connection to the brain-mediation system. Within a month her grossly deranged endocrinal system had returned almost to normal. A few days later she began to menstruate. That pleased Barnes most of all. An idea had formed in his mind. She would have her child. As soon as consciousness returned they would discuss it. He knew this was what Karen wanted most. In all their conversations since the accident this was the one thing she had always asked for.

He looked around. Sister de Villiers was at her desk. She was a good nurse, he thought, but she seemed oblivious to Karen's rapid improvement. She and the other two nurses didn't notice when Karen opened her eyes. He had asked them to report any body or eye movement but they claimed to have seen nothing. Odd that it only happened when he was with her. Perhaps that was Karen's way of saying she wanted to be with him. 'We understand each other, my darling,' he told her, and patted her hand. He felt her fingers briefly hold his before they fell back to the bedcover. She knew he was there and this was another means of communicating her feelings. His heart ached with the need to hold her, to caress her and tell her how much he loved her. 'Soon, my darling, soon,' he whispered.

Sister de Villiers stirred and began a ward check. Since Karen's dramatic improvement there had been enthusiastic support from Andy Anderson who immediately routed another three patients to ward D7. The first to arrive was a young girl with brain damage from a drug overdose. A week later the trauma unit suggested they take care of a middle-aged woman who had gone into a coma after a brain haemorrhage. The third was a black man with massive brain damage after a gunshot wound to the head.

Barnes rose to go. He found that his conversations with Karen seemed to upset the staff, almost as if there was something abnormal in talking to her. He had been at pains to remind them that comatose patients continued to hear and often understood what was going on around them. Staff were encouraged to talk to Karen while carrying out nursing routines but they seemed too embarrassed to do so in front of him. It didn't matter. Soon she would be well enough to keep up her own end of the conversation and the staff would understand why he had talked to her all these months.

'Any changes, Sister?'

Startled, Helen looked up from her clipboard. She had tried not to take any notice of the one-way conversations Dr Barnes had with his patient. It was part of the therapy, he said, but she had the feeling it was as much for his own benefit as the patient's. 'Yes, Dr Barnes. All three of the latest admissions are improving rapidly,' she said, happy to have him talk to her instead of another long monologue with Karen.

He checked the clipboards and noted there had been rapid change in the condition of each patient. When first admitted, it had looked as if they were deteriorating rapidly, but all three had shown progress from the moment they were connected to a black box.

Kapinsky obtained tiny pieces of brain by perforating a needle biopsy through a small burr hole in the skull of the baboon. A microscopical examination showed no histological evidence of rejection. 'Now we have a ready supply of donors,' he crowed.

Barnes had allocated a patient to each doctor to get the full team involved. While he looked after Karen, Alex Hobbs took over the black man, Des Louw, the young girl and Jan Snyman the middle-aged woman. Kapinsky, in charge of the black boxes, ran a twice-daily check on the perfusion systems and was on constant call around the clock should anything go wrong.

The report-back meeting to the Ethics Committee was almost as stormy as the last one had been. The members had hardly sat down when Professor Thomas stood up. 'I demand to know the exact details of this mediation system and absolutely refuse to go along with the ridiculous idea that the brain-dead patients are for organ storage and, even more serious, are potential experimental subjects.'

This caused gasps around the table: the idea of experimenting on brain-dead subjects had not been discussed at the previous meeting.

'And where did you get all this information from?' JJ asked, staring at Thomas.

'Oh, even though, as a respected member of the Medical Faculty, I am not allowed access to Kapinsky's den of iniquity or sections of Dr Barnes's ward, I have ways and means of acquainting myself of diabolical intentions,' Thomas replied with a sneer.

Turning to face Kapinsky, JJ asked, 'I must ask you to explain in detail exactly what you have in mind.'

Barnes replied before Kapinsky could speak. 'Gentlemen, I think you will all agree that it would be preferable to test the effectiveness of new drugs in humans rather than on animals—'

But JJ interrupted, 'Experiments performed on humans without their consent are reminiscent of the behaviour of the Nazi doctors who sheltered under the mantle of science.'

'I'm aware of those atrocities,' Barnes replied. 'But in the camps experiments were not performed on humans that had been certified dead. They were alive'

Kapinsky sat listening to these arguments without comment. What could this bunch possibly know about what happened in the camps? The occupants may have been alive but they certainly could not be classed as human. They were a disease that could have destroyed the purity of the Third Reich. They had to be eliminated, and whether this was by means of the gas chambers or scientific research didn't really matter.

In a voice that sounded as if he was delivering a sermon, Thomas announced, 'Man was created in the image of God and even after death this image should not be desecrated.'

'You should stop doing autopsies,' Professor Bills was quick to point out to the professor of pathology. 'Cutting up corpses on the post-mortem table is a desecration of God's image every bit as much as the work that Dr Barnes wishes to do.'

Thomas realized he was cornered and started to sulk.

JJ moved on to the legality of the proposed experiments and the question was put to Dr Leonard Hertz, professor of medical jurisprudence, who replied, 'Just off the cuff, I can see no legal reason why these experiments may not be performed, but I will investigate the matter and inform Dr Barnes if I come up with a different opinion.'

After a few more questions Barnes was given the necessary permission. Pleased that it had gone so well, he called an immediate meeting of the heart team but found a hotbed of dissension.

Alex Hobbs had admitted a patient desperately in need of a heart transplant, who tests showed was compatible with Des Louw's patient in D7, the young girl. Louw abruptly refused to use her as a donor, which almost resulted in a fist fight.

Barnes soothed them by pointing out that Kapinsky was working on an alternative source of donor organs. In the meantime, he told them, ward D7 subjects would be used for non-fatal experiments. 'Four projects have been given the blessing of the Ethics Committee and I have allocated one to each of you,' he told the group. 'You will be required to set up the protocol for your experiment and present a paper on your findings. I can assure you this is high-level work and, should your initial results show promise, it will attract major funding.'

He had their attention.

'I have allocated Dr Louw an interesting project in testing the efficacy of a new antibiotic called amomycin for the treatment of a gram negative septicaemia.' Louw frowned but made no comment. 'This antibiotic is a metabolite of a fungus found only in the soil of the Amazon jungle, hence the name. The Swiss company which isolated the drug claims it's the answer to gram negative infections which are so often fatal.' He waited. There were no questions. 'Dr Hobbs has been allocated a project requested by our own oncologist. He asked if we could test the cytotoxic effect of a herb used by a Hungarian doctor for the treatment of cancer. Near miraculous cures have been reported but there's no scientific evidence to substantiate the claims.' Hobbs said nothing, but wondered privately how he would be expected to create a cancer in his patient. 'The third project, which I would like Dr Snyman to oversee, is to test a drug called AZS in the treatment of myocardial irritability especially in ventricular arrhythmias.' He picked up three folders and handed one to each man. 'Here is all the basic information you need. The pharmacist has been alerted to provide drug and herbal supplies as needed. I would like to have your protocols within two weeks, please, after which we can proceed to set up the experiments.'

There was an immediate flurry of questions but Barnes shook his head and referred them back to the written material. They would meet for a further discussion when they had completed some solid background reading, he said. Uneasy but intrigued, they left. Nobody remembered to ask about the fourth project.

Kapinsky was silently furious and headed back to the lab. He had put effort and time into developing an efficient method of organ storage, a means of keeping donors alive so that they could have a permanent organ bank, only to have it kicked to pieces by this piece of gee-whizzery dreamed up by Barnes.

Barnes had changed his tune without consulting him. The original plan was to use the resources of D7 for organ storage. Now, the donors were to be used for risky experiments that could just as easily be carried out on expendable animals. Dr Hobbs's patient had died, waiting for a donor, just because of this absurdity. What the hell had got into the man?

Barnes could have told him but he felt he could confide in nobody. His pleasure at seeing Karen's amazing progress was paralleled by a growing fear that she would be required as an organ donor. That was something he would never permit. Now that he had sent them all off on separate projects he could logically claim Karen as his personal research project and stave off any other requests that might threaten her survival.

Samuel swabbed out a cage and wondered if perhaps it was time to say goodbye to the city and retire to the homeland with his wife and children. He had enough money to eke out an existence and all he was doing now was making himself richer than his neighbours. Life in the city was no longer such an adventure, work as a surgeon for the white doctors was becoming a strain, and he was beginning to think that it would never lead to any other kind of medical practice.

He no longer felt threatened by the creature. After Kalolo's death he had waited for weeks, nightly expecting the 'thing' to burst through the door of his room. As time went by, however, his fears subsided, the nightmares stopped and he began to relax. After all, he told himself, the affair had nothing to do with him. Why should he spend sleepless nights and even perhaps risk his life to find out more about the half man? He would do the work that was given him and life would once more be enjoyable.

And that's the way it was: blissful days of satisfying work, except when Dr Barnes got notice of an execution. Then he had the pleasure of flying in luxury to Pretoria mixed with the fear of offending the soul of the dead. But things were changing. Steadily the number of tolerant baboons built up until Dr Kapinsky began to complain that he had too many animals under his care. He refused any assistance, other than Samuel's. The baboons in which he had induced immune tolerance, he said, should be housed in the department's animal room after they had been operated on. As these were valuable animals, Samuel was assigned responsibility for their welfare, which led to a running joke from Victor: 'These are your private patients, Dr Mbeki.'

At first Samuel had felt proud of the honour. After all, Dr Barnes had selected him and had entrusted him with more responsible work. He had also done most of the surgery on the animals under his care. Even the executions could be handled with professional detachment, he found. Seeing nothing of the executed person but the uncovered chest, he developed a totally dispassionate approach to removing the heart, as if it was just that of another donor.

Now he had a 'ward' of these animals under his care. The storage program was such a clinical success that several of the animals already had donor hearts stored in them and some had other organs such as kidneys and livers. Dr Barnes had given him a major increase in wages and he now earned an amount undreamed of only a year before. But for the fact that his wife and children lived in the homelands while he lived in the township, his life would have been rich and full.

So why did he have this dragging sense of doom, this constant anxiety that seemed to blanket his thoughts? He couldn't put his finger on anything definite but there was something about the behaviour of some of these animals that puzzled him. As soon as they recovered from surgery they clutched nervously at their necks.

The storage of hearts in the tolerant baboons had been so successful that Barnes decided to employ the same technique to store hearts from accident victims when a suitable recipient was not immediately available. In the past, these hearts had been wasted.

Samuel was watching one of these animals recovering from surgery when his blood ran cold as the answer came to him: the unexplained behaviour only occurred in recipients of hearts taken from executed prisoners: these animals were attempting to remove an imaginary noose. It must have been the last urge of the hanged man as he lost consciousness.

When he reported his observations to the doctors they laughed and pulled his leg about his tribal superstitions. A heart, Dr Barnes said, was just a pump. But as time went by he came to believe that something was going on that the white doctors couldn't comprehend. He was convinced that some memories had been transferred to the animals with the transplanted heart. He did not believe the white doctors' claim that the heart was just a pump. His grandfather had told him his spirit was inside his heart. That was why it jumped in the chest when a man felt strong emotion such as when making love to a woman or when afraid, or even when happy. He knew the old man had been right – and that was why Samuel tried to find out the reason for each prisoner's execution. All the men had been hanged for some crime, usually murder. But it was the case of the last prisoner that bothered him most. In a fit of rage the man had beaten his wife to death with an axe. As Samuel had expected, the baboon into which the man's heart was transplanted became vicious and dangerous.

Some weeks later he confided in Victor, who laughed but also agreed to look at the baboon. They watched it in its cage for a few moments as it flung itself about, pulled on the bars and bared its canines at them. 'This animal,' said Victor, retreating from the cage, 'is a killer.'

Barnes, who had always been a great supporter of the work in the laboratory and an invaluable source of encouragement, had become disinterested and even, at times, hostile. It was all due to this woman. Kapinsky had closely observed his friend's behaviour until it was clear that Barnes was beginning to lose contact with reality: according to him, the living brain of the baboon was going to help Karen to such an extent that she would regain consciousness. Barnes did not want to accept Kapinsky's argument that the conscious state depended on the normality of a special centre in the mid-brain.

'You know, Rodney, the question is not why we are conscious, but rather why we are not unconscious. We are not unconscious because there is a continuous stimulation to consciousness from that area of the mid-brain.'

'But if memory has a chemical component, why not consciousness?' Barnes insisted.

'Of course there is a chemical component to consciousness as neural transmitters are necessary for this area of the brain to fire continuously, but the nerve cells must be alive for these chemicals to be released and the responding cells must similarly be alive to react.'

Kapinsky concluded that, before his friend was driven to destruction by this woman and the research ground to a halt, he would have to act. He kicked at the waste basket, which skidded across his office floor. But what to do? He looked at his watch. It was going to be a long day. Quietly, he began to plan. It had to happen tonight, if possible, and look like a natural death.

Suddenly, he realized it was Friday. He had arranged a visit to Carol's luxurious pad and a drop-off of the product of his laboratory, the heroin analogue. Bugger it. Now that he had a plan of action for Karen he didn't feel like getting his rocks off but the research funds could do with an injection of cash. Ward D7 was turning out more costly than he had anticipated. Then there was the problem of Susan. He looked through the office window. She was engrossed in the centrifuge, head slightly bent, those incredible breasts jutting out under her white lab coat. The coat was riding up slightly at the back as she bent over, showing the perfect legs and the curve of those tight buttocks.

Her appearance didn't mean a damn thing, he thought. Like all dykes, she could get quite ugly when thwarted. Always the icy-cool professional in the laboratory, she had once grabbed him by the genitals when he told her he would be in Europe for several weeks. And she'd done it right here in the office while other staff worked outside, unsuspecting.

His resolve weakened at the memory. She had gripped him tight while he grimaced in pain, cursing him in whispers until he almost blacked out. Incredibly, as soon as she let go he ejaculated and had to sit down. She could press his buttons at will, he thought, which was why she was so bloody good as a dominatrix.

'You sent for me, Dr Kapinsky?' She stood in the doorway of the office, holding a clipboard.

The bitch must be psychic, he thought. He looked at her. She was at her prim and proper best, hair scraped back, face devoid of make-up and lips pursed. Might as well get this over with, he thought. 'Yes, Susan. I can't make it tonight but I'll arrange the drop-off.'

She said nothing, eyes icy. He felt his insides turn to water. Slowly she walked into the office, letting the door swing closed behind her and stood facing him with her back to the door. Holding the clipboard tightly against her breasts with one hand, she reached down with the other and, without taking her eyes off him, opened the bottom button of her lab coat. One-handed, she spread the coat slightly to show she was naked underneath. She motioned him forward until he was close to her. Then suddenly she grabbed hold of his hair and pulled his head down. Her pubic hair glistened blonde in the light. As her orgasm flared she gave a long sigh and released her grip. 'Thank you, doctor,' she said, buttoning her coat and turning to go. Over her shoulder she added, 'Next time I might not be so lenient.'

Thank God, thought Kapinsky. He'd fobbed her off without too much drama. She was such an unstable bitch that anything could happen. He'd seen her throw a major tantrum with Carol that had wrecked the apartment.

The day couldn't end quickly enough for him. At the end of

the shift he waited until both Susan and Nat Ferreira had left the lab. 'I'm coming, my son,' he called.

These meetings with Josef in the locked animal section next to his laboratory gave him so much pleasure that he found it more and more difficult to spend the days in the lab. He could not wait to end the day's work and head for the animal room to spend a few hours with his son. On a growth hormone program since birth, Josef's physical development had been so stimulated that he was almost Kapinsky's height and build. More powerful too, as Kapinsky had discovered in their play-wrestling matches.

Josef had shown some grasp of language and had the vocabulary of a small child. Much of Kapinsky's time was spent in teaching him to speak. He still couldn't pronounce words clearly but could understand spoken commands and answer questions in a series of growls and grunts.

Kapinsky had been delighted to discover that Josef insisted on walking upright, human fashion, almost as soon as he could stand. His face, feet and hands resembled those of his father but he was covered in a fine fur of body hair. To Kapinsky he was a handsome young man despite his small eyes, prominent eyebrows, flat nose and protruding upper jaw. Only when Josef laughed and showed his large lower canines were his simian features more evident.

One Friday night he had accompanied Kapinsky on his mission to Carol's house, closely watching every turn of the road and happily carrying the briefcase. While Kapinsky was inside he had waited patiently in the shadows until his father returned. His father had promised to send him on his own, one day. And it looked as if tonight was the night, Kapinsky told him, to a series of delighted squeals and growls. He explained that he had to go and see someone urgently but that Josef could make the drop-off at Carol's. He need only knock and leave the briefcase at the door and depart immediately without being seen.

More squeals from Josef and a brief wrestling match before Kapinsky broke off to show Josef his new wardrobe – a heap of his father's shoes and cast-off clothing. Minutes later, outfitted in suit and tie with a hat pulled over his brow, he could easily have been taken for a human male. A pair of dark glasses completed the outfit and Josef was ready for his first outing on his own. Kapinsky coached him on how to get to the house and back, and what to do when he got there. The boy had a kind of animal intelligence that was in many ways superior to that of a human. He seemed able to grasp concepts of space and distance quickly.

They waited until dark before Kapinsky quietly let him out of the rear door of the research block. Excited, and eager, Josef set off, his mind full of half-formed ideas. This was the first time his father had allowed him to go out on his own and the excitement was almost more than he could bear. He had been warned to watch out for people and to talk to no one. He had barely gone a hundred metres before he sensed that he was not alone – not only that but other animals were stalking him. His entire body switched to full alert. An age-old defence pattern, built into the genes he had inherited from his mother, took over. He did not look back but sniffed for a trace of odour that would give him some clue to the animals' intentions. He was lucky. A light following breeze gave him all the information he needed. His stalker was human, male, aggressive and fearful and although he himself was visible, his stalker wasn't. He had to do something about that.

He stopped in the shadow of a large tree, circled the trunk and shinned up it with the skill of an ape. Using his powerful arms he pulled himself into the cover of the foliage and crouched out of sight on a large branch. Now he was the hunter. The adrenaline coursed in his veins, causing all the hair on his body to stand up.

Half a block behind him, the man with the moustache paused and drew a revolver. He had been assigned the pleasant task of executing this Polish scum. He had waited for weeks for this moment, every Friday night ... He had followed the movements of his target meticulously, just as the cell leader had instructed him. Better to intercept him now and take him out while he was still on the deserted medical campus.

He braced himself. He was now a highly respected member of the Observatory cell, a man who had identified and executed his mark on time and as directed. It was unfortunate that the attention of the police had been drawn to the medical school but the phone calls had kept them off his trail. The Dubofsky case had received a lot of attention from the media. They blamed the police for not trying to bring the culprit to justice as the Government had considered the victim an enemy of the state. He smiled at the thought.

This henchman of the devil just ahead of him was about to meet his Maker, and may God have mercy on his soul. Soon he would be able to report back to the cell, wherein he was gaining status, that another mission had been successfully completed. The cell members had been receptive to his request for their judgement on this doctor from Poland, who was carrying out devil's work in his infernal laboratory. At first, when he had told them that the Pole was keeping people alive with baboon brains they had thought it funny, and he caused a roar of laughter when he said that if the doctor was keeping blacks alive like this then nobody would notice the difference. However, when he told them that Kapinsky had taken fertilized eggs from white women and implanted them into female baboons, there was outrage. The originators of the Mixed Marriages Act fumed at the idea of a human womb carrying a child of a different colour. How much more evil was the notion of a baboon bearing a human infant? Particularly if it were white. The man with the moustache was given the go-ahead to plot the madman's movements. He reported that every Friday night the evil doctor would leave the laboratory and walk several kilometres to a house party held in a wealthy suburb. He would return to the laboratory about two hours later; he always carried the same briefcase. He was usually alone, except on one occasion when an unknown youth had accompanied him. The contents of the briefcase were a mystery but he assumed that they were notes of his work that he did not want out of his sight.

317

The group agreed that he must die. This was worse than all the pornographic filth which was pouring into the country and corrupting the youth. This was genetic engineering at its worst, a form of corruption that reached into the very genes of the nation.

But where had the target gone? The man paused, put the revolver back in his pocket and peered into the darkness. He cursed the stinginess of the university administration, which had economized on street lights on the campus, leaving large pools of darkness between them. He hurried on, stopping at the tree where he had last seen the target. There was no sign of anyone in the darkened roadway ahead. Something rustled above him. He looked up just as a black shape dropped down, knocking him flat on his back and winding him.

The moon came out from behind the clouds and he found himself staring into a face with a prominent snout and deep-set tiny eye-sockets. Suddenly the man's breath returned. He shrieked and leaped to his feet. Almost as tall as he, the creature opened its mouth and revealed two massive canines. The man shrieked again as it lunged at his throat. Moving on pure fear reflex, the gun in his pocket forgotten, he threw himself backwards. The slashing canines missed his throat and plunged into his body just below the breastbone, ripping him open to his pubic bone, his intestines spilling out in an untidy heap. Screaming in agony and fear, the man grabbed at them with both hands and held them tightly. The creature hesitated and then ran off into the darkness.

Back in his office, Kapinsky focused on what he had come to think of as the ward D7 problem. There was only one way to solve it. All he had to decide on was the method. It had to be foolproof, undetectable and apparently natural.

He stood up, walked to the lab drug cupboard and unlocked it. Pausing just long enough to put a syringe kit and phial of potassium in his jacket pocket, he headed for the Ward of the Living Dead.

*

Barnes was ecstatic. There was no longer any doubt about it. Karen had opened her eyes and spoken to him. He stared at her beautiful face and pleaded with her, 'Darling, once more, please. Just a glance.' She did not respond but he knew he had until midnight with her. Sister Cathy Browne hadn't been able to believe her luck when he'd offered to take over the rest of her shift so that she could go to the Friday night rave-up at the nurses' quarters.

'I'll be taking a series of readings at intervals until midnight, Sister Browne,' he told her. 'There's no point in both of us being here so why not take off for the evening?'

Who better to receive such an invitation from than the head of the department? she thought, and left with alacrity.

As soon as she was out of the door Karen opened her eyes and smiled at him. This was proof, if ever he had needed any, that she was responding only to him. He sat by her bed and told her of his plan for their child. She smiled several times as he spoke. When he said that he had monitored her cycle and she was at her most fertile she opened her eyes and said: 'Yes, Rod, I know. I've been waiting for you.' He flung his arms around her. She felt warm and responsive. This was their moment, their time together. He had waited so long and endured so much. Tonight their love would create the child they both wanted.

Kapinsky couldn't quite credit what he was seeing. He had stopped just outside the swing doors of the ward and had peered through the upper door panes. He had taken a quick glance to see who was on duty. All he needed was a few seconds with Karen and it would all be over. It would look completely natural. But it wasn't Sister Browne in the ward, it was Barnes. And he was stark naked, screwing his floozie. Kapinsky was fascinated. There could be no doubt that's what the poor benighted bastard was doing.

So this was his bloody project – impregnating her! He felt he wanted to laugh. He watched until the whole episode was over, hardly believing what he saw, and then silently walked back to the elevators.

This had put an entirely different slant on things. He felt a rising excitement. Barnes was pathologically obsessed with the idea that Karen would recover and had even dreamed up episodes of consciousness for her. That was his problem, poor bastard, but it would certainly create some interesting findings.

Kapinsky's eyes gleamed. There were several reports in the literature of brain-dead women giving birth but usually only those who had been in the final stages of pregnancy when brain-death occurred. He had never heard of a woman becoming pregnant after death and then carrying the baby to full term. This could be the first time life was *created* after death. Life out of death! The idea fascinated him. He would certainly be observing this one closely. He let himself into the lab and turned on the light. Now for some serious reading.

He walked to the book-shelf and gathered a pile of reprints on brain-death that he had collected over the past few weeks. He settled himself comfortably in his chair and was soon lost to his surroundings. Every so often he felt a stab of anxiety and thought of Josef: he had sent his son out alone, anything could happen to him – he had no road sense and could easily get himself knocked down by a car. Worse still, if he met a police patrol he could get shot.

At last, unable to concentrate, Kapinsky put his head in his hands and wept. Never again would he allow his thinking to become so muddled. And all because of that stupid bitch of Barnes's. Perhaps there was still time to put an end to her.

A whine at the door brought him bolt upright. He ran out of the laboratory down the corridor of the research block to the rear door, unlocked it and found Josef crouched outside. He pulled him into the darkened corridor and, without a word, hugged him while the boy whimpered. Together, holding hands, they walked back to the special section where Kapinsky locked the door behind them.

'What happened? How did it go? Any problems? Did you make the drop?'

Josef put his hands to his ears. He was talking too much. One question at a time. The boy looked all right but a bit frightened. And he should be too, all alone out there in the city at night.

'Tell me about it, Josef. Did everything go OK?'

Josef suddenly erupted in a rush of growls and grunts, waving his arms. Slowly Kapinsky pieced it together. He had been followed by a man. He had climbed a tree and jumped on the man. After that he had walked all the way as he had been told, dropped off the briefcase and the note, and walked back home.

'Did you kill him?'

It was important that nobody had seen Josef. At least not yet. Kapinsky questioned him further. No, he hadn't killed the man but he had hurt him, perhaps badly.

Kapinsky soothed him and warmed up some milk, Josef's favourite drink. When he was quiet Kapinsky began to think. He had to find the man. Josef had told him the spot where the attack had taken place. It wasn't far away. The man might still be around somewhere. Kapinsky took a torch, locked Josef in his room and began a search of the medical-school grounds.

At the tree he spotted a few drops of blood. A few metres further on he found more. The man was obviously still con-scious and capable of walking. He followed the trail out of the medical-school complex where it turned uphill towards the hospital. Of course! The man would head for the place where he could get medical attention and that would be Casualty. Kapinsky quickened his pace.

First-year intern Dave Gill had been there when the man stag-gered in carrying his small bowel in his two cupped hands. He was incoherent and hysterical, screaming about a man with teeth like an animal who had ripped him open.

'I'm Dr Gill –' That was as far as he got before the man screamed again and pushed him away. Clearly this was one for the orderlies, Gill thought. If he didn't get him to surgery he would soon be in deep shock from blood loss.

'Zac! Willem! Get in here fast,' he called on the intercom.

They were there immediately, wrestled the man onto a stretcher and had him strapped down in seconds. Once sedated, he gave no further trouble. For them, this was a normal Friday night in Casualty.

The wound, Gill found, extended all the way from the sternum to the pubis. It ripped through all the layers of the abdominal wall into the peritoneal cavity. Most of the small and part of the large intestine had escaped through the opening. Although the coils of bowel were uninjured they were covered with dirt. The patient must have fallen several times on his way to the hospital.

It was imperative to clean the abdominal contents thoroughly before replacing them. Fortunately the trauma surgeon on duty was already here, thought Gill. He wasn't sure if he wanted to act as long stop on this one. The shock from the blood loss and trauma was severe so he started the patient on an intravenous drip, took a sample to determine his blood group, ordered a few litres of blood and took him to the theatre where the surgeon and his staff were gowned and ready.

As the bowel was not perforated, the surgeon returned it to the peritoneal cavity after washing it several times with warm saline to remove all foreign material. He stitched the ragged wound layer by layer and the patient was transferred to the general surgery unit.

The nursing attendant responsible for checking the patient into the hospital went through his pockets to look for identification and to secure any valuables for safe-keeping. All she could find were his wristwatch, a false moustache and a loaded revolver, still cocked. As soon as she left the ward to take the items to the chief nurse for safe keeping, a doctor in theatre garb and still masked, entered.

The patient was brought back to consciousness by a familiar voice. Where had he heard it before? He opened his eyes and stared up at a face, the mouth and nose covered by a green cotton mask. He must be in surgery already. No, it was all over and this was the anaesthetist coming to ensure he was awake.

The doctor pulled off his mask. 'Goodbye, Professor Thomas.' Kapinsky smiled, plunged the long needle between Thomas's ribs directly into the heart and emptied the syringe. His heart stopped before Kapinsky reached the door of the ward, heading back to the research block to give Josef the good news.

CHAPTER 25

Barnes savoured his breakfast coffee, leaning with one hand on the balcony rail and staring across the bay. To the rest of the city it was just another beautiful Cape morning. To Barnes it was a day like no other: it was the first day of his fatherhood.

The thought sent a thrill of delight through him. He was a father! He knew it as firmly as he knew his own name. He didn't need any test to prove it. Karen and he had conceived a child and now they had the rest of their lives together to enjoy their offspring. He couldn't wait to talk to her. There was so much to discuss.

He put down his cup, picked up his jacket and briefcase and headed for the elevator, where he punched the code button which cut out all the other floors and gave him a high-speed ride to the basement garage.

As he swung out into the traffic a niggling anxiety crawled into his consciousness. How was he going to explain the pregnancy to his staff? What reason could he give? He had a sudden recall of a serious student discussion on parthenogenesis, a condition in which an unfertilized egg develops into a foetus genetically identical to the mother. He shook his head. Not likely. Nobody believed in immaculate conception any more.

No, as an explanation that wouldn't fly. If his staff were half as sceptical as he had been when he was first shown the turkeys that had hatched from unfertilized eggs ... He let the thought trail off. There was only one approach. He would call the team together and tell them that Karen's level of hormonal recovery while on the brain-mediation system was to be tested. Pregnancy would be a major indicator of normal hormone levels and this could be effected by artificial insemination. Yes, that was the answer. He would talk first to Kapinsky. No need to tell him about what happened last night.

Lost in his own fantasy world and lulled by the soft music from his car radio, he was suddenly jerked back to reality by a news flash. 'It has just been reported that a member of the medical staff of Groote Schuur Hospital was viciously attacked during the night while walking home from the medical school. The doctor concerned underwent an emergency operation but later died of a heart attack. The name of the victim has not yet been released.'

Suddenly Barnes realized it was Saturday morning. 'Please, God, not Kapinsky,' he muttered. But who else could have been wandering in the vicinity of the medical school on a Friday night? It must have been Kapinsky who was attacked while out on one of his mysterious missions.

Fear gripped him: if his collaborator had been killed then Karen would also die. Her life depended on the black box – and its maintenance depended on Kapinsky. He cursed himself for not having insisted on learning how to service the system. Why had he put Karen's life in this man's hands? He should have known that sooner or later Kapinsky would let him down.

Barnes put his foot down on the accelerator. The hell with speed limits. If he were stopped by traffic police he would ask for an emergency escort to the hospital.

He had a sense of *déjà vu* as he pulled into the medical-school grounds where he found several parked police cars with their radios still squawking. Fortunately, his parking bay was empty. He halted with a screech of breaks, flung open the door and ran to the research block. At the entrance he took the steps two at a time, ran down the corridor and burst into the laboratory. There was no sign of Kapinsky. At the far end of the lab Nat Ferreira and Susan Bates were loading the self-analyser with specimen bottles. They both stopped and stared at his sudden entrance. 'Sorry,' he half apologized, 'but I'm looking for Louis – Dr Kapinsky.'

Susan Bates slowly raised her eyebrows and focused on him as if he were some kind of insect. Christ, the woman was bombproof. She looked as cool as an iceberg while all hell was breaking loose outside. 'Dr Kapinsky hasn't been around, Dr Barnes,' she said, and turned back to the analyser.

Ferreira smiled and added, 'Good morning, sir. It's quite early yet. Have you tried the animal room? Dr Kapinsky might still be there.'

Obviously these two hadn't heard the news. He thanked Ferreira and sat down at Kapinsky's desk. What to do now? Phone the hospital. He should have thought of that earlier. Casualty would give him the name of the patient who had died. As he picked up the phone he heard Kapinsky's voice at the other side of the door that provided the entrance to his animals. 'Bye-bye, Josef. Don't make a noise, there's a good boy,' he said.

Relief flooded Barnes. Kapinsky hadn't been attacked. But if not Kapinsky, then who was it? And who the hell was Kapinsky talking to? He must be having one of those weird conversations with the animals he'd heard about. Kapinsky spent so much time with them that he probably talked more to them than to people.

Kapinsky came out, locked the door behind him, saw Barnes and smiled. 'Good morning, Rodney. To what do I owe the honour? It's ages since you visited me so early in the morning. Not another drama, I hope?'

'Which doctor was attacked last night?' Barnes said, ignoring the greeting.

'Doctor attacked? Who? You know more than I do. I've been in here all night.' Kapinsky looked genuinely worried, and added, 'Weren't you at the hospital last night?'

'Er – no, I wasn't. I had an early night.' Barnes was almost stuttering and wondered why he was lying. Kapinsky could easily find out from Cathy that he'd been in D7 for most of the evening.

A cough sounded behind them. He swung round. Des Louw was standing in the doorway. 'Am I disturbing anything?' he asked, courteously.

326

'No, not at all. Come in,' said Barnes, glad of his appearance. 'We were trying to find out who the victim was in the attack reported in this morning's paper.'

'You haven't heard?' Louw asked, surprised. They both stared back at him, expectantly. 'You won't believe it but it's our old arch enemy and greatest critic, Professor Thomas.'

Barnes glanced at Kapinsky but his face showed only concern. 'What happened?' he asked Louw.

He told them that, according to Casualty staff, Thomas had come staggering into the emergency room late at night with his abdominal viscera protruding through a large vertical wound down his midriff. Obviously delirious and in shock, he had insisted that he had been attacked by an animal. However, the surgeon who operated concluded that the wound looked to have been inflicted with a sharp instrument such as a knife.

'But it gets even stranger,' said Louw, pausing for effect. 'The nurse who collected his personal effects found a revolver and a false moustache in his jacket pocket.'

'Why didn't he shoot the person who attacked him?' asked Kapinsky.

'There's no explanation for that. And clearly it wasn't robbery or, at least, the mugger must have been disturbed. Thomas still had his gold Rolex and a few hundred rands in cash. And listen to this! One of the nurses told me that she had heard a policeman say that the calibre of the revolver found was the same as the one that killed Dubofsky.'

'Well, I'll be damned,' said Kapinsky, shaking his head and looking amused. 'Who would have expected this from such a God-fearing gentleman?'

'Why would Thomas want to get involved with this sort of activity?' wondered Barnes.

'He had a thing about Communism in general and the Russians in particular,' said Des Louw. 'I heard he blamed the Russians for the death of his father during the war.'

'How was that?' asked Kapinsky, suddenly seeing that he and his professional opponent had been on the same side.

'I got all this from the nurses' staff room this morning so take it with a pinch of salt, but it seems that Thomas's father was a sailor on the North Sea supply route to Russia. His ship was torpedoed but he managed to get into a lifeboat with fourteen others. After three days in icy conditions they were spotted by a Russian patrol boat which ignored their pleas to be rescued and sailed past. Two days later a single survivor was picked up by a British destroyer. He told the story to Thomas's mother.' Louw had their full attention, and both Barnes and Kapinsky were engrossed. 'Thomas was only a boy but he swore he would avenge the death of his father and had been violently anti-Communist ever since.'

'I never had the opportunity to get to know him,' said Barnes regretfully. 'He was always so antagonistic that it was hard to have a conversation.'

'I think I now understand him a little better,' said Kapinsky, with a faraway look. 'He saw me as a Communist because of my Polish origins and because of that we crossed swords from day one.'

'Sorry, didn't mean to play the gossip, but I found the whole story very interesting,' said Louw. He turned to go and then added, 'Oh, there's more drama. Samuel asked to see me this morning. He wants me to take a look at the baboons in which we store the human hearts.'

'What's the problem?' asked Kapinsky, suddenly alert.

'Oh, that old story about a murderer's heart makes a murderous baboon. I'll talk to him. I think all he needs is a sympathetic audience,' said Louw, smiling.

'That black man is imagining all sorts of things.' Kapinsky snorted. 'He has the whole cleaning staff believing things about transplanted organs that are physiologically impossible.'

Barnes realized with sudden clarity that this jibe was aimed at him, but said nothing. He waited until Des Louw had left before he said, 'Louis, I've thought of a fascinating research project for which Karen would be a perfect subject.'

'And what is that?' Kapinsky raised an eyebrow as he spoke, but Barnes ignored his quizzical look.

'We have studied the return to normality of various systems in the donor bodies when connected to the live brain. It occurred to me that one of the best means of testing the recovery level of the endocrine system would be to test whether or not the brain-dead donor can become pregnant.' Kapinsky said nothing and Barnes hurried on. 'After all, ovulation and fertilization – and the development of the embryo in the uterus – depend on the normal operation of several endocrine systems.'

Kapinsky grinned. 'How do you think we should impregnate her?' he asked, his grin widening.

'Well, by artificial insemination, of course,' said Barnes quickly.

'Why don't you just fuck her?'

Barnes coloured and bit back his anger. He needed this man to ensure that Karen stayed in good health so that one day she could recover completely and deliver her child normally. 'Don't be so crude, Louis,' he said, forcing himself to smile in light reproof.

That wasn't your opinion last night, my friend, thought Kapinsky, but said nothing.

'Actually, I should discuss this with Aubrey Miller,' said Barnes, getting up to go. 'You won't know him. He works part-time at the hospital and is an authority on the subject.'

'Yes, I agree,' said Kapinsky mildly, and waited until Barnes had gone before heading back to the animal section.

Once inside, he relaxed. Here with Josef and the other animals he felt at home. Thomas was dead. Only Karen and Boots remained to be dealt with. He should talk this over with Josef. He unlocked the door to Josef's room and found him fast asleep.

No hurry. A cup of coffee is what's needed, he thought. He poured it and began to go through the events in logical order when an idea struck him so suddenly that he nearly spilled his coffee. Why hadn't he thought of it earlier? Karen should give birth to Josef's baby! Now that *would* be a worthwhile project.

He turned to look at the sleeping Josef and said quietly, 'You don't know it yet, my son, but you're going to be a daddy.'

It was late afternoon before Barnes could call the heart team together for what he told them was a report-back meeting on the D7 projects. They packed into his office and looked at him expectantly.

'I thought it about time we had a progress report on the projects we allocated a week ago,' he said. 'Who'd like to start?'

There was a rustling of papers but nobody volunteered.

'How about you, Dr Hobbs?'

'Yes, I have a few ideas on how to test the anti-cancer effect of the Hungarian herbs,' he said. Kapinsky thought he heard a note of sarcasm in his voice. 'The first hurdle to cross is how to produce a malignant growth in the subject. I think you will all agree that it should not be a disseminated tumour, for two reasons. First, the response would be difficult to measure, and second, if the herbs don't show the miraculously curative properties claimed for them then we have lost a valuable donor.' Hobbs paused and looked around. There were no questions. 'For the reasons given, I decided that a skin cancer would be the lesion of choice.'

Barnes, his thoughts on Karen and listening with only half an ear, nodded.

Hobbs looked down at his notes before continuing. 'I read abstracts of the more recent papers on the subject and it appears the most effective way to produce a malignant lesion would be to apply an anthracene derivative, such as coal tar, to an area of the skin.'

Of course, thought Kapinsky, the old chimney-sweep connection. In Victorian times it had been common for chimney sweeps to develop cancer of the skin of the scrotum, from constant contact with soot, which was anthracene based.

'How long would it take for the subject to develop a lesion?' asked Des Louw.

'Months or even years,' Hobbs answered. 'But the period

could be considerably shortened if growth in the same area were stimulated, for example, by means of a wound or the use of a growth promoter such as Croton oil.'

'The onset of malignancy could also be promoted by inhibiting the immune response,' Louw interjected.

Hobbs agreed but pointed out that this again would have a generalized effect and would endanger the life of the subject. A general discussion ensued which Barnes patiently allowed to continue: this was the cosmetic job he needed to put the team in the right frame of mind. He wanted them to emphasize the research aspect of ward D7.

'I think it's a well-thought-out protocol,' he told Hobbs. 'Congratulations. Shall we move on?'

'Just one question, sir,' said Hobbs. 'Do you have any information on how the herb is administered?'

'No, but I'll get all the data you need from Oncology. You should run the idea past them first before you proceed any further.'

Hobbs nodded and Barnes turned back to the group. 'Who's next? Dr Louw? Yes, let's hear from you.'

'As Dr Hobbs said, one would not like to cause a generalized lesion that could endanger the patient,' said Des Louw, frowning at his notes.

God, they're all mad, thought Kapinsky, burbling on as if they were endangering the lives of living persons. They don't realize their precious patients depend on me for life. A small adjustment to the black box and it would be a case of goodbye, patient.

'I've decided to make an incision in my subject's right calf and introduce an infection with Pseudomonis or Klebsiella bacteria. When the infection has become established I will begin treatment with the amomycin.' Just like it was in Auschwitz. Kapinsky remembered. 'If the antibiotic cannot control the infection I can always amputate the leg and save the subject's life.'

'Isn't that a bit drastic?' asked Barnes. 'Why not just clean up the wound by cutting out the infected flesh?'

'Have you considered the possibility of a blood dissemination of the gram negative organism?' Hobbs asked.

'Yes,' said Louw. 'That's why I intend introducing gentamicin as soon as it appears that the amomycin is not controlling the infection. It's a risk but does anyone have a better idea?'

That started a major discussion which Barnes cut short. 'Gentlemen, time to give Dr Snyman a chance.'

Jan Snyman looked up from his notes with a rueful smile. 'To my surprise, I find it extremely difficult to produce ventricular arrhythmia in a normal heart.' A few eyebrows went up. Clearly he wasn't the only surprised person in the group. 'For this reason I intend to produce a reversible pathology,' said Snyman enjoying the attention of his seniors.

'What about using a beta stimulant such as isoprenaline?' asked Alex Hobbs.

'I had that in mind,' said Snyman. 'But it appears it will only work if there is an area of ischemia or circulation blockage in the heart muscle.'

'Go on,' said Barnes.

'This is the plan. I will introduce a small balloon catheter into one of the smaller coronary branches and then inflate it to cut off the blood supply to a small area of the heart muscle. That done, I'll infuse the isoprenaline and, when ventricular arrhythmia is detected, I'll inject the AZS.'

'Won't that cause myocardial infraction?' asked Barnes, frowning over the problem of the destruction of the heart muscle.

'No. I don't have to keep the balloon inflated that long,' said Jan Snyman, looking sure of himself.

Kapinsky felt irritated. Why the hell could all these experiments not be done on animals? Why use brain-dead humans and risk losing them as donors? It was all due to Barnes's obsession with that bloody woman. The man was cunt-struck. Only when Kapinsky got rid of Karen would he get some sense out of Barnes. He thought of Josef, and realized he would have to go along with these buggers playing at being scientists. He couldn't deny Josef the chance to become a father and it looked as if Karen was his best hope.

His thoughts were interrupted by Barnes. 'You've probably wondered what I had in mind for my subject,' he said, looking at the group and carefully avoiding the use of Karen's name.

Here comes the real reason for all this bullshit, thought Kapinsky resentfully.

Barnes gave a lengthy background talk on the importance of the endocrine system and the need to test its return to normality.

Kapinsky was acidly amused to note that most of the heart team stirred restlessly. They weren't accustomed to being lectured to at student level and were wondering what Barnes was on about.

'For those reasons, I intend to see if the subject can conceive and give birth to a normal child.'

There was dead silence. The group appeared to be in total shock. Kapinsky was alarmed: perhaps Barnes had overstepped the mark. He and Barnes had been so close to this project for such a long time that it was difficult to remember what was accepted as normal and what was beyond the pale. Perhaps it was time for him to step in in support.

'You must be joking, sir.' Hobbs was the first to recover his tongue.

'Not at all. I've already discussed this concept with Dr Kapinsky and he can see no objections.'

All heads turned to Kapinsky. He nodded encouragingly towards Barnes.

'What's the stance of the Ethics Committee on this?' asked Louw, looking uneasy.

'Fully in support. They've already given us permission to set up the ward and carry out any experimental work we deem appropriate.'

There was another silence. Barnes pointed out that the work was unusual only in that they were working on brain-dead humans, subjects who were legally regarded as corpses. Because of the success of Kapinsky's brain-mediation system the bodies were in a healthy state, which perhaps was misleading them into personalizing the subjects.

'Sure, no problem,' said Kapinsky, looking sourly at Barnes.

The big questions – how would the subject be inseminated and what would happen to the foetus – went unasked. It seemed as if everybody was aware they were balanced on the edge here and no one wanted to rock the boat.

After everyone had left, a strangely quiet Fiona brought Barnes a cup of tea. He wondered how much she'd overheard. He was well satisfied with the outcome of the meeting. Tomorrow he would bring a sample of his semen to Kapinsky to ready it for use in the artificial insemination of Karen. Dr Miller had been fascinated when Barnes had telephoned him with the idea and was ready to help. Barnes knew he would have to carry through the charade to the end, but there was no need to disclose himself as the semen donor – he'd had enough of Kapinsky's uncouth remarks.

Kapinsky was having almost identical thoughts but getting a lot more amusement out of them. Barnes, he knew, would be bringing him a semen sample, which would be a simple matter to replace with fresh semen from Josef. Once the semen had been introduced into Karen it would be a lottery as to who would be the father of the child – Josef or Barnes. The Kapinsky strain would triumph, of that he was sure.

Now to teach Josef how to masturbate. It was instinctive in most primates, including man, so he didn't expect difficulty in getting a semen sample.

Late the following afternoon Barnes came to the lab with a small specimen jar in a brown paper bag. 'Here's the semen sample from the donor. Could you get it ready for this evening?' he said, making it sound like a routine request.

'Sure, no problem,' said Kapinsky. 'Shall I bring it up to D7?'

'No, no. I'll collect it myself at about eight o'clock,' replied Barnes, and left.

As soon as he was out of the door, Kapinsky took the glass jar from the bag, and flushed its contents down the sink and placed it in the sterilizer. From his desk drawer he took another jar and held it up to the light. Josef's semen had already liquefied. With a pipette he added culture medium, transferred the contents to a centrifuge tube and spun it for ten minutes. On inspection he found that a small pellet of sperm had collected at the bottom. He decanted the superannuitant fluid, again added culture medium and repeated the process. This time he placed the resulting pellet of sperm on a small glass plate, and dripped culture medium over it. He then put it in the incubator for twenty minutes at just under blood heat to allow the mobile sperm to swim into the liquid.

Satisfied with the results, Kapinsky drew the fluid up into a syringe. That was the specimen Barnes proudly collected that evening.

Sister Helen de Villiers was the duty nurse. When Barnes and Professor Miller arrived she wasn't curious about the reason for their visit and looked pleased at being given an hour's break.

They waited until she had left the ward before Barnes raised Karen's legs into a knees-up position and separated them. The obstetrician inserted a speculum into the vagina to expose the cervix, and Barnes handed him the semen-filled syringe. Miller attached a catheter and carefully expelled its contents into the entrance of the cervical canal and over the cervix itself. Satisfied that all the semen had been expelled, he withdrew the speculum and looked up at Barnes. 'Easier than the real thing, hey?' he said, smiling.

'Perhaps. But not so enjoyable,' said Barnes, forcing a laugh.

Back in the laboratory Kapinsky visualized the scene. He had no doubt that Miller would have done a competent job but he would be happier if the insemination didn't take. That would enable him to ensure that next time only Josef's sperm would be used.

Over the following month he kept a close check on the patient. She did not menstruate and a few days after her period should have come a blood test showed that she was pregnant.

Kapinsky cursed. Now he would have to wait until the child was born before he could be sure it was Josef's. Only then would he know whether he was a grandfather or not.

Helen de Villiers hated night duty. Ward D7 got on her nerves even in daytime and after-dark duty was a nightmare. At first she had been happy to sign on to the night shift because of the extra pay. She and Brent had planned to get married at the end of the year and every cent counted. Now that was all over and here she was without the man she loved, working at a job she hated.

She had thought she was handling the break-up with Brent rather well, until last week in the hospital cafeteria when she had found herself weeping and unable to stop. The senior sister had been very understanding and had sent her home for a couple of days, but being in her flat alone was even worse. She had asked to come back to work and the sister had promised to move her from D7 to more congenial duty in the heart unit.

Thank God, this was her last night. She could never quite explain, even to herself, what she disliked so much about ward D7. It was just that there was something creepy about the place. The patients, who were not really patients but more like warmed-up corpses, were bad enough but the experiments being carried out on them didn't seem right to her.

On the one hand there were doctors who saw the bodies as a place to store organs, while on the other there was Dr Barnes, who came in sometimes twice a day and talked to his patient, often for over an hour. The things he said made her uncomfortable, almost as if he was making love to the body on the bed. She now made it a practice to stay at her desk in the office cubicle at the far end of the ward when he arrived. That way she didn't have to listen.

She busied herself at the computer. She had to check all these pointless readings every fifteen minutes even though the computer was hooked up to the monitors. The whole thing was automatic, yet Dr Kapinsky insisted on seeing a printout every time he came to the ward. There was no medication to be given and no positional changes; nothing to do but this mindless clerical work and basic nursing. Why Dr Barnes insisted on staff with intensive care qualifications to look after this lot was a mystery. All they had to do, really, was to suction the bodies regularly to ensure that the airways stayed clear. They could train a baboon to do that. The thought made her chuckle.

She looked up at the sound of footsteps. It was Dr Kapinsky, who smiled and nodded. She smiled back, pleased to see someone during the graveyard hours. Normally she felt uneasy when he was around, but tonight she would have welcomed practically anyone for company.

'Take a break, Sister. I'll be here for at least half an hour,' he said. She could have hugged him. A half-hour break would take her close to midnight and the end of her shift. She didn't need a second bidding and headed for the elevators and a cosy chat with whoever she could find in the cafeteria.

Kapinsky carefully checked each black box, testing the cannulae to ensure they remained firmly in place, examining the tubing and connections. He had reduced his regular maintenance routine to a fine art. Satisfied, he closed all the boxes and cast a brief glance over the donor printouts. Everything seemed in order. He was about to call the cafeteria to tell Sister de Villiers he was leaving when she walked in. He said goodnight and went back to the laboratory feeling a little uneasy, as though he had forgotten something but couldn't think what it was.

In the ward, Helen settled down to the last half-hour of her shift. Thirty minutes more and she would be quit of this damn ward for good. She pulled a paperback novel from her bag. Reading as a means of passing the time was a total no-no for intensive care staff, she reminded herself, and felt deliciously guilty.

The computer clock buzzed softly. Time to suction the

patients. She began to get up but stopped, half-standing. A noise was coming from one of them. Perhaps he was choking. She moved swiftly to the bed and realized the noise was coming from the black box. It was a kind of gurgle, almost as if there was something locked inside it.

Kapinsky was checking through his day's work, mentally reviewing the service steps for the black box when he remembered. He hadn't started the anaesthetic again before closing the black box connected to Hobbs's patient. The head was going to wake up! He raced out of the building, searching his pockets for his car keys. It was several hundred metres to the hospital and it would be quicker to drive.

His fingers touched something in his pocket. He pulled it out, not daring to believe what he saw. It was the padlock of the black box. He had forgotten to start the anaesthetic *and* to replace the lock.

Back in D7 Helen was hypnotized by the noise. Should she phone Kapinsky? All the staff had strict instructions not to touch the boxes. Suddenly the box began to rock backwards and forwards, the door flew open and the baboon head stared at her – eyes blinking and teeth bared.

Fear froze her to the spot. Suddenly, the head growled. She screamed and ran in blind panic, out of the door and down the corridor to the elevator and hammered helplessly at the doors.

Several floors below, in the swiftly rising elevator, Kapinsky heard the commotion and swore under his breath. The stupid bitch must have looked inside the black box. She had become a dangerous woman.

Driven by panic, Helen turned and saw the door to the balcony standing open. Without thought she rushed towards it, flung herself half over the railing and screamed again – a fear-filled shriek that echoed off the surrounding buildings and pierced far into the night.

The elevator doors opened and Kapinsky leapt out. The scream was coming from the open door to the balcony. He ran up the corridor and found Helen. She was unaware of the man behind her until powerful hands gripped her ankles and she found herself falling, arms and legs outstretched like a skydiver.

The scream became a long, fading cry, which stopped abruptly as her body struck the road four floors below.

Kapinsky didn't bother to look over the edge but ran immediately to the ward and saw the open door of the black box. 'You naughty thing! You gave the poor girl a fright,' he said to the baboon head as he locked the door and started the anaesthetic. The growl stopped almost immediately.

He made a quick check. All boxes locked and anesthetics on. He heard the elevator start up, realized he had to move fast and headed out of the fire escape.

The bloody woman had only got what she deserved, he told himself.

CHAPTER 26

Detective Sergeant Du Toit wasn't in the best of moods. This was the third time he had been called to this hospital to investigate a violent death and, as on the two previous visits, he was getting nowhere. To make things worse he was saddled with Lieutenant Pienaar.

He looked sourly at Barnes who looked back at him with equal distaste. They had spent the last hour going over the events leading to the death of Helen de Villiers. He had grilled everybody in the department who could have had the slightest contact with the dead woman on the day of her death, including that weird Polish bastard who seemed to spend his time living with the baboons in the animal house.

He looked down at his notes. In the background Lieutenant Pienaar sat quietly, apparently engrossed in the framed degree certificates that lined the walls of Barnes's office. Sergeant Du Toit wasn't fooled. Pienaar would insist on a full report from him before he went home tonight – if he ever got home tonight – and would then spend the rest of the week tearing it to pieces. He sighed. Pienaar was pushing for promotion. Perhaps the best thing to do was to help him along by ensuring he got the credit for any success they had on this case. That way he wouldn't have him breathing down his neck.

He flicked his notebook closed. According to what he'd written, there was a simple non-criminal explanation for the nurse's fall. She had been dumped, on the verge of marriage, by her fiancé, gone into a severe depression, threatened suicide and, in spite of fooling everyone into thinking that she was feeling better, had jumped from an open balcony on the top floor of the hospital while alone on night duty. That's what his notes told him. His experience said that the whole story was bullshit. Everybody he had questioned had such perfect explanations. It all fitted too well. Real life wasn't like that.

Pienaar coughed. The smarmy bastard had sat in that chair for more than an hour, saying nothing. Now he was making it clear it was time to go. Fuck it. No point in breaking your balls on a case that your superior thought was open and closed.

Du Toit stood up, pocketed his notebook and looked at Pienaar who nodded at Barnes and got up to leave. Du Toit thanked Barnes for his co-operation and that of his staff, and followed Pienaar out of the door. Detective Sergeant Du Toit was, if nothing else, street-wise. As a child he had been taught the biblical wisdom of knowing when to hold onto something and when to let it go. This was a time to let go. The Americans had a phrase for it. What was it again? Ah, yes, don't buck City Hall!

Helen's body was released after the post-mortem, which indicated she had died instantly from injuries sustained at the fall. All members of the heart team and nursing staff who were not on duty attended the cremation service where they exchanged a few words with her bewildered and grieving parents. Kapinsky said he was unable to go but sent flowers instead, with a little note praising Helen's high standards of nursing and her care for her patients.

Afterwards, in the special animal section, he discussed the situation with Josef, who grunted his approval. Josef also got excited when Kapinsky brought up the question of Samuel. The *kaffer* hadn't been taking any interest in what was happening in their domain, said Kapinsky, but he was still a danger and would have to be eliminated.

Josef barked loudly in agreement and had to be quietened by Kapinsky, who had already begun to work out a way of dealing with Samuel.

As the weeks passed, Karen's pregnancy was carefully monitored. Barnes was not aware of the rumours flying around among members of his team about this extraordinary state of affairs. He considered having an amniocentesis done to check for chromosomal abnormalities but was warned off the procedure by Aubrey Miller. 'No need, Rod,' the obstetrician told him. 'She's well under the age at which those kinds of abnormality become a probability. I suggest an ultrasound scan, which presents no risk to either the patient or the foetus.'

Barnes agreed. To his delight the scan, carried out by moving a sonic device across the surface of Karen's swollen belly, showed that the foetus was not only healthy but also male. My parents have always wanted a male heir, he thought. But now was not the time to tell them. He would wait until Karen recovered consciousness.

Barnes wasn't the only one following Karen's progress with great interest. Kapinsky pretended pressure of work when he was asked to watch the scanning process. Better to appear at arm's length. God knew how Barnes would react when the child was born, but he would deal with that when the time came. He too was delighted to learn that the child was male. Another Kapinsky! Then came a niggling doubt. Perhaps Josef's sperm hadn't succeeded in fertilizing Karen. The idea kept him sleepless for nights. He cursed Miller for talking Barnes out of the amniocentesis, which would have given him proof positive that the child was Josef's. For days he argued the issue in his head. The amnio would certainly have given proof of fatherhood but then Miller might have interpreted the results differently: if it were Josef's child growing inside Karen, Miller would see the test results as abnormal and most likely interpret this as some kind of mental handicap – which might mean Barnes wanting an abortion.

It was a no-win situation, he decided. Better to wait and sweat it out.

The pregnancy breathed new life into Barnes's work. Where for months before he had paid little attention to routine surgery, leaving much of it to his team, he was now his old self – vital, interested and enthusiastic. The baboon donor pool was also paying dividends in that there was now no shortage of organs, resulting in a major expansion of the transplant program.

Within a few months the transplant unit became one of the world's busiest. Media attention was, once more, attracted to their work, but Barnes easily fobbed off enquiries about the source of donor organs, sheltering behind the privacy laws passed after the first heart transplants.

'I never thought I'd approve of anything the Nationalists did in Parliament,' he told Fiona, after putting down the receiver on an enquiry from the Prime Minister.

'How's that?' she asked, pausing in his office doorway.

'They got on the bandwagon quick-smart, after we started the transplant unit, and passed the Privacy of Organ Donors Act. That was about the most intelligent thing they did in twenty-five years of government. It certainly gets us off the hook when it comes to awkward questions about donor sources.'

Fiona's face closed up. She turned to face him. 'The problem, I suggest, is not awkward questions. Perhaps what we need around here are a few answers.'

Taken aback, Barnes could only stare at her. This was a new side of Fiona. Come to think of it, she had been very off-hand of late. Since the project had been launched she had become more and more brusque. Gone were the jokes and the daily humour that had been so much a part of her vivacious personality. Now she was simply the cool and efficient secretary, a person who arrived on time, did her job and went home on time – a far cry from the dedicated Barnes supporter he once knew.

'Come on, Fiona, you know the public would never understand. If it were to take on board all the emotionalism and mythology about body parts that you read about in the press we'd never be able to function. Just over a hundred years ago it was illegal to dissect dead bodies, but now every medical school expects their students to do it as a basic part of their training.'

Fiona set her jaw, and Barnes saw that this wasn't going to be just a simple disagreement. Whatever it was she had seen or heard in the course of her work had clearly made her unhappy with the project. He smiled. 'Lighten up, woman. This isn't witchcraft, this is medicine. We're operating on the frontiers of human knowledge here and we're attracting criticism from uninformed people for that very reason.'

'Have you considered that you might also be operating on the frontiers of human morality?' she fired back, and turned to leave.

Alarmed, Barnes half rose from his desk and held up his hands placatingly. 'Hold it, Fi. We've obviously got a communication problem here. You know very well that the project has been approved by the Ethics Committee and that includes methods of organ and body storage. You also know we have legal clearance from the Department of Justice to approach relatives of executed criminals for organ donation.'

She stared at him for several seconds. Barnes found it impossible to hold her gaze and dropped his eyes. Then she said, 'Dr Barnes, I'm well aware of what goes on here. And I'm also well aware of what isn't recorded in your official diary. What you and Dr Kapinsky are doing is wrong. You may be able to fool yourself but you can't hope to fool me.' She spun on her heel, then stopped, turned back and added, 'Don't expect me to approve of it.'

Back in the laboratory, Kapinsky leafed through the property section of the morning newspaper. He had to get Josef out of here. The animal room and the lab were drawing so much visitor interest that sooner or later he and his work were sure to be exposed. It was a lot more difficult to convince visiting scientists of the need for isolation than it was to frighten off badly paid policemen.

A final notice of an auction caught his eye. The old Buchinsky property was up for sale. Located on the slopes of Table Mountain, high above the city, it had been unoccupied for years and looked after by a series of caretakers. It stood on ten acres of land and was now offered as a 'developer's dream'. The auction was scheduled to take place the following week unless the property was sold in the interim. He picked up the phone and called the number listed. Within seconds he was talking to the auctioneer who realized immediately he had a serious buyer on the line.

'Sir, I'll meet you at the property in half an hour,' he said.

The moment he drove through the massive iron gates Kapinsky knew this was what he was looking for. The whole property was securely fenced in Victorian wrought iron – massive railings that stood well above head height. Old Buchinsky must have been paranoid, thought Kapinsky.

The house was a Victorian relic, two-storeyed and rambling. Solidly built and expensively finished, it spoke of an era of craftsmanship that was long gone. At the rear were stables, several garages and a workshop with an inspection pit and remarkably clean concrete flooring. The grounds were overgrown with shrubs that completely concealed all the buildings from the road. The place was purpose built, he decided.

A call to a valuer before leaving his office had given him an idea of the price range, leaving him shaken. He hadn't known that large city properties were climbing into that bracket. He made an offer below the lower end of the range. The auctioneer quoted a price in the middle, which he thought his client 'might be interested in looking at', and offered to ring him immediately on his car phone.

The client turned out to be a city lawyer entrusted with the sale of the property by the family, who had been overseas 'for several years', he was told, and were anxious to sell. They had a three-way haggle, sitting in the front seat of the auctioneer's car as he loudly transmitted Kapinsky's bid into the receiver. Finally, the lawyer agreed to split the difference. Kapinsky, sensing a bargain, stayed quiet.

The auctioneer, alarmed at the prospect of his cash buyer losing interest, jumped in. 'The house is fully furnished and most of the kitchen appliances are fairly modern. My client will throw it all in for the price.'

Kapinsky furrowed his brow, and said nothing. But the auctioneer was an old hand at reeling in customers. He added further bait. 'That offer goes with an industrial cleaning team to spruce up the house from top to bottom, and a landscaper who will get those lawns into shape and trim up the shrubs.'

Kapinsky could hardly believe his luck. They shook hands on the deal and Kapinsky followed him back to his office to sign the agreement and pay a deposit. Possession was immediate on payment in full. Two drops at Carol's house would more than pay for this, he thought. As he signed the papers, Kapinsky realized he was in for the busiest few weeks of his life. And so it proved. It wasn't only the increasing number of visitors but Josef was becoming impatient at being locked up and was agitating to be allowed out during daylight. The purchase couldn't have come at a better time.

A month later they moved in, Josef making the journey in the back seat of Kapinsky's car late one night. Kapinsky had spent hours preparing his son for this moment and had taught him how to use the phone to dial his private line which he'd installed in the laboratory. He was taking no chances. Josef had been warned not to leave the house while he was away and to ring him if any visitors came. In turn he would call Josef during the day and in this way they could keep in touch.

On their first evening at home Kapinsky and Josef sat grandly in huge easy chairs on the wide first-floor balcony overlooking the lawns that swept down to the driveway. While Josef drank a milk shake, for which he had developed a passion, Kapinsky allowed himself the rare pleasure of a whisky. He took a sip, allowed it to slip warmly down his throat and looked around.

The trees shut out all view of the nearby suburb. To the right the sheer wall of Africa Face rose from the city, bathed in a pinkish glow from the setting sun. On the left was the conical peak of Lion's Head and in front the city spread out towards the sea. Table Bay, stretching away to the north, was as calm as a mill pond. 'Space, privacy, security – just like the advert said. Eh, Josef?' He looked at Josef, who gave a grunt of pleasure and wiped milk from his chin. Kapinsky felt his skin tingle with pleasure. This was going to be the home of Dr Lodewick Kapisius. Here his children would grow up and be trained for the important work he had in mind for them.

The change in Kapinsky's routine didn't go unnoticed at the research block but everyone agreed it was a good thing. He had been too engrossed in his animals, even to the extent of living with them. He must have become tired of such cramped and unhygienic quarters and taken the obvious course of moving out. He claimed to be renting the old Buchinsky property up on the hill and that was probably the best place for such an oddball, they said.

Barnes, scanning his afternoon's mail, was also feeling pleased at the change in his colleague. The old bugger had become almost human, he thought. The phone rang, interrupting his train of thought.

It was Fiona. 'Dr Hobbs on the line for you, Dr Barnes,' she said coolly, and switched the call through. There was a time when she would have put her head around the office door to deliver a message – and have called him by his first name, he thought.

Hobbs asked if he would come up to the intensive care unit and have a look at a patient, a forty-six-year-old male in severe cardiogenic shock. Barnes agreed, pushed the heap of mail to one side and headed for the door. Fiona didn't look up as he passed her desk.

In the elevator he reflected that the bloody woman was making him feel guilty. Perhaps he'd better discuss it with Kapinsky. Then he pushed away all thought of Fiona: she wasn't going to affect his day. He was on top of his world and feeling good, he told himself. Karen was nearly ready to deliver their son.

The patient was almost comatose. Barnes flipped through the notes on the clipboard: the cardiologist had tried to assist

347

circulation with balloon counter-pulsation. This acted like a small pump in the descending aorta, assisting each heart-beat. The problem was that the patient had frequent extra heart-beats which triggered the balloon pump in the wrong sequence and was of little help.

Barnes swore under his breath. He had sent in four requests in as many months for the piece of equipment that could have solved the problem, a left ventricular assist device. The Administrator, as usual, had pleaded poverty.

He noted the cardiologist had already sent blood to the laboratory for tissue typing. As soon as the results were available Jan Snyman had phoned Dr Kapinsky as this was a grade one emergency and no human donor was available. After studying the results Kapinsky had informed the hospital staff that the heart of the baboon in cage number four was an excellent match.

When Barnes read this an alarm bell rang in his brain. Wasn't that the baboon which had become so vicious?

Kapinsky confirmed his suspicion.

'But Boots insisted this baboon is as dangerous as the man whose heart was implanted in it. Don't we have something else?' he asked.

'Jesus, Rodney, not you too. And, to answer your question, no we haven't got a better heart. I'm running a lab down here not a marriage bureau.' Kapinsky laughed and hung up.

Barnes considered his options. Kapinsky was right, of course. The fact that the animal-room cleaning staff walked in fear of this animal, fed by lurid tales from Boots, really made no difference to its suitability. That it carried the donor heart of an executed murderer was also irrelevant. The important thing was that the heart was an almost perfect tissue match for the patient.

In the lab, Kapinsky had stopped laughing. Barnes's call had suggested an answer to the problem of Samuel Mbeki. The more he thought of it, the more he felt this would be a way to deal with the damn *kaffer*, to get rid of him once and for all. He had been quiet for months now but that didn't mean a thing.

The black bastard was like a time bomb. He could go off at any moment and start pointing fingers. The immediate danger of Josef's discovery was past but Boots was a loose end, and Kapinsky didn't like loose ends.

His phone rang. It was Barnes again, mind made up and barking orders. 'Stop Boots from going off duty and tell him to get that baboon ready on the operating table. I'll come down and remove the heart while Hobbs prepares the patient here in the hospital.'

'OK. What time can we expect you?' Kapinsky made his voice sound laconic, almost off-hand even though his adrenaline had already pushed up his heart-rate.

'Let's see. It is now half past five, and it will take at least three hours to get everything ready up here and all the paperwork completed. So let's make it eight thirty to be on the safe side.' The new Transplant Co-ordinator he had appointed to replace Karen was not as good as she had been, and the processing time was slower than it used to be.

Kapinsky assured him they would be ready, softly replaced the receiver and stood still for a moment. He waited until his pulse levelled off, forcing himself to keep calm. This had to look like a completely normal procedure. He didn't want to spook the black bastard before he could close the trap. The afternoon's operation had taken much longer than they had anticipated and although the day staff had already left, Kapinsky knew that Samuel was still in the operating room clearing up, with at least an hour's work still ahead of him. He went into his office to think, to plan. After half an hour, he made his way to the operating room.

'Boots! Glad to see you're still here,' said Kapinsky, with a smile.

Samuel, surprised and uneasy at this unusually friendly approach from Dr Kapinsky, stopped his work and stood still. He would ask this man no questions. It was better to wait to hear what he had to say.

'The boss has just phoned me. They have to do an emergency

transplant tonight and he has asked me to tell you to get a baboon ready. He will be down later to help you take the heart out.'

Samuel asked nervously, 'Which baboon? One of the transgenic baboons or –'

'No, they're too valuable.' Kapinsky cut his question short. 'This time, we have to use one of the animals under your care.'

'But I thought the boss had decided not to use these hearts until he was sure –'

Again, Kapinsky stopped him half-way through the sentence. 'I have not come to discuss the merits of the donor with you. That is entirely our decision. All you have to do is obey my instructions.'

A cold shiver went down Samuel's spine but he decided to keep quiet while Kapinsky continued, 'I will go down to the animal room to have a look at the donor. In the meantime, you finish clearing up this mess, and then get the room ready for the next operation.'

Kapinsky left Samuel wondering which of the baboons they had selected. He prayed that it was not 'the Killer'.

Before Kapinsky went down to the animal room, he went to his office to fetch the strong iron rod that he carried as a weapon when he went on his Friday night sessions. He preferred this to a firearm as it was quick to use, and deadly, and as he did not need a licence he could not be traced as the owner. Because he did not want to be seen with it, he slipped out of the building by the fire escape and made his way to the animal room in the basement via an outside door.

He unlocked the door that led into the area where the baboons were housed. It was quiet except for the occasional rattling of cages. He knew that the Killer was in cage number four, but was not quite sure where it was positioned. He slowly walked down the line. The cages were made of quarter-inch iron rods spaced about two inches apart in a stout metal frame. The floor was lined with steel mesh so that the cages could be hosed down, and excreta and left-over food could be washed out without opening the doors. Each cage was securely closed with a strong lock.

Every animal retreated to the back of its cage and stared inquisitively at Kapinsky as he passed by them. When he came to the second last cage on the right-hand side, he stopped. The large male had also retreated to the back, but Kapinsky could clearly see the hate and hidden fury in its face. As Kapinsky stepped nearer, the animal lunged to the front with a fearsome screech, gripping the bars of the cage with both hands. It rocked it with such force that the heavy metal construction moved backwards and forwards on its wheels.

Kapinsky looked up. The cage was number four. 'Tonight you can satisfy your murderous lust, my beauty,' he addressed the baboon.

First Kapinsky hit the Killer a sharp blow across the fingers clasping the bars so that it jumped back and retreated to the back of the cage. Then he put the iron bar into the lock and with a sharp downward thrust, snapped open the lock. He backed away carefully, the iron rod raised in front of his body to ward off any attack if the animal escaped prematurely. But there was no further movement in cage number four. After leaving the animal room, Kapinsky locked the door behind him. The trap was set.

When Kapinsky returned to the operating room, Samuel had set out all the instruments and everything was ready for the donor baboon.

'Dr Barnes has not phoned yet?' he asked.

The black man shook his head.

'I will give him a call and see whether he is ready to come down. Why don't you go down to the animals and give the donor some ketamine? I will be there in a minute to give you a hand in bringing him up to the operating room.'

'But you haven't yet told me which of the baboons you have selected,' Samuel said with bated breath.

Kapinsky took a piece of paper out of his pocket and

pretended to study it before replying. 'According to compatibility tests, it should be the one in cage four.'

'The Killer,' Samuel groaned, before taking a syringe and drawing up some ketamine hydrochloride.

Kapinsky went back to his office and rang the sister's office in the ward.

There was an immediate reply. It was Barnes. 'Ah, Louis. I was just about to phone you. The patient died about ten minutes ago, and we could not restart his heart,' he informed Kapinsky.

Kapinsky's own heart missed a beat. He couldn't let this chance slip away. 'But Samuel has already gone to anaesthetize the baboon.'

'Well, stop him!'

But Kapinsky did nothing to stop the black man who was on his way to the Killer.

When Samuel reached the entrance of the animal room, he stopped to sum up the situation. All the cages were fitted with a squeeze-back: the back of the cage could be moved forward so that the animal inside was immobilized against the gate to such an extent that there was no difficulty in giving it an intramuscular injection.

He was pleased in some way that the choice was number four. If his theory was correct, the animal should calm down after the heart of the murderer was removed and, with only its own heart beating, would return to being the tranquil, lovable animal it had been before the operation. Then a sudden thought made him stop again at the door. What about the patient who would receive the heart tonight? Would he turn into a murderer? Had the boss ever given this some thought? Maybe he should go back and phone Barnes and warn him.

But it was none of his business. After all, he was just a laboratory assistant. Samuel unlocked the door leading into the animal room, but did not lock it again after him. An expectant silence reigned. He walked quickly down the familiar wide passageway that ran between the two rows of cages to number four.

The animal, with its habitual vicious look, sat huddled at the back of the cage. Samuel took the handle and started moving the back panel of the cage forward. The Killer resisted and he had to use all his strength to squeeze him towards the door. Slowly, the resistance was overcome and the animal was forced closer and closer to the gate.

Samuel nearly had him immobilized against the front when he noticed the broken lock. He attempted to scream but no sound came. Like a hunted buck who had sensed the danger, he ran back down the passageway towards the door of the animal house. Half-way to safety, he heard the clang of metal on metal as the cage door flew open, and then he was knocked flat on his face by the weight of the animal as it landed on his back. With the force of the attack, the syringe, with the needle still attached, spun out of his hands under the row of cages.

Samuel knew that this was his end. He could feel the long fangs biting deeper into his neck muscles. He prayed that death would be swift. That he would not be torn to pieces, bit by bit, the way a pack of wild dogs finished off their cornered prey.

Suddenly the animal let go of him. Samuel spun round on his back as the powerful hairy hands went for his throat. For a brief moment he stared into the eyes of the Killer. Images of his past flashed by as he sank slowly into the dark valley of unconsciousness for ever.

Kapinsky had made himself a cup of coffee. He sat at his desk, slowly enjoying the brew and waiting to hear from Samuel. Twenty minutes had passed since the black man had left with the syringe of ketamine. As he had heard nothing, he was sure that by now the bastard must be dead.

Armed with the same iron rod he had used before and a syringe newly charged with tranquilliser, Kapinsky went down to the animal room. Somewhat to his surprise, he found the door unlocked, and put away the key he had brought with him. He pushed the door open a crack and peered in. Samuel was lying motionless on his back, half-way down the passage, the Killer sitting on his bared stomach. It appeared that the animal had torn a large piece of flesh from his abdomen and its mouth and hands were stained red.

The Killer's lust for blood was obviously not satisfied. He had turned his head at the sound of the door opening, and had then left Samuel's body and charged down the passageway. Kapinsky sprang back, slamming the door shut behind him. He knew immediately that he had to tranquillize the animal and then kill it, but there was no way he could get close to it. The only chance was to use the dart gun.

His hands shaking – because he, too, had seen the glint of hatred and murder in the killer baboon's eyes – he loaded the dart gun, which was housed in the emergency cupboard outside the animal room. Then, returning to the door, he pressed his ear to it. He could hear the grunts of the Killer at some distance from the door and knew that the beast was still with its prey. Kapinsky realized he had one chance only, but if he scored a hit, the animal would be immobilized within minutes. If he missed, he would have to confront the animal armed only with the iron rod – otherwise it would become a problem for police marksmen.

He turned the door handle quietly, releasing the catch, then opened it just enough to peer into the room. His target was too occupied in tearing at Samuel's flesh to detect the new danger. Kapinsky's luck was holding. He saw that the animal was bending over the body with his back to him, presenting his buttocks as an excellent target. He manoeuvred the gun through the slit opening, aimed and fired. With a rush of relief, he saw the dart hit home, and the baboon jump as the needle entered its flesh. Before the Killer had time to turn round, Kapinsky closed the door. He looked at his watch and decided to give the tranquillizer five minutes to take effect. He discovered that he was shaking and sweating. He had to think quickly. Earlier, he had not planned further than sending Samuel down to the animal room, knowing that the Killer's cage was unlocked; after all, he had had no real idea what the outcome would have been.

But now he was well satisfied: the black bastard was dead, and now no one but himself knew of Josef's existence.

There were several important decisions to make within the next hour or so. Should he kill the baboon or just put it back in its cage? Should he report the accident tonight or leave it until tomorrow morning? Kapinsky decided to take one step at a time. He looked at his watch again. It was time to act.

He opened the door and peeped into the animal room. The Killer lay sprawled across Samuel's body. He could now be handled without posing any danger. Kapinsky pushed open the door, then reached back to snatch up the iron bar that was resting against the wall. Next, pausing only to kick the door shut behind him, he went down the passageway to the two bodies.

There was no need to examine the black man: the torn ends of the two carotid arteries were clearly visible through the gaping wound in his neck. The baboon was lying dazed, but if Kapinsky did not do something soon it would start recovering from the effect of the tranquillizer. While it might become an excellent donor one day, Kapinsky could not forget the hatred he had seen in the animal's eyes. Had Samuel been right after all?

With deadly accuracy, he dealt a mighty blow to the baboon's temple, a blow from which Kapinsky knew that it would not survive. He registered that its breathing stopped immediately, and knew that in a few minutes the two hearts would also cease to function.

Leaving the two bodies where they were, Kapinsky walked out of the animal room, locking it behind him in the usual way. He returned to his lab, deciding that he must phone Barnes. There was no reply. Barnes was probably up in the ward with Karen. Should he beep him there, or should he inform the police? He realized that if the police were brought in now, he would be at the medical school all night answering stupid questions from the dumb bastards but he was keen to get back to Josef to tell him about the evening's events.

Suddenly he got up from the chair where he was sitting,

turned out the lights and left the building. Samuel was dead, the Killer was dead, and reporting this now could only serve one purpose and that was to keep everybody from a good night's rest.

CHAPTER 27

In the morning, Kapinsky was in a hurry to get to the medical school but got stuck behind an accident as he drove in. When he arrived he was not surprised to find the lab heaving with a mixture of stunned staff, police and various others he concluded had to be the press since they were clutching notepads and microphones. He pushed through the throng of people milling around an ashen-faced Rodney Barnes.

'There you are!' Barnes screamed. 'For Christ's sake, Louis, where the hell have you been? We've been trying to contact you since seven thirty this morning but there was no reply from your phone or your bleeper.'

'I've been at home and as far as I know there's nothing wrong with my phone,' Kapinsky replied truculently, 'but I did happen to leave my bleeper in the lab last night. But the question is where were *you* when I tried to report Samuel's death?'

For a moment, there was a hushed silence. This was broken by a police sergeant saying, 'Now, sir, if you could –'

Kapinsky shrugged. He had used the time sitting in the traffic jam to rehearse his words and he knew he had to act his usual self. 'When you informed me that the operation was not going ahead last night, I phoned the animal room, told Samuel not to prepare the baboon, and to come back up to the operating theatre. When he didn't appear, and didn't answer the phone, I went down to see what had happened. I found his body and the mad baboon on the loose. As one of the cage doors was open I imagined the animal must have broken out and attacked him –'

Barnes interrupted him, 'You went in alone, knowing the beast was dangerous? Why didn't you call for help?'

'I knew that all the staff had gone home and since I wasn't to know if Samuel was still alive, I had to act quickly.'

As Kapinsky explained to his gaping audience, who were absolutely still apart from the journalists' scribbling pens, how he had used the dart gun to tranquillize the animal, he paced up and down and ran his fingers through his hair to accentuate his agitation. 'When I realized that poor Samuel was dead, I am afraid I lost control, and took up the iron bar that Samuel had obviously taken down with him, and I killed the fucking animal.' He swung round to face Barnes. 'I immediately phoned you but there was no reply from your home.'

'And why did you not notify the police?' the sergeant interrupted.

'To do what?' Kapinsky snorted. 'I had already done your work. I caught the culprit and executed him. What more could you have done last night that you cannot do today? Now, if you don't mind, I have work to do.'

Samuel's long-time friend Victor, with distress written all over his face, now stepped forward. 'Boss, Boots was always saying how much he hated that baboon. We all heard him say it was a murderer. Do you think that he perhaps decided to kill it?'

'It's possible, I suppose, but we shall never know,' said Barnes. He turned to the sergeant and suggested that they went into an office to take statements – and told everyone else to get back to work unless directed otherwise.

As the sergeant followed Barnes, he half turned and said over his shoulder to Kapinsky, 'We'll need a full statement from you, sir.'

And there the matter of the death of the animal room's black attendant rested. Kapinsky was severely reprimanded for not having reported it immediately, and at the meeting a few days later between Barnes and the Dean of the medical school, they concluded that the tragic accident could not be ascribed to negligence on the part of anyone other than Samuel himself. A report on Samuel's funeral service in the township took up one paragraph on the back pages of the newspaper.

*

Barnes had always considered the black man an exceptionally gifted technician, who had become a vital part of the research team. Now that he was not present in the laboratory a number of projects ground to a standstill.

Kapinsky did not miss him: his departure was a blessing. Only Karen still stood in his way. Thanks to her continued presence in ward D7 and Barnes's obvious infatuation with her, his plans for establishing a donor pool had been thwarted, diverted with the ridiculous experiments that were of no use other than as a device to keep Karen from becoming a donor herself. She would have to go, but he would wait until the birth of the baby before dealing with her.

Unexpectedly, a new ally emerged to support him: the Administrator of the hospital. All the research projects undertaken by the three members of the surgical team turned out to be dismal failures. Alex Hobbs could not cure the skin cancer or even slow down its growth with the Hungarian herb. He eventually excised it widely and closed the wound with a skin graft.

The amomycin turned out to be totally ineffective against the gram negative infection. Des Louw had to resort to a wide assortment of antibiotics to stop it spreading and amputated the leg to get rid of the primary source.

Jan Snyman found repeatedly that the ventricular arrhythmias induced by ischemia and beta-stimulation were not controlled by AZS. The irritability disappeared only once the balloon in the coronary artery was deflated and the blood supply restored.

For a few months the hospital authorities accepted the extra expenses in ward D7 with remarkable tolerance but then Dr Webber went to see Dr Barnes. In an amicable way, but with no uncertainty, he pointed out to Barnes that the original plan for ward D7 was to have a bank of human donors. All investigations had to be directed with this in mind. The experiments that Barnes's group had now completed with little success were out of line with the original plan. After all, the hospital was for patient care and not for testing new drugs. He insisted that from now on the inhabitants of the Ward of the Living Dead should be used only as donors for eyes, hearts, lungs, kidneys and livers.

Barnes's hopes for the future were shattered by this encounter. How could he ever allow Karen's beautiful eyes to be removed? How could he sacrifice her to donate vital organs? He did not bring up the matter of the pregnancy and unborn child, but surely they would not allow her to die while a life was developing inside her body. He still had some time.

Barnes had changed his lifestyle. He gradually became more and more withdrawn and spent less and less time in the operating room. Instead, he would sit with his hand on the expectant mother's belly and a smile of satisfaction would light up his face when the child kicked or turned. With the help of one of the ward nurses he spent days fitting out a nursery at his house and he booked a trained nurse to care for the child once he came home.

This unusual interest in the unborn child was noticed by the staff of D7 and raised certain questions but no one had the audacity to ask Barnes on ward rounds why he always talked about Karen's little boy and pretended that it was because she was the mother that he felt duty-bound to look after the child.

Barnes was awakened by the shrilling of the telephone. A call at night was unusual for him these days as he operated only occasionally and the intensive care staff always called the doctor whose patient had developed complications. He sat up in bed and felt around for the phone next to him in the darkness.

'Yes, what is it?' Barnes enquired without greeting.

'I'm sorry to worry you, doctor, but Dr Kapinsky instructed me to notify you.'

'Notify me about what?'

'She's bleeding, doctor.'

'Who is bleeding?' He recognized the high-pitched voice of the nurse he had left in ward D7 only a few hours ago.

'Karen is bleeding,' the reply came back.

'How can she be bleeding? She was not operated on!' Barnes asked, puzzled.

'No, Dr Barnes, she has started to bleed from her vagina. When I suctioned her I noticed blood on her sheets.'

Barnes remembered enough obstetrics from his student days to realize immediately that Karen and the baby were in serious trouble – Karen from the haemorrhage and the baby because it was seven weeks premature. 'Nurse just keep her quiet. I'll be there in a few minutes.'

The nurse rang off wondering how one keeps a dead person quiet.

Barnes replaced his receiver then picked it up again and dialled Miller's number.

A sleepy voice answered, 'Aubrey Miller speaking.'

'Karen has started to bleed,' Barnes shouted. 'What do you think's gone wrong?'

Miller could hear that Barnes was beside himself. 'Just calm down, Rodney, and tell me what's happened in more detail. What about the pulse-rate, the blood pressure, and how much has she bled?'

'I don't know. The nurse just phoned me at home and told me Karen had started to bleed. Do you think they'll be OK?'

Dr Miller was not prepared to venture a prognosis on such scanty information. 'I'll meet you in D7, Rodney, and we'll assess the situation.'

'OK, but please hurry,' Barnes begged and hung up.

He got to the hospital, in record time. The drive from his house had been a reckless race with scant regard for traffic rules or speed limits. He ran down the passage and up the steps, arriving out of breath in D7. Aubrey Miller was already there examining Karen.

'What do you think?' Barnes panted.

'Just give me a few minutes. I've only just arrived myself.'

The expectant father paced up and down the corridor while the obstetrician examined his patient. After five minutes he called Barnes. 'She hasn't lost a lot of blood and the bleeding has stopped.'

'What about the baby?' Barnes interrupted.

Ignoring the question, his friend continued, 'Her blood pressure is a hundred and ten over seventy and pulse-rate eighty-five per minute.'

'And the baby?' Barnes pleaded.

'The child is fine. The foetal heartbeat varies between a hundred and twenty and a hundred and fifty depending on whether the uterus is contracting or not.'

'The uterus is contracting – so she's in labour,' Barnes shouted hysterically.

'Take it easy, Rodney, everything's under control. The contractions are false labour contractions and will not dilate the cervix.'

'But why is she bleeding?'

'You remember with the last ultrasound scan I mentioned that the placenta was situated fairly low down.'

'Yes, but you said it wouldn't cause trouble.'

'I remember saying that, but with a lower segment of the uterus now being taken up by false labour contractions a small section of the placenta must have become detached resulting in the bleeding.'

'So you were wrong!' Barnes shouted.

Miller realized that his friend was not himself. 'Rodney, we can all make mistakes.'

'So what do we do now to correct the mistake?' Barnes could think of nothing else but the danger in which Karen and her son – their son – were in.

'All we can do is wait. At the moment there is no immediate danger to mother or child.'

'Wait for what? Wait for her to bleed again?'

'Yes, or not to bleed again,' Miller responded carefully. 'I can do a Caesarean section now, but I would like the child to mature as much as possible. Every day that we can wait will lessen the chances of his developing complications after birth.'

'What kind of complications?' Barnes had calmed down a little and spoke less vehemently.

'The problem with these premature babies is that their lungs have not developed fully. They're prone to run into pulmonary complications. I suggest we give Karen some cortisone, which will reduce the risk of breathing difficulties after birth quite significantly.'

'OK.' Turning to the nurse Barnes was again the conscientious surgeon. 'Nurse, I want you to observe her like a hawk. Half-hourly pulse and blood pressure. Look out for bleeding and call me as soon as there is the slightest change in her vital signs.'

He started walking away, then turned back. 'Oh, yes, and count the foetal pulse-rate every half an hour.'

The two doctors left the ward. When they reached the corridor Barnes stopped. 'You don't think we should operate straight away? Surely the life of the mother is more important than that of the child.'

For several weeks Miller had sensed that Barnes was thinking of Karen as a living human being. He would probably suggest that they do the Caesarean section under epidural anaesthetic. 'There are two schools of thought on when to operate on a patient with a placenta previa. One school thinks like you, believing that as soon as the mother bleeds one should remove the baby. I belong to the second school, which feels that one should wait as long as possible before operating.'

'Why do you want to wait?'

'I've already answered that question. The longer we can delay the birth of the child the better the chances for the baby to recover. Look, Rodney, we can have Karen in the operating room within thirty minutes if need be. In situations where the facilities for careful observation and immediate surgery are not available, I should agree with those who want to operate at the first bleed.'

Karen was carefully monitored while Barnes left the hospital for a bath, a shave and a change of clothes.

Friday night expeditions to Carol's house had stopped. Susan Bates spent her days in fury. Her hold over Kapinsky seemed to have disappeared and, try as she might, she couldn't tempt him to attend another bondage session. Worse, now that Kapinsky was no longer interested in visiting her, she herself was forced to play the risky role of drug courier. This was something she had been determined would never happen.

Something must have changed in Kapinsky's life, she thought. It couldn't be another woman, unless he had met a new dominatrix and that was unlikely – she knew every pervert in this goddamn city and she would have heard it on the gay grapevine by now. Kapinsky's name simply didn't figure in that world. He had been very careful until he met Susan and their professional interests had meshed so much that it was in their mutual interest to keep it that way. The set-up with Carol was perfectly balanced for all their needs, she thought. Now the bastard was endangering them all with his strange behaviour.

The clients were getting more demanding too and a once-weekly drop was not enough for some. Carol had ensured that there were at least three distributors between themselves and the clients, which gave them a fail-safe triple drop system, but even with that she was feeling the pressure. Something had to be done about Kapinsky.

In the old house on the hill, life for Kapinsky had never been sweeter. He took Josef on daily early morning jogs along the bush tracks on the lower slopes of the mountain. There was never anyone awake just before dawn and they wandered and climbed the hillsides each day until the sun was up. Kapinsky was amazed at the speed of Josef's physical development from a well-built adult to a large, powerful male with massive shoulders and thighs. There was no doubt that he had inherited a number of characteristics from his mother, not the least being his incredible agility at rock-climbing and his continuous sense of alertness.

That last quality had once saved Kapinsky from stepping on a puff-adder. These ever-present dangers for rock climbers were slow-moving snakes that frequented the sunny slopes of the mountain and attacked immediately when surprised. Josef's sudden bark of alarm had caused Kapinsky to stop immediately a pace away from it.

Josef's grasp of language remained poor. He and Kapinsky understood each other perfectly but it had as much to do with Josef's animal sense of body language as it had with any understanding of grammar or vocabulary. He could barely comprehend abstract ideas, though he understood the passing of time and could successfully carry out simple tasks when required. Kapinsky resigned himself to the fact that, in human terms, his son would always be mentally subnormal. Yet he found himself loving his child with a fierce intensity that burned deeply within him. Josef, in turn, was affectionate, kissing and hugging his father with a warmth Kapinsky had never experienced from any other human being.

Occasionally he found himself wondering at his own sexuality. Throughout his adult life he had been driven by the guilt of having watched his parents die and having made no effort to save them. Always the shadow of his father was at his shoulder, saying nothing but making judgements on how well he succeeded. As a teenager, he had found the guilt came in cycles, growing stronger until he felt he would break under the burden. If only he could be punished for what he had done wrong. But there had been nobody to turn to, no one who understood.

Then he had met a prostitute who abused him for his poor performance, which gave him a peculiar sense of relief. On the next visit she beat him with a light cane, setting the pattern for years of sadomasochistic sex routines. Recalling the incident brought back thoughts of Susan Bates. A mental picture of her naked breasts and leather-clad thighs stirred his loins but he realized with pleasure that he could examine the idea without desire.

Once, after a wrestling match with Josef in which the boy easily subdued him, Kapinsky laughingly called a halt. Together they relaxed on the grassy slope in front of the house. Kapinsky felt his breath slow as his heart-rate dropped to normal after the exertion. He looked across at Josef, who was lying with one foot in the air and idly examining it.

Suddenly, he found himself filled with a sense of peace, a feeling like no other he had ever experienced. He felt somehow worthy, a full person. All his life he had fought the sense of inferiority, driven always by the image of his powerful father. His father? He probed the idea. His father was gone! No, not quite gone but hard to remember. The feeling of freedom was so heady that he braced himself on the grass with his hands, surprised that the earth wasn't moving.

The weeks passed. Barnes no longer made any pretence of administering his department. He had ceased daily surgery and he did not attend teaching rounds, concentrating almost full-time On D7 and Karen's advanced pregnancy. Administrator Webber called him in twice to explain his behaviour and eventually suggested that he take long leave.

Barnes exploded. 'Dr Webber, you are well aware that I cannot leave my patient in D7. She is almost full term and requires full support in this critical phase. You'll note we have asked for nothing beyond basic running costs in the past two months. All other costs are being borne by sponsors.' He rose to go, then leaned across the desk so threateningly that Webber shrank back. He growled, 'So don't quote your fucking budget at me – I don't need it,' and slammed out of the door.

Webber sat thoughtfully for a few moments then lifted his receiver and punched in a number. 'Dr Webber here, put me through to the Dean of Medicine, please,' he told the receptionist. Barnes was clearly out of touch with reality, he thought while he waited. This was a council decision and the Dean should carry the can. Barnes had international standing and – no matter which way they handled it – when the story broke, the media would have a feeding frenzy.

Barnes told Karen about the incident, assuring her that he would let nothing harm either her or the baby. If necessary they would move out and into a private ward in a city clinic. She had only a little while to go and seemed more relaxed, he thought. He spent the last hour of the day shift with her and left just as the night nurse came on duty.

He arrived home, tired but pleased that he had come to a decision. Another word from Webber and he would move Karen out of the hospital and let the Dean have his resignation. He still had the power of attorney given him by Karen's relatives and the hospital authorities couldn't legally stop him. Barnes stripped off his clothes and was asleep almost as soon as his head touched the pillow.

He wasn't the only one who had come to a decision. Susan Bates, simmering with frustration, had made up her mind. She would pay a surprise visit to Kapinsky's house and find out for herself what was going on. The bastard had never been able to stay away from her like this before so he must be having his rocks off somehow.

She dressed carefully in front of the tall, one-way mirror in her bedroom, knowing that Carol was watching from the other side. Carol and God knows who else, she wondered, feeling her hormones quicken. She clinched the chain-link garter belt about her waist, feeling the metal cold against her skin, drew on the wire mesh stockings and clipped them tight to the black leather suspenders. The high-heeled black knee-boots came next before she stepped back and considered the effect. The garter belt framed her pubic hair perfectly. Now for her breasts. Working carefully, she rouged the nipples to make them stand out from the milky skin surrounding them. Her forearms needed emphasis she decided, and buckled on a pair of brass-studded leather arm-guards. She pirouetted in front of the mirror and looked over her shoulders at her tight buttocks. Satisfied, she wrapped herself in a full-length fur coat. When she was ready, she felt herself begin to lubricate. Dressing up in dominatrix gear had always been a turn-on, and dressing up in front of an audience even more so.

She considered what to take for Kapinsky and chose the choke-chain with the ankle and leg cuffs. The frustration fuck, a perfect choice. With his wrists chained behind him to his ankles, and linked again to the choke-chain round his neck, he would still be able to get into her but would have to fuck slowly. Any sudden movement would tighten the chain – and she could always arrange that, she thought, laughing.

There was an answering laugh from the watchers behind the mirror. Susan flashed open her coat and allowed it to swirl, showing naked buttocks and breasts, dipping into a curtsey as if taking a curtain call. The difference was that the show hadn't started yet, she thought, picking up her briefcase. This was going to be a night to remember.

Kapinsky had just finished his nightly romp with Josef. The horseplay had taken them around the house and upstairs, ending in Kapinsky's bedroom. He was exhausted. Josef was now so strong that perhaps it was time they gave up this rough-and-tumble, he thought. A few years ago he would still have been upright and smiling after this kind of exercise. He turned to ruffle Josef's hair, found him already fast asleep and felt a sudden rush of love for him. He was always surprised by Josef's feral ability to sleep anywhere at any time, another of the animal qualities inherited from his mother. Normally, he would have wakened him and led him to his own room but this time he gently slid the boy's arms out of his shirt, drew the coverlet around him and switched off the light. That done, he stretched his arms above his head, feeling them ache, and headed for the spa bath. Time for some heat treatment for tired muscles.

The spa was a recently acquired luxury, installed in a circular room at the end of the verandah. Kapinsky always found the massaging effect of the surging water bliss after a day at the laboratory. Tiredly, he now staggered down the stairs, shedding clothes at every step, stopping only at the bar to pick up a bottle of whisky and a glass.

In the spa room, he turned on the bath, set the jets to a single point and lowered himself in. The water, kept at a constant heat, pummelled his body into instant relaxation. He sighed, filled his glass again and swallowed half of it at a gulp.

The liquor warmed him all the way to his toes. He decided to sip the rest and by the time he had finished he decided he was feeling no pain. He slid deeper into the water and felt himself become erect. Interesting! He deliberately moved his body into the jet swirl and let the water massage his erection. Life, for Louis Kapinsky, was almost perfect. Right now, he decided, all he needed was an orgasm.

A shadow fell across the bath. Alarmed, he turned his head and saw Susan Bates. 'How the hell did you get in?' he spat.

She was smiling, holding the black fur coat tightly closed at the throat with one hand while carrying a briefcase in the other. Slowly, she set the briefcase on the floor and allowed the coat to fall open.

Her perfect breasts jutted clear of the fur, erect nipples standing high and proud. His eyes went immediately to her pubic hair. It glistened wetly. 'Yes, Louis, it's hot cunt and it's all yours,' said Susan, allowing the coat to fall to the floor.

Kapinsky's mood changed. He sat up, intrigued, feeling his desire heighten. What did she mean? If she meant what he thought she meant this was an incredible change in their relationship. He had never been allowed to fuck her before. He had never been *able* to fuck her anyway – his erections had always come after the pain but here he was with a raging erection and a woman who wanted to use it.

His mind dulled now after the whisky, he climbed out of the bath, oblivious to all else but that, for the first time in his life, he was about to copulate with a woman. Susan picked up her briefcase, took him by the hand and led him into the living room. Passing Kapinsky's desk she noticed the answerphone and, without pausing, nudged a button with the corner of the briefcase. The indicator light winked out, showing that the call signal had been switched off. There would be no interruptions to this little interlude, she thought. Lights blazed in the huge

369

living room. Susan looked around and spreadeagled herself on a huge bearskin rug stretched in front of the massive stone fireplace. As she sank into the warm fur she pulled Kapinsky down on top of her and, behind his back, flipped open the briefcase. As he straddled her she slid the choke-chain around his neck, snapped the linked cuffs on his right wrist, pulled his left over behind him and closing them together. Blurrily he objected but she pulled him down on her, kissed him on the mouth and snapped the cuffs on each of his ankles.

He began to thrust desperately with his hips, vaguely aware that he hadn't entered her. She opened her legs wide and guided him in. As he thrust home she pulled his legs up hard by the ankle cuffs and slid the end of the choke-chain through the cuff-keep, an ingenious device that allowed the chain to move one way only. A trigger allowed her to release it at will.

'Dr Kapinsky,' she said in his ear, 'if you poke hard you choke hard.' The chain tightened with each thrust and his breath began to whistle in his throat. 'Make up your mind,' she whispered. 'You can breathe or fuck but you can't do both.'

She was totally in control. The sense of power thrilled through her and she felt her body gather itself for the orgasm. This one, she knew, was going to be a rocket ride and the big dipper all rolled into one. Never before had she felt this potent.

Karen had started to bleed again. Aubrey Miller phoned Barnes and told him that this time he had decided to operate although the child was still premature.

'So you *were* wrong,' Barnes blurted out as he rushed into ward D7.

Miller decided to give him something to do to keep his mind off the problem. He realized he was treating the man like an expectant father but, what the hell? He was behaving like one.

'I'll scrub up while you and Sister take her to theatre,' he said, patting Barnes's shoulder.

At that moment Dr Ohlsen walked in. Ever cool, he nodded to Barnes, had a word with Miller and headed off to the theatre to set up his anaesthesia machine, Since the death of Helen de Villiers, each bed in D7 had been set up with clamps to hold its own black box so that the donor and box could be moved as a unit. Kapinsky, as always far-sighted, had arranged for each to have a small battery-operated power pack that could run its own box for several hours in the event of a power failure. The sister had already rigged a plasma drip. Within minutes they had unplugged the bed's various power systems and had taken it to the elevator.

As they wheeled Karen into the theatre, Miller was still scrubbing. He had decided to use the bed as an operating table so that there would be no need to move her.

Helped by Barnes, the sister slid the padded boards beneath Karen's unconscious body to give a firm platform for the operation. The scrubbed nurse cleaned the operative field and covered the patient with sterile sheets, leaving only the swollen abdomen exposed. After setting up the instruments and refocusing the overhead lights on the bed, the sister also went off to scrub up.

On his way back from the dressing room Barnes suddenly remembered Kapinsky. He would be furious if they delivered this child without him. 'Please ring Dr Kapinsky and tell him we're about to operate on patient van der Walt in D7,' he asked the floor nurse.

She smiled and nodded. Barnes headed back to the bedside to join Miller and Ohlsen. Miller had already marked off the operation site. Barnes looked at Karen's exposed belly and saw that it was to be a vertical incision. He couldn't let that happen: Karen was so proud of her body and wouldn't want a scar that could be seen. 'No, Aubrey, she'd prefer a bikini cut,' he said quickly, before Miller could pick up the scalpel.

The obstetrician looked startled, seemed about to say something, then shrugged and marked a transverse incision along the upper border of Karen's pubic hair. An anaesthetist – for a brain-dead organ donor? And now a cosmetic incision? He'd heard the rumours about Barnes but had ignored them. Now he wasn't so sure, but Miller, a disciplined surgeon, put all such thoughts out of his mind and concentrated on the work before him.

The nurse could get no reply from Kapinsky's home number. She got none from his laboratory either so walked back to the theatre to report.

Josef relaxed as the buzzing of the bedside telephone stopped. His father had warned him never to answer the phone unless it rang in a certain way. This telephone had just kept ringing so it couldn't be Father.

Father? Where was Father? Josef looked around the darkened room and realized he was in his father's bedroom. A sound carried clearly to his ears. It came from below. He felt happy. Father was nearby and would be up soon to tuck him into bed as always.

He lay back on the pillow and suddenly tensed again. That smell. There was another person in the house. He sniffed again. It was a human female. Curious, he climbed off the bed and went out into the big landing above the stairs. The sounds increased. He moved closer, trying to make some sense of them. One was a female voice making a moaning sound. The other was someone in distress, breathing hard.

Father! He bounded down the stairs and stopped in the doorway of the living room. His father was trying to get away from the female who was holding him with her legs and hurting him. She was choking him, killing him.

At that moment Susan felt herself engulfed in an orgasm like none she had ever experienced. It was like falling off a cliff. She threw back her head and screamed in ecstasy.

Josef gave his alarm bark and then followed with an attack growl. His father needed him, he was being hurt by this creature who was gripping him and wouldn't let go. He leapt over the big dining table and landed beside the struggling couple.

Kapinsky, still plunging into Susan, was fighting for every breath. Josef barked a 'go away' warning to the female who seemed to stop moving for a moment and then turned her head to look at him. He bared his canines, growled the attack signal and lifted his arms to make himself look as big as possible. Then she screamed with a sound that hurt his ears.

Susan's world had moved in a split second from pure pleasure to sheer terror. A nightmare beast, half man and half ape, was so close she could feel its hot breath on her face. Huge canine teeth bared, it was about to lunge for her throat. Trapped by Kapinsky's weight, hands flailing, she tried to get away. One hand, the chain held tight in a panic grip, jerked the choke tight, cutting off Kapinsky's airway. He began to thresh wildly, making sounds of desperation deep in his throat.

Josef attacked immediately. Pushing his father off Susan, he lunged at the woman's body and sank his canines deep into her throat. Her screaming stopped immediately but she doubled up convulsively, curling long legs under him and thrusting him away with her feet.

They rolled across the living room, Josef growling and ripping flesh from the body until it stopped moving. For a long moment he crouched beside the bleeding remains, now barely recognizable as human, let alone female.

Slowly, his hate cooled as he realized the threat had gone. He turned to look at his father.

Kapinsky lay on his side, tongue protruding from a purple face. Josef lifted him up and cradled him, picking in puzzlement at the chain buried in the flesh around his neck and trying to release the cuffs from his ankles. He crooned quietly, nibbling softly at his father's ears, asking him to wake up. The female hadn't bitten him, there was no sign of wounds and no blood. This was strange.

Josef held his father tighter and put his face against the naked chest. He had often done this after they had gone swimming in the pool. It felt good to listen to his father's body. It always made a steady thumping sound that started off fast and then slowed down as he listened.

There was no sound. No sound from his father's mouth. No

sound from his chest. No movement, just coldness. Still clutching his father Josef put back his head and howled his loss into the night.

The sound carried far in the still summer air, drifting beyond the walls of the old house, a lonely cry of grief and rage that echoed along the lower slopes of the mountain.

Barnes watched tensely as Miller made the first incision. The next few minutes would determine many things. If the child died there would be no need for Karen's survival and she would become another donor. If the child lived he had reason to maintain Karen on the brain-mediation system on the grounds that it was unfair to allow the child to grow up without a mother. And what about the baboon brain? Did it provide all the necessary chemical messengers to ensure normal foetal development? What if the child were born with congenital abnormalities that would not allow it to live? A hare lip, cleft palate or even a hole in the heart presented no real problems, but what if it were born with a malformed brain, or as a monster without a brain? And where the hell was Kapinsky? He was supposed to be here. He had been on round-the-clock call for weeks now and yet there was no answer when the nurse called. Perhaps he had picked up the news from somewhere else and was on his way, Barnes comforted himself.

He watched as Miller carefully cauterized the bleeding points on the skin and tissues before cutting further. Barnes was glad to see that the arterial blood was bright red, indicating that Karen's lungs were in good condition and keeping the blood well supplied with oxygen. With the sister silently assisting, Miller carefully separated the rectus muscles vertically and incised the peritoneum. A self-retaining retractor now held the wound open. Barnes could feel the pulse in his head as he peered down at the gravid uterus.

Hidden in that cavity was his future. Another minute, and Miller would deliver their child, he silently told Karen. He added a prayer that all would be well with him.

A gush of amniotic fluid signalled the beginning of the birth. Ohlsen leaned forward, gripped like the other three by the momentum of the event. Four pairs of eyes stared down at the incision in the uterus. First a tuft of black hair came into view and then a perfectly formed human hand appeared.